Dying
for a Family

A.L. Nelson

Dangerous Offer is a work of fiction. The story, all names, characters, dialogue, and incidents portrayed in this production are fictitious and a product of the author's imagination. All incidents, dialogue and characters are products of the author's imagination. No identification with actual persons (living or deceased), places, buildings, and products is intended or should be inferred.

Printed in the United States of America

DEDICATED TO A SPECIAL HORSE

In what may be an unusual dedication, I would like to credit a horse I used to share my world with, Shaman. He inspired Spark, not in appearance but in personality. He simply loved people and followed me wherever he could. He was the best horse in the whole world and not a day passes that I don't think of him.

ACKNOWLEDGMENTS

I would like to acknowledge the continuing support and encouragement of my family and friends. They are amazing and always willing to help.

Contents

Thanksgiving

ONE

"Mom! Wait, Mom!"

The call came with such insistence, it compelled Lacey to look. A teenager dressed in khaki pants and a deep blue athletic jacket jogged over from the uptown Charlotte Mecklenburg Government Center, where she worked. He waved his arms through the early morning air, coming to her as if he belonged. No one else was in the immediate vicinity, which began the mystery.

The resemblance was uncanny, even the smile. His hair was shorter, but identical to hers with soft waves of dark, carrying lighter streaks of strawberry blond from exposure to the sun. His streaks hung with fortitude, whereas hers had faded. Cooler temperatures over the past weeks kept her mostly inside.

Eyes of soft gray with a subtle hint of green in bright sunshine were also like hers. They were more alike than different. He could be her son. But she didn't have a son. Or any children at all.

Sorting out the birds and the bees had been more complicated than she'd imagined. Kids had been a desire, but the right man had yet to cross her path or vice versa. Not even close. It left her wondering if something was wrong with her or if fate had other plans.

"I'm sorry; you must have me confused with someone else," she said.

His smile widened, revealing braces with orange bands. The eyes danced with excitement, his body cutting a lean figure barely taller than hers. "Lacey Freemont?"

"Yes." This stranger knew her name.

"My name's Russell Collier. I'm your son."

Her stomach cramped up for a split second, even without reason. "That's impossible; I don't have any kids. Your name doesn't even ring a bell." Lacey's eyes narrowed. It was the day before Thanksgiving, not April Fools' Day. Still, people often pulled pranks, with her a gullible target. "Is this a practical joke? Did one of my friends put you up to this?"

"No ma'am. I'm your son." The oversized grin continued unabated.

"It's possible for a man to have a child and not know it. Happens all the time, I guess. But it's completely *impossible* for that to happen to a woman. I would know if I'd ever given birth to a child; let alone having experienced nine months of pregnancy, which I haven't. So, there's no way possible you're my son." She glanced around, expecting to see friends videoing the encounter.

"You're right, but I am."

This had to be a practical joke. But who'd go to all the trouble of setting up something so off-the-wall? It made no sense. Most of her coworkers had taken today as a vacation for traveling to visit family. Lacey was one of the few working, her usual for holidays. "Who brought you here?"

"I came mostly on my own. My dad and I researched until we found you. I flew to Charlotte this morning and paid a driver to bring me here so I could meet you." He gestured toward her jacket. "That looks like a biker jacket. Do you ride motorcycles? Do you have tattoos?"

Reflex shifted her glance to the old black leather jacket she wore. "No, on both counts. Do your parents know where you are?"

"My mom died when I was five." The words vanquished his grin.

"Listen." The lapse was understandable, considering the circumstances. "I'm sorry, what was your name again?"

3

"Russell."

"Sorry. Listen, Russell, I'm sorry about your mom. I don't know how old you are, but..."

"Fourteen," he said.

Trepidation set in. A juvenile left his home to visit her. Did that make her an accessory to a crime? She should take the kid into her office and call the police. Couldn't just leave him outside all alone. That wouldn't be right. She had no idea what else to do. "Aren't you kind of tall for fourteen?"

"I take after my dad. He's six feet, two inches. Here, see?" Russell fished the cellphone from his pocket and swiped it a few times, then held it out for her to see. "It's mostly his face, though. It doesn't give you an idea about how tall he is."

Her heart nearly choked her at the sight. The attraction was immediate, all-encompassing flames of desire. Heat radiated out from Lacey's stomach to broil the rest of her body.

It was just an image, but the animal magnetism charged straight into her. His father was an attractive man, mostly because of the smile he wore, the skin around his eyes crinkling at the corners. The depth of those lines showed he spent a lot of time outside or he smiled a lot; or both.

His facial features were strong and angular and a prominent nose. The man's skin had a strong olive undertone, like the boy's. The hair and eyes were dark and appealing, the tan cowboy hat adding fuel. If he were standing there, he'd melt her into a puddle just from the expression. As it was, the photograph had Lacey's throat dry.

"Nice cowboy hat," she managed.

"It's a Stetson. Dad's tall, but it makes him look taller. You're short for a woman, aren't you? What are you, five-five? My mom was six feet even."

"I'm five-nine, above average for a woman. Not short." The kid was a masculine version of her in many ways. His facial features were stronger, more angular, rather than petite; likely his father in him. But there was no connection to her thus far. Perhaps he was the

4

child of a relative she'd never met.

"You're on the thin side but you've got muscles, like an athlete." He studied her with a critical eye. "I play baseball, like my dad. My mom was a model in college; she didn't play sports, but she liked board games on family game nights. What sports do you like?"

"What about your dad? Where is he?" Continuing to deny being his mother wasn't proving to be a beneficial tactic. She needed contact information. The boy's father could pick him up.

"He's away on a business trip to Montana. He's gone to buy some bison for our ranch. He won't be back until early tomorrow."

Bison? Did he just say bison? This must be a practical joke after all. He seemed sincere, though. "Isn't there a tracker on your phone?"

"A tracker?" His face scrunched up.

"An app showing your location."

"Oh, yeah. He's not checking it; he thinks I'm home." He gave her a tentative smile.

Runaway. Lacey had trouble processing the situation. "Won't you be in trouble if he checks the app? Even if he doesn't, he'll notice you've gone missing when he goes home. What's your plan for that?"

Logic might get to the truth. "You said you came all this way to meet me. Didn't you have a plan for when your family found out you left? I'd imagine they're going to come looking. Not to mention the whole getting from here back to your home if they don't. If you're going to do something this elaborate, you need to cover your bases."

"It depends on you. If you don't want to have anything to do with me after I explain, then I guess I'll have to head back home." His face fell.

The kid had no grasp on the gravity of the situation. "Why don't we go inside, and I'll call your father for you?"

He cast his eyes to his feet. "He's going to be mad."

"I'll talk to him." An uncomfortable conversation loomed.

"I don't think it'll help. He'll still be mad."

"It's how parents are. It's their job to keep their kids safe. If you were my son and you left home without permission, I'd be angry, too." There. Logic.

"I *am* your son." His lower lip pooched out. "You're going to turn me in, aren't you? The way I imagined it, you'd be happy and excited. And I didn't even think about my dad."

Looking at this boy was almost like staring into a mirror. If she'd been born a guy. She tried to maintain emotional distance, but the idea of hurting Russell's feelings gave her pause. All the kid wanted was a mother. Lacey wouldn't have the first clue how to be one, making her a poor candidate for the job. "He'll be afraid if he gets home and finds you gone."

"I know," he mumbled.

"Come on then." She gave him a smile meant to encourage. "Have you had breakfast yet?"

"No ma'am." He studied his shoes again.

"Let's go inside and see what I've got squirreled away in my desk. I keep snacks on hand for the munchies. You and I can talk until we reach your dad."

"Okay." His raised to meet Lacey's.

They went inside and made their way through the mostly empty building. They hung their jackets on the coat tree in Lacey's office space. After putting her purse away, she pulled out a box of toaster pastries. "How about these? There're two in each package."

"Are they cherry-flavored with frosting? It's my favorite kind."

"Yes. They're my favorite, too." Mere coincidence. Liking the same flavor of store bought pastries couldn't possibly be an inherited trait. Ridiculous enough that she had to quit thinking about it. "We'll toast them in the breakroom." Considering what she'd always heard about teenagers, especially boys, she grabbed two silvery packages. One package for him. One for... one for them to share if he needed three pastries of his own.

He followed her down the hallway while she asked another question. "When did your flight get in?"

"Almost an hour and a half ago."

The lever on the old toaster squeaked when depressed. She snatched a few napkins. "How long have you been waiting outside for me to get here?"

"Maybe thirty minutes."

"Good grief. You must be chilled to the bone. You're only wearing a light jacket." The thought of a kid outside alone early in the morning gave a twist to Lacey's stomach. Anything could've happened.

She pointed to his locks. "But from the looks of those light streaks, you must spend most of your time outside. My hair does the same thing when I'm outside a lot." She hadn't thought before speaking. Too late.

He laughed. "I'm outside most of the time, no matter what the temperature is. There's always work to do at home."

"It's healthy to be outdoors." Mercifully, he seemed not to have noticed the remark about their hair.

Russell studied her. "It's not just the streaks; your hair is exactly like mine, only longer."

So much for not noticing.

"Your eyes are just like mine, too." The hesitation gave way to a grin of satisfaction. "If you're not my mom, how do you explain us looking so much alike?"

"It's just a coincidence." She didn't mean to snap at him, but she had. He was a kid. She needed to keep her emotions in check, no matter how stressful the situation grew. All the things the boy had pointed out were details she had already noticed on her own. Details that nagged at her, demanding to be explored and answered.

She removed his two pastries from the toaster and inserted her own after sliding his over. "Here you go; be careful, they're hot."

"I'm sorry, Ms. Freemont, I didn't mean to upset you. It's just that I've come all this way..."

"It's okay. I'm sorry, Russell. I'm not mad. And you can call me Lacey, all right?" He was a kid. And without a mother. "Speaking of coming here, how'd you find me?"

"I found your workplace and home address online. Is your apartment big?"

A kid stalked her. Maybe it should bother her, but it didn't. "It's mid-sized. I share it with a friend of mine. We each have a bedroom. Where do you live?"

"Near San Antonio."

"San Antonio? Do you mean you came here all the way from *Texas*? That's in a different time zone." This was getting more complicated by the minute.

"That's right. I have a smartwatch. That means I didn't need to change the time when I got here." He held it up for her to see.

Don't freak out in front of the kid. "I've always wanted to go there. Texas seems like a fascinating place to visit, but especially San Antonio. I've seen pictures of that River Walk they've got."

"It's a great place to live, not just to visit. You'd like it." His enthusiasm grew. She already wanted to visit his home state. Maybe she would come to visit their ranch.

"I'm sure. Do you like it?"

"Yeah, but I've never lived anyplace else." He took a huge bite of one of his pastries. It had her thinking he'd definitely need one from her package. She could never eat two pastries in one sitting anyway.

"I can relate. I've always lived in Charlotte. I can't say I love living here. It's just a place to be and a job to do. I'm a GIS Analyst for the government here."

"What kind of job is that?" He frowned.

"I make maps, different from what's on computers and phones. Everybody always thinks that's what we do. We help other departments analyze situations and solve problems with maps and data. I'll show you once we're done with breakfast. Why don't you tell me about your ranch? How big is it?"

"Dad bought the neighboring ranch a few years ago, which made it a lot bigger, around ninety-three thousand acres, give or take a few hundred."

"Ninety-three *thousand*? That's huge." Like Lacey's eyes must look as her brain tried to visualize that number in land area on a map in her head. "Is it pretty?"

"I guess so. We have horses and cattle, and tourists come. Sometimes we do cattle drives. They're dirty but fun. And we get to camp out. Grandpa still helps my dad with cattle drives. We don't have as many cattle as we used to, though."

"Why not?" Lacey's nostalgic view of Texas ranches showed nothing but cows as far as the eye could see on arid, open land.

"My dad went to college and got his head filled with crazy ideas, according to my grandpa. He learned about the damage cattle did to the land and when he took over running the ranch, he made changes. He sold some cattle and fenced off areas where he didn't want the rest of them running. The water is cleaner now and wildflowers are spreading.

"The tourists like it better. We have dude ranch vacations and a bed and breakfast. Dad gives tours to groups, even schools. He tries to give city folks an appreciation for the environment. He's been doing it for close to nine years now since he built a huge addition to the ranch house. He added cabins by this big lake we've got, too."

"Does your grandfather not approve of what your dad's doing?" It sounded like a nice place to visit, but busy. Why wouldn't the grandfather like having the land protected and his business growing?

"The ranch has been in our family for generations. Grandpa doesn't like some of dad's changes, but we still have cattle, and he likes having the ranch bigger."

Lacey collected her breakfast and led the way back to her desk, Russell inhaling another bite as they walked. "Why'd you leave home without telling your dad?"

"About six months ago, my dad told me my mom wasn't really my mom. When I found out I had another one, I wanted to learn about her, so my dad showed me the paperwork he had. I asked him to help me find out more, so he did some checking around. It took a while, but he found her... I mean you. I've been asking him to bring me to meet you, but I don't think he wanted to. I don't know why."

Confused, Lacey didn't know what to say at first. "Oh." She motioned the boy to pull up a spare chair and slid aside a stack of folders to create more room before retrieving a couple of bottles of water.

He accepted the water with a nod.

"It must've been a shock for you to find out about all that, about you and your mom." Lifechanging. Had to be hard on a kid. This one seemed to have dealt with it well enough. Except for the whole running away thing.

"It was. My dad talked to me about everything. I know my mom loved me."

"I'm sure she did."

"I wish she was still here, but I don't have many memories of her. Mainly, I remember her smile. And how she complained about the heat all the time." He grinned. "My dad made fun of her wanting to spend all summer in the air conditioning. Dad said she liked it when he did that. It made her laugh real hard.

"Where was she from?" Lacey nibbled at her pastry, hanging on Russell's story.

"Minneapolis. Dad said she missed the snow. She went back to visit her parents and sister up there a lot in the winter. She took me once, but I don't remember."

"Where she came from explains her not liking the Texas weather. How'd your parents meet?" She figured it would be good to keep him talking and get him comfortable before bringing up the inevitability of calling his father.

"In college. My mom couldn't have a baby the regular way and she didn't want to adopt. She wanted their child to be my dad's."

"So, they used your father's..." Lacey stopped to clear her throat. It wasn't her place to give a sex lesson to a kid she didn't know. "Sorry, I don't know if they've taught you about stuff like that in school yet."

"They did. I took my first class on health a couple of years ago, and they taught us about human reproduction."

"Good grief." She choked on dry pastry and embarrassment. "Seems awfully soon. Not having a child, I don't know the timing on stuff they teach you in school. It's been a long time since I was in middle school." She took a drink of water since the bite of pastry remained reluctant to go down.

Russell grinned, stifling a snicker with another gargantuan bite of pastry.

"Take it easy before you choke from laughing. I doubt I'm as old as your dad, I'll have you know."

He downed a gulp of water, wiping his mouth with the back of his hand. "You're not; I know your age from the research. Anyway, I'm not my mom's child biologically. They used a donor's egg combined with my dad's sperm. My other mom had cancer and they removed her ovaries when she was a kid about my age. Her sister, my Aunt Kate, had hers removed, too. She said she was worried about cancer. But I think the main reason is that she doesn't like kids."

The conversation's course needed to change before Lacey got herself into trouble somehow. His story had her curious, though. "We should be thinking about calling your dad. We have to let him know what happened."

He grinned. "I embarrassed you, didn't I?"

"No," she lied, the warmth of a blush making its presence known. Russell's skin tone leaned toward olive, which wouldn't show a blush as much.

"We need to get moving on this to let your dad know where you are. It's like a bandage; rip it off and it won't hurt as bad. After that, I'll take you on a tour of a museum or two while we wait for him because I'd imagine he'll be coming to pick you up right away. Would you like me to make the call?"

He pulled the phone from his pocket and laid it on the desk, the joviality gone. "No, I can do it." He swiped and tapped the screen until his father's face appeared. Russell's finger hovered, giving Lacey another glimpse of the heartthrob.

Lacey hoped the father would be gentle on his son, although she didn't know if she'd be able to do the same in his shoes. She'd go crazy finding out her son had run away. But he didn't run *away* from something, he ran *to* something, someone. Her.

Russell's forefinger descended to the phone symbol under the face.

"If you need me to talk, I don't mind. I'd like to help you. I can let him know where you are, who I am, and tell him you're safe with me. You could put it on speakerphone."

"Thanks." Russell activated the speakerphone.

Four rings later, a sleepy man answered. The father's voice was deep, accompanied by a slur from sleep, and laden with sex appeal, especially when combined with the photo. Lacey shook her head, trying to keep her train of thought where it belonged. It was a difficult task.

"Hey, Russ. You're calling early. What's up? Is something wrong?"

"Not exactly. Did I wake you up, Dad?"

There was a pause on the other end. "Yes, you did, but that's okay. What does not exactly mean?"

So, despite having just been awakened, he caught that part. Lacey wondered if she would have.

"Well, Dad. You know how we went over the information about who I am?"

"Son, you are the person, the young man, you've always been. Knowing about the woman who donated the egg doesn't change anything, especially the way I feel about you. You're my son and you always will be. I'm proud of you and I love you. I'll be home tomorrow, and we can discuss this then, okay? As much as you want."

He sounded like a kind, reasonable man. He hadn't been hit with the two-by-four upside his head yet, though.

"Dad, I did something you're not going to like." Russell glanced at Lacey and back to the phone.

Again, a moment of silence passed before he spoke. "What would that be?"

"I studied everything I could find about my mom." Russell winced. "The donor, my other mom, I mean. I wanted to find out more about her, so I'd know more about myself."

A heavy sigh came from the other end of the line. "Son, it's understandable. It makes sense you'd want to know about her. Since there's no school today, I want you to focus on helping your grandpa around the ranch. I'll be home before you know it and we'll work through this together. Don't forget tomorrow's Thanksgiving."

"I can't help grandpa today, Dad."

"Tell me why, son." Concern hinted around the edges of his voice. The father had the sinking feeling he should have postponed his trip to purchase a herd of bison. It had been long-planned, but now the timing felt wrong.

"Those records we got about the infertility clinic where you and mom got the egg to make me. I read the news articles again, the ones about the eggs that were stolen and sold on the black market and how the people involved were in jail. They got some of their eggs from universities, remember? And one of them was in North Carolina." Russell paused.

Shock took hold. Lacey's mind reversed time. Donated eggs for experimentation and money to help pay for part of her college expenses, something her elderly parents were unable to afford on their social security. It couldn't be.

"Your lawyer found my donor's name and some stuff about her. She's Lacey Freemont, and she lives in Charlotte, North Carolina. You remember all that, right?" Russell's eyes were on his mother's as he spoke.

Lacey's mouth gaped open as she forgot Russell's phone. She blinked, slow and long. "What?"

"The people I spoke with named you as the donor for my parents. You really are my mom. They have documentation to prove it. They emailed it to me. I can show it to you."

"It's not possible. This is a mistake. It has to be. I never donated eggs to be used for..." Her mind attempted to solve the puzzle.

The breach of trust, of contract, was enormous. Her eggs, a part of her, were stolen for the black market. Sold. How could someone do something this terrible to another human being?

"Someone at your university got a load of money for stealing extra eggs they had frozen in storage, the best ones they had, from four different women, including you."

"Who is it you're talking to, Russ?" Russell's father asked with a sense of urgency.

"It's my other mom, Lacey Freemont. I got a plane ticket and flew to Charlotte early this morning."

"You did *what?* You're in *North Carolina?* How did you get a ticket? You aren't old enough to buy a ticket." How had everything fallen apart like this? He'd only been gone three days. His only child had run away from home. Momentary panic and a sudden sense of helplessness overwhelmed him.

"Aunt Kate bought it for me and drove me to the airport. She signed the papers they gave her to let me fly alone. She thought you'd never let me meet my mom. She said you were afraid my mom would probably reject me. She said she'd take care of you and me if that happened."

"No. She had no right. Where are you this minute?"

The puzzle pieces fell into place for Lacey. Her donor eggs, Russell's uncanny resemblance, it connected. Russell could be her son, was her son. She had a son. What should she say to him? She'd wanted children, but not like this. She didn't even know how to be a mom.

"Are you all right, Lacey?"

Shaking hands gave her away. She licked her tongue across her lips. "I... Russell, I think I know what happened. Some of it, anyway. I can't believe this."

"Russell, tell me what's going on there. Is that the woman, the one you said before? What's her name again?"

Russell rested a hand on Lacey's, an anchor stopping her from falling into complete panic, pulling her back. She needed to snap out of her daze and man up, or woman up. Was that even a thing?

"Mr. Collier, I'm Lacey Freemont." She paused for a swallow. "I can't tell you what a shock this is to me. I honestly didn't know about any of this. I participated in an experiment in college, for research only. It was an ordeal to go through, with multiple injections that made me physically ill.

"Back then I was basically on my own and I needed the money to help pay for tuition. I never heard about the theft from the University. I don't keep up with the news much, and no one contacted me about what happened.

"Russell came to me at work this morning. I've got him in my office with me right now. He's safe and sound. I won't let anything happen to him. I'll figure out a way to get him back to you, don't worry."

There was a long pause. "Ms. Freemont, I apologize for all this. We can talk about it as soon as I get there. I just... I don't know what to say to you."

His words barely registered. "You don't have to say anything. Russell's a good kid."

"He is. This is out of character for him."

"Did you say you're coming here?" She needed to stay focused. A massive load had just been deposited on her shoulders, but the kid needed help. Time to get over herself and be a responsible adult. A parent.

"Yes. I'll get a flight to Charlotte. I'll contact Russell as soon as I find out what time the plane will arrive there."

"Okay." The ability to form coherent speech left her. She'd suddenly become a mother. What did that mean? What should she do? Was this what it felt like to take one of those at-home pregnancy tests, seeing the color of the stick the first time? Unprepared for the results. Total shock.

"I'm sorry for this intrusion into your private life, Ms. Freemont.

Russell, I need you to go somewhere safe until I can get there. I'm thinking you should go to the police station."

Police station? He didn't trust her with his son? *Their* son? It hit her. She had a son with a handsome man she'd never met before. Unless she'd gone insane. This was getting more bizarre by the minute. At least preceding a pregnancy test would have been the likelihood of amazing sex with the child's father. Why was her mind so tumultuous? Why couldn't she focus?

"Didn't you say I could stay with you, Lacey?" Russell's words were a plea for help.

A deep breath helped to calm her. "Yes, of course. We've got a lot to talk about. Besides, I still have to show you what I do for a living. Mr. Collier, would it be all right if I keep Russell until you get here? I'd feel better knowing where he is. I promise you I'll keep him safe. I've fed him breakfast and I'll get him to you at the airport." Lacey's concern shifted to Russell's father. She'd caught something in his voice. He didn't trust her.

"Ms. Freemont, I don't know anything about you. And I don't want to impose on you. You've already endured an emotional blow as it is. I appreciate your offer, but you're a stranger. The police would be a better solution under the circumstances."

"It's no imposition. I want to spend time with Russell. I didn't know I had a child. I didn't know." Get ahold of yourself and focus. This wasn't encouraging trust.

"Ms. Freemont..." Russell's father began.

"I'm going to show him what I do at my job." Think fast Lacey, change his mind before he closes the door all the way.

"How's this for starters? I work for the local government here. Right now, I'm making a map for the Police Department that my supervisor assigned to me. After I'm done, we can go for the walk I promised him. I want to take him to a couple of museums. You can look up my name on the government's website under the Planning, Design and Development Department. Then just look for Online Mapping. You'll see my name, work email, and office phone number.

"I'll have Russell text you my phone number and email address, and Russell can do the same for me with yours. Then it'll be on my phone. I've never been in trouble or broken the law my entire life. There's a church I go to, and I have friends who'd give me excellent character references, plus there's my employer. I can have Russell text you their names and phone numbers, and even for the church, although I have no idea what time the pastor comes in. Does any of this make you feel more comfortable?"

"I suppose it'll be okay. Sounds like you've got a lot of references. I'll check on you, but just the website, nothing else." He paused to avoid laughing. She might take it the wrong way. It sounded like she was serious about taking care of Russell for him.

It was strange but she got the feeling he now wore a smile, just from the sound of his voice. It was working. She didn't understand why her world would end if she couldn't keep Russell with her for the day, but it would happen, no doubt about it. The two of them needed time to talk, to get to know each other. Lacey and her son.

"I appreciate that you're willing to look after him. I just don't like leaving my son with a stranger, to be honest."

"I'm sure you don't. I'd probably feel the same way in your shoes, even though I don't have any kids myself. Well, until now, I guess. If you'd prefer, I could take him to the police and see if he can stay there. I'd imagine they'll have to call Social Services since Russell would be labeled a runaway and he's a minor.

"I don't know if there'll be any repercussions for either of you. I'll do my best to help, but I don't know that many people in our Police Department. This is a big organization. I'd rather keep him with me. We can check in with you regularly and send you lots of updates and photos. It'll let you know he's okay."

There was a brief pause before the father spoke again. "I like the idea of the photos and it's a good point about the police. I hadn't thought about Social Services getting involved. I don't want trouble over him running away, considering the circumstances." The sigh was audible. "All right, Ms. Freemont. I appreciate your help."

"Dad, can you tell her the story?"

"The story? What... oh, that story. Now?"

"Yes, please. I want you to tell her." Backup for what he'd already told his mother.

"There isn't an ideal time for this conversation, Ms. Freemont, so I'm going to do my best but keep it brief since I've got to find a flight out. It's about how Russell came to be. Is that alright?"

"Yes." The quiver in her voice came through, much to Lacey's chagrin.

"My wife, Karen, and I went to an infertility clinic when we decided to have a baby. There were lots of tests for both of us. Then we selected a donor. They only had a small number of eggs from Karen's top pick, but once she'd made up her mind there was no alternative. The first attempt with that donor worked. We got an embryo, and the implantation was a success." He couldn't help smiling to himself at the memory.

"We were happy and excited. And grateful to the donor. That woman had no idea the gift she gave, the power of it. Karen studied the donors for a full month before she chose. The woman selected had outstanding grades in school and graduated in the top five percent in her college class, so she had intelligence."

Lacey's head tilted. She'd been in the top five percent.

"There was no photograph, just a physical description from the time of the donation: five feet, nine inches, one hundred thirty pounds. My wife was a little jealous over that, by the way." He smiled again before refocusing.

This would have gone much better in person. He should have taken Russ to meet Lacey Freemont months ago. There was no one to blame but himself.

"The donor had the hair and eye color Russell has, naturally. I guess that was obvious when you first met him. Something you'll probably like is that Russell played baseball from the time he was four. They called it tee-ball then. He's still playing. Baseball, that is. I did the same as a kid and all through college. Just like the donor.

You. The paperwork said you loved the sport. It also said you were a strong hitter and played third base."

"Yes, I did." Her eyes remained wide as the boy's father spoke. The confidence had left her as the facts settled in. A naturally light skin tone had turned pasty, and she was visibly shaken. Her hands clutched the arms of the chair she sat in as she attempted to control the trembling.

"When Russell had too many questions about why no one else in the family had hair and eyes like his, I told him the truth. Naturally, he wanted to know more about his biological mother than what little the records Karen and I were given could tell. Begged me for two months until I gave in.

"Our family attorney and a private detective checked into it for me and found out the previous owners of the clinic Karen and I had used were in jail. The records they kept had been unsealed due to a court order.

"It turns out that the owners got some of their eggs from a North Carolina university lab, sold by an employee who went to jail for what she did. She'd been operating a black market in human eggs, getting rich off of it. Because of the court order, the attorney was able to get the name of the donor.

"It was a relatively simple matter to trace your name and find your address after that. Phone number, too. What my son has told you is true. He has the same proof of everything on email, just like I do. He can show it to you if you want to see it for yourself."

"Are you okay?" Russell asked Lacey.

She nodded, releasing her grip on the chair. "Yeah. It's just... a lot. But I'd rather know the truth. I'm okay."

"Russell, can I talk to you? Just you, I mean, off the speakerphone? I'm going to need to explain all this to your grandpa and he'll want to talk to you himself."

The dad probably wanted to check on Russell without her around, just to be sure he wasn't being coerced into anything. No need for feeling paranoid, even though she did. "I'll go for a quick walk and be back in a few minutes, Russell. You go ahead and talk to your dad. Take as much time as you want. I won't be far away. Just holler if you need me."

His eyes widened. "Can I take a quick picture of you? Then my dad can see how much we look alike. It might make him feel better."

"Oh, okay. Go ahead." The pale, cold gray of the wall would be a dead giveaway for a government building, helping verify the work location.

"It'd be better if we do a selfie." Russell waved her over.

"All right." She came around the desk to lean her head by his, her hands on his shoulders. He tilted his head toward hers as he took the image.

"This came out good, but you should've smiled bigger. You've got a pretty smile."

"Thanks, Russell. I'll be back in a minute. You be sure and stay right here, okay? If anybody comes looking for me, tell them you're with me and I'll be right back." She walked out.

"I will." He looked at his phone. "Okay, Dad. Did you get the photo I just sent?"

Lacey hesitated in the hallway just outside the door, where she'd be out of sight.

"Yeah, I think she's beautiful, too. And she's been really nice to me," Russell said.

A smile came over her. As soon as she delivered Russell to his father, the next step would be to check on the fertility clinic and the university. It sounded like a lawyer might be needed. She had to make sure there weren't any more children of hers out there. The thought of it sent her hand diving for her stomach, to rub it into submission.

The most pressing issue was that she had no idea how to be a mother, especially to a teenager, not to mention a boy. Russell's appearance gave her little doubt his story was true. To say her life had changed didn't even begin to cover it.

TWO

Amid the chaos of the Charlotte Douglas International Airport, Russell and Lacey found a place to settle in with their dinner at a small table in a crowded restaurant.

"Is that going to be enough food for you?" She sent him a mischievous grin. Lacey's appetite had recovered after spending the day getting to know the teen.

They'd seen a few of the many sights to see in Charlotte. In between, they sat on a park bench where they perused Russell's emails and news articles about the clinic and the theft. He proved it to her, made her believe. He also made her feel comfortable with him. That part had come easy.

"I'll be helping you with your sweet potato fries. There're way too many of them for you. You don't eat much, do you?"

"We'll see about that. I happen to love sweet potato fries. And I eat plenty, for your information. This food probably isn't as good as what you're used to on the ranch." Lacey started in on her fries before her son ate them all.

"This is good, just not as healthy. It's early for dinner, but I'm starving after all the walking we did. The hotdogs didn't hold me long."

"It's early, but your dad's flight should be here soon, and I wanted to have you fed before he got here. It'll show him I'm a responsible parent."

Russell sent her a radiant smile.

"Do you eat burgers a lot?" Lacey popped some fries into her mouth and picked up her massive cheeseburger. Russell was right. It was an ambitious amount of food.

"Yeah. We have burgers or steak at least once a week."

"Oh. I figured growing up on a cattle ranch you'd have them every day." Burger juice escaped her lips when she took a bite, so she grabbed a fistful of napkins for each of them from the dispenser on the table.

"We don't," he paused to swallow, "but people think we do. My dad says it's how he grew up. He likes to say his intestines are probably crammed full of twenty pounds of undigested red meat." Russell snickered, covering his mouth with a napkin.

"Gross, Russell." Lacey's forehead crinkled.

"Not half as gross as the painting we saw. What was that place called?"

"The Bechtler Museum of Modern Art. And it wasn't gross. It was art." She couldn't come up with better terminology. It had been a bit hard to take when escorting a teenage boy she barely knew. "You don't get exposed to a lot of art in school, do you?"

"Not like that one!" He burst into a fit of laughter.

"Great. Your dad will probably never let me see you again after he hears about it." Why hadn't she given thought to the possibility of seeing something like that in an art gallery? How did mothers handle all this? There were many more life variables to consider now.

Russell's eyes went wide. "I didn't think about how my dad would see it. I won't say anything, I promise. I want you two to hit it off so you can visit. When could you come? Christmas?"

"I have no idea, Russell. We'll have to wait and see what your dad says. Christmas is a family holiday."

"But you're family now; you're my mom. Wow. I've changed all our lives, haven't I? My dad's going to be upset I ran away to do this without him."

"Most likely. I'd be upset too. I don't want you to do anything like this ever again, all right? You have to promise me." Remembering what her parents had looked like during lectures helped with pasting on the frown and the stare, both of which they seemed to have mastered so well.

"Okay. I've never done anything like this before and you're the only mom I've got. Besides, dad will ground me for the next four years, anyway."

"Four?" Odd number. Why four?

"In four years, I'll be leaving for college."

"I didn't think about college. What do you want to study?" A few fries found her mouth, but it was hard to taste them through everything that was going on. Her son would soon be old enough to go to college. Yet again he'd stunned her. The realization of having missed out on his life crept in. First steps. First words. First day of school.

"I'm not sure. I've been thinking maybe modern art." His expression was unreadable.

Lacey hesitated, trying to sort it out, staring at him. Then her skepticism kicked in and her eyes narrowed. He was pulling her leg. "Yeah, right."

He laughed again. At least she provided him with plenty of

amusement. She shook her head and joined in the laughter, realizing she had a lot to learn.

"I'm interested in becoming a medical research scientist or a doctor. I like biology and chemistry and math. I'd like to find a cure for what killed my mom."

The mood crashed to earth. "What happened to her, if you don't mind my asking?"

"No, I don't mind. The cancer wasn't gone. It spread and they didn't find it in time."

"I'm sorry, Russell. I guess your aunt doesn't have children, does she? Because of having her ovaries removed, I mean."

"No. She never wanted children, but it's all my mom ever did want. Aunt Kate had surgery to remove it all so she wouldn't have to deal with it, is what she said."

"Wait. She had a hysterectomy?"

"That sounds like the name she used for it."

"Did she have it done before you were..." She hesitated, wanting to say conceived, which he probably knew about already, but she'd pushed his knowledge base far enough. "I mean, did she have the surgery before you were born?"

"A couple of years before."

"She didn't freeze her eggs, did she? Preserve them, I mean. If she had, your parents could've used them to..." Yet again, she'd started down a path she shouldn't have. "They could've used eggs genetically close to your mother's, instead of mine."

"Aunt Kate said she didn't want to risk having any screaming brats running around, sucking her bank account dry in the future. She didn't save any eggs. She likes telling that story."

"Harsh." Ironic indeed.

"I guess so, but dad said it was her right. Besides, my mom didn't want to risk passing on the cancer gene to a baby. She wanted a healthy donor to make me with, so I'd have a chance of being in better shape than she was."

"Your mom was smart to think about it that way."

The boy studied her closely. "She picked you. Of all the donors on the list, she liked the results of the tests that were run on you and your family health history and the description they gave of you, what you looked like, all that stuff my dad told you about."

Tears came to her eyes. A stranger had decided Lacey Freemont was the best choice to be the mother of her child.

"It's true. You can ask my dad if you don't believe me."

"I believe you." The words were whispered. The conversation needed to take a turn so Lacey could avoid crying. "Your aunt. Is she the one who bought you the plane ticket and drove you to the airport?" Lacey hadn't met her but didn't like her much.

"Yes. She helped me."

Lacey drew in a long, slow breath. "Why'd she do that?"

"She wanted to help me find you because you were my dream. She also wanted to make sure I got here safe."

"That's nice, Russell. But I guess what I meant was, why didn't she come with you herself? I know you're a teenager, and a boy, but it's still risky to put you on a plane by yourself with nothing more than an address. Anything could've happened to you. Not everybody in the world is a nice person."

"Aunt Kate says I'm big enough to be responsible for myself. She's always letting me do things dad wouldn't." He sat up straight in his seat, chin jutted out.

"Is that wise?" He wasn't getting the point and she wasn't sure how far to press the issue.

"She treats me like an adult."

"Being treated like an adult has a lot of appeal to a young person, I'm sure. But she should keep your real age in mind. And she needs to think about your dad since he's the one who's responsible for you. You're not her child." The lecturing came naturally. Was that a parenting instinct?

"No, I'm yours. What would you have done?"

"Well, I've never had a child before this morning. I'm not sure what I would've done, but after spending the day with you, I know you're important to me and I don't want anything bad happening to you."

He smiled, averting his gaze to his food and back. "I like that." He took another bite.

"Good. Now, I want you to be prepared when your dad gets here. I doubt he's going to want to listen to anything we have to say about me coming for a visit. He's going to be upset and off-balance enough already, I'd imagine."

Russell stopped chewing to stare.

"It's not like I'm not going to go see you. I promise I'll come. But I think your dad will need some time to get used to the idea of me being in your life. Let me call him a few times to talk and send him some emails or texts. It'll make him comfortable with me before I ask him if I can come."

"Okay. Will you call him right away?"

"I don't want to push. I'll maybe call or text sometime tomorrow to make sure you got home safe, but I'll keep it brief since it's Thanksgiving. I'm not pressuring your dad. I don't want you to, either. Do we have a deal?"

"It's a deal." He resumed eating.

"I'll send you at least one text a day, once your dad clears it." A twinge of nerves hit her stomach. What if it wasn't okay? It couldn't be possible; there was no reason to worry. "Now, finish up your food and help me eat these fries while you're at it."

"Told you it'd be too much." He grinned, snatching a fistful of fries, piling them atop his own before cramming some into his mouth.

"Maybe the next time you and I have dinner together, we could have salads. They're healthy." She should try to get him to develop good eating habits, right? Be a good example.

"My dad makes sure we eat healthy. He has a big garden every year and grows vegetables for us and the tourists. We make a meal out of salads or something vegetarian twice a week. My grandpa cooks our meat meals. The best ones are his steaks. He oversees the cooking for our guests. He says he's found his calling after all these years."

Thinking of it brought a smile to her face almost as big as Russell's. "It sounds like you've got a good family."

"You're my family too, Lacey. I'm going to miss you."

"And I'll miss you. We'll see each other again; you don't need to worry about it." It was true. She would miss him. This morning she had been single, no serious commitments to anyone, free to do as she pleased. Now, she had become a mother to a teen. How to handle this was a mystery.

**

Russell's fingers tapped out a fast rhythm on the arms of his chair, so Lacey decided against pacing. Didn't need to add to the anxiety level for either of them. Her toes bounced on the floor instead, though not in sync with her son's tune, whatever it was.

She couldn't help wondering what Russell's father would think of her. The strain to make a good impression mounted. What if he didn't like her? That could make it difficult to see Russell. Would he try to stop her from having a relationship with her son? None of this was her fault.

"My dad's flight is here."

"What?" She hadn't been paying attention, lost in thought.

"My dad's here." Russell stood and Lacey followed, watching passengers emerge.

"There he is," Russell nodded.

His father was tall and broad-shouldered, his face just as pleasant to gaze upon as his image on Russell's phone. He carried a leather satchel over his shoulder. He wore a black T-shirt covered by a light tan jacket, faded jeans that have seen better days, much like the western boots on his feet. Just under the sleeve of his jacket, she noted what looked like an expensive watch. Very expensive.

The curiosity of the watch was forgotten as Lacey's heart pounded with butterflies that tickled, then slammed repeatedly into the lining of her stomach. Wings of steel, tipped with razors.

A big sigh of relief came over Reid Collier when he spotted his son. He followed it up with a smile. He couldn't help noticing the woman standing just behind Russell. It was remarkable, the similarity in hair and eye color, a few other features, including the smile. But where the boy was almost gangly, the mother was perfectly proportioned, and her beauty almost made Reid trip over his own feet.

Seeing the dad triggered something vital. "Russell. What's your dad's first name? I forgot to ask you."

"Oh, his name's Reid."

"Reid," she whispered to herself, afraid of forgetting during the deer-in-the-headlights moment about to envelop her. "Reid." Rats. What was his last name? How could she forget that? Same last name as the son. Mental paralysis had her momentarily. "Collier," she whispered as the information offered itself up. "Reid Collier. Reid Collier. Come on, Lacey. You've got this."

Reid was on them as she uttered her self-encouragement. He gave his son a warm embrace. Lacey bit her lower lip as she waited, nerves escalating. There was a tear in Reid's eye. The man was even better looking in person. How could that be possible? She bit her lip harder.

"I'm so glad to see you, Russell. You gave me a real scare." The deep voice broke.

"I'm sorry Dad. Lacey pointed out how lucky I am to have such a great family. I should've trusted you and waited until you got back to ask for your permission to contact her. She's been great, honest."

Why did she have to be beautiful? Reid was finding it difficult to remember what he'd planned on saying next. They had found a single photograph in their searching.

It had been an image of her in a newspaper article when she'd been in a softball game in college, a championship her team had lost. The team photo was with an injured player held by half the team, including Lacey. She wore sunglasses and what looked to be an infectious laugh, her hair in a high ponytail. Seeing it had brought a smile to his lips, lightness to his heart.

The sight of her now, in person, had temporarily robbed him of speech. He wouldn't make an impression on her this way. And his focus needed to partially remain on his son, to help him through whatever happened next. Reid had decided to leave it up to her.

Reid's eyes shifted and Lacey's breath left her as she tried to decide if it was from nerves or because she'd briefly visualized Reid shirtless. It just popped into her head. That happened sometimes to people, didn't it? Was that wrong? Probably. Was she breathing yet? She'd forgotten to breathe. Yes, that's what happened. Something about his eyes made it difficult to remember to breathe.

What was his name again? How long had he been staring at her? By now he must be concerned that she had a social anxiety disorder.

"Hi, Mr. Collier." Her lungs resumed their job. She extended her hand and tried to produce her best smile. Calm down, for crying out loud. He's probably dating some lucky woman back in Texas. "I'm Lacey Freemont."

"It's good to meet you, Lacey." Reid smiled, shaking her hand. Her skin was soft and smooth, confirming his imagined version. The way she licked her tongue over her lips had his thoughts straying.

Lacey noted his grip was like Goldilocks, not too firm, not too weak, just right. Perfect. Like him.

"And please, call me Reid. I'm grateful to you for taking care of my son and I'm sorry this happened. I would never have imagined he'd go off and do something like this." Reid took a deep breath and finally remembered to release her hand. Slowly.

"Russell has been excited about meeting you, and he obviously lost patience with me and my timetable. I didn't think news like this would be good coming over the phone. It should be delivered in person, by me. And Russell. I had intended to approach it gently, the two of us coming here to meet you together. As gently as news like this could be given, anyway."

"Can Lacey come for a visit, Dad?" Russell's face filled with eager anticipation as he blurted out the question he and his mother had agreed to wait on.

"Well, I don't know son. We need to talk about this first. And you have to consider Lacey's feelings on the matter. You're a surprise to her and she just found out. She helped your mom and me be able to have you, but that doesn't mean she's ready to suddenly jump in and be a part of your life. Give her time to process."

Reid needed that, too. All he could think of was asking her to spend Christmas with them. But that was a family holiday and she probably had plans already. A woman like her probably had a boyfriend. It would be pressuring her, something she likely didn't need right now. She'd been through a tremendous shock today.

Besides, he hadn't dated a woman in all the years since his wife passed away. Never could bring himself to sever that connection. Why was he thinking about doing so now?

Russell hadn't considered the possibility before. Could his mother not want to be in his life? His face fell.

The father's words came as a shock to Lacey. Her son didn't need to be hurt, thinking she hadn't meant what she'd told him, that she didn't care. Why would Reid say something like that? Was he driving in a wedge on purpose, or was it an accident?

"Mr. Collier. Reid. I've enjoyed being with Russell. And up until today, my family's been small, basically just my cousin and his parents."

"I'm sorry we put you through this," Reid said. There. This had indeed been upsetting for her. She might never want to see either one of them again. If only Russell had waited. Or if Reid had pushed himself into cooperating with his son's need to meet his biological mother, rather than putting it off.

"No. That's not it." She sped up her words since he'd cut her off. "What I meant was, this was a great surprise. Who'd ever imagine they're going to meet a child they never knew they had? And we've had the best day today. *I've* had the best day. I wouldn't trade it for the world.

"What I'm hoping is that you'll give me the chance to get to know him. I'd like to have your permission to talk to him on the phone or text him if it's all right, to keep in touch. It'll only be in the evenings, so I can find out how his day went. I won't keep him up late or interfere with his homework or studying or anything. I'd like to come out to spend time with him, too."

Keeping in mind that she'd be calling for Russell would be difficult, considering the attraction he was already feeling toward her. And the visits would bring her there to see his son, *their* son, not him. Could he deal with that?

The jolt passing through his body every time their eyes met gave him the answer. It would be challenging to maintain his distance. Maybe while she got to know Russell, she could get to know the rest of the family, too.

It registered with him that her face had fallen and that Russell was staring at him, mouth sagging open. How long had he left her request hanging in the air, unanswered, while his mind began drifting toward contemplation of a potential future with a woman he only just met? She must think he didn't want her around when the opposite was the case.

"I don't know about that." Reid rubbed a hand over his unshaven chin. He needed time to think it over for himself, to sort things out. He needed to step back, think logically about this, think about what might be best for Russell. "I'll need to give it some thought."

Did he truly need to think about it? Had she done something wrong? "Reid, please. I just found out I have a son, almost a grown man. I've already missed out on so much of his life. Please, don't shut me out of the rest of it. I can just call for now or fly out to visit sometime since Russell is too young to fly. Whatever it takes." Did she sound desperate when she needed to be calm and reasonable?

Reid's brows inched closer together as her eyes searched his. They lived far apart. He had to make sure she was serious about Russ, that this wasn't some momentary novelty for her. Russell would be devastated if that were the case. Still too soon to tell for sure about that, or her.

"I'd like to get to know you better myself first before you and Russell begin having conversations. I hope you can understand that Lacey."

There was the hope she'd been searching for. Her smile blossomed. "Oh, I definitely can. That'd be great. I'd like to get to know you, too. Here." Lacey reached into a back pocket and handed him a business card. "I already put my cell number on the back. Please, call me anytime, day or night. We can talk about anything at all."

Reid had been concerned she would reject Russell. So far, so good. The caution remained, however. He looked from her face to the card and withdrew his wallet to put the card into an empty slot, then flashed her a warm smile. "I'd need to have my head examined if I turned down the opportunity to get to know a beautiful woman who also happens to be the mother of my son."

Her eyes widened just before the shy smile came, followed by a rising blush. "Oh. Thank you. I mean, thank you for giving me a chance."

"I owe you for taking such good care of Russell. Speaking of which, can I reimburse you for whatever you spent on him today? You must've had to take the day off from work, too."

"Most of it, but I was happy to spend time with him. I don't want anything for it. You've done a wonderful job raising him. He's great."

"I appreciate it. I'm going to leave the initial phone contact up to you, Lacey. Call me whenever you're ready. We'll wait on you, however long it takes." He dug into his shirt pocket and removed a wrinkled business card, handing it over.

Then he turned to his grinning son. "The screen shows our flight's about to board. Time to tell Lacey bye," Reid said.

"Already?" Russell asked.

"I've got us on a flight out to Atlanta, then Dallas-Fort Worth. It boards in about twenty minutes. We've got to hurry to get to the gate because it's on a different airline and it'll take a while to get there through these holiday crowds."

Shock gave way to near panic as Reid's words registered with Lacey. "You're leaving already? I was hoping maybe we'd have more time, that we could talk for a while."

"I think we've taken up enough of your time as it is, Lacey."

Was he shutting her down? "You haven't; not by a long shot."

"Well, I have tickets and we need to make it home in time for Thanksgiving. It's a big event on the ranch and we're needed there. And Russell's grandfather is worried. Maybe some other time, all right?"

He wasn't sure what to do next. A hug seemed presumptuous, while a handshake was too formal. In a move that felt bold for him with a woman he didn't know, Reid extended his hand to pat her shoulder. Life had become confusing over just a few minutes.

Lacey glanced at his hand as he patted her shoulder a couple of times, as an adult might console a young child who'd just dropped their ice cream cone. It raised suspicion. "Can I at least walk with you to the gate you're heading for?"

"I'm thinking it would be best if you didn't. We can move faster that way." Without any indication, Reid allowed himself to become a brick wall. The conflicting emotions were waging a war in him. Did the ideas scampering through his head and the attraction he felt mean he was being disloyal to the memory of his wife? Life had been so simple just yesterday.

It was difficult for Lacey to grasp what could have crawled up the man's rear all of a sudden. Her eyes narrowed in response. If Russell weren't around, she'd light into Reid. He seemed intent on separating her from Russell. He had no idea how stubborn she could be, but he'd find out pretty quick if he kept this attitude up.

"Bye, Lacey." Russell wrapped his arms around her shoulders, interrupting the internal tirade each adult was processing.

"Goodbye, Russell." After allowing a prolonged hug, Reid exerted a steady pull to get Russell back from his mother.

"We need to get moving. Thank you again for taking such good care of my son, Lacey."

"No problem." He's my son too, she wanted to counter but refrained. "Russell, I'm glad you decided to come and find me. Be good for your dad and remember what I told you. I'll see you again. I promise."

"Okay, Lacey. Bye!" Russell threw up his free hand in a wave as Reid nodded politely, taking hold of Russell's arm to lead him away.

The brief encounter had been so odd that Lacey realized she'd neglected to get their home address. But it wasn't like she could just walk up and knock on the front door, anyway. Watching them disappear into the throngs, an idea took shape.

Maybe she *could* knock on their door if it came down to it. She didn't trust Reid Collier, even though part of her wanted to give him a chance to prove her wrong.

THREE

"What did he have to say for himself?" Connie Cha's large brown eyes were already narrowed when she looked up from her computer screen. She tucked sleek black hair that barely brushed her shoulders behind her ears. She'd been Lacey's friend and roommate since college.

"It went directly to voicemail." Lacey flopped down into the uncomfortable spare chair by Connie's desk, her rear end immediately regretting the decision to flop.

"Again? Isn't this like the twentieth time in three weeks? It's almost Christmas."

"It's the forty-second time. I've called twice a day, every day; including today."

"So why isn't Russell calling you?" Connie leaned her elbows on the desk. "Have you tried calling or sending a text message?"

"I can't call or text Russell. I promised. I'm waiting on his father. They both have my number. Maybe Reid confiscated Russell's phone as punishment for running away." She shrugged. "I'm supposed to talk to Reid before I call Russell. I'm trying to respect Reid's wishes." Lacey drummed her fingers on the chair, suddenly feeling like a moron. An angry one.

"It's not fair, and I'm thinking he doesn't have the right to do this to you. What about a text message to Reid?" Connie asked.

"I've tried texting as many times as I've called; more than that even and that's not counting all the emails to the ranch website. And since it's almost Christmas, I sent cards with long notes; and a gift card for Russell, because it looks like Reid's not inviting me to join them. You're right about this not being fair, but I'm trying one more time, on the ranch phone."

"Why? He doesn't want to talk. What're you going to say that's different from any of the other times?" Connie rolled her chair back.

"It's time to change tactics."

"Ooh, can I listen in? Are you going to make him mad? Because I'd make him mad if I were you. Just hearing about this all the time makes me mad, and it's not even me or my kid."

Lacey's eyebrows rose. "Do I talk about Russell all the time?"

"Not all the time. A lot, though."

"I hadn't realized. Sorry." Lacey concluded she must sound like the receptionist in a neighboring department, carrying on endlessly about her grandson to anyone who held still for more than two seconds.

"Don't be. You just found out you have a son, for crying out loud, which makes you a new mom. And he's your only child, according to those records the clinic gave you. I'd be talking about him all the time if it were me. That goes double if his father wasn't allowing me to see him or even talk to him. And there's no telling what he's saying to Russell without you there to defend yourself."

"What do you mean?" This was going somewhere unthinkable.

"He might be telling Russell you don't want to have anything to do with him." Connie stood, coming around her desk to perch on the edge of it.

Lacey's blood boiled. She stood, clamping her hands on her hips. "That'd be evil."

"So? Some people are evil. Talk to anyone who has kids and has been through a divorce." Connie raised an eyebrow for emphasis.

"I didn't think about it like that. I've been worried about how to be a mom. Even checked out a couple of books from the library to help me figure it out. But Reid won't give me a chance. Can I borrow your phone?"

"Of course. Why?" Connie stood, pulling the phone from her back pocket.

"You've got a different area code. They won't tie the incoming call to Charlotte...or me." Lacey sent her friend a half-grin as she took the phone and dialed, holding up a finger for tolerance from her impatient audience of one.

On the other end, someone answered on the second ring. "Hello?"

"This is Lacey Freemont. I'm an acquaintance of Mr. Collier and I need to speak with him, please. He'll know why I'm calling." Lacey's eyes were wide, her eyebrows high.

"All right Ms. Freemont. Hold on and let me see if I can find him for you." The woman on the other end of the line was polite, even cheerful.

Unbelievable. She'd gotten through to a real person this time. It had to be a good sign. Progress. She paced as her eagerness and nerves grew.

Maybe she'd start by being sugar-sweet and see where it got her. She could ask Reid how he was, how Russell was. The weather could be another topic. It would be awkward, but she'd have to ask what was going on there, why she hadn't received any return communications. It would be wise to keep a strong check on her emotions with that part of the conversation. Nerves were getting the better of her as the silence persisted.

"Ms. Freemount?"

"Freemont. I'm still here."

"Naturally. Mr. Collier cannot be disturbed at this time." The haughty voice undoubtedly came from a different woman.

"It's important. I've been trying hard to reach him." Lacey's disappointment at coming close and being denied overwhelmed her self-control.

"It can't be helped," the woman said.

Choking back the letdown, she paced faster. "I'm getting worried. Is Russell okay?"

"He isn't any of your business. And there's no one available to talk to you, Ms. Freedman." The voice chilled her hand through the phone. Lacey's teeth clenched and her free hand fisted.

"Freemont. Free*mont*." For crying out loud. "Can you at least tell Russell and Reid I called? And when would be a good time for me to call back?"

"There is none."

"What does that mean? Who are you?" Whoever the woman was, she didn't have the personality to handle the public. Lacey felt her patience slipping.

"Who am I? You have a lot of nerve, don't you?"

"What's your name?" Lacey lashed out as she seethed.

"You don't need to know my name. You don't need to call here and ask to speak to Mr. Collier anymore, either. What goes on here is none of your concern."

"It isn't up to you to decide. You don't know who I am to him."

"You're nothing to him, I know that much. He doesn't want to talk to you. Not ever. And you're not to call his son, either. If you do, we'll be pressing charges."

"Charges? What're you talking about?" Just as she'd feared, Reid was keeping her away from Russell. That wasn't going to work out well for him, as he'd soon discover. "I haven't done anything wrong. If there's anyone pressing charges, you should be aware they'll be coming from *me*, against Reid Collier. You can tell him I said so."

"You have no right."

"I have every right. He's got my son and won't allow me to see him. We're going to have to work out a custody arrangement. I won't let Reid keep us apart. I think Russell needs me, especially after the way I've been ignored the past few weeks, not to mention the way I've been treated just now, by you." The mystery woman on the other end of the line couldn't see or hear it, but Lacey stomped her foot for emphasis.

"I'll forewarn you, if I catch you anywhere near Reid Collier, there'll be hell to pay. I'd advise you to reconsider your ideas. You'd better watch yourself, Lacey." She pronounced Lacey's name with the hiss of a serpent.

"Are you threatening me?" Lacey's voice elevated, despite being at work.

Connie bounded to her feet, ready to jump in.

"Oh, I don't threaten. I promise. And I keep my promises, little girl."

Memory combined with suspicion kicked in. Aunt Kate. "I think you'd better watch yourself there, *Kate.*" Two could play at this game.

The call ended abruptly on the other end. Did Kate mean what she said, or could it have been an empty threat? There was only one way to find out. Time to put the backup plan Connie had helped create into motion.

Birthday

FOUR

The San Antonio airport bustled with travelers and noise, leaving Lacey anxious to get outside. She shifted the padded strap of her old satchel over her head to wear it crossbody. The faded denim jacket that once belonged to her father covered her white camisole and plaid shirt. Plaid was a stereotype for ranch attire since she had no idea what to wear.

After snatching her duffel bag from the carousel, she moved through the throngs to the exit. At the curb sat a Jeep emblazoned with Collier Ranch. She'd been informed it would be waiting when the plane landed, to pick up a father with two teenage sons and her, all guests at the ranch.

A handsome young man stood waiting. His shirt sleeves were rolled up and he wore a cowboy hat tilted back on his head at a casual angle. Dark hair, skin, and eyes were topped off with a friendly smile. He removed his hat and gave her a nod. "Welcome."

He glanced at a small notepad pulled from where it had been tucked into his shirt pocket. "You must be Connie McCall, from Rock Hill, South Carolina."

"Yes, that's me." In the real world, it was the first name of her friend, the maiden name of Connie's mother, and the home address of Connie's parents. Cha wouldn't have worked well, considering the lack of Korean heritage in Lacey's blood.

"Can I take your luggage for you, Connie?"

"Yes, thank you." She handed both bags over.

"No problem at all, ma'am. You're the only single we've got at the ranch this week, which means you'll get all the special treatment we can dish out. You'll have a herd of new friends in no time. Right this way, gentlemen." He waved a father and his two teenagers over. "Who wants shotgun?"

"Me!" I edged out the boys. Their disappointment was fleeting.

The luggage was stowed in the rear of the vehicle, then everyone piled in for the ride.

"First off folks, my name is Jayden. I've been working for the Colliers for three years now and I've loved every minute of it. Have any of y'all been to the Collier Ranch before?" He glanced in the rearview mirror to see the boys on their cellphones.

The adults responded in unison. "No."

"Well then, you're in for a real treat. The Collier family runs a wonderful place. It'd be impossible not to enjoy yourselves. You can participate as much or as little as you'd like. Most people are active, but some folks like to relax in the rocking chairs out on the front porch and take it easy to enjoy the view. How many of you have ever ridden a horse before?" Jayden asked. "Show of hands."

The adults raised their hands.

"You kids don't need to worry. We'll teach you everything you need to know and have you riding like real cowboys before you leave us."

"How long is it until we get there?" one of the kids raised his head from his phone long enough to ask.

"It depends on the traffic. Around an hour this time of day."

"A whole *hour*?" The amazement was clear.

"Yep. There isn't anything I can do about it. Sometimes it's longer. Just sit back and relax. I'll tell you about the history of the San Antonio area. There's a lot to tell, so I'll just hit the highlights. It'll take about as long to go through all that as it takes to get to the ranch. But we'll intersperse it with some trivia for fun. My favorite to start with is about my job. Who knows what percentage of cowboys, historically speaking, were African-American?"

"Dad, you didn't tell us there'd be tests on this trip. Especially not math," the oldest boy whined.

Lacey's curiosity was up. "What was it?"

"Estimates put it at around twenty-five percent," Jayden said.

"I had no idea. They didn't teach history right, or comprehensively enough, back when I was in school. What's it like to be a cowboy?" Lacey asked, her anxieties temporarily forgotten.

The kids groaned.

***

"Here we are," Jayden announced as he turned off the main road and passed beneath a high, arching sign reading: Collier Ranch. The black iron script set it off, giving it a Texas feel. And twisted the knot in her stomach tighter.

According to Jayden, they'd been driving alongside the ranch for several miles. Lacey had never seen terrain like it before. Many of the trees were low-growing, but in a mass, they formed a near-impenetrable wall on one side of the road. The silvery green color of some of the vegetation fascinated her. It was so different from the greens back east. She hoped to have the opportunity to explore the sloping hills around them.

The focus naturally shifted to a massive building around a curve in the driveway. The original home was connected by a long, enclosed breezeway to a much larger three-story addition. Both structures drew heavily from Spanish architectural influences, with white stucco exteriors, arches, and chestnut brown barrel-tile roofs. The old homestead had two stone chimneys, whereas the new building had only one, but it was colossal.

They rolled up to the wide wrap-around porch of the guesthouse and stopped there, noting a solar farm in the distance. The front door stood open and welcoming, built of dark wood like something out of a history book, or a movie, with ornate carvings and metal trim. A middle-aged couple rode by on horseback as a few people watched from the porch.

Oversized sunglasses hid Lacey's eyes, her hair tucked under a floppy hat. Reid wouldn't recognize her; perhaps not even Russell would since she was undoubtedly the last person expected to show up. Lacey waited by the Jeep as Jayden unloaded the luggage, wringing her hands and glancing around.

The new arrivals followed Jayden up the low steps and across the porch flanked by two dozen rocking chairs, brightly colored plaid blankets draped over their backs. Inside, the massive main room had floors of hand-scraped walnut, the walls white. Floor-to-ceiling windows along the back wall showcased the expanse of land beyond, including a large pasture and a two-story barn. The view through the windows served as a backdrop for the dining area, with rows of long wooden tables, simple straight-backed chairs, and colorful cushions. An empty buffet line promised food for hungry guests later.

At one end of the room stood the towering stone fireplace, with rows of rocking chairs fanning out in front of it. Plush chairs and couches were nearby for alternative seating. Flat-screen televisions were strategically placed, one of them bigger than Lacey knew existed. Paintings of wildlife and the Old West adorned walls that soared upward three stories, ringed by an interior widow's walk on each floor.

Doors leading into guestrooms lined the walls above, with hallways branching off and away, out of sight, holding additional doors to more guestrooms. Dark, hand-hewn beams spanned the ceiling, while a multitude of stout, squared-off support columns added to the hacienda appearance. A wide, open staircase led to the second and third-floor guestrooms. A young couple leaned on the second floor's decorative black iron railing, gazing at the activity below.

Lacey's fingers moved to release the buttons on her outer shirt, confronted with heat from a combination of warm air and rising nerves. The family she'd arrived with registered at the front desk ahead of her, their luggage in a mound nearby. It was all she could do to stand still while waiting for her turn.

The woman behind the counter, a young redhead, was pleasant and had a warm smile.

"Here's the boss," Jayden announced.

The knot in her stomach yanked tighter and she sucked in a deep gulp of oxygen. The sunglasses still hid her eyes from recognition. But the man approaching was a stranger. He wore jeans, cowboy boots, and a brown shirt. The older gentleman was as tall as Reid and had similar features, but silver hair. She released the breath she'd held, removed her sunglasses, and hooked them on the front of her camisole.

"Welcome to Collier Ranch, folks. My name is Robert Collier. We're going to do our best to make sure you leave us relaxed and happy. After your check-in, stow your gear and then come back down and we'll take a walk around the grounds for orientation. We'll be joined by some other folks who came in earlier today."

So far, so good. She'd keep her hair hidden and her sunglasses on during the orientation. The objective was to speak with father and son alone. If she couldn't make Reid see reason, she might not get to know Russell until he was eighteen and independent of his father. She'd miss out on so much.

And she'd already done that.

***

The tour for a total of ten transitioned from the interior of the guesthouse to the enormous barn, with almost as large of a footprint as the guesthouse. The loft held bales of hay, while the ground floor had two long rows of stalls, one on each side. At one of the short ends of the barn, a door stood open, revealing an office with a large desk. The open doors and stall windows throughout the barn gave the structure an airy feel, mixing with scents of hay, grain, and horses.

A few animals poked their heads over the stall doors, nickering a greeting, hoping for a head rub or a treat.

"Most of our horses are in the pasture. We'll be bringing some of them in for tomorrow's ride. It'll be led by my son, Reid. He's going to show you some of the pretty parts of the ranch."

That had to be a reference to Reid's effort to return the reach of the natural environment. His father didn't seem to approve, from the tone of voice and his expression.

A buckskin horse nudged Lacey's shoulder over the stall door. The need for caution evaporated, forgotten in delight as Lacey rubbed the animal's face and ears, whispering to him. She'd been in love with horses all her life. He blew a soft breath against her shirt, his eyes half-closed.

So engrossed was she in the horse it escaped her attention when a man whistling an upbeat tune entered the barn from up ahead. As the sound registered, along with a trace of memory, the man himself proved startlingly familiar. Reid.

He wore his Stetson and a light blue shirt with worn jeans and work boots. He held a bale of hay in his hands by two loops of twine, nodding as he approached the group. His sleeves were rolled up, revealing muscles enticingly bulged from the weight he carried.

Swallowing at a lump in her throat, Lacey's focus returned to the horse, keeping her back to Reid. His whistling stopped just behind her, bringing with it a reluctance to move for fear of drawing attention to herself. Was her ruse at an end already?

"That's a nice horse. He favors female riders, which makes him smart in my book. He's the one we brought up for you to ride, Miss. He'll do an excellent job for you." Reid's voice sounded just to her left, perhaps a foot away.

Her stomach somersaulted, her body stiffening. She was unprepared, despite having rehearsed for weeks. How could that happen? Had to be the pressure. A sudden reversal of plans came to her, to speak with Russell first. That way, if Reid threw her off his property, at least Russell would know she'd tried to connect with him.

"This is my son folks. His name's Reid," Robert said.

The distraction was welcome, and the timing couldn't have been better.

"Glad to meet everyone. It's time for these horses to have their afternoon hay."

The thump of the hay bale on the ground indicated a glance might be safe, so she risked it. Reid wore a smile as he withdrew a pocketknife, slicing the rough cords holding the bale together. Thick slices of the hay flaked apart, slumping to the ground like dominos, now freed from the rope joining them. Reid resumed whistling as he closed his knife. One of his favorite activities was coming up tomorrow: teaching people the importance of protecting the environment.

A quick decision in support of her plan had her leaving the horse to weave her way among the tourists studying Reid's work to the front of the line and Robert. "Where to next?" She kept her volume low.

"We're taking a quick look outside to show you where we wash the horses; then we'll see the paddocks and the pasture. I doubt any of the other horses are at the front of the pasture just now, but we'll check. Then you can all relax before dinner. Let's move out."

Once outside, Robert pointed out a few of the trails, spreading away from the barn, like wobbly goat paths. There was also a large, fenced pasture that reached out to disappear over a low hill beyond. By the front of the pasture were several paddocks, smaller fenced areas to contain an individual animal while giving them more freedom than a stall. The wash area was easily the nicest she'd ever seen. Everything here was.

"Do we get to pick our horses?" The boy who asked scanned the field ahead, shielding his eyes from the glare with his hand. "I want a white one."

"Well, I want a black one," his younger brother said, mimicking his older sibling's stance.

Robert's face hardened. "We do all the selecting of the mounts you'll ride. We match them in size and personality to you and your riding ability, as noted on your forms. We'll watch real close tomorrow as you ride in the exercise ring to make sure those matches are good ones. If they're not, we'll switch them out with safer mounts. Color doesn't matter. Safety's all that's important. And speaking of safety, we have riding helmets in a variety of sizes. We require kids to wear them while on horseback. It's optional for adults but strongly recommended."

It might not have been wise, but Lacey glanced toward the barn. Reid walked by just then, carrying hay flakes. He glanced in the direction of the group as he passed the doorway, shifting his load to give his hat a tip. Lacey threw a hesitant wave before lengthening her stride to catch up to the others, who had moved off.

"Hey there, Russ! How was school today?" Robert called, gaining Lacey's full attention. "Everyone, this is my grandson, Russell. Russell, this is our newest group of arrivals."

There was no way possible to dim the light on her face as Russell jogged over, a couple of medium-sized dogs at his heels. "Hi, everyone." He wore jeans, tennis shoes, and a green T-shirt. Lacey's attire stood out like someone trying to fit in with a stereotype. Several other guests were dressed like her, making them stand out from those who lived and worked on the ranch. Newbies.

"This place is huge. Does it have Wi-Fi?" one of the boys asked.

"We do, but only up in the main house. You're supposed to enjoy the outdoors, not cellphones. Right, Grandpa?" Russell responded.

"Absolutely. You can play with those anytime. Your father signed you up to get you away from the electronic gadgets, I'm sure. You should spend time in the great outdoors with him. It'll be good for you."

Russell made the rounds, shaking hands with each guest, taking a minute to speak with them, being personable. Due to positioning, Lacey calculated that she should be the last one greeted. Luck was on her side.

"All right, folks. You can wander around as much as you'd like, inside or out, just not off into the brush without a guide. We do have wildlife out here and some of it isn't friendly. Dinner will be served promptly at six. Don't hesitate to stop any of us if you have a question or a concern. It's good to meet you all." Robert strode toward the barn.

The other guests moved in the general direction of the main house, many of them in discussions about whether there might be a policy for cellphone use on a trail ride, wondering if they could get reception away from the main house. Russell extended his hand, the timing near to perfect. If she could delay her revelation for a few seconds, until the tourists were a bit farther away and Robert was out of sight, this part of the plan could work.

"Ma'am, I'm Russell Collier. I'm pleased to make your acquaintance. Are you here alone?"

"Hi. And yes, I am. My name is Connie McCall." Her dark sunglasses worked, although he gave her a curious look. Could he have recognized her voice? Then she noticed he'd grown in the brief time since she met him.

"Well, welcome to the ranch. There's plenty around here to keep you occupied. You'll make new friends before you know it. You don't have to worry about being alone. I've got to go now to help bring more horses down for tomorrow morning's trail ride; if you'll excuse me."

"Sure Russell." Beyond, Robert disappeared into the shadows of the barn's interior.

Russell started toward the barn. The other tourists seemed far enough away.

"Russell?" Lacey called.

He returned to her right away. "Yes ma'am?"

She took a deep breath and released it before removing her hat, which allowed her hair to cascade past her shoulders. She followed the hat with the removal of her sunglasses. The expression on his face was priceless. Lacey responded with her biggest smile. "Hey,

Russell."

"Mom!" He lunged forward and threw his arms around her, giving her a bear hug so tight it bordered on pain. One of her bones popped. "I missed you."

"I missed you, too." He'd called her mom. She liked being called mom more than she'd ever imagined. A wave of warmth and belonging swept over her. Strange how it made her want to cry.

It took a minute for his grip to loosen. It broke her heart at the sight of tears in his eyes. She gave him another big smile. "It's only been a few months, but I think you've grown since you were in Charlotte."

He liked the observation, squaring his shoulders. "I have. I've grown two inches and put on ten pounds."

"I'll bet you could pick me up. Don't try it, though," she added, extending a hand for restraint as she remembered he was a teenage boy who'd probably enjoy proving his strength to his mother.

"You're going to be tall, like your dad." Then she remembered Reid wasn't far away. Lacey's eyes darted to the door and back. "And I see you've cut your hair. I like it. It makes you look more grown-up, though." Her eyes narrowed for effect. "I'm not sure I like that part of it."

"Dad said the same thing. What're you doing here, Mom? Is this a surprise for my birthday?" His grin just wouldn't stop.

Her face fell. Something else she'd never considered. "No, Russell. I'm sorry. I never even thought to ask you when your birthday was. When is it?"

"March third."

Her brain stumbled into a quick calculation, not simple considering how taken aback she was already. "Saturday. I didn't know. I should've asked you back in Charlotte."

"It's okay. I didn't get to Charlotte in time to celebrate yours last year. It came right before I got to you. Even if you didn't come for my birthday, I'm glad you're here. But why'd you come? And why haven't you called me? Or texted? You promised you would.

"Dad said he hasn't heard from you, either. He wouldn't let me call you. He said you might've thought about the situation and changed your mind. He said it was your right, and I shouldn't have invaded your privacy in the first place." His smile had vanished.

"No, Russell, no. That's not what happened. I sent your dad tons of texts and left voicemails, all this time we've been apart, multiple times every day. He never responded. I figured in all the excitement when he picked you up in Charlotte maybe he'd lost the business card I gave him and forgot where I work." Which was ridiculous to contemplate, let alone say aloud. Reid Collier had some serious explaining to do.

"I told your dad I wouldn't contact you until we'd gotten to know each other the way he wanted. I don't understand why he never got back to me. I plan to find out what happened while I'm here."

"My dad wouldn't have done that on purpose. He would've called you back." Russell wore a frown.

"It seemed strange to me, but I don't know your dad. So, I decided to give him the benefit of the doubt and some time. After a while, I got mad and found the ranch phone number on your website. I left multiple emails through the site and voicemails on the ranch phone, but there was no reply." That was enough. It would be better to discuss this with his father instead.

"I don't understand. We've never had a problem with our phones before. Dad will have to check on it. He's in the barn." Russell grinned and took her by the hand, but she pulled free. "What's wrong?"

"He doesn't know I'm here yet. I paid for everything and came under the name of a friend of mine, as a tourist, in disguise. I wasn't sure how your father would react to me being here. But I had to see you. It's why I came here under an assumed name. All I could think of was getting to you."

"You didn't need a disguise. My dad wouldn't keep us apart. Come on." He walked off, forcing Lacey to move if she wanted to keep talking with him.

This had to be confronted; might as well be now. She moved faster to catch up. "Did you get the Christmas card and present I sent you?"

"Card? No. There wasn't anything. I checked the mail every day after dinner once we got back from Charlotte. Especially since we didn't hear back from you."

"I sent a card. Two of them, one to your dad and one to you. His was in a regular envelope, but yours was in a padded mailer because of the present. I didn't want to risk someone feeling something inside the card and maybe taking it.

"Since I don't know much about you, I sent a gift card to a big sporting goods store. I checked online first, to make sure they had one of them in San Antonio. I remembered how much you said you liked sports and being outside."

"A gift card would've been nice. But my dad always says it's the thought that counts. And my aunt gave me a bunch of stuff for Christmas from a big sporting goods store, so it worked out. She's spent a lot of extra time with my dad since we got back from Charlotte, seeing as how you never contacted us. She's been nice to me, too.

"She said she could tell we were disappointed and needed special attention because we'd been rejected, especially my dad. He took it harder than me, I think. I don't know why. He only talked to you for a minute at the airport. Aunt Kate said you didn't know what you were missing out on, but she did."

Lacey's jaw clenched tight enough to make speech difficult. "What did she give you?"

"Let's see. There were three athletic shirts, a nice all-weather jacket, and some new cleats for baseball."

Interesting. Lacey had visited the same chain store herself in Charlotte and checked on the prices of similar items for Russell before purchasing the gift card, to make sure there'd be enough money on it. Those items would add up to about the amount on the card she'd sent. "Does she shop for you there a lot?"

"No. This was the first time she bought me stuff I liked for Christmas. She usually gives me a book. She's not into sports, but she came to one of my games once, a long time ago."

The barn loomed large and scary. "Books are good presents." Lacey tried to find something positive to say about the woman since the aunt was a relative of her son. Her thoughts shifted to the moment. "Russell, listen. I'm worried your father will be upset with me."

"Come on, dad will understand. We'll talk to him. This is great!" He was about to explode from excitement.

The foreboding doorway to the barn loomed, voices emanating from inside. Reluctance held her back. A deep breath didn't help, so she kept her eyes on Russell. "Okay."

"It'll be all right. My dad's a nice guy."

Skeptical and anxious, Lacey followed Russell in. As her eyes adjusted to the light level, it became apparent where the voices were coming from. Robert, Reid, and Jayden stood at the far end of the barn near the office, talking and laughing.

The borrowed hat crumpled in her hand. She'd have to buy Connie a new one. There was no longer a disguise to hide behind.

As they drew closer, her pulse rate increased as the change came to Reid's face in slow motion. Since she didn't know him, she couldn't predict his reaction. It was likely someone could push him over with a feather right about now. Lacey's trepidation grew with each step. Would he call the police?

"Connie, what can we do for you? Reid, Jayden, this is Connie McCall, a newly arrived guest," Robert said with a smile.

"Yes sir, I remember. I brought her in from the airport this afternoon. Do you know what? She came here with one small bag to last her a whole week! I couldn't believe it."

"Lacey." The name trailed off Reid's tongue. Standing in front of him was the woman so lovely he'd been momentarily at a loss for words in the airport. He thought her lost to him, after such a long time with no contact. Rejected. Not an hour in a day since then had passed without seeing her smiling face in his mind. And now, by some miracle, she stood in front of him.

"Dad, she came to see me. She had to come in person because..." his words spilled out, running together as he tried to mediate.

This was something Lacey knew she had to handle. She placed a hand on Russell's shoulder and shook her head, facing down Reid. Russell's presence gave her courage.

"Mr. Collier, I came here to visit my son. I've tried to contact you daily, repeatedly, since we met in Charlotte, but you never answered any of my text messages, emails, phone calls, or voice messages, of which there have been plenty. I apologize for coming here under false pretenses, but it was the only way I could think of to see Russell. I wanted him to know I'd tried my best. I wanted him to know I cared."

"She sent Christmas cards to you and me, Dad. We never got those, either."

"No, we didn't. We didn't." Reid appeared stunned. Did this mean she wanted to be part of their family? She'd been trying to contact them, all this time? What could've gone wrong?

"I don't mean any harm and I'm not attempting to undermine your authority here, Mr. Collier. Even knowing you might have me forcibly removed from your property, I couldn't leave Russell thinking I didn't care about him. You have my apologies for the ruse."

She'd never been in trouble with the law before. Reid Collier held her future in his hands, with a choice to be made. Which one would it be? Fear gripped her, so she bit down on her trembling lower lip in a failing attempt at control. One large tear slid down her cheek. She hated crying, particularly in front of strangers, or men, or men who were strangers.

"No Mom. It's okay, please don't cry. He wouldn't kick you off the ranch. Would you Dad?" Russell's hand moved to her shoulder in a show of solidarity.

Reid's astonishment shone clear. "No, of course not," he

stumbled. "It's just... this is unexpected. I assumed you'd changed your mind. I never imagined we'd see you again."

Assumed or wished? She didn't trust this man at all. Those deep brown eyes spoke to her, tried to take her into their depths. She blinked the thought of it away. Resentment had her, but she couldn't help the attraction she felt, though she wished she could.

"Mom? Do you mean this is the woman who..." Robert seemed at a loss for words.

"She's my mom. The only mom I've got left. Lacey, this is my grandpa, my dad's father. Grandpa, this is Lacey Freemont."

She extended her hand for a shake. Robert hesitated but took it. "It's a pleasure to meet you. I've heard a lot about you from Russell. He said you were both pretty and cool; for your age."

Age? Did her son think she was old? That took her aback and she turned to Russell.

"I didn't mean it like that. I didn't mean you were old or anything. You're just older than me and my friends. You're younger than my dad." The focus shifted to Reid.

"Thanks a lot, Russ." Reid rubbed a hand over his chin and the approaching five o'clock shadow. His voice lowered, softened. After close to forty years of being around horses, starting when he could walk halfway decent on his own, the reaction was instinctive. "I'm sorry about all this, Lacey. I have no idea what might've happened. I never received any texts or voice messages from you, though. I made sure to check every evening before I went to bed, at least until sometime after the new year started. There weren't any emails, either.

"It sounds strange and probably hard to believe, but I've never even been able to find the business card you gave me. I remember putting it on my dresser, tucked into the edge of a framed photograph of Russell and me. Something happened to it, a breeze or something must've blown it off.

" I even moved the dresser after I searched for the card with a flashlight. It upset me I'd lost it, and it was Thanksgiving Day. I wanted to call you, to let you and Russell have some time to talk. I figured on calling you at work that next Monday. But then you didn't call us over the Thanksgiving holiday, so I didn't pursue it. I should have." He sighed.

"I apologize you felt you had to go to these lengths to visit Russell. You and I will need to put our heads together soon and see if we can't figure out what went wrong to prevent it from happening again. We'll make sure of it."

"Do you mean she can stay?" Russell's voice went high, filled with hope.

"Of course, she can stay." Reid seemed bewildered that the question even needed to be asked.

"Thanks, Dad!" Russell charged into his father's embrace. If the man hadn't been standing by a wall, the impact might have sent them both to the ground.

Reid grunted from the collision before recovering to pat his son on the back. He turned his gaze to Lacey. Russell stepped aside to allow his father to pass. "I'm sorry, Lacey. We'll figure it out, whatever happened, and fix it, okay? I don't want any more communication breakdowns between the three of us."

"I'd appreciate it." She hadn't imagined he'd be nice about everything. She'd been braced for a battle. Slowly, she released the breath she'd been holding since boarding the plane in Charlotte that morning.

"There's not much left of the day, but why don't you spend it with Russell? Russell, you can teach Lacey the proper way to brush her horse. Then, the two of you could go for a short ride. How does that sound for a start?"

Since Reid was staring intently into her eyes, not turning to Russell, Lacey assumed he meant her. "It sounds wonderful, thank you. I'll take whatever time I can get with him."

"You'd better get started. Dinner will be on the table before you know it. I'm sure Lacey must be hungry after her plane ride. We'll keep something warm for you both, so you don't have to rush to be at the table by six." He glanced at Russell. "But do your best and don't have Lacey out riding after dark if you can help it. At least stay on the lighted trails."

"Okay, Dad."

Russell grabbed her hand and charged away with her to Spark's stall, the others trailing along at a distance. They stopped several feet away to observe, making Lacey feel like a mouse in a laboratory. She stood ready for the challenge, though still tense. She tucked her sunglasses onto her camisole again.

"The color of this one is called buckskin. He's got a light coat, kind of like a palomino, but with dark points instead of white. His are almost black. Sorry, Mom. Points are what they call the colors on the mane, tail, and legs.

"His name is Spark, for the cluster of white hairs up near the top of his head. Here, look." Russell lifted the horse's forelock to reveal the burst of white. It looked for all the world like the sparklers she'd played with one Fourth of July when she was a kid.

"He'll be yours while you're here. He's an easy horse for girls to ride. Step back and I'll show you how to get him out of his stall."

Time to change this up and make an impression, to show them what she was made of. Lacey jammed the hat onto her head. "Hang on a second, Russell. Let me give it a try."

Russell's eyes widened, but she moved too fast for him to stop her. She opened the latch on the stall door and swung it aside just enough for her to fit through. Spark nickered, lowering his head. Lacey took hold of his halter and rubbed him underneath, taking care to spend time behind his ears, while he pressed his face against her abdomen. Then she led him from the stall and over to a set of crossties, hooking the clips on the ends of each rope to rings on his halter that served to hold horses in place for grooming and saddling.

"Where're his brushes?" she asked, one hand fiddling with Spark's mane and a sly grin on her face. First test passed.

The men stood wide-eyed at what they'd witnessed.

"You know your way around a horse!" Robert, the first to recover, said with clear approval in his voice.

"Yes sir, I do. It's been a long time, though. Twenty years, give or take."

"It's like riding a bicycle," Robert said as Jayden dashed off to return with a five-gallon bucket holding supplies, passing it to her with a big grin and a quick wink.

"Thanks, Jayden." The young cowboy was easy to like. Lacey's first friend at the ranch.

"You're welcome, ma'am."

Reid and Robert observed as Lacey worked. Russell stuck close, telling her what a good job she was doing as if their roles of parent and child were temporarily reversed.

She curried and brushed, then plucked mud, a couple of small stones, and debris out of his hooves with the hoof pick until they were clean. All the while, she made sure to talk to the animal. Lacey patted him as she moved around his body, helping him keep track of where she was. He behaved well, but she didn't want to risk being kicked.

"Where're the saddle and blanket?" she asked.

"I'll get them," Russell offered.

"No, Russ. You'd better go ahead and take care of your horse. It looks like she's going to beat you to it." Reid chuckled.

"Okay, Dad!" Russell skidded as he scrambled for a horse farther down the line.

Robert approached with a bridle slung over his shoulder and handed over a striped blanket, which Lacey arranged on Spark's back. Jayden brought the saddle.

"I'll get this for you, ma'am. It's smaller and lighter, but overall Western saddles are heavy."

"I know, but I can do it myself, thanks."

They both looked to Reid, who laughed and nodded. Jayden handed off the saddle to Lacey. "Could you hook the far stirrup over the saddle horn for me, please?"

"Yes ma'am." He performed the task, which kept the stirrup clear for swinging the mass of leather up and across the horse's back, then easing it into place. Saddles were heavier than she remembered, but she was stronger now than all those years ago, not to mention determined not to ask for help or make a mistake.

Once the girth was fastened and everything else arranged, she measured the stirrups to length and adjusted them to fit her legs. Throughout the process, she smothered her nerves by focusing on the tasks at hand and talking to the horse.

Robert laughed heartily, clapping his hands. "She's perfect! I'm giving you a ten out of ten on the spot, Lacey. It's amazing to me you can remember everything after such a long time. You must've paid close attention."

"I did. I love horses. I've wanted a horse since I saw one in a book when I was a kid. Every book I checked out for pleasure reading until I turned eighteen had to be about horses. My all-time favorite author was Walter Farley. He wrote The Black Stallion books. My parents never had the money for a horse or lessons. I rode a couple of times with a friend from school when I was older. I cleaned the barn and tack in exchange for the privilege." She slipped on the bridle and rubbed Spark's forehead as he mouthed the bit.

"Well, I think Spark loves you. He's always been fond of the ladies," Robert said.

"He's thrown many a man who tried to ride him; never a female, though," Jayden added.

"How odd." Spark pawed the floor and Lacey jiggled the reins. "No."

His head rose to meet hers and his near eye blatantly stared at her, as though taken aback at being subjected to discipline from the woman who'd given him a nice rubdown. But he stopped pawing.

"Well done. You can't let them get away with misbehaving," Robert said.

"You about ready, Russ?" Reid called, leaning against an empty stall, his eyes taking in everything. She was so much more than he'd imagined. Or dreamed. But he had to maintain his distance to make sure she wasn't here just for herself. This had to be about Russell, too. He didn't want his son hurt.

"Yes sir," came the reply.

"Do you want to go on outside and mount up, ma'am? I can take you," Jayden offered.

"I'll take her out. You and I will be bringing in the horses for tomorrow's ride, Jayden. You can get started. I'll be right there. Follow me, Lacey." Reid led her outside to the mounting block, which made getting onto the horse easier.

"Thanks again for allowing me to stay here and spend time with Russell."

Reid held the reins to ensure the horse remained steady, though the animal didn't give any indication of being otherwise. "You have a right to get to know your son. I just..." He stopped.

"You just what?" She swung up into the saddle and settled.

"I just hope you're serious about Russell, about being there for him. If this is merely a curiosity for you, you'll destroy him. I don't want to see that happen. He's handed you the key to his heart."

"He's got mine right back. I'll never let him down. He means a lot to me. I'd never do anything to hurt Russell."

"I don't know you very well, but I'm giving you some rope here; don't hang yourself with it. I'm entrusting you with my son."

"I won't let you down. I promise." Lacey had the strong impression he didn't believe her. Maybe he didn't even like her.

"I'm going to hold you to it. *I* promise." Reid's expression held firm. His son was more important than anyone else.

The seriousness of the moment was broken by the arrival of Russell. She could understand Reid's concern. He'd decided to hand over what he held most precious in the world to a stranger. While she didn't know anything about being a parent, she knew she'd feel the same way in Reid's shoes.

"Okay, Mom. Let's go. I'll show you around this part of the ranch." Russell moved his horse off.

"You two stay safe." Reid patted her horse's neck as they moved by, maintaining eye contact with her. He was attracted to her, but his son's well-being remained paramount.

Lacey simply nodded, taking up a position beside Russell.

"We will. Follow me, Mom."

Overall, this had turned out better than she'd hoped. Lacey smiled, knowing she'd follow Russell Collier anywhere.

FIVE

Friday morning arrived bright and early, just the way Lacey liked it, being an early riser and lover of a new, sunny day. The beautiful blue sky and expansive views through the large windows of the dining area distracted her from a review of the previous night's events.

The investigation had ended on a discouraging note, leaving Russell, Reid, and Lacey unable to figure out what happened with the calls, texts, and emails she'd sent. Lacey's phone provided concrete proof, a record of her many efforts, with Reid verifying the numbers she'd used were correct. Her number in his phone and Russell's, however, was one digit off. Very strange. She went to bed with suspicions intact. Communications had mysteriously vanished on Reid's end.

Lacey didn't dare hurl accusations. It wouldn't help her situation, or make Reid like her. Which he didn't. It was easy to tell last night. He'd been anxious, despite the bounty of smiles he'd given, relief apparent when she'd surrendered the effort in favor of sleep.

On a happier note, the breakfast in front of her was proving as good as the dinner had been, both served buffet style. Russell told her they had even larger spreads on weekends, due to additional bed and breakfast guests. It was great sharing another meal with her son.

Relaxed and happy, Lacey munched on a perfectly cooked slice of bacon as she discussed her favorite breakfast foods with Russell.

"Anything with bacon, especially as outstanding as this, is always a favorite for me." She studied the slice clasped between her fingers as Russell chuckled. It was her third slice and three more waited on her plate.

"Good morning. Is this seat taken?"

When Lacey glanced up, it was into Reid's beaming face. The joviality went out of the air for her like an inflated balloon, let loose so the air inside gushed out. Effort forced the corners of her mouth upward.

"Morning. Here, please sit down." She patted the seat cushion. Why did he want to sit beside her instead of taking the vacant spot next to Russell? Would he subject her to questioning, maybe with a side of subtle threats? Probably not with Russell around.

Reid sat with a mounded plate as a waitress filled the nearby coffee mug. In her other hand, she held the steaming mug of tea Russell had requested for his mother. "Is there anything else I can get for you, ma'am?" She sat the mug by Lacey's plate.

"No, thank you. Tea's all I needed. I appreciate it."

"Let me know if you change your mind or want a second cup." She moved to the mug of another guest, filling it with strong black coffee. The aroma from Reid's wafted her way.

"You're a tea drinker?" Reid asked.

Was there disdain in his tone or was it her imagination? She still couldn't shake the sense of being judged.

"Yes. English Breakfast is my favorite. I like the smell of coffee okay, but I've never enjoyed the taste. Do you drink it black?" There was little else she could think of to say in the way of small talk with this man. Everything felt uncomfortable around him.

"No, I have a sweet tooth. Sugar and creamer are fattening and unhealthy, but I can't resist. Excuse me, please." He reached for both condiments, stationed in clusters down the center of the table. In between those were clear vases filled with spears of bright yellow spring flowers.

As he reached past her, she smelled manly soap and had to

Dying for a Family – A.L. Nelson

refocus her attention from imagining him taking a shower. That brought on a rush of heat and increased her heart rate. "Well, you must work it off during the day, because you look like you're in really good shape." There went her nerves, invading her mouth. Hopefully, he wouldn't take it other than how it was intended, but Lacey wouldn't blame him for thinking she was being forward.

He turned to her with a definite gleam in his eye as he poured creamer. Was she interested? It sounded that way. His heart rate increased. "Thank you, Lacey; that's nice to hear, especially coming from such an attractive woman."

Wrong way. But how could she recover? Wait. Did he just call her attractive? Under the circumstances, she could've heard the attractive part wrong, but he did call her beautiful on the phone before. When she shouldn't have been eavesdropping.

"You're welcome. I doubt there're many heavyset ranchers around, though. Are there?"

"There are, just like in the general population. But there aren't many in the immediate vicinity; not too bad, anyway. I encourage everyone working here to stay healthy. It keeps our healthcare costs lower and it's good for the employees, too. We have a gym for them to use, which is also open to our guests. Do you work out, Lacey?" He plunged his fork into a pile of scrambled eggs.

"Yes. We have a small gym in my apartment complex. I go there at least five days a week. I jog on the treadmill and lift weights occasionally." Polishing off the last bite of the bacon she held, Lacey tore off a chunk of homemade buttermilk biscuit to taste before slicing it open to slather on jelly.

"Even a little weightlifting helps keep the body toned. It gets plenty hot enough here in the summer months for you to wear shorts and a tank top around the ranch or a bikini for our swimming pool. You may not have noticed the pool yet. It's a big one, with a waterfall, a slide, and a splash pad we just had put in last year for the young ones who aren't ready for the big pool yet."

What just happened here? Bikini? Did she miss something? She must've missed something. Reid didn't even like her. She licked her tongue over dried lips and cleared her throat to seek clarification. "The summer?"

"I thought I'd go ahead and extend an invitation for a long vacation for you this summer if you're interested. You could stay a month or even the entire summer. Bring your bikini and anything else you want. You'll be able to get to know us better, since it's a slower time of year as far as the guests go, and Russell will be out of school."

Reid must not have been against her after all. While the invitation came as a huge relief, she wasn't sure about the bikini part, which would be uncomfortable. For her, anyway. "It sounds wonderful. I won't be able to do a lengthy stay, but maybe I could do a long weekend in there somewhere. I'm hoping I'll be able to come every quarter for a long weekend visit. If it's okay. I'll be able to keep up with Russell's life better than two weeklong vacations."

"They don't give you a lot of time off where you work, do they?" Reid couldn't contain his disappointment and it crept into his voice.

"It's on par with other governments. But now that I have a son to get acquainted with, it's nowhere near enough."

"Maybe you could get a job here," Russell suggested.

"Oh, I don't think so, Russell." Lacey brushed a hand across his shoulder. "At least, we don't need to be making any plans right now." She got the words out fast, wanting Reid to know she wasn't trying to wedge herself into their lives full-time. Not that she wouldn't like to, especially now that Reid seemed okay with her presence. He was a difficult man to figure out. But then, most of them seemed to be.

"Why not?"

"Well, I think we all need to get to know each other better before I even consider making such a big move. I don't even know anybody in Texas except you two." Lacey glanced to the mug of tea she'd love to quench her thirst with, but steam still gushed from it. The glass of ice water beside it did the trick.

"We're all you need." Russell's eyes begged.

"That's nice to say, honey, but it doesn't help me with a job." How could she explain this to a child?

"You could work here on the ranch. Dad will give you a job, won't you Dad?"

This wasn't a direction she'd intended for their breakfast conversation. She turned to Reid in her rising sense of fluster, but he didn't look upset. Lacey didn't want to be the bad guy, but under the circumstances, Reid shouldn't be the parent who was forced to say no to Russell.

"Russell, this isn't the kind of work I went to school for. I don't want to cook or clean for a living, and I don't have the necessary toughness and coordination to be a cowgirl. And this ranch is too far away from a city I'd be able to work at. The best I could do is see you for a brief time on weekends since this is a busy place and your dad and grandfather need your help around here. And I'd be starting over in my life and career."

"But you wouldn't be starting over. You know us. And at least we'd see you on the weekends. You could spend the whole weekend with us, every weekend," Russell pleaded.

She'd already managed to hurt him. Great mother she was turning out to be. "You understand, don't you, Russell? It has nothing to do with you, I promise. I'd love to live closer to you. Let's just take it slow and see how everything works out, okay?"

"Okay." He toyed with his eggs.

After a long pause and a couple of slow sips of coffee as he stared out the big wall of windows, Reid added his thoughts. "Well, I hope you'll at least spend the major holidays here with us, Lacey. It'd be a good start for you and Russell. For all three of us."

Her mouth sagged open for a moment. "Yes, thank you." Three?

"Good. Then it's settled. We'll see about adding on from there." One step at a time.

"But the holidays are a long way off," Russell complained.

"Not too far. Easter's coming." She forced an upbeat tone. It seemed long to her, too. "What I can do is combine my visits here with holidays and a day or two of vacation, like Memorial Day. I'd be here for maybe two or three full days and a couple of partial days. It won't be more than that, because the travel takes up part of the time I'll have off."

"Oh."

The disappointment continued. Lacey felt it, a twinge in her heart. Had she made her parents feel that way? Probably more than once.

"Let's see the glass as half full, son. It's better to have her here for a little while than not at all, right?"

"Yes sir."

"Do you like grits, Lacey?" Reid asked, diverting the conversation. His eyes took in the full mini bowl by her plate. Knowing her favorites would ensure they were around every time she visited. The familiarity might add to a sense of comfort and home.

"I adore grits. The consistency of these looks promising."

"They're the best I've ever had, personally. Our head cook could stand with the best in New York or Los Angeles. She's amazing. What is it you've put on them?"

"I just add a pad of butter and a sprinkling of brown sugar. I discovered it when my parents took me to Disney World for a long weekend when I was a kid. It was the only real vacation we ever had. It was wonderful."

"I've never taken Russell there, but I've always meant to."

"Could the three of us go, Dad?" Russell's face shone with excitement.

Lacey's mouth fell open, her throat instantly going bone dry. The three of them? On a vacation with her newfound son *and* his father? His handsome father. It would be kind of awkward; more than kind of... and more than awkward. Again, she decided to say something to handle this for Reid, who must've been equally taken aback. "Russell."

Reid spoke simultaneously, his voice brimming with enthusiasm. "That's a great idea! If Lacey wants to, that is. I'm sorry, Lacey. I didn't mean to put you on the spot." Reid rested his hand over hers, squeezing it before moving away.

"Oh. No. I'm fine. You're right, it... sounds great." She licked her dehydrated lips with a moisture-starved tongue. "I'd love to." The words came with so little enthusiasm it should generate concern on Reid's part. Yet, he didn't seem to notice. Why did this feel like a blind date? It was incredibly uncomfortable, worse than a blind date. There was much more at stake.

"Then it's settled. All we need to do is select a time of year for our first family trip. When do you think is best, Lacey? You're the lone one of us with experience. That means you're officially in charge of the details."

This was fantastic. Before she knew it, he'd have her moving in. She seemed genuinely interested in Russell. The boy's father was the next logical step. If she lived here, they could go for long horseback rides, strolls at sunset, goodnight kisses. Long ones. Kisses that would lead to other things.

Lacey momentarily had no words. Their first family trip? Why was it so infernally hot in here? Couldn't someone open a window or two, or maybe all of them? Or turn on a ceiling fan? A glance to the ceiling showed all the fans spinning. Could a person sweat to death in the span of one extraordinarily long minute?

"Well, I'm no expert. It was a long time ago. We were there for Christmas. It was beautiful but crowded, so it was hard to get on as many rides. I'd want you guys to ride a lot since it's fun. Summer would be difficult because of the heat.

" It's a different kind of hot from what you're used to here. The East Coast has humidity. I don't want to risk either of you having a problem with the combination of heat and humidity, but we should also find a time when Russell won't miss school, I assume."

"We'll figure it out. I think it'd be okay if he missed school, maybe in conjunction with a holiday or school break." A grinning Reid leaned past Lacey to see his son's face.

"Can we Dad?" Russell's eyebrows reached toward the ceiling.

"Sure. Why not? It'll be special for all of us." Reid's grin remained wide.

"This'll be fun! I can't wait!" Russell exclaimed, taking off nearly half his huge biscuit in a single bite.

***

Lacey lingered by the registration desk, awaiting Russell's arrival. Reid spoke with guests near the front door. When their eyes met, he sent her a bright smile. She responded with a wave.

"So. You must be Lacey Freshman."

The words, painstakingly articulated, were long icicles stabbing in her back. Lacey turned.

A tall woman with brown eyes and dark hair extending to her waist stood nearby. Her eyebrows had been groomed into tight, perfect lines, the makeup bordering on heavy in Lacey's opinion. Cherry red lipstick topped it off.

The woman was lovely in her bright blue dress, even if it was on the tight-and-revealing side. The pushup bra performed its job to perfection, yet there were no lines indicative of panties. Couldn't hide them with a dress as clingy as hers. Exceedingly high heels matched the color of the dress, putting her on eye level with Reid, no doubt. She wasn't dressed like anyone else around. She stood out, contrasting with Lacey's jeans, T-shirt, and worn jacket.

"Yes, I am. Hi." Lacey offered her hand for a shake. It would be pointless to argue about the name when it was being mangled on purpose. The hair on her neck stood on end as voice recognition came. Instincts from that phone call were on target.

The woman's grip held like a vice, leaving Lacey rubbing her fingers when the woman let go. "I'm Reid's sister-in-law, Kate Sandler. I run the ranch for Reid since I'm a member of the family and all, plus considering he and I are close."

"Oh. Kate." Lacey enunciated the name as Kate had just done, sizing the woman up. "Yes, Russell mentioned an aunt. You're taller than I'd imagined. Nice shoes."

"We may as well go ahead and cut the pleasantries."

"I'm sorry?" The look in Kate's eyes gave Lacey pause. Good thing looks couldn't kill. The new mother fought the instinct to take a step back.

Kate took a single step closer, dipping her head toward Lacey's. "You very well might be. Stay away from Reid."

"Excuse me?" Lacey leaned back from her, angry with herself for relinquishing any ground, however small.

"You think I don't know why you're here? When I arrived at work this morning, I was told how you'd conned your way onto our ranch like a wolf after my lamb. You're after Reid and he's *mine*. You'll steer clear of him if you know what's good for you. Texas is a beautiful place, but it can be dangerous, too."

"Whoa, now." Kate had just taken this, whatever *this* was, too far for Lacey's comfort. "You need to hold on with your threats and accusations. I have no interest in Reid. I'm here for Russell. He's my son."

"I'm aware. But you've wormed your way into the family holidays." Her eyes narrowed into slits.

"Reid asked me. It wasn't my idea."

"He's innocent and too nice to everyone he meets for his own good. He hasn't seriously dated a woman since my sister. You come here and start flirting with him, flaunting yourself in front of him because you're low enough to sell your eggs…"

The aunt had just crossed the line, venturing into dangerous territory. Jaw set, Lacey leaned toward her opponent this time. "Now you wait just a minute. I haven't been flirting with Reid. I told you, I'm here for Russell. And what happened with my eggs isn't any of your business."

"I saw you at breakfast, laughing at everything Reid said, blushing, touching him, batting your eyes. You listen to me, you little thief. You don't belong here. This is my turf and I'll have you know that Reid and this ranch belong to me. You can forget about getting your greedy hooks into him. You're a gold digger after my family and my ranch.

"This place is worth almost a billion dollars, including what's under the ground and in the bank. And it'll never be yours. You have no idea who you're dealing with. I'll do whatever it takes to keep what's mine."

Kate smelled of an overdose of expensive perfume and had lipstick smeared across her upper teeth. Lacey didn't enjoy being close enough to notice any of those things. "Your family? Funny how you've mentioned Reid but not Russell in your family."

"Reid's mine." The snarl showed the reddish tinge to her teeth. And maybe her eyes. She was intimidating.

"Hold on a second. First of all, I'm no threat to you because I have no interest in Reid as I've already told you. More than once. But you should remember he's a grown man, capable of making his own decisions. Second, your family technically includes me now, since I'm the mother of your nephew. Third, I'm not going anywhere. You might want to keep *that* in mind."

Russell jogged over. "Good morning, Aunt Kate. Have you met my mom?"

She bristled. "*Mom?* You mean Ms. Freidman. We were having a lovely conversation, weren't we?"

Lacey's teeth were still clenched. It took a few seconds to unlock her facial muscles enough to enable a response. "I guess it depends on your definition of lovely, but sure. Are you ready to go, Russell?"

"Yes ma'am. We'll see you later, Aunt Kate."

"Have a good day, you two!" she said with exaggerated enthusiasm as they left the building.

Lacey shook her head as they left the female Janus. "So, your aunt is in charge of running the ranch, huh?"

"No. Dad and Grandpa do most of it. Aunt Kate helps make sure everything that needs doing gets done. My dad gave her the job a long time ago. She does what my mom did, along with Becky. She's the nice lady who checked you in when you got here. She handles the paperwork and answering the phones and taking reservations. Becky's my aunt's assistant."

"Who's in charge of the ranch's website and email?"

"Aunt Kate."

"Interesting." She'd be willing to bet Kate also signed for packages and opened the mail. It would be wrong to accuse Kate of keeping her from the Colliers without tangible proof but maybe there was some to be found. She wished she'd had a recorder or a witness for the conversation a few minutes ago. "She seems busy to run a website in addition to everything else she must have on her plate."

"A professional company designed it not too long ago. There isn't much for anyone else to do."

Which meant Kate wasn't a computer geek like Lacey had always been, which would help with the plan rolling around in her head. One of these days, she'd get her hands on that computer and teach Kate a thing or two. "Does she handle finances?" The shadowy barn interior added to the early morning chill.

"Let's grab our gear first. And Dad wanted you to wear this old white riding hat we've got that he thinks might fit you. It'll protect your skull in case of an accident. He says it's just until you're comfortable. He's worried you could fall and get hurt." He veered toward the tack room. "And my dad takes care of the finances. He's smart with numbers."

"That's good to hear." At least there wasn't a worry about Kate siphoning money away from the ranch or Russell's college fund, assuming he had one. As close as college was getting, the question needed to be asked. Lacey would contribute what she could.

"I'm sure those good math genes got passed along to you. Math is important for almost anything you want to do in your life." They carried the gear to the outside saddling area to take advantage of the sun's warmth.

"Hey, my dad says that, too."

"Russell, I've been thinking about something." They deposited their gear and returned to the barn for the horses. "I was thinking whenever your aunt is around you shouldn't call me mom."

"Why not?" He turned to her, wounded.

Because Kate didn't seem stable, and the word mom might add to her volatility, but she couldn't put it to him like that. "Because her sister was also your mom, and it might hurt her feelings to hear you calling me by the same name. Come to think of it, you should ask your dad about it. I wouldn't want to cause anyone pain." Except for Kate. If Lacey could hold her own against the woman, she wouldn't mind causing Kate a little pain.

"I never thought about it like that. I'll check with them."

"Not them...just your dad. He's the one whose feelings matter the most. Or better yet just call me Lacey all the time. At least for now, okay?"

"Okay. How about when we're alone? Can I call you mom then?"

One corner of her mouth rose. "I'd like that."

***

They rode along a narrow path, Russell checking over his shoulder for his mother's progress, even though Lacey was close enough for them to carry on a conversation. A deep sense of joy came every time he smiled, which he did whenever he looked back. Sometimes, his voice cracked or came out high and squeaky.

Lacey didn't laugh unless he did, which was often. The scenery was wonderful, but she spent most of the ride studying Russell. He carried himself well astride his horse. And he had many of the same mannerisms his father possessed.

"Here it is, Mom. What do you think?"

The path widened, enabling her to move Spark alongside Russell's horse. The land ahead slid away in a long, gentle slope. The vista was unlike anything she'd ever seen. "Wow."

"It's pretty now, but in a month or two it'll be a million times better. This isn't just ours. Parts of it belong to a couple of neighboring ranches, too. We've got loads of sunflowers, blue bonnets, which Texas is famous for, in case you didn't know. And we've got Indian paintbrush. Those flowers are bright red. There're lots of other wildflowers, too. And Texas sage on the hills over there," he pointed. "It's beautiful all year but spring and summer are the prettiest."

The farthest hills were a wispy violet, while the sky was deep blue with a scattering of cotton balls for clouds drifting past on a lazy breeze. The land stretching out toward those violet hills had begun greening up for spring, bright and cheerful, even without the benefit of flowers.

"This is such a great place. You're lucky to have all this. And your father. He strikes me as a good person."

"He is. He's busy with the ranch, but he always makes time to help me with my homework and spend time with me. He goes to my awards at school or baseball games and practices. Last year, he was an assistant coach. Hey, maybe you can watch me play one of the times you're here." Russell's horse swiveled his ears to listen to his owner at the change in tone.

"That would be wonderful. When you get a schedule, email a copy to me so I can arrange time off from work. I'll be looking forward to it." The idea of watching her son play baseball filled her mind. She couldn't imagine anything in life more exciting. It was a big change from spending all her time with friends at the movies, window shopping, or just hanging out. This would blow all that out of the water. She'd need to take lots of photographs.

The grasses waved like the surface of a big lake as a breeze whistled through scruffy, gray-green shrubs clinging with determination among rocks and bare soil on a nearby hillside, waiting for spring growth to fill it in.

"Even though all we're doing is sitting on our horses, admiring the view, I can't think of anything I'd rather be doing, Russell. Except watching you play baseball. That'll be fun." Sitting astride a horse in the wide-open spaces with fresh air blowing and budding flowers all around, not to mention the company, had Lacey happier and more content than she ever remembered being.

"There're plenty of things more fun than watching me play baseball. My games are okay, but if you want real fun, you should go to a professional baseball game. Dad takes me to see an Astros game twice a year. He's done that ever since I could walk. Do you like baseball?"

"I love it. I go to a few minor league games every year with my friends." Most of them had gotten married over the past few years and some were expecting babies. They wouldn't be attending those minor league games for a year or two, at best.

"Maybe you could come with us to the next Astros game. Dad will love it when he hears you like baseball. I thought you might since you played softball."

Lacey winced. Another family outing. She wasn't ready for Disney, but it was almost on the calendar. An Astros game in addition to Russell's? Responsibilities were piling up fast. She'd never anticipated any of this.

There'd only been the challenge of getting onto the ranch and seeing Russell. Now there were commitments. The air felt hot again. "I don't know about going with you and your dad to an Astros game. We'll have to see. I can't just leave work any time I feel like doing it."

"If you can't make a game, there's something else you could come out here for. It's called Fiesta. You need to come for that, even if you can't make an Astros game. We have fun when we go. Lots of people from all over come for it. They hold it in San Antonio by the river."

"What's the Fiesta?" She'd never heard of it before.

"It's a big celebration with a lot of side events connected to it. It's mostly along the River Walk, near the Alamo. They have parades, music, and food, and all the shops are open, and they have booths with even more things to buy. You can stay at the hotel with us. It's our annual family vacation; it's tradition. Dad's been going since he was a kid, just like me."

"I've heard about the River Walk but I've never seen it. I don't know about going with you, though. We should talk to your dad first." This whole new family situation was getting out of hand, and part of her liked it despite the pressure. The other part had her fanning herself with her hand from nerves. Connie's squashed hat would've worked better, but it had already been thrown out.

The horses shook themselves against a pesky fly buzzing around, but it looked for all the world like they were reprimanding her.

"Okay. He won't mind. He'll love the idea. You'll see."

***

Saturday dawned late, for Lacey anyway, with early morning cloud cover blocking the sunrise. Since she was tired and stiff from helping Russell with some of his Friday evening chores, she didn't mind sleeping in. Yesterday had given her some one-on-one time with her son, well worth sore muscles.

She slid over to the side of the bed, then stumbled, bleary-eyed, and almost ended up face down, tripping over slumped covers and the guest robe, all of which had dropped onto the floor in a tangled mass sometime during the night. The steps into the small bathroom were more deliberate. The water in the shower heated fast, the dial set for a much-needed pounding massage.

Once finished, she dried with a thick, soft towel, warmed by a heated rack. It would be easy to get used to luxury like this. Reid took good care of his guests.

After tugging a brush through her hair until it was smooth, Lacey wrapped the towel around herself and stepped out to the dresser for clothes. A knock came at the door.

Pulling the towel tighter, she crossed to the door and opened it. "Reid. Good morning."

"Good morning." His eyes scanned her briefly before dropping to the floor. Don't imagine what she'd look like if that towel fell. Don't do it. "I'm sorry; it looks like I pulled you out of your shower."

"No, just finished. Great shower facilities here, by the way."

His eyes met hers and he smiled. "I'm glad you like it."

"I do, very much." The conversation would be more comfortable if she were wearing more than a towel, though.

"Well, I'll leave you alone then. We were getting worried since you hadn't come downstairs yet. Russell's got your mug of tea steeping at the table. We thought maybe you'd overdone it yesterday."

Her nerves calmed as he spoke, his voice deep and reassuring. It probably helped with skittish horses. "I appreciate the concern. I overslept, probably from being tired, and the clouds blocking the sunlight didn't help. I'm usually up around sunrise, even without an alarm. It always helps to see the sun, though. Sleeping late annoys me."

"It does?" He chuckled, leaning against the doorjamb, trying to make it seem casual. Nerves were rising, along with his internal temperature, being close to her in such a state of near undress. He couldn't help feeling momentarily envious of the towel. "Me, too. Russell's a teenager. He used to get up before dawn, part rooster, my dad said. Now, he'll sleep in if I let him. Most days he gets right up with his alarm, though. He's a good kid."

"Yes, he is. You've raised him by yourself most of his life. You should be proud of how he turned out."

"Thanks. I'm prejudiced, but I couldn't ask for better. I've been blessed. I'll let Russell know you're coming down in a few minutes, I assume?"

"Yes. I just need to get dressed and throw on some makeup. I'll be sure to set my alarm clock tonight. I really thought I'd done that last night."

He chuckled and moved to close the door, but paused, clearing his throat. "By the way, it's just my opinion, so take it for what it's worth to you. You don't need any makeup, Lacey. You're a natural."

He closed the door. She listened as his footsteps faded away, her smile spreading from ear to ear.

SIX

Russell and Lacey participated in an afternoon nature ride, assisting Reid in guiding a group that included most of the guests. Lacey didn't do much, but she enjoyed herself. Reid insisted she ride alongside him most of the way.

In between pointing out features to the group and discussing the local flora and fauna, or the history of the ranch, he shared stories with Lacey from his upbringing there, and Russell's. They explored the hills, as hoped for when she'd first arrived. And she ended up more worn out than the day before.

Upon their return, Lacey found dismounting difficult. Painful even.

"Do you need some help, Mom?"

A glance showed Reid preoccupied assisting other guests, some groaning, some laughing as they made the attempt. She didn't want Reid to see her like this.

"No, I can do it. It's just that my rear end isn't used to a saddle. I was okay this morning, just a little sore, but after today I don't know if I'll be able to walk normally tomorrow. Or the rest of today."

As her son snickered while trying to hide the fact that he was doing so, Lacey managed to get off Spark without falling. But not without groaning. She'd need some over-the-counter pain meds before bed.

Mother and son shared the duty of cleaning horses and tack,

helping a few of the ranch hands with the task. When they turned the last of the animals out to pasture, they leaned on the fence to watch them walk off in search of greener grass, which reminded them of their dinner.

"The horses are glad to be free for the night," Russell commented.

"Do they have to work tomorrow?" Lacey asked as they left the pasture behind, walking toward the house.

"No, grandpa likes to give them a break after a long ride. Did you have fun?"

"Except for the pain in my rear end from riding all day, which my rear end isn't used to, I most definitely did. Spark is a great horse. I'm having the best time of my whole life out here with you."

"Me, too. But speaking of fun, have you decided to come with us to Fiesta?"

"To be honest, I've been preoccupied with today's activities and getting to know your dad." Every time Reid had smiled at her or touched her arm, her interest in him, as more than just the father of her son, had grown. He was almost as easy to like as Russell, just in a vastly different kind of way.

"Aunt Kate usually meets us there on the day when they have the boat parade."

"Oh, I didn't know that. Come to think of it, I'm not sure about your Fiesta, Russell. I probably have to work anyway." She'd been contemplating it until the mention of Kate.

"Plus, I don't want to interfere with your family tradition, and I'm sure Kate needs time with your dad." She didn't know if anything was going on between him and Kate but didn't want to risk getting caught in the middle.

Besides, Russell was the priority, not his father. Lacey could tell herself that all day long and still not believe it. She often imagined what he must look like shirtless.

"That doesn't matter. He said he wants you to come."

"Your dad said that? When?" Considering how well the afternoon ride had gone, it was possible.

"Yeah. He meant it, too. We talked on the trail ride while you were taking photos of all the families against the hills for a backdrop. Dad liked the way you handled the guests. You got everybody relaxed and comfortable. He said he feels bad about whatever happened before you got here that stopped us from talking on the phone. He said if he'd known you cared, he would've flown you out to spend Christmas and New Years with us.

Russell stopped walking. "He also said you shouldn't miss out on a special event like Fiesta. He's excited about it. Dad said you'll need to take a few days off from work, though. Will you do it? Please?"

"I'd like to hear all that from your dad first." Even if Reid told her that face to face, she wasn't sure she'd accept. Not if Kate would be there.

"You don't believe me? He even said he'd insist if you turned him down. He's already making plans." Russell paused to glance toward the big house. "He's set on giving you a vacation you'll never forget. That's exactly what he said."

Lacey laughed. "If he lets me know he's serious, I'll think about it. You have to remember I have a job and it's a long way from here. I'll have to check at work when I get back. But I want you to know I'd rather spend Thanksgiving and Christmas with you, Russell. When will this Fiesta take place?"

"It's in April this year."

Her eyes widened. "That's next month. I don't know if I can get the time off so soon." She sighed, running through it in her head. "I'll try. But only if your father asks. And it has to be genuine, not from you bugging him until he does it. I'll be able to tell the difference." One eyebrow rose in a warning.

"Okay. You'll see."

"Hey, you two! Dinner's ready. Come on, get a move on!" Reid cupped his hands to his mouth, hollering from the kitchen doorway. He disappeared inside without waiting for a reply.

In the expanse of windows by the dining area, Kate stood with her hands on her hips, staring out at Russell and Lacey. Or maybe those daggers were just aimed at Lacey. "Russell, you go ahead. I'm tired; I think I'll turn in early today. I'll go in through the front entrance since it's closer to the stairs leading up to my room. You go ahead; your dad called you."

"He called both of us. And we were going to watch the sunset together, remember? I have to go back to school on Monday. One more day is all we'll have."

Her mouth dropped open. "I didn't even think about you having to go to school. I don't know why I didn't. So, that means I won't get to spend time with you after tomorrow?" The words squeaked, her eyes stinging with the sudden onset of moisture.

"We can in the evenings after my homework's done. I get most of it finished on the bus ride home because it takes a while. And we can sit together at dinner and breakfast."

"Homework and school never occurred to me when I made this grand plan to sneak in here to see you. I thought I was being so clever." School should have entered her thoughts. How would she ever get to know her son like this...a few short visits a year? At this rate, he'd be grown and gone before she knew it. She'd never get to know him.

"Mom, are you crying? What's wrong?"

Lacey swiped the tears away, but they kept coming. What was happening to her? She'd become so emotional. Was this what normal parents went through? "Nothing. I'm fine. I'm just disappointed at not getting to spend as much time with you as I was hoping for."

He hugged her and more tears fell. She couldn't allow Kate to destroy whatever relationship she'd be able to carve out with her son. Kate would just have to get over it. And Lacey had enjoyed spending time with Reid today. The two of them needed to know each other better for Russell's sake, if for no other reason. Kate could fume if she wanted.

"Okay then, let's go inside. Together." His face beamed when Lacey took his hand and tugged him toward the house.

"Should I go back to calling you Lacey when we get inside? You know, for my aunt's sake? Dad says he likes the idea of me calling you mom and I should call you whatever you and I feel comfortable with. Other people don't matter, even if they think they do."

Could Reid have been referring to Kate when he said those words? Russell was more important than anyone else in the world to Lacey now, his feelings and needs more significant than those of an angry, territorial woman. "In that case, I don't care what anybody else thinks about it either. You can call me Lacey or mom, or both. It's up to you."

"Then let's go have dinner, Mom."

Lacey squeezed his hand in response.

They stopped in the kitchen long enough to wash their hands, then entered the dining area. There, everyone had gathered around the longest of the dining room tables where a massive cake sat, decorated with a baseball diamond and in the colors of the Astros. Fifteen orange candles burned, and the cake was surrounded by a slew of cupcakes, each with the miniature figurine of a baseball player atop it. There must have been somewhere near one hundred team player bobblehead figurines to dole out to friends and guests on another table, near a pile of colorful gifts.

"Happy birthday!" the crowd yelled.

Russell was completely taken by surprise, like Lacey. The day had been too busy. All she'd managed to get out was a happy birthday at breakfast. Lacey was thrilled she'd decided to come inside with Russell. She squeezed his hand again and mouthed those two words as everyone clapped and whistled.

Reid approached, and Lacey released Russell's hand, stepping to one side. Reid gave his son a bear hug, then pushed back to study his son, proud of the man Russell was becoming.

"It's easy enough to see how hard you two have been working today," Reid said. "You shouldn't have to do so much work on your birthday. And you shouldn't be doing it at all, Lacey."

"Russell's all that matters. I'm happy to help." Russell and Lacey shared a smile.

Kate shoved her way between them to embrace Russell, but it seemed awkward. Perhaps it was just Lacey's imagination.

"You're my nephew and the son I never had. You and Reid are my family. I'm in love with both of you. Happy birthday, Russell." She held on, shedding crocodile tears while glaring at Lacey, baring her teeth.

Lacey couldn't believe it. If Kate had been near enough, she might've lashed out with those teeth for a bite. A rabies shot would've been called for afterward, no doubt. Lacey winced at the thought of it. She wasn't an enthusiastic fan of needles.

"Thanks, Aunt Kate." Russell frowned when his aunt took a few steps back, clasping her hands in front of her chest before wiping at her tears with a silk handkerchief.

What was she doing? Lacey watched in confusion. Was she fooling anyone? The performance was overdone in Lacey's opinion. She stared, finding the idea of having Kate around Russell unsupervised less appealing by the minute. Taking advantage of their proximity, Reid stepped in front of Kate and grabbed Lacey's arm, pulling her up against Russell, initiating a group hug between the three of them.

They squished her, but she loved the show of family affection. Reid kissed Russell's cheek and then Lacey's, soft and extended. Jostling indicated the presence of a new arrival. Lacey opened her eyes to see Kate's face a few inches away. Kate made eye contact with her rival before grinning, her hand pulling Reid's face around to kiss him on the lips.

Russell and Lacey let go fast and staggered back, their eyes wide, mouths agape. Lacey had no idea the two of them were so close, figuring Kate had lied. From the looks of him, Russell didn't know, either. This trip had been full of surprises.

It may have been news to Reid as well, considering the speed with which he disengaged himself from Kate. He didn't appear to have enjoyed the experience.

Lacey's attention was diverted as the group called for the birthday boy to blow out his candles, which were on their way to burning themselves to stubs. Instead of waiting for Reid, who had Kate's arms pinned at her sides as he spoke to her with a low voice and a scowl, Lacey escorted Russell to the table. Reid and Kate followed a minute after, Kate well behind Reid, smoothing at her hair and tugging on her dress, her smeared red lips pursed. Reid wiped away the lipstick with a handkerchief as he walked.

"Okay Russell, make a wish," Robert instructed, ensuring he had the boy's attention before nodding with a wink toward Lacey. "And make it a good one."

Russell smiled. In a single, massive breath, he extinguished all the candles to a round of applause.

"What'd you wish for?" one of Russell's friends asked.

"He can't say, or his wish won't come true," another kid, much younger, stated with certainty.

Becky made quick work of removing the candles and Russell cut the first slice. It wasn't the corner. Instead, it was along the edge near home plate, where his name was written in orange letters. He handed it to his mother, grinning. "Here you go. I want you to have this one."

"No, no. This one is yours." She pushed his hand back. "When it's your birthday, you're supposed to have the first piece."

"But this is my first birthday with you."

"It's okay. I'll never miss another one; I promise. I'll cut the rest." Lacey removed the knife from his hand. "You go get your ice cream and eat with your friends. I'll have their cake ready in a minute. And I'll see you by the fireplace, and at dinner. After we eat, I hear the sunsets out here are not to be missed."

"Thanks, Mom." The smile on his face could never be surpassed by any sunset.

"You're welcome, honey."

"Wow. She's your mom?" a boy asked in awe as Russell walked off, scooping in a mouthful of cake while nodding his head in the affirmative. It was the best accolade Lacey had received in months.

Reid put a hand on the boy's shoulder as Russell headed for the fireplace. "Yes, Clay. She is."

"She's pretty," Clay said.

"You're right about that," Reid concurred, deepening the color in Lacey's cheeks.

Kate seethed nearby. She could explode at any second. Bits of her scattered all over the place, including the cake, wouldn't be good for anyone's appetite. Yet, a part of Lacey that she wasn't proud of enjoyed imagining it. After flashing Reid a quick, shy smile, she passed Clay his slice.

Reid patted the boy on his shoulder and accompanied him to the vicinity of the fireplace to find a place to sit near Russell. Laughter erupted from the gathering soon after. Lacey couldn't wait to join them, fearing she'd miss out on too many interesting conversations.

Nevertheless, she continued until the cake was nearly obliterated, leaving the skin of her fingers stained orange. Kate stood on the opposite side of the table, the final person in line. "There isn't much left to choose from. Would you like the last corner piece, or are you aiming for a cupcake?"

"What I'd like is for you to stop interfering in my life," Kate said. She took a deep breath and let out a snarl.

"This is my family, not yours. You'd never even know about Russ if not for an accidental discovery. All you did was sell an egg. What respectable woman does something so unseemly anyway, selling your body for money? I've raised Russell since my sister died when he was seven years old. He's more mine than yours and he always will be. And soon, you'll be leaving the ranch."

Lacey raised an eyebrow, wondering how Kate could speak clearly with her teeth clamped together so tight. It was both impressive and uncomfortable.

"True, partially. But not the part about me interfering in your life; you're doing an outstanding job of that on your own. And your sister passed away when Russell was five, not seven. What I'm doing here is getting to know my biological son. We're growing closer by the minute. If it bothers you, that's your problem. I won't allow you to make it mine. Here." Lacey slid the corner piece across the table. "You could use some sweetness."

Kate glowered, seething with anger.

Lacey felt the woman's eyes on her as she continued working. At least Kate didn't have possession of the knife.

Carving out two small pieces from what remained, Lacey wiped her hands on a damp cloth and walked to a smaller table with the cake, leaving Kate alone. At the ice cream station, Lacey scooped out generous portions and added toppings. Then she thrust spoons into the bowls and wound her way over to where Russell sat with his friends and family on couches and rocking chairs near the roaring fireplace.

"This is for you, Reid. The ice cream was beginning to melt. These'll hold it better than a plate," Lacey said.

His smile blossomed as he accepted the bowl.

"Thanks, Lacey. Here, sit next to me." He scooted over to give her space on the oversized plush chair with him.

Knowing it would add fuel to Kate's fire, Lacey sat anyway. Kate couldn't be allowed to ruin their lives. Sitting with her body pressed tight against Reid increased her heart rate and sent a quiver through her body.

"I hear our son has already invited you to join us at Fiesta."

Lacey could scarcely get past the shock of hearing Reid call Russell 'their' son to answer him without a delay so long it might cause him to question the working capabilities of her ears. "Yes, he did."

"He beat me to it. He also tells me you might not come."

"Well, I don't know if I'll be able to take more vacation time just then; other people might've spoken for it already, and we need at least one mapping analyst available in case of an emergency. It's an important job. Besides, it sounds like it's more of a family trip and I don't want to cause problems for anyone."

"You're just as much a part of our family as my father," Reid stated matter-of-factly.

He didn't say anything about Kate. Had she become closer than Kate now? Then the weight of it sank in, warm and comforting. She had a new family. Robert sat nearby and sent her a smile, nodding with approval as he ate.

Reid scooped up some melting ice cream, savoring it. "You have to be with us. There's no logical argument you can make against it. You're going to fly in early that Wednesday. Russell and I will pick you up at the airport and bring you back to the hotel. We're going to make sure you have the time of your life. And you'll only be taking three days off from work. I'm sure they can spare you for three days."

"Probably." Lacey's voice grew soft. She hadn't expected any of this and wasn't sure how to react since there seemed to be no choice in the matter. Not that she wanted one, deep down. "But I'll still have to ask first. I can't make any promises."

"That's fine, you go ahead and ask when you get back to work. Russell and I will see you on the Wednesday before the big day. No later than Wednesday. We can't risk you missing the Flambeau Parade. You should also know I've already purchased your airline tickets, both ways." He took a bite of cake. "This is good, isn't it?"

"Delicious." Lacey caught sight of Kate, watching from nearby. Spinning on her high heels, the furious woman stormed off.

"It's about time for you to open your gifts, Russell," Robert prodded.

"I'll have to get you something later, Russell. I'm sorry." She should have thought to ask her son such a simple question when he was with her in Charlotte.

"Are you kidding? You've already given me the best gift in the whole world."

"I have?" What could he mean?

"Yeah... you've given me a mom."

"Oh, Russell. You're going to make me cry." Tears rushed into her eyes. It used to take a lot to make her cry. She handed her bowl hastily to Reid and squirmed free of the chair to stand for Russell's embrace.

"This is the best birthday ever," he whispered in her ear.

"I love you." Lacey squeezed him tight.

"I love you, too. Mom."

The title that also served as a name had come again. Mom. "Okay, now go ahead and open your presents." She reclaimed both her seat and her bowl, using one hand to wipe at her eyes. This had been such a wonderful day. Reid gave her a pat on the leg and a kiss on the cheek, sending a jolt through her belly.

***

On Monday morning, Russell left for school as some of the guests prepared to leave. Reid told Lacey to take it easy all day, that she'd done enough work over the weekend. Still, she'd risen early to see Russell off after their breakfast, and then proceeded to help where she could. After all, she was family now.

For a couple of hours, she bussed breakfast tables. A bonus came at the sight of Kate's face every time their eyes met. Kate shot daggers at Lacey, who responded with her best smile in return, adding in a jovial wave whenever she had a free hand. Kate bristled and slammed things.

Reid witnessed some of the exchanges. He frowned at Kate's display of temper, unable to comprehend what the woman was angry about this time. It couldn't be that she was upset with someone as pleasant and helpful as Lacey, but it appeared that might be the case. Hopefully, she'd get over it without needing Reid to set her straight.

Seeing Lacey around, helping anywhere she was wanted, warmed his heart. She'd fit in well here with the rest of the family. He sent smiles Lacey's way. Sometimes, a blush swept across her face, depending on Reid's proximity. He liked that since it showed interest.

After the breakfast shift, Robert said Lacey could either accompany the tourists about to leave for a morning nature trail ride or do her own thing. She opted for the latter, to groom Spark and go for a ride, just the two of them. When the last family left, she jogged to the barn.

It didn't take long to figure out Spark loved people who showered him with attention. Maybe it wasn't so much the women as the doting they piled on him. How could they help themselves? He was sweet and a joy to ride.

"This is confusing me, Spark."

He angled an ear back, listening.

"I like Reid a lot, I do. He makes my heart pound. No guy I've dated has made me feel like this before. Not that Reid wants to date me. But I came here to spend time with Russell. I need to get to know him; he's the most important person in my life, in my entire life. While we're out, I'll talk to you about it and maybe you can find a way to let me know what I should do.

"It would be great if I could get to know Russell and Reid at the same time. I'll have to be careful about it. I don't want to risk a relationship with Reid and have it end up going bad. That could make it awkward when I visit Russell. Plus, it's been a long time since Reid has dated. What if he's not a good kisser?"

She envisioned kissing Reid, his big, rough hands pressing her body against his, those lips brushing over hers before plunging in. Not a good kisser? Impossible.

Spark snorted and shook his head at a bothersome fly, which Lacey promptly shooed away. It returned, so she waited until it landed. Then she smacked it with the bristly end of the brush against Spark's ribs. The horse barely flinched but the fly dropped to the floor, stunned. Lacey put an end to the little troublemaker by using the bottom of her shoe.

"There. Problem solved. No more pesky fly. We're going to go nice and slow on our ride. Did I tell you how much I love horses? And thus far, you're my absolute favorite." She patted his neck, and he gave her another snort and a flick of his tail. Lacey led him outside, mounted up, and he ambled off.

Rounding the side of the barn, they approached a small assemblage of trees, where clusters of yellow flowers stretched skyward among the roots. Horse and rider moved toward one of the easy trails, a short, manageable expedition. Spark pricked his ears and turned his head, having spotted a sizeable group on horseback a football field away, embarking on the nature ride. Reid and Robert led the way.

They wouldn't have noticed if not for the sharp snort from Spark that carried farther than Lacey had imagined. The two men looked her way. Not wanting to be rude, she sent them a wave, which they returned.

All she'd wanted was a solitary ride for some peace and quiet on this last day at the ranch, listening to the creak of leather, talking to the horse, enjoying the scenery. Some finagling had enabled Lacey to switch out her Thursday morning ticket for Tuesday. It left Russell disappointed until Lacey pointed out that it would give her two extra days to spend with him during the summer or at Christmas when school was out. There'd be no school to interfere with their time together then.

Clucking her tongue, Lacey squeezed her legs and Spark broke into an easy lope. In less than ten seconds, their view of the tourists was obscured by additional tree cover. Spark slowed at a mere tug on the reins.

"You're such a good boy, Spark." She gave his neck a couple of pats. "We're going to have a great time, aren't we? This is such a beautiful place. I want to get to know every square inch of it. Well, except for the parts where there could be snakes. I guess that means you and I will be sticking to the trails."

The horse's ears flicked back as he listened to her words. He even shook his head, seeming to nod in the affirmative, which made her giggle and adore him more.

The pounding, rhythmic drum of hoofbeats announced a rider

coming up fast behind them. It was Reid, his horse in a gallop. The horse slowed to a trot and then a walk as they neared.

"Uh oh," she muttered to Spark. "I'll bet you our plans are ruined now."

Spark snorted as Lacey pulled him to a halt on one side of the trail. Reid stopped his mount alongside them, the animal's sides heaving from the exertion. "Where're you going all alone?"

"I was just taking Spark out on a solo ride for my last day. We weren't going far. He's a great horse and I thought it would be good for the two of us to get better acquainted. Russell brought me here for my first real ride; it's got a pretty overlook. I wanted to see it one more time." She patted Spark's neck again and he pinned his ears against his head, reaching out to nip at the neck of Reid's horse.

"Hey now, watch it Spark," Reid reprimanded as his horse threw back his head to get out of the reach of those teeth, his eyes showing their white rims.

"He's just agreeing with me is all; about the two of us getting better acquainted, I mean." Lacey gave a quick tug on the right rein to straighten out Spark's head while trying to contain a smile. The horse did seem to be reading her mind.

"You think so?" Reid looked from her to the horse. "He does seem to be fitting you like a glove. He's a good horse, unflappable with women. But he seems to have an extra flicker in him with you. I'm thinking we might have to make this union legal."

"I'm sorry?" He had her confused.

"I mean, I'm going to make him your horse. Officially." As much as she loved horses and this one, in particular, it would make her happy and keep her coming back. This could eventually serve as an extra incentive to convince her to move in. Her own horse to ride as often as she wanted. He was getting ahead of himself but couldn't help it.

She'd been focused on Spark, fiddling with his mane, hoping Reid might clue in on her body language and go back to the tourists. She enjoyed spending time with him, but he had work to attend to. What he said caught her attention, though. "He'd be mine? My horse?"

"Yes, yours. If you want him."

She squealed with sheer delight and reached forward around the saddle horn to hug Spark's neck. The application of pressure with her right leg moved him left, allowing her to lean sideways and hug Reid. He gave her an irresistible, warm squeeze. And he smelled nice.

"Thank you so much! This is the best present anyone's ever given me; besides Russell, naturally." Excitement had her blood pumping. A childhood dream had come true.

Reid rubbed a hand across her back as he laughed. "You're welcome. Now that ownership is settled, how's about you join us on our nature ride? It'll give you and me extra time to get acquainted."

He had just fulfilled her lifelong dream of owning a horse, after all. "Okay. Thanks, Reid."

"No, thank *you*. This way, I'll be assured of having good company on the ride."

Obediently, Lacey turned Spark back the way they'd just come, moving up alongside Reid. He was talking, but it was hard to concentrate. Her focus would improve if Reid didn't have those dreamy chocolate-colored eyes. The horse didn't hurt, either.

Fiesta

SEVEN

"I sure wish I was going on a trip to a huge party, especially with an attractive man like Reid Collier. You're lucky," Connie said.

"Hey now, don't forget about Jonathan. Besides, I'm going there to be with my son, not his father."

"Sure you are. Even if it's true, the dad's a nice bonus." She gave Lacey an exaggerated wink. "He's been calling or texting you or both every night since you got back to Charlotte, which says something, I hope you realize. You could use a good man in your life."

"I do like him, but I want to focus on getting to know my son. He's the reason Reid's been calling. I've spoken with Russell every time."

"Come on. You can't tell me you wouldn't respond or care if Reid Collier tried to put some moves on you."

"I didn't say that. I'm very attracted to him. But he seems... reserved. It's probably because of Russell being young and all. He wants to set a good example and behave appropriately. I think he'd want to keep the pace of a new relationship slow. If there ever is a relationship. I'm not sure about that yet."

"Appropriate behavior is for the pilgrims, not the modern era. And a relationship might be nice, but I'm talking about a roll in the hay. You said it's a farm, right?" She winked again. "Pretty funny, right?"

"No, it wasn't. And it's a ranch, not a farm, but yes, they do have hay. He doesn't strike me as the roll in the hay type. His priority is making sure I'm a good mom. He loves his son and he's watching out for him."

"Regardless, he invited you to come along on a traditional family vacation, a vacation he bought you non-refundable airline tickets for. Non-refundable left you with no option. He made sure you'd go along on the trip."

"I'm just worried about starting a romance and having it go bad between us. He has the power of the law behind him, and he could prevent me from being able to see Russell as much as I want to."

"You told me he was a nice guy. Coming between you and Russell would make him vengeful. Did he seem like that kind of a person to you?"

"No. Maybe I'm worried about nothing." The phone beeped, and Lacey's lips curved upward when the display showed her son's image. "It's Russell. He's texting to make sure I'm leaving the apartment in plenty of time to make my flight. He's a sweetie." Lacey's fingers sent a simple yes in reply.

"You sound like a proud mama to me. Speaking of which, you planned on getting to the airport almost two hours before your flight. Not like you're excited about it or anything. Do you have a book to read while you're waiting?"

"I have the paperback you gave me. I've got plenty of thoughts to keep my brain occupied if I need anything else. And I think Russell will text me a lot while I'm waiting for my flight. He's been texting a lot since I left Texas. He's excited about the trip, too."

"Loaned. I loaned you the book, I didn't give it to you. I don't give away my Nora Roberts books. I read them over and over." Connie's hands rested on the kitchen countertop, fingers strumming.

"Easy enough to tell from the worn-out cover. I'll take good care of it." Lacey patted her satchel.

"I'm sure you will. My library has an unforgiving return policy, don't forget."

"I won't. I'll see you when I get back." She moved past Connie with the duffel in hand.

"Text me when you get there so I know you made it safely." Connie followed her to the door.

"Okay, *Mom*. I'll bring you back something cool from the Fiesta." Lacey opened the door and threw up her hand in a wave.

"Make sure you do that, funny girl!" Connie hollered down the breezeway after her friend.

The morning was perfect, not a cloud to be seen, which should mean no problems with the plane taking off on time. Shoving her phone into the satchel, Lacey tossed her bags on the backseat. The engine of the aging yet reliable Ford Escape started right up. Fifteen years and two hundred eighty thousand-plus miles, still going strong with regular maintenance. Spring air and birdsong wafted into the interior through the open windows.

As she shifted into reverse to allow the little SUV to roll backward out of the parking space, awareness of a problem came immediately. She applied the brake and shifted to limp the few inches back to the curb. The entire right side of the car leaned substantially down, something she should've noticed on approach from the building. She'd been too caught up in thinking of the trip and about what Connie had said concerning Reid.

Relationships. To have a chance at one, she'd need to get there in the first place.

Connie emerged from the breezeway a minute later to find her roommate standing at the passenger side of her car, studying the dilemma, hands fisted on her hips. "What're you still doing here?"

"I've got two flat tires."

"You're kidding me!" Connie stepped around, mouth agape, and squatted by a tire as she removed her sunglasses. "You're *not* kidding. They're..."

"Flat as a pancake. I don't know what to do. I can't change two tires with one spare. This can't be happening; I can't miss my flight. Did Jonathan have to go to work this morning? Maybe he could take me to the airport, and I'll deal with this when I get back in town.

Paying a driver to take me would cost a small fortune at the last minute like this, I'm sure."

"Jonathan's been working the graveyard shift; he won't be off for another couple of hours. Come on, I'll take you. Jonathan can come by later and take your tires to the shop for you and see if they can patch them. Maybe they're salvageable." Connie straightened from examining the front passenger tire, repositioning her sunglasses.

"It'll make you late for work." The protest was weak since she was thrilled with the offer.

"It's all right. I worked late almost every day last week. Chuck will cut me some slack."

"But what if he doesn't?"

"If he doesn't, I'll let you know and you can make it up to me by getting me something extra nice at your Fiesta. Sound good?"

"Works for me. I'll do it anyway since you're sweet enough to drive me yourself."

"Grab your bags and toss 'em in my car so we can get this show on the road. There's no way I'm letting you miss that plane." She spun on her heel, key in hand, then stared across the drive aisle to the next row of parking spaces to where her car sat. "Oh, no."

Lacey turned, eyes widening. "This can't be happening."

Connie's teeth ground together. "That's no coincidence. I'm going to get some payback when I find whoever did that to my car. They don't know who they're messing with."

***

"Mom! Here we are! Over here!" Russell and Reid each waved an arm through the air.

Her face beamed as she cut across the intervening space and fellow passengers to reach them. Russell gave her a big hug as Reid slipped the satchel from her shoulder.

"I'm glad you're here, Mom."

"Me too, honey. I'm excited about this vacation. I've never seen the River Walk before."

"How was the flight?" Reid put an arm around her shoulders, leaning in to hug her and apply a kiss to the top of her head, sending the butterflies in her stomach into frenzied flight.

"Fine." She'd gone all dreamy over Reid again. It couldn't seem to stop. Not that she tried much.

"Good. I'm glad you didn't have any problems. Baggage claim is right this way." He guided her with a hand on her lower back, reveling in the close physical contact she was allowing him.

Lacey hoped he'd keep his hand there. It was warm and a little electric.

"I guess you remember the location of baggage claim from the last time you were here," Reid said.

"That part of the trip was a nervous blur." Although having Reid touching her now didn't eliminate any anxieties.

"Well, you don't have to be nervous anymore. We'll grab your bag and then there's a nice restaurant we like with great Mexican food. We'll eat something light because dinner's going to be special. And we're planning to drive you around the city for an overview." Reid gave her lower back a gentle caress. "You left your car in a good, safe spot at the airport where it could stay longer than originally planned, right?"

"Well, not exactly. I mean, sort of." Why would he ask a question about her car?

He gave her a frown. "You've given me a rather convoluted answer to a simple question, don't you think?"

"Probably. What I should've said was, I don't need to worry about it. I couldn't drive my car. Didn't drive it." Lacey winced at her poor choice of words.

"You couldn't drive it? What does that mean?" Reid asked.

"It had two flat tires. I didn't notice until I tried to leave the apartment this morning. My roommate Connie drove me to the airport. She saved me from missing my flight."

"Two flat tires? All the way flat?" Reid asked, eyebrows high.

"All the way."

"You must've run over something pretty serious. You'll need to get a new set of tires, or at least two, to balance it out."

"I'm hoping to get replacements for free, or at least discounted. They're practically brand new since I bought them a couple of weeks before Russell came to visit me. My old ones wouldn't have passed inspection, which left me with no alternative. I had to get new ones."

Reid gave her a look. "You shouldn't drive around on bad tires, ever; it's dangerous. But two new tires going flat isn't normal; you must've hit nails."

"I didn't notice any when I checked them this morning. And as far as the condition of my tires goes, I'm still paying off my college loans, they raised our rent on the apartment, like every year at lease renewal time, and I just finished covering some family debts last year from my mom's passing, including the funeral." Reid had some nerve, telling her what to do. He didn't seem to understand that some people had trouble making ends meet.

"Life's different when you don't have money to spare, even for safer tires. My roommate's boyfriend, who also happens to be my cousin, took one of the flat tires in to be fixed for me. He was texting me about it as the plane taxied to the gate here."

"Lacey, I want you to know from now on I expect you to let me know whenever there's something important you need, especially where your health and safety are concerned. You're extremely important to us and I won't risk anything happening to you for want of money. Was your cousin able to get the tires patched for you?"

"They couldn't do it." They needed to talk about something besides tires.

And there was no way she would ever accept money from Reid. They'd spent a lot of time talking on the phone, but they didn't know each other well enough for him to give her money. Even if they did, she wouldn't accept it. That wasn't how she'd been raised. An explanation would come later, without Russell around to overhear.

"Why not? How could nail holes be irreparable, even

temporarily?" Reid asked.

"It wasn't nails."

"What was it, then?" He seemed fixated, like a dog playing tug-of-war.

"Why'd you need to know where I parked my car?" Maybe asking him a question would allow her to make a shift in the conversation.

Something that would lead to others, perhaps a question about Fiesta or the sleeping accommodations or dinner. He'd forget it completely by the time Lacey was finished. She wasn't going to allow the conversation to return to money, nor would she have him thinking where she lived might be too dangerous for Russell to visit someday. There hadn't had a problem like this one before at the complex. Nothing she'd heard of, anyway.

"It was in case we managed to keep you with us longer since the weather's supposed to be nice. We were thinking we could talk you into coming back to the ranch with us, even if it's only for a day or two. You'll need the rest after we're done here."

"So, I'm assuming there'll be a lot of walking? I've been walking and jogging on a treadmill at least an hour a day every day in preparation since I got back to Charlotte from my first visit to the ranch. I can't wait to see the River Walk and the Alamo."

Threading them smoothly through the crowds in the airport, Reid wasn't diverted. "I'm glad you're enthusiastic, and yes, there's a lot of walking involved. So, back to the original line of questioning. What did they find out about your tires?"

The heavy swallow didn't help Lacey's tension. "They were cut by something bigger than a nail."

"They must've had a guess as to the cause for you." Reid hiked her satchel higher on his shoulder.

May as well go ahead and finish it, since he wasn't giving in. Lacey gave a sideways glance to Russell, who seemed disinterested in the conversation. "The mechanic thinks somebody cut my tires on purpose, with a knife. A big one."

Reid was shocked. "Who would slash your tires? You can't

possibly have any enemies."

"Yeah, Mom. You're such a nice person." Russell's brow furrowed.

Lacey sighed. "Everyone has enemies; it's just a matter of how dedicated they are to the cause. But that aside, there's no telling. It was probably random."

"So, it was somebody playing around then. Sick little..." Reid glanced to his son and selected a different word, "...individual. Did they cut anyone else's tires?"

"Connie's. My cousin had left his old pickup in the apartment's visitors' lot, and Connie had the spare key. She drove me to the airport in the truck and then took it to work."

Reid walked along deep in thought, with no apparent intention of letting the subject go.

"Well, I'm extra glad you're here with us now, Mom. You don't have to worry about your car for a while." Russell patted his mother's shoulder.

***

The hotel amazed her. Lacey stood in the center of the lobby, making a slow rotation, studying details. She loved everything about it. There were deep arches, a sweeping grand staircase, and luxurious furnishings, with ornate mirrors and artwork adorning the building like expensive gems set in a stunning necklace.

"What do you think?" Reid asked.

Her gaze lowered from an examination of the ceiling. "This is beautiful and elegant; I can't believe it. I've never been to any place like this before."

"I'm glad you like it. They have a Latin version of the British high tea starting in about an hour. They serve roasted Mexican coffee with a light cinnamon flavor, the best coffee I've ever tasted. For those like you and Russ, they serve other beverages, including hot cocoa. Plus, they have Mexican cookies our son happens to be crazy about."

"Speaking of Russell..." Lacey scanned the room.

"He's over there, waiting." Reid gestured to a spot near the registration desk. "He wanted to take our picture when he saw how enamored you were with the hotel. Why don't we pose for him?"

Reid placed her bags at his feet, put an arm around her waist, then tugged her tight against his side. Lacey decided to go with it, wrapping both her arms around his waist and pressing the side of her face to his chest. Reid imitated her pose, his chin resting on her head.

Russell approached them, grinning. "Great posing. Now a selfie!" He positioned the three of them to his liking and took a few images.

"Hey, I got a couple of good shots of the two of you; take a look. You look good together. See?" He swiped through the photographs of his parents, then of all three as a group.

"You're right about that, son."

"We look happy, all three of us. I know I'm happy." Lacey patted Russell's back. "Good photography. This trip is going to be so much fun. What're we going to do first?"

"Well," Reid stooped to retrieve her bags, "first we're putting your belongings away. Then we can walk around."

"But we're sticking close to the hotel for the tea, right?" Russell reaffirmed.

"Absolutely. Afterward, we'll do some exploring and then have dinner. Let's get upstairs and show your mom our room."

***

By the time they'd reached the room, Lacey was ready to start the adventure outside. It surprised her that all three of them were sharing a room but liked the implication of family and belonging. "Would it be okay if I stepped out on the balcony first? I can unpack fast."

"That'd be fine," Reid said, returning his hand to her lower back, just where she was growing accustomed to its presence. "Come on,

I'll show you. We've got a pretty view of the River Walk."

"Yeah, Mom." Russell grabbed Lacey's hand, pulling her away from his father. "I'll show her, Dad. You'll love this, Mom." He opened the glass door, leading the way. "What do you think?"

Through the trees, other tall buildings were visible across the way. The water in between was dark and still, reflecting the bright blue of the sky and the underside of a stone bridge spanning it nearby. People crossed from both sides of the bridge. Farther down the river stood another one.

The idea of calling it a river piqued her interest. Its bed wasn't typical of a river. The water had been hemmed in by man, confined, channeled by concrete and stone. But somehow it worked with the buildings, trees, and splashes of bright colors, creating a mystical environment, charged with excitement and energy. It was artificial and natural at the same time, flowing past buildings of varied architectural styles.

Below them was a hive of activity. Clothing in vibrant colors was as diverse as the people wearing it all, weaving in and out of shops or strolling along the river. Most everyone carried shopping bags. Some clutched ice cream cones.

"I've never seen anything like this before. Look at all the people."

"Lots of people come here all year, but way more for Fiesta. It's popular." He gestured along the river and her eyes followed.

"Ooh!" She grabbed Russell's arm, pointing. "Look down there! Look! It's a boat. It's so pretty with the bright colors. There're lots of people riding on it. Does that mean we can take a ride, too? Can we, please?"

Russell grinned. "Sure Mom. Dad's got everything all planned out."

"Reid..." Lacey turned but he wasn't there. "Reid?"

"I'm coming." He stepped out to join them, laughing. "I heard you. We're going for our boat ride in the morning. Tonight, we're dining at Russell's favorite restaurant. I'm glad to hear you're excited about everything, Lacey."

"Excited doesn't even *begin* to cover it. Which restaurant is your favorite, Russell? Is it here or do we have to drive somewhere?" Lacey's eyes were wide, and her words rushed together. Calming down wasn't likely to happen anytime soon.

"It's called the Rainforest Café. I know you've never eaten there before since this is your first time coming to the River Walk. It's going to be fun for you, Mom."

"It's a franchise, son. There're more than this one," Reid offered.

"I still don't think I've ever eaten there before. The name doesn't sound familiar," Lacey said.

"They have one at Disney," Reid said. "You got me eager about the family trip coming up at Disney World Lacey, so I went online and found the restaurant while I was perusing the food offerings at the different parks."

"They do?" She paused to think back, putting a finger to her lips. "It still doesn't ring any bells. Disney was a long time ago. If we do end up going to Disney together one of these days, we'll have to be sure to eat there. Since it's your favorite, Russell."

"If? That's not an if, Mom. It's a when. All we need to do is pick a week. Right, Dad?"

"Absolutely. The trip is definite; we settled on it the last time we saw you." Reid stood by the railing, his hands on his hips and one eyebrow reaching for the sky.

"Then, who am I to argue with my two favorite men in the entire world?" she asked.

Reid looked like a happy kid on Christmas morning. Was it because of what she'd said? Was he looking forward to the trip that much? She hoped so.

***

Lush, tropical foliage seemed to grow impossibly from the interior walls, interspersed with brilliant flowers. Everything was artificial, just like the animals, but fascinating, nonetheless. There were faux gorillas, monkeys, big cats, elephants, colorful birds, large serpents, and poison dart frogs, among other creatures, all hanging from sturdy vines or trees, perched on boulders, or peeking out from the vegetation. The air felt almost humid, like back home in Charlotte during the sweltering summer months.

Russell and Reid checked their watches and whispered conspiratorially while eyeing Lacey whenever they incorrectly believed that she was sufficiently distracted not to notice.

"This is remarkable. It's no wonder this is your favorite restaurant, Russell." Curiosity was difficult to control as she gazed between people standing in line ahead of them.

"Just wait, it gets better," Russell said.

"It does? How?" Lacey raised her head as high as she could, even standing on her tiptoes while using Reid's muscular arm as a willing brace for her hand. It allowed her to eye the restaurant's gift shop, brightly lit and filled with all manner of vibrantly colored, interesting items. "Do we have to wait until after we eat to go in there? Is it a part of the restaurant?" she asked her companions.

"Collier, party of three," a waitress called.

"Over here," Russell spoke up, raising one hand while using the other to take hold of one of Lacey's.

Reid came along behind them as they made their way to the table.

It was a fascinating journey as they moved deeper into the restaurant's jungle. Surrendering to her imagination, it became real without much effort. Rainforest animals entwined among the vegetation helped flesh out the illusion. Although created for children, adults fell under the restaurant's spell just as easily. The waitress seated them near a massive gorilla.

"Sit here, Mom. I want you to have the best view of the show." Russell pulled out her chair, positioning his mother to put her back to the wall. He wanted a clear view of her face.

"Thanks, honey." Reid slid into the seat next to Lacey's and she leaned over to him as Russell moved to the opposite side of the table. "What kind of show do they have?"

"Oh no, you don't. I'm not going to spoil it for you. Here you go. Peruse this instead." He handed her a vivid, laminated menu. The woman was so intensely curious about everything that it was going to be a challenge to keep her distracted. "Looking through that'll keep you occupied, young lady."

She took it with a smile and began searching through the interesting names the restaurant had come up with for relatively common meals.

"Is it time yet, Dad?"

Reid glanced at his watch and gave Russell a wink. "Not yet; soon, though."

As Lacey lifted her head to study their surroundings, Reid held up a few fingers to Russell. She caught the move but didn't pay it much mind, not wanting to spoil their surprise. The anticipation for this one had her antsy, though. "There doesn't seem to be enough floor space in here for any kind of a show. The tables and chairs are packed in pretty tight."

Reid chuckled and patted her thigh a couple of times beneath the table, adding in a gentle squeeze. "Just be patient. You'll see." Then he leaned in to kiss her cheek. It seemed like a good opportunity for it, and he'd take whatever excuse he could find. "You're cute."

Any thoughts of a floor show fled her mind as the heat rose through her core and into her head, bringing on a blush. She gave Reid a shy smile. "Okay. What do you recommend for dinner?"

"Everything's good. People come here for the atmosphere more than the food. Order whatever strikes your fancy." As he watched her, the corners of his mouth rose.

"There sure are lots of families here. That's almost all I see." Anticipation made it difficult to focus on the menu. Children, most of whom danced in their seats with building tension, were everywhere.

A waitress took their orders. Reid asked for the largest of their burgers, as did Russell. Lacey opted for chicken.

Her attention faltered then, taken by a passing waiter who glided among people and tables while balancing a dessert she'd never seen before. Her mouth dropped open as she leaned forward. It was a mountain carved from vanilla ice cream with slabs of chocolate cake, topped by a sizzling sparkler. The firecracker on a stick threw a cascade of brilliant sparks across the waiter's tray and onto the floor. The scene captured Lacey's imagination. "Whoa. What's that?"

"They call it a Volcano. We'll order one so you can try it," Reid said.

"It's a lot of food. I'm assuming we'll all share, right?" Lacey kept her eyes focused on the family who had placed the order, sitting at a table not far from theirs. The sparks reflected in the wide eyes of their three lively children.

A flip to the back of Lacey's menu showed the Volcano dessert. Room in her stomach must be saved for that lusciousness. She licked her tongue across her lips.

"Sure, Mom. They'll bring us extra plates and spoons." Russell said, his eyes shifting to something above her and then to his father, his expression anticipatory.

The smile she wore faded as she observed him. And she noticed the changes around them. It wasn't her imagination.

The sounds of the jungle came alive all around them, widening Lacey's eyes and capturing her attention. The din of human voices lowered with the lights. A mechanically generated fog cascaded over rock formations and tumbled from the vegetation.

Brilliant lights flashed as thunder cracked and animals she'd assumed to be solely decorative grew agitated. They snorted and squealed and roared, coming to life with movement, including the gorilla they were seated by. He pounded his chest and roared.

Childlike wonder took hold. She'd never been swept up in anything as captivating as this, except as a kid on her family's magical trip to Disney. The scene transported her back to that innocence as she immersed herself in the adventure. She was hardly alone; most everyone had the same reaction.

Reid and Russell glanced around periodically but kept their eyes on Lacey, reveling in the experience with her.

Once the animatronic animals and the manmade storm eased back to the status quo and the lights came up, she found it difficult to stop smiling. "That was great! I can see why this is your favorite restaurant, Russell. Do they do this a lot?"

"Yeah, they do. I told you it was fun!" Russell grinned.

"Every half hour, there's the big storm like we just went through, Lacey," Reid explained. "On the quarter-hour, some of them move around a bit, with a little sound thrown in. It's just a preview of what's to come. I timed our reservation so that we'd be here for at least two of the big shows, possibly three if we take our time eating."

"This is wonderful. Thank you for bringing me here." Joy overcame common sense. Lacey placed her hand on Reid's far cheek to angle his face to hers for a firm kiss on the lips. It was a far bolder move than she'd imagined in her daydreams of kissing Reid, with no idea such a minor, brief act would make time stop. She wasn't sure what had possessed her to kiss him, beyond allowing herself to get overly excited.

"Well now, we may have to come here more often," Reid said with a broad smile when Lacey released him, the taste of her still on his lips. He hadn't seen that coming. He wanted another.

"Could we, Dad?"

Reid laughed. "Depends on how often your mom gives me a kiss like that one just for bringing her to this restaurant."

Her cheeks reddened as she smiled and averted her eyes. Russell's big grin was impossible to miss, though.

The waitress interrupted by bringing their drinks. "Here you go. The food should be along in about twenty or thirty minutes. Sorry, but we're packed tonight."

Russell was still grinning. "It's fine. We're not in a hurry. Right, Dad?"

"Definitely. We're in no rush at all." The waitress nodded, moving to the next table. "We've got all the time in the world. We're going to take this nice and slow to let us see more of the show your mom liked so much. I want this trip to be memorable." Reid took her hand in his, resting them, joined, on her thigh.

"It's already been that," Lacey said.

***

After dinner, they roamed around the River Walk, browsing in some of the multitudes of shops, and debating which restaurants they'd most like to try the next day for lunch or dinner. Every time Reid pointed out something, he put an arm around her and leaned in close as he made sure whatever it was didn't escape her attention. He held her hand most of the evening. She had no idea how she'd ever get to sleep.

One shop with souvenirs had a T-shirt she liked, so Reid bought it for her. Just as he had purchased a colorful ceramic mug with a poison dart frog emblazoned over it in the restaurant gift shop. He carried the bags in one hand, holding her hand in the other.

He was enjoying himself as much as she was. It had been a long time since his family had felt complete. He wondered briefly if he was moving too fast mentally before dismissing the thought. Impossible.

When they returned to their room, a small piece of chocolate lay on one of the pillows on her bed, with one on each pillow of the other bed. The covers had been turned down for them.

On her side of the nightstand, which sat between the two beds, sat a dozen soft pink rosebuds in a shapely, etched crystal vase. It refracted the light from the lamp above it into a myriad of rainbows. At its base sat a small box wrapped in embossed silver paper, tied up with a frilly, soft pink bow overflowing the box it was attached to.

"Oh! They're beautiful!" She fingered one of the tender blooms-to-be, then faced Reid. "Did you do this?"

He was already smiling, hands on his hips where he stood by the foot of the bed. "I did. Or rather, we did. Russell helped. We thought you might like them. It's a welcome to San Antonio for you."

"You're so sweet! Thank you for the flowers." Lacey moved to Reid and threw her arms around his neck, pulling him down to rest her cheek against his. Her eyes closed as his arms encircled her waist and he applied two quick kisses to her neck. Warmth rose inside her.

He eased back from her to study the beautiful, delicate features he'd first memorized at the airport in Charlotte. He still had the photo of her and Russell, taken at her office that day Russell ran away. He studied it multiple times a day, every day. "Anything for the woman who gave me such a wonderful son."

"Do you like the flowers, Mom? I picked the color. I chose pink instead of red. You know, since you're a girl and all."

"Oh, Russell. You're as sweet as your dad." Lacey released her hold on Reid to hug Russell.

The man had taken the hug in stride. The son was embarrassed.

"Now you need to try the candy. It's great." Russell darted around her.

"You've had these before?" She took the one Russell plucked from her pillow, offering it to her on his outstretched palm. She unwrapped it as he scrutinized her, anticipating her reaction. A single bite of the succulent treat had her eyes closing. "Mmm. You were right, Russell; this is delicious."

"They always have these for the guests." Reid grinned. This trip was having the desired effect. Not only was she relishing the experiences, but everything, including the feelings, were being imprinted on her heart. At least, he hoped so. "They're imported from Venezuela. Grab yours, Russ. You'll need to get into your pajamas in a few minutes."

"Okay, Dad. I want to see her open the present first, though. Hold out your hands, Mom." He retrieved the gift, placing it on her outstretched palms.

"The packaging is beautiful; it's almost a shame to disturb it."

"You have to open it, Mom." Russell's eyes were wide, eyebrows raised. How could anyone not want to tear into a present? Grownups said the weirdest things.

"I will." She smiled, opening the gift with great care to find silver-backed diamond stud earrings resting on the black velvet interior of the box that had been concealed by another box, this one silver. The earrings took her breath away, catching the light, shooting back miniature rainbows.

Part of her wanted to protest, to say they were too much, but she pushed the urge down. Gratitude was a better response, especially to the excited faces watching her. "Oh! These are gorgeous. I've never had earrings like them before."

"Do you like them, Mom? Dad picked them out."

"They're a half-carat each. I wasn't sure how you'd feel about them, Lacey. But the jewelry store sales clerk promised me you'd love them. They're supposed to be perfect on every scale," Reid said.

"Like you, Mom."

"Oh, Russell. You're the sweetest son in the world." She embraced him again, not wanting to let go. Until Reid cleared his throat repeatedly, the volume and duration rising each time.

"I *am* the one who bought them, after all." He gave her a huge smile, opening his arms.

"They're wonderful." She filled those open arms, with her own going around his waist. He kissed the top of her head.

"Try them on, Mom!"

It would be more pleasurable to continue hugging Reid instead, but he released her. That allowed her to comply with their son's request. Lacey removed the small silver hoops in her ears and replaced them with the gift. She couldn't wait to get to a mirror.

"What do you guys think?" She tucked her hair behind her ears and turned her head from side to side. "Do they sparkle?"

"They sure do, Mom."

"They look fabulous on you, Lacey," Reid said.

"I may never take them off. I love them. You two are so good to me."

"Like you are to us. You'd better get going, Russell. We've got an early boat ride in the morning. I've checked to make sure the guy we rode with last year still works there and he does." He winked at Russell before facing Lacey. "I managed to get us on with Russ' favorite boatman, Joey. He's very funny, you'll love it. He gives a great tour."

"I'm looking forward to it." She smiled at Reid as Russell moved past them.

"Good job, Dad. Joey's the best." He popped the candy into his mouth and chewed as he grabbed for his pajamas on his way to the bathroom. Reid placed his candy at the base of the flowers.

"That's yours, Lacey, for later. Russ, I'm taking your mom out on the balcony to look at the lights while you're showering. Come on, Lacey."

They emerged onto the balcony just as a boat cruised by below, its lights reflecting in the water, just as those of the hotels and shops were doing. It was like something out of a dream. The rippling water made the bright mirrored lights dance in the darkness.

"It's so pretty at night from up here. This place is beyond belief, like you and Russell. I'm glad you two are in my life. It's not the presents, it's the two of you. I've never been this happy; not even close to this, not ever." The gushing might have been excessive, but it was genuine.

"We're sure glad you're in ours. You make us happy, too, Lacey." He faced her and gave her shoulders a rub. His hands glided to her waist as he leaned in to kiss her cheek. The kiss lingered, his lips sliding along her cheek, making her stomach flutter. He eased back.

Their eyes met, then his settled on her mouth, his head dipping to hers. The temptation was too much to pass up. He didn't even care to try, still remembering the kiss in the restaurant, still wanting more. The desire for her was too much to overcome.

Warmth swelled in her, along with a rush of nerves and a rapid pulse. She tilted her head to meet his and closed her eyes, feeling the warmth of his breath, of his lips. There came the barest contact, a hint of chocolate cake and ice cream.

It ended far too soon for her and was nowhere near enough. Reid rested his forehead against Lacey's and sighed. "I promised myself I wouldn't do that. Not until maybe your next visit. You and I can wait. Time with Russell is more limited. College will be here before you and I are ready for it."

He traced a finger over those sexy lips of hers. "Russell is happy having you in his life. He missed out on so much with you, and with his other mom. He barely remembers her. I want to tell you a little more about it if that's all right."

"Sure." She didn't know what he meant by "it", but they'd just taken a big step toward a relationship. Whatever he wanted to tell her was something she wanted to know.

"Karen and I were happy and excited, not to mention grateful to the donor. You have no idea the gift you gave, the power of it, even though it was unintentional and stolen from you. We didn't know that at the time, of course.

"Anyway, when Russell had too many questions about why no one else in the family had hair and eyes like his, I told him the truth. Naturally, he wanted to know more about his biological mother than what little the records Karen and I were given could tell. He wanted to find you. Begged me for two years until I gave in."

"You know the rest, how our attorney found about out everything. Found you, too. I'm glad Russell pressed me into finding all the information on you, glad he had the nerve to do what I was afraid to do. He found you for both of us, as it turns out. But he's the priority, and I understand that."

"You're right. The most important thing to me is getting to know my son." She turned away to place her hands on the railing, looking down but not fully noticing the river and the people. Reid had kissed her and yet he grasped that her focus was on Russell for now. It didn't seem real, the opportunity to both have her cake and eat it.

Reid rested a hand over Lacey's. "And maybe his dad, too?"

Lacey smiled and angled her head to meet his gaze, then leaned into him, resting her head against his shoulder. "Definitely his dad, too."

A sharp knock came to the room's door just then, breaking the moment. Whoever it was paused for less than three seconds before escalating to pounding, much as Lacey's heart had been immediately preceding the interruption.

"I'll go see who it is. Don't move from this spot, all right?" Reid whispered, studying her face before brushing his fingertips across her cheek.

"Okay." She watched him go before turning to enjoy the sights and sounds of the River Walk at night. The kiss from Reid Collier had the world's butterfly population in a tumultuous flight in her stomach.

Reid opened the door.

"Oh, my goodness! Won't this be fun?"

EIGHT

The butterflies vanished in an instant as her stomach twisted into knots with lightning speed. A glance over her shoulder revealed the tall brunette pushing past Reid, trailing a hand across his chest as she went. Her towering high heels of choice tonight made her a fraction above eye level with Reid.

"Kate?" Reid's surprise carried in his voice. "What're you... you're not supposed to be here."

He stepped back, unintentionally opening the door wider for the impatient valet and a long, wheeled cart crammed with luggage. The valet pushed past and into the room with the load.

"And you're not staying with us," Reid added.

"Pardon me, sir. Where would you like these?" The thin young man behind the cart was clearly exhausted. And frustrated.

"Good grief. Are all these yours?" Reid asked.

"No, silly. You can place them over by the dresser. Be careful with my garment bags. I'll unpack as soon as I've scrunched the boys' clothing together into one drawer. They take up far more room than they need. Most men do that; it must be genetic." She winked at Reid.

The valet removed two large pieces of luggage, one large suitcase, and two leather garment bags, placing them all to one side of the dresser. Then he stood in front of Reid, waiting.

Reid fished in his pocket, withdrawing a few bills, placing them in the valet's hand.

"Thank you, sir. Have a pleasant evening." He maneuvered the luggage cart from the room, closing the door after.

"What is all this, Kate? What're you doing here?" Reid demanded.

"I decided it was high time I took a real vacation and I wanted to spend it with you. Oh, and Russell, too. Where is my little darling boy?"

"Bathroom. But why are you moving into our hotel room? You know this was supposed to be a special trip."

"It's precisely why I told myself I had to get out here, for our special family trip. The timing also made it a good opportunity to have my house painted on the inside. You know what terrible headaches paint gives me."

"No., I don't." What just happened? How would he and Russell get to spend time with Lacey now?

"Well, it does. Terrible. I'm forcing myself to be out of it for at least a few days, maybe a week. And don't think I haven't heard about the other family trip you're planning for us in Disney World, out in California."

"Florida." Lacey allowed irritation to creep into her voice as she corrected Kate from the balcony doorway. She leaned against the doorframe with her arms crossed. She wasn't sure why she'd bothered to speak up. As sure as the sun shone in the sky, Kate wasn't going on that trip. If she did, Lacey would remain in Charlotte instead.

Kate's eyes widened. "Oh, Lacey, dear! There you are. Since I didn't see you when I came in, I thought for a minute maybe something terrible had happened and you'd missed your flight. It would've been such a shame."

The look she gave, aside from the usual hatred, had Lacey's curiosity up. "What would make you think I'd missed my flight?"

"Oh, I don't know. All sorts of nasty, unplanned possibilities spring to mind. You just never know what'll happen when you travel."

Russell emerged from the bathroom; wet hair tousled. "Aunt Kate. What're you doing here?"

"Russell, you're delightful. You sound just like your father. I've surprised you both. And that pleases me to no end. Tell me, when is our family trip to Florida going to take place? I have to make sure to put it on my calendar." She faced Reid with her eyebrows raised.

"*Our* family trip? Kate, the trip is just for the three of us," Reid corrected. Why was she doing this? Why was she even here?

"Oh, I'm sorry! I shouldn't have brought up something painful, but I didn't know." She turned to Lacey then. "Poor little Lacey. You weren't able to get away from the job in South Carolina at the Courthouse, were you?"

Lacey's eyes were slits. It seemed to be their natural state around Kate. "It's North Carolina, at... never mind. We haven't even set a date for the trip yet. And when we do, I'll be going. I'm the tour guide for the family on our Disney vacation. It's going to be special like this one was supposed to be." She hadn't meant to let the disappointment slip out.

"This trip is still going to be special, Lacey. I mean it," Reid assured. "So will our Disney trip." He faced Kate, a scowl on his face. "That trip is just for Lacey, Russell, and me."

"I'm not sure I understand. Did you not think I'd be able to take time off from work when you started making the plans?" Kate switched her focus to Lacey, eyes narrowing. "You should've consulted me, Lacey. Reid wouldn't dream of keeping me from a vacation like Disney. I'll be able to get the time off. I'm well connected to the boss." She sent Lacey an exaggerated wink.

The frown on Lacey's face was exchanged for amazement. Was she clueless or did she honestly believe she could pull this off and finagle an invitation on the trip? Reid didn't seem to be going along, judging from his expression.

"Aunt Kate, the Disney trip is for my dad and me to get to know my mom better. We're the only ones going, right Dad?" Russell's voice rose, as did his eyebrows.

"Yes. The Disney trip doesn't include you or anyone else, Kate." Reid crossed his arms over his chest. "Immediate family only."

Kate wandered toward the nightstand between the beds. "Oh. Well, that's okay. I'll just have to get to work changing your mind before then, Reid. Look at the chocolate! I love these." She snatched it up, ripping off the paper to take a dainty nibble before anyone thought to say a word through the disbelief.

"That was supposed to be mom's," Russell announced.

"It's all right, Russell. She can have it," Lacey said.

"Oh, you mean this was supposed to be yours?" She feigned innocence, one hand moving to lie on her chest.

"It's fine, go right ahead and enjoy yourself."

She sat on the bed and took another nibble, inserting low moans to accompany the act. "This gives me the same reaction as something else." She glanced to Reid. "You know what I mean, Reid?"

Lacey's eyes narrowed further. The creases in her forehead were bound to become permanent from being around Kate.

"I'll take this side of the bed, Lacey, next to these beautiful rosebuds. They're exquisite. Pink is my favorite color, as Reid obviously knows. I adore them, Reid."

The absolute last straw. Lacey strode into the room and over to Kate. Since the dark-haired woman was seated, Lacey could stare Kate down for a change.

"Russell is the one who chose the color and they're *mine*. They're something I'm not sharing with you, Kate. And there's no table, no place for them on the other side of the bed, which means you'll sleep there. This is *my* spot." Control slipped away, even as Lacey attempted to hold on.

"Oh, I'm sure we can figure out something. We can pull over the chair from the little desk against the wall. Then I can sleep here. I'll sleep better this way, since Reid will be right across from me, just like at the ranch, but closer in here, instead of in separate rooms." She sent Reid a sultry glance.

Lacey's teeth were clinched. "No. I've already selected this side and that's how it'll be. There's no discussion."

"Aunt Kate, why did you have to come?"

Kate stood and crossed the room. "Russell, you're such a cute little kid. Family trips include me, don't forget. I don't want to be out at the ranch working when I could be with my family on vacation." She clapped her hands together. "Now, it's time to unpack. I'll move your clothes around, don't worry. I may need to stuff a few personal items in with yours, Reid."

A snarl took hold of Lacey's face. No way that was going to happen. Reid was too polite for his own good. Lacey would handle this herself. "Hold on!" She ordered in a verbal gunshot.

Kate stopped; one drawer open. Lacey's volume and intensity had surprised her.

"If you absolutely have to be rude and have your own way, allow me." Lacey moved Kate aside with a shove from the hip.

She rearranged Reid's clothes to make them occupy less of the drawer. Opening the second drawer, Lacey removed her undergarments and shorts, placing them in the top drawer beside Reid's clothes. Next, she shifted Russell's clothes from the third drawer down to the second drawer, where Lacey had left her shirts and socks.

"Problem solved. Now you can unload whatever of yours will fit into the two bottom drawers. Plus, you can have the closet space. I have a shirt in there, but I'll just fold it and put it in a drawer. I'm not a prima donna; a few wrinkles don't bother me."

Reid beamed, on the verge of laughter, and maybe clapping. This was the first time he'd witnessed anyone hold their own with Kate and come out on top. It was upsetting to have Kate ruining their plans, but this was great entertainment.

Lacey had lit Kate's fuse. "Sweet little thing. You're thoughtful. And don't you worry too much about those wrinkles. Some women just naturally age faster than others."

Kate got in a zing, even though she wore crow's feet in

abundance, whereas Lacey carried few. Lacey regretted the new scowl that covered her features, however brief the reaction to the attack.

"Hey, my mom's way younger than you, Aunt Kate."

Bingo! Lacey shot a triumphant smile at Russell as Reid turned his back, his shoulders moving from the heaves of laughter he struggled to keep silent.

"Russell! Where are your manners? Besides, how do you know how old I am?" Kate snapped, forgetting to coat her words in a dose of sugar.

"I know how old my mom is," he paused, looking to Lacey, "my other mom, I mean, would be now. I calculated by the documentation how old Lacey is, which makes her six years younger than you are."

"Well, now. Aren't you just a clever little human calculator? Excuse me, I need to use the facilities." She rushed into the bathroom, slamming the door.

"Russell, turn on the television and see if a game is on. I'll let you watch it for a few minutes while we all get ready for bed."

"Okay, Dad." As the sound filled the room and Reid approached, Russell asked in a hushed whisper, "Did I hurt her feelings? I'm sorry, but she tried to hurt mom's first. It wasn't nice of me, but she made me mad the way she talked to mom. She was being mean on purpose. I saw her getting in Mom's face that first morning Mom came to visit us. I didn't let you know I saw that, Mom."

Lacey put a hand on his shoulder to give it a quick squeeze. "That's okay. I can take care of myself."

"You're fine, son," Reid added. "Don't worry about anything you've said. I'm not sure what's gotten into Kate lately. I'm going to have a talk with her about it one of these days. I'm sorry all this happened, Lacey."

"Can I speak to you out on the balcony for a few minutes, Reid?" Lacey asked.

"Sure. Russell, you stay right here. Watch some television."

"Yes sir. I'll stay here and guard mom's side of the bed." He sat at the foot of her bed, his back rigid, jaws clenched, and arms crossed.

Reid closed the slider behind him, joining Lacey at the railing.

"I'm sorry, Reid. I'm going to put you in a difficult position. I have to be honest with you. I don't like Kate and she definitely doesn't like me. I'll go ahead and tell you I have a strong suspicion she's the one who blocked my attempts to contact you after you picked up Russell in Charlotte. I could get proof easy enough, but I'd rather let it go. Let bygones be bygones, as they say.

"I don't blame you for any of this, but she's got to get herself under control. I don't have to put up with the way she treats me, or the way she talks to Russell.

"My whole purpose in coming to the ranch is to spend time with my son and get to know him. I'd like for my son's father to be included, but it's not a requirement. It's up to you. She doesn't have any reason to be here in this hotel room with us. Her goal is to interfere with you and me getting to know each other better."

Lacey didn't want to say more than she had to. The main point was all that needed to be made. "If you have feelings for her, fine. I might question your taste in women, but it's not my business. Just say so. That's all I'm asking."

"No. No, I don't. Far from it. I've never thought about her romantically, even for a minute, and never would. Ever. All I did was give her a job which she performs well enough. But I have no interest in a future with her."

"In that case, are you going to ask her to leave, or do you plan to let her stay here in the room with us? I'm sorry, but if you don't ask her to go elsewhere, I'm leaving. I regret any hurt it'll cause Russell, but I'll have to find a hotel somewhere, a room of my own."

"There aren't any more rooms. At least, not anywhere around here there aren't." He rubbed his hands up and down Lacey's arms to soothe her. If she left them, they would lose precious time together.

The physical contact wasn't going to be enough, not after Kate's unexpected arrival and Reid not yet insisting she find a room of her own. "I'll do whatever I have to, even if it means flying back to Charlotte tomorrow. I'm not putting up with her sharing a room with us. I got more than enough of her the last time I was at the ranch. Besides, she'll behave better if I'm not around, and I know for a fact it'll make my life more pleasant not being near her."

"You're not leaving us. I'll handle it. I didn't invite her. I even told her if she wanted to show up for the parade this year, she'd have to make other arrangements, because this time was special. Just for Russell and me to spend with you. From what she said, she can't go to her home, but she can always go to her room at the ranch.

"I'm going to call and get Gil to pick her up here at the hotel. I don't think you met Gil, but he's a good, hard worker, like Jayden. Friend of his. Tall guy, blond hair, gray eyes, and a long mustache ending in a goatee. Good at entertaining kids, dependable.

"I'll introduce you next time you're at the ranch. You'll like him. Everybody does. He's been with us for almost twenty years now. He handles afternoon or evening issues that crop up. You and Russell stay out here on the balcony while I talk to her. She's not going to spend the night here. I'll take care of everything. I promise, Lacey."

She disengaged her arms from his hands and leaned on the railing. "Reid, you don't owe me anything. Make sure before you talk to her. Make sure it's what you want. If you want her in your life as anything more than an employee, it's your choice. But I won't be around for it.

"I'm not trying to pressure you. You barely know me. Russell and I can have our visits working around you and Kate. Maybe I could stay at a bed and breakfast here in San Antonio and Russell could come and spend with me there. I shouldn't have gotten upset. It's not my place."

"It *is* your place. It's a long story, but I'd never want to be with her. She's been working at the ranch for years. I'd always hoped she'd warm up to Russell, at least try to be some kind of a mother figure to him because of her sister, but it never happened. She's never shown interest in him. And there's more to it, but I won't go into it now, not here. Not with Russell close by."

"I don't want to hurt him or you. I don't want to hurt anyone or cause problems. The most important thing to me is that I get to know my son."

"And you will. We'll all get to know each other." He smiled, his eyes crinkling at the corners. He couldn't risk letting anything or anyone drive her away. She belonged with them. He was certain of that. "We're a family now, whatever happens."

Reid applied a quick kiss to Lacey's forehead, then stepped into the room. "Russell, go outside for a little while with your mom. Kate and I need a few minutes to talk."

Russell rose from the bed and walked out, turning to watch as his father closed the door. "What's going on, Mom?"

"Your dad's asking Kate to leave, I think."

"Oh. She wasn't supposed to come here in the first place. I'm glad. I wanted it to just be the three of us." He stepped to the rail and looked at the activity below with his mother.

"Play some music on your phone for me Russell, something festive. It'll give them some privacy in there. And you and I can enjoy ourselves out here. So, tell me how school is going."

***

Reid paced the room while Kate ran water in the bathroom sink. He talked with Gil while he waited for Kate to emerge. Then he phoned the front desk, asking for someone with a luggage cart. By the time he'd hung up, he heard the music with a strong Latin flair coming from the balcony and watched as his son and his mother bobbed their heads to the rhythm. He longed to join them. First things first.

The bathroom door opened. He stuffed the phone into his back pocket and took a deep breath. He loathed confrontations. It was a failing, he knew, but getting past it had always proven difficult. He wanted everyone happy, with no anger or hurt feelings. Little hope of that now.

"Oh," Kate purred, dragging out the word. "Have we been left alone?" She approached Reid with an extra sway in her hips.

It didn't appeal to him or change his mind. He extended a hand to keep her away. She stopped.

"Listen, Kate. I told you long before Russell and I left on this trip that it was going to be different this time. Special."

"I know. That's why I had to come." She gave him her biggest smile.

"No. It's why I told you *not* to come, more than once. I don't care to know why you defied me. You're free to attend Fiesta if you so choose. But you're not staying here or spending time with us."

"But Reid, I already told you they're painting my house…"

"I know. Nice timing on that, by the way." He took another deep breath and strode for the television. He grabbed the remote and lowered the volume. It didn't matter if his family overheard, just that Kate got the message.

"You're not staying here with us. Russell and I need and deserve time alone with Lacey. And we're going to have it. I've called Gil. He's on his way here to pick you up and take you back to the ranch. Someone from the hotel will be here momentarily to pick up your luggage. You can wait for Gil downstairs. Order anything you want at the bar or get some food and charge it all to my room. But you're leaving this room. Now."

The smile transformed in slow motion to tears as Kate gave the appearance of struggling to hold them back.

Reid shook his head. "It doesn't matter how much you cry or if you throw a temper tantrum. You're not staying. Get your things together."

A knock came at the door. Reid moved around Kate, careful to avoid physical contact. He grinned when he opened the door to find the same young man who had delivered Kate's luggage not long ago. Reid pulled out his wallet and gave the man a hefty tip. "Load her luggage and take her back to the lobby," he indicated to Kate with a tilt of his head. "She's leaving."

That wasn't as bad as he'd built it up to be in his mind. A part of him enjoyed it.

***

The next morning was bright and sunny, the breakfast tasty and filled with laughter. They went for an early walk beside the channeled river to the Go Rio Cruises boats. Lacey's guys positioned themselves on either side of her as took seats on a boat. "I wish you never had to leave," Russell said. "When's the next time you're coming out here, Mom?"

"The Fourth of July, I guess."

"What about Mother's Day?" Russell frowned.

In a flash, it came to her, the special day she hadn't observed since her mother's passing was now her own to claim. "Mother's Day? It didn't occur to me. I've never been a mother before."

"You can't be away from us on Mother's Day, Lacey; you simply can't. This will be the first Mother's Day Russell gets to spend with you. We don't relish having to say goodbye at the airport in a few days as it is. July is too far off."

"I hadn't given it any thought. It's an important day for a mother and her child." Lacey couldn't afford to squeeze in a whirlwind trip to Texas for Mother's Day, but a glance at Russell's face altered her thinking on the subject. What she couldn't afford to do was disappoint the most important person in her world on that or any other day. "I'll be here for Mother's Day."

Russell and Reid hugged her at the same time, each kissing one of her cheeks, making her laugh.

"Thanks, Mom!"

"You're a wonderful mother with a big heart." Reid kissed her cheek a second time as the boat trolled away from the dock.

Mother's Day

NINE

"See you late Sunday night, Connie!" Lacey waved with jubilance as they parted ways. Connie was heading out to spend the weekend at her mom's, while Lacey jogged off to retrieve a large map she'd printed on the plotter down the hallway. It was the final task to be taken care of before leaving for the airport and wouldn't take more than a few minutes.

The packed duffel bag waited in the trunk of her car. There didn't seem to be another soul in the building, though the cleaning crew should arrive soon if they weren't already inside, somewhere.

"Enjoy your first Mother's Day! Hurry up and get out of here!" Connie shouted.

"I will. You have a good weekend at your mom's." Lacey hurried to the new copy room where the large map-printing plotter sat. Her excitement had grown through the week, sleep eluding her most of last night.

Reid and Russell were supposed to spoil her rotten all weekend, and they had tried to prod her into staying with them on Monday. She'd had to refuse, but it was sweet of them to try. Reid had bought her airline tickets as a Mother's Day gift.

The final task remaining was to get the map off the plotter, roll it up, and place it on the boss' desk. She removed the rubber bands from her wrist after noisily rolling the map. The job couldn't be done in silence. Using two rubber bands, one near each end, was taking better care of the product, showing how much pride she took in her work. "There, all finished. Texas, here I come!"

The door behind her slammed shut. Lacey whirled. She'd been standing in plain sight, directly across the small room from the door. And no one else was around. As she stared at the narrow glass pane in the doorway in shock, the lights went out, including those inside the copier room.

"What in the world?" She tossed the rolled map back into the plotter's catch tray, strode to the door, and tried the knob. Locked from the outside, impossible to unlock from the inside.

"Hey!" She pounded with both fists. "Hey! Open the door! Don't leave me in here!"

A doorstop had to be removed from under the door before it could be closed. Someone had been in the doorway to perform the act. They saw her standing there, rolling the map. And the process of rolling the large, thick sheet of paper generated a fair amount of noise.

Someone had done this on purpose. If intended as a prank, it wasn't amusing. If they left her here for long, she'd miss her flight. Connie had worked late with her but was likely exiting the building now. No help there anyway without a phone, which she'd left at her desk.

The automatic lock on the door could only be unlocked with a key; a decision made due to the new, expensive equipment stored within. Who could've done this? She and Connie had been the last employees working in the area. Maybe in the building.

At least that they were aware of.

Why would anyone lock her in? *Everyone has enemies; it's just how dedicated they are to the cause.* She'd said those words to Russell and Reid on her last visit to Texas. She didn't know anyone at work who would do this to her, to frighten her to this extent. Or slash her tires and Connie's.

Yet, someone might hate her just that much. Being trapped brought the realization that whatever had been going on was directed at her. Connie was collateral damage.

As her eyes worked on adjusting to the darkness, she peered through the elongated pane of glass in the door but there was no one visible. Someone had physically closed the door and turned out the lights, knowing a person was inside. And then they'd run off. The sole illumination came from distant windows and scattered emergency lighting, none of which helped in the copy room.

The perpetrator must still be out there. Everyone who knew her was aware of how much she hated practical jokes and the importance of this trip. Her first Mother's Day. Russell. She closed her eyes for a moment of regret.

Her purse, holding her cellphone, car keys, and airline tickets, was in her unlocked desk drawer, ready to grab and go. The culprit could have the cash and even the credit cards, but not her tickets. There'd be no reason.

If not for deciding to print the map, she'd be walking to her car with Connie. The map was important but wasn't expected until the end of the day on Monday. Lacey had wanted to impress the boss by preparing it in advance.

The man had said he planned to swing by the office late Sunday afternoon, once he left his mom's house. He'd been joking about filling her position soon since she'd be moving to Texas. That was despite her telling him how much she liked her job and that she intended to stay.

He'd countered that she used to say she loved her job and pointed out how she'd rarely taken a vacation in previous years. Since meeting Russell, her vacation requests for the months to come would drain her reserves before this time next year. Not quite, but close.

The objective had been to show commitment to the job. And she'd gotten trapped for it, at least until the cleaning crew came through in a couple of hours. She'd never make it to the airport on time.

Reid had snagged the last ticket on the sole direct flight to Dallas-Fort Worth this evening. The next one wouldn't be until noon tomorrow, but the schedule was iffy, considering the severe weather forecast to sweep through the southeast on Saturday. Lacey would've been safely ensconced on the ranch by that point.

There was no way to break down the heavy door; not for her. And no knowledge, or even guesswork, of how to pick a lock. Not to mention there were no such tools around. Instead, she used her hands to probe the darkness, finding the counter against the opposite wall, working along it until she found her way to the desk phone.

When lifted, the receiver emitted no sound. There should've been a dial tone and an illuminated display, but there wasn't one. Her fingers probed for the cord at the rear of the phone and found nothing.

Connie had used the phone a few hours earlier, while they were searching for supplies and had to resort to calling for assistance. Further exploration found no connecting cord anywhere. If it had been stuffed behind the countertop, there was no way to retrieve it. The cabinet was anchored to the wall and the rear of it stretched to the floor.

There had to be something she could do. She couldn't give up because Russell was counting on her. But what options were there?

Then she remembered. People from the IT department had been in the room that morning, measuring and marking off the exact spot for installing a new cabinet to hold a wall-mounted server. The room had been built to house two plotters, several printers, high-tech computer equipment, and specialized drones. Construction on the room was still ongoing.

Maintenance workers had cut a substantial hole in the wall near the ceiling to hold the server cabinet, following the markings drawn by IT. Other employees had complained about the location, concerned they'd knock dents in their skulls, not being used to a sharp-edged aerial obstruction at head height.

In the ambient illumination leaking through the window slit in the door, a dark object high on the wall stood out. The maintenance workers had put a blue tarp on the pale gray wall and taped it in place. A rolling cart used for moving computer equipment was parked in a corner of the room. After making her way there and rolling it into place, Lacey clicked the wheel locks into position and climbed aboard.

Stripping the tarp away, her hand reached inside with caution, afraid of electrocution. The only contact came with the back of the wall on the other side of the gap. What was over there? It came into her mind, as she visualized herself walking along the hallway, rounding a corner, and moving into a suite of offices. If she was right, it would be a reception area. There was also a door leading out into the corridor. And a desk phone.

Lacey hopped down and began feeling along the countertop in pursuit of a tool. A sturdy box cutter was kept on the counter to open boxes and the large rolls of paper to feed into the plotter. It wasn't there. How could she get through the other wall without a cutting device?

Then she remembered the second box cutter. They kept it in a low cabinet. On her knees, she dug around until she found the small plastic toolbox.

Inside it rested what she was after. Once the box cutter was clutched in her hand, she returned to the cart, climbed aboard, and extended the blade on the box cutter. Then began the slow, awkward process of sawing through the sheetrock.

The job took longer than she'd imagined and was noisy. It sent particles of dust flying that she hoped wouldn't give her a sneezing fit to draw unwanted attention. Once finished, something in her couldn't resist the opportunity to blow off some steam by punching the irregularly shaped square free.

The angry act stung her knuckles. But it worked. The square landed on the other side with a thud. Then came the sound of a thump and multiple objects pinging, rolling, more pinging.

More noise that might attract unwanted attention if someone was in the right place to hear it. After a moment of pausing to listen, she resumed her escape. The room on the other side of the wall seemed brighter than the copy room, but not by much.

Retracting the blade, Lacey shoved the tool into her back pocket. Just in case she'd need it again. There was no sense in taking unnecessary chances, considering what had happened already. The current predicament was proof of that.

Pausing, she assessed the situation. There was no way to be sure what she'd find beneath her on the other side. If there wasn't anything to break her fall, she'd drop anywhere from six feet or more, headfirst, from the base of the cutout.

The fall could result in a broken hand, arm, or neck. The plan she came up with to avoid killing herself wouldn't be easy to achieve. She'd have to become an acrobat in short order, contorting her body like a pretzel to enable her legs to go through the hole first.

Only one way to do that.

Hopping down, she moved the cart away and dragged over long, heavy boxes containing rolled plotter paper one at a time. She stacked them side-by-side and one on top of the other. The next step was lifting the cart to the summit. It was heavy, but Lacey was motivated. An attempt to topple it proved to be unsuccessful, though it did wobble.

The stool kept by the plotter allowed an easier climb to the top of the cart, though it was still unnerving. Once there, it took an effort to lift her legs high enough to get them into and through both holes. Hands and straining arm muscles provided stability for the precarious position, bracing against the sheet of drywall.

Not knowing what lay beneath her feet was unsettling. A push forward served to drop her dangling body over the edge, knocking her forehead hard against the opening in the process. The sensation of falling came next, but too brief of a one for panic.

Her feet smacked onto the curved edge of a countertop. But that wasn't the end of the journey. A plethora of small, unstable objects that were both long and round cost Lacey her tenuous balance and sent her ricocheting to the floor.

The thin layer of carpet provided little cushion for the subsequent impact. Her face hit a fraction of a second after her shoulder took the brunt of the blow. At the sound of a pop, she cried out against the excruciating, severe pain in her left shoulder. Her teeth clamped together, gritting, to avoid additional outcries in case her tormentor remained inside the building. If he was, he wouldn't have to be all that close to have heard her exclamation.

Blood trickled from a scuffed lip on the outside and from the inside where her teeth cut into the inside of her lip. Her right hand took over, pushing her to a seated position. Her left shoulder, unable to move, was on fire.

She leaned back against the cabinets, groaning as she caught her breath. It gave her mind time to wonder how seriously her shoulder might be damaged. The need to call for help became clear when she realized she probably couldn't escape the building on her own.

The first order of business was to find a working telephone. Standing brought on a cascade of pain and nausea acute enough that she questioned her grip on consciousness. After a moment of leaning against the counter to allow most of the nausea to pass, she felt ready to explore.

A few feet away was a desk, complete with a chair, easily rolled out for sitting. The meager illumination provided by the nearest emergency light revealed a phone. Lacey slid it closer and dialed, noting the time. It had taken longer than she thought to escape the copy room.

"Nine-one-one operator, please state the address of your emergency," a strong, calm female voice on the other end steadied Lacey immediately.

"I've hurt my left arm bad. It might be broken." Lacey paused to gasp for air against the unending pain.

"Can you give me your address?"

"I'm trapped in here." Alone and helpless, focused on pain and fear.

"Where? I need your exact address, please."

Had the woman asked for that already? Maybe. Some focus was needed, but that proved difficult. "I'm in the government building."

"Downtown Charlotte?"

"Yes. Look at the phone number on your readout. I need help." She'd never worked a dispatch job but knew the desk phone's number would display on the woman's phone or monitor.

"You're a government employee?" The woman's fingers flew, typing on her keyboard hard enough for Lacey to hear it over the phone.

"Yes. Not in this department, but yes. I cut a hole in the wall."

"You did what?"

"I cut through a wall to escape. Somebody locked me in the new plotter room. I had to get out of there and that was the only way." Couldn't she just call for help? Why the conversation?

"What room did you say it was?"

"There's no time for this. It's the new copy room, then. I don't know what number the room is. Please, he could still be in here." Her voice was getting too loud. And a little whiny.

"Who?"

Lacey paused to close her eyes and take a deep breath, which set off a new wave of pain in her shoulder. "Listen to me. I need help."

"I've already dispatched EMS to your location."

"I need the police, too." The words were rushed, but she kept her voice low.

"The police?"

"Yes. I told you, someone locked me in the room. The plotter...copy room. They disconnected the phone cord to prevent me from using it to call for help. They turned out all the lights, too, at least the ones on this floor."

"You mean your assailant is still in the building?"

"Might be. I don't know." She winced as she leaned forward.

"I'm dispatching two additional patrol units; one is already en route. Can you give me a physical description?"

"Of him? I never saw him. He slammed the door, and the lights went out."

"It's well past seven o'clock. Isn't it possible someone closed both the door and turned off the lights, not knowing you were inside?"

"No, it's not. They would've had to see me in there; I was in plain sight, right across from the door, maybe ten feet away, moving around, making a lot of noise. There was a doorstop to remove, too. Plus, I banged on the door and yelled to be let out." Why did the questions keep on coming? She just needed to send help.

"Take a few deep breaths and try to stay calm. I'm going to remain on the line with you until help arrives. What's your name?"

"Thank you." Lacey was still alone, but it felt better with someone on the other end of the line. She closed her eyes to try and calm herself, as the woman had suggested. "I'm Lacey Freemont."

"And you are employed with the local government, Ms. Freemont?"

After a couple of deep breaths, she did feel calmer and opened her eyes. They riveted to the glass on the door across from her, which showed a dim reflection of light. Odd. For it to reflect like that, the light would have to be coming from... behind her. Lacey's eyes widened as she rotated the chair slowly, terror building, trying not to make noise.

The hole in the wall showed black. Maybe it had been her imagination. The little voice in her head disagreed. Strongly.

"Yes. I work in GIS." She whispered the answer, just in case.

"G-I-S?"

No one ever knew who they were, let alone what they did. "Geographic Information Systems. I made crime analysis maps for the police department not too long ago."

"Oh really?"

The woman may never have seen them. Didn't matter since the mapmaker's name was never on the maps they created anyway. "Yes. Please, can you tell them to hurry? I'm hurt and I'm scared. If he's still in here and he wants to hurt me, there's nothing I can do to defend myself."

"Ma'am, you got lucky. I had a car near your location already, and the officers have already entered the building. They'll reach your location soon. They're required to use caution with the possibility of an unknown threat inside. A second patrol car is arriving now, and the ambulance has already pulled up right on the heels of the first patrol car. They're in the building now, too."

"I appreciate you sending help." God, please let them get here in record-breaking time. Her voice returned to a normal level. Help was coming. Everything would be fine now.

"You're welcome. It's what we're here for. Now, just remain on the line with me. Help will be there before you know it."

"Okay. I can't wait for them to get here. This is nerve-wracking." She couldn't help wondering why someone would be doing this to her.

"So, do you normally work late on a Friday?"

"No. I was finishing up a project for my boss. It's a map of the downtown, with some changes the planning folks have been thinking about."

"What kind of changes?"

"Figuring out transportation options that don't involve gasoline-powered cars. We've already got that going on, but this is an expansion, and working in some design considerations for the autonomous vehicles to come, freeing up parking spaces to use for something different."

"I don't know about you, but I don't trust those things. They crash, you know. I've seen reports on the news about it."

A long, narrow beam of light caught Lacey's attention as it played about from side to side, approaching her location. "Hey, someone's coming. That was fast."

Lacey needed to get to her phone to call Reid. Then would come a visit to the hospital. There was no doubt the weekend plans would need to be adjusted, but not eliminated. The trip couldn't be eliminated.

This had to be a simple sprain. And the weather had to hold off for a flight tomorrow. So many things needed to fall into place to make the weekend work. The odds were stacked against her.

"Ms. Freemont. Are you telling me you can see someone?"

"A flashlight. Someone's coming down the hallway, sweeping the beam around. I guess he's looking for the man who did this. Should I go out there to meet him, or open the door and call out, or just wait for him to get here? I don't want to do anything that might get me shot."

The dispatcher hesitated. "Ms. Freemont, I want you to listen to me very carefully and remain calm. The officers haven't reached your location yet. They're close, but not there."

"What does that mean?" The stiffening body incited Lacey's shoulder to scorch. The realization of looming danger dawned.

"If you're seeing someone approaching your location, it isn't someone with emergency services. It isn't anyone who's come to help." The woman's voice rose, her words clipped, adding to the warning.

Lacey's mouth dropped open as she tried to breathe. "Oh, God. Is it him? Is he coming to get me?"

"Stay calm. Is there someplace you can hide? I'm communicating with the officers now. They're speeding up their approach. They should reach your location in less than one minute."

Stay calm? "He'll be here before then; way before then. There's no place to hide, except this desk."

"Get under it. Don't talk, but don't hang up."

"I have to hang up." The woman didn't seem to understand the dilemma.

"No. Don't do it. You have to remain on the line with me. Let me hear what happens."

"Then you might hear him kill me. He'll see the light from the phone. It's dark in here; he'll see it, he'll know, he'll get me." Panic escalated as control slipped, but she couldn't stop it. An image popped into her head then. She had to stay calm for Russell, she had to survive for him.

When Lacey spoke again, her words were slow and measured. "Don't call back or you'll be the one who killed me. I have a son to live for; he needs me." Lacey put the receiver back in place and the phone's light dimmed to dark.

The flashlight was close. The person, assumedly a man, clutched a cellphone, which held half his focus. Shadows eliminated details but the person was tall, slim, skulking. He took his time, clearly unaware of the impending police presence.

He must have gone back to retrieve her from the room but found the escape hatch and determined where his quarry had logically gone. The faint light from moments before would have been his flashlight sweeping over the hole in the wall. What did he intend to do to her?

The pain in her shoulder stabbed at her efforts as Lacey scrambled beneath the desk and pulled the chair back into place. She withdrew the box cutter, extending the blade. It was sharp but short, allowing a shallow cut, only enough to make a person angry. Or maybe sever an artery. She tried to guess where those were located on the human body.

Go for the neck or maybe his wrist. Or an eye. Lacey pushed her back against the front panel of the desk, her feet resting on two of the chair's wheels, ready to shove it into the man.

It might provide the element of surprise. But she hoped the police would arrive before she was forced into an attempt to protect herself.

In the thick, suffocating blanket of silence, it was easy to hear the doorknob turning, to feel the shift in the room's atmosphere with a rush of fresh air from beyond as the door opened. The person responsible for the influx of fresh air made only the slightest of sounds from feet on the carpet, muffled to the volume of a mouse.

The light scanned the room and Lacey hoped he couldn't see her jeans in the sliver of a gap at the bottom of the desk. His beam rose, passing the hole in the wall. Then it stopped to return to the spot, shining steadily on it. "You were right," he whispered. "Got her now."

Wanting to cry, Lacey bit her still-bleeding lower lip instead. And closed her eyes. The words came into her mind as though he'd be able to hear them, unspoken, from such a long distance. *I love you, Russell.*

"Police! Freeze! Hands up!"

"Shit!" the assailant spit into the air.

"Hey, you! Stop!"

Lacey's eyes popped open, her breath catching in her throat. The commanding voice was followed immediately by booted feet, charging down the corridor toward her, then past where Lacey sheltered as the door to the room swung closed.

The police were after him. What about her? Should she run? She was afraid of running but just as afraid to remain. Faced with the dilemma, she chose to stay put.

The atmospheric change came to the room again as the door pushed open.

"Hello? Hello, is anyone in here?" A man's voice came from the doorway.

Her insides instantly twisted into knots. Did he double back? Would he kill her now? The urge to rock back and forth came at her strong. She wished Reid was here to protect her, soothe her, something. Or Connie, who'd keep Lacey so distracted trying to keep her friend from rushing out into the fray that there'd be no time to panic.

But there was no one else. It was all up to her. She'd kill him if she had to. If she was able. She'd live to see her son again.

"Ma'am, are you in here? We're the paramedics."

Her hopes rose, but the fear remained intact. She opted for silence.

"Lacey Freemont?"

"Hey," another voice said.

There were two of them. Fear was replaced by a fragile sense of hope. But she decided to wait.

"What?" the first asked.

"Look up there, on the wall."

The hole she'd made was illuminated by a flashlight. Again. On her side, this time.

"This must be it. Dispatch said she was in a room where she'd cut a hole in the wall to get out. They said she was hiding, and the brute was coming after her. Speaking of which, even though they've got him on the run, you'd better close the door."

The men had moved inside the room. They'd see her. Maybe they were telling the truth. Please be telling the truth.

"Lacey? Is it okay if I call you Lacey? The man who was after you is being pursued by the police. Other officers are on their way in. Another patrol car pulled up behind us. No one's going to harm you."

One of them came around the desk, his shoes giving him away. The footsteps sounded different from the first man, the bad man.

"We were told you might have a broken arm. We're here to help you." He bent at the waist, shining his bright light on her. Lacey shielded her eyes with her right hand, still holding the box cutter. He immediately cast the beam to the floor.

"Over here. I've got her. It's okay, Lacey. I'm Jim. My partner is Mikey."

"Stop calling me Mikey, for God's sake. You're such a juvenile." The second voice sounded irritated.

The one who called himself Jim grinned. "It's okay; we're not going to hurt you. We're here to help. Why don't you crawl out of there, nice and easy, and let us have a look at your arm?"

The second one shone a beam on the floor at her feet, enough to see by. "She's got a knife."

"I know; I saw it. She's scared. It's okay, Lacey. Come on out, please. Look, I'm going to take the chair and roll it out of your way. Okay? I'll move it real slow."

Jim narrated everything he did, moving slowly like he was dealing with a frightened rabbit. She guessed there were similarities. If there'd been room to maneuver, she would've taken off running already.

"There we go." Jim knelt and Lacey studied his uniform and badge.

She released those knots inside her, closed the box cutter, and tossed it out, away from the man.

"Good girl. Come on, slide this way. You can do it. Go as slow as you need to. You don't want to cause yourself extra pain." He extended a hand to her and gave her what must be his most earnest expression, enhanced by red curls and ruddy cheeks with freckles.

Teeth clenched, Lacey slid from beneath the desk, inch by painful inch, until he had her.

"Okay now, good enough. Mike, shine the flashlight to let me see what I'm doing. Good. Right there, thanks. I wish somebody would turn on those lights. Now, you just tell me where it hurts."

"My left arm, my shoulder."

"Left shoulder, huh?" He studied the pain in her face and the way she cradled the arm.

"Yes. I dropped from the hole up there and hit the countertop behind you."

Mike shone his light on the wall, then the countertop, just as the lights in the area turned on. He extinguished the flashlight.

"The momentum sent me over at a bad angle and my left shoulder hit the floor first."

"That's impressive," Mike said, adding a low whistle. "Looks like you probably landed on these pens. There's a bunch of them spilled here. That would've cost you your balance for sure. I think the cutout piece from the wall hit this blue plastic cup, which was likely holding the pens. The cup and most of what was inside it are on the floor here."

Jim poked and prodded while Mike conversed, distracting Lacey until she yelled and leaned away.

"It looks like you've dislocated it. We're going to make sure you're stabilized before we move you. I won't lie to you; this whole process is going to hurt. We'll minimize your pain as much as we can and immobilize your arm. Afterward, we'll transport you to the hospital. Do you want something for the pain? I know it's gotta hurt like the dickens."

"Yes, it does. I'd rather go without medication, but it hurts."

"Don't worry," Jim said. "We'll take the edge off it for you. You won't be using the arm much for a while, except for physical therapy. That won't be any fun, either. The doc at the hospital will give you an approximation of how long you'll be out of commission."

The men set about their work, taking her vitals, checking her memory and reflexes. "We'll get you to the ambulance in no time."

***

"Here you go, ma'am. Is this your purse?" The young police officer, looking all of sixteen, handed over Lacey's purse inside a plastic evidence bag. "We found it out back of your workplace by the dumpster. Your wallet is in there but it's empty, I'm told."

The wallet was of comparatively little concern to her. "Yes, this is mine. What about my tickets? They're all I care about. Are my tickets in my purse?"

"Tickets? Tickets to what?" a second officer, only slightly older than the first, asked as he came up behind his partner.

"Airline tickets to Texas. I was supposed to spend Mother's Day weekend with my son."

"Oh. I'm sorry. There were no tickets. No tickets, no cash, no credit cards, no driver's license. Can't fly without tickets and a license. When's your flight scheduled to leave?"

The wall clock delivered the bad news. "Hours ago."

The tests had been run, the bad arm repositioned and strapped into a sling. They were waiting for the discharge, for the doctor's evaluation of the last-minute decision to take x-rays on her head. The head was bruised but swelling. The pain medication had her drowsy, but the loss of her tickets countered it.

"We'll have to see what we can do to get you on another flight if the doctor says it's okay. With a busted-up shoulder like yours, a plane ride won't help, no doubt about it. Just prepare yourself for the eventuality." The second officer gave a sympathetic grimace.

"That's nice of you, but the doctor isn't allowing her to fly; we already checked on it," Connie said, peering at the contents of another plastic evidence bag. "I see what's left of your phone. Here you go, take a look."

It had to be handled with caution to avoid getting cut on the sharp pieces through the clear bag. "My phone's been broken; the face is smashed to bits. It won't even turn back on. Can I take it out of the bag?" The second officer took it from her to examine for himself.

"No ma'am, I'm afraid not. It's evidence. The person who grabbed it took the time to break it, so we're hoping there're some prints. We needed you to identify everything, verify it's yours."

"It is, all of it. I need to get a message to someone, please."

"All right, who are we calling?"

"His name is Reid Collier. He's my son's father."

"Ah, okay." The second officer scribbled the information in his notepad. "Go ahead."

"He needs to know I'm not going to make it this weekend. I'll miss my first Mother's Day with my son." Her chin dropped to her chest, and she shut her eyes, pursing her lips, trying hard not to cry.

"Your first Mother's Day? Congratulations. You don't look like you've had a baby recently."

"I haven't. It's a long story," she added before they could ask.

"All right then. What's Mr. Collier's number?"

Her eyes went wide, staring at the man. "Oh no. I don't know what it is. I always just push the icon on my phone. It's a picture of Reid and our son." Tears slipped past her resolve. "Why did this have to happen? Why this weekend? My son will be disappointed. I'm letting him down."

"Hey, now, it'll be okay. We'll look up this Reid Collier the old-fashioned way. Where does he live?"

"San Antonio, Texas. Close to it, anyway. He's the owner of Collier Ranch. You can look it up the number is on their website. You've got to reach them before they leave. They were picking me up at the airport tonight." Lacey turned her head away, to stare at the wall and cry.

***

"Well, I've got some news. It isn't good, though," Jonathan warned as he entered the room. Her cousin stood only a couple of inches lower than Reid, with a lean, muscular build. His hair and eyes were a match for Lacey's. It ran in the family. Distant Irish heritage, supposedly.

"What is it?" Connie asked before Lacey could.

"The police officer reached someone at the ranch, a woman. Reid and Russell had already left. A long time ago."

"Oh no," Connie exclaimed. "But she can reach them by cellphone, right?"

"That means they would've gone early. Why'd they have to leave this early?" Lacey interrupted. The medication had made her foggy.

"I don't know, sweetie. The woman refused to give out Reid's cellphone number, said she'd call him herself with the message." Jonathan patted her leg.

"She refused to give his cellphone number to the police when this is an emergency involving a crime perpetrated against his son's mother?" Connie raised an eyebrow. "Sounds like Kate. You know, I'd like to visit the ranch with you one of these days, Lacey. I just want one crack at Kate. One. Please."

"Connie." Jonathan started in on his reprimand. It rarely worked.

"No, Jonathan. You don't understand. She's downright evil. I wouldn't trust her as far as I could throw her, and believe me, I'd love to try and see just how far I could throw her. Like maybe down the side of a steep hill and see how many times she'd bounce on her way to the bottom."

The resulting outburst of laughter brought on shoulder pain. "Ow. Stop, you're hurting me."

"Sorry, Lacey," Connie said.

"I tried to warn you, Connie," Jonathan said. "You want me to get a nurse, sweetie?"

"No, I'll be all right. Thanks anyway. I just want to talk to Russell. I don't want him to be scared. He and his dad will be worried when I don't show up. They'll be upset and they'll try to call my phone, but it's broken. Why'd he break my phone? He didn't need to do that."

"We'll get Russell on my phone, just as soon as Reid calls. Uh-oh." Connie's eyes went wide. "Jonathan, did the cop tell the witch..."

"Connie," Jonathan warned.

"Okay, okay. Did the officer tell *Kate* that Lacey's cellphone is broken? And did he give them another contact number to use for reaching her?" Connie asked.

"Yeah, he did. Yours. He read the name and number to her twice, directly from my phone."

"I don't know what I'd do without you. You're the absolute best boyfriend in the whole world." Connie rose from the edge of the bed.

"You're right. I am." Jonathan put his hands on her lower back, pulling her in and up to her toes for a long and loving kiss.

"I'm such a lucky woman." Connie's eyes had gone all dreamy.

"Yes. Yes, you are." He kissed her again.

"Do you two want me to stagger out into the hallway and close the door to give you some privacy?"

"Don't be ridiculous. We'll have plenty of privacy when we get back to the apartment," Connie said.

"Am I going to have to listen to you two having sex all night?"

"You won't hear any of it. You'll be conked out from the medicine."

"I certainly do hope so," Lacey closed her eyes.

TEN

The smell of fresh coffee and bacon roused Lacey from sleep. She'd pulled the covers over her head since it was frosty. Jonathan had stayed overnight to help, which explained why Lacey could almost see her breath. He and Connie were no doubt working up a sweat, which meant he'd cranked the air conditioning to compensate.

The pair had wild and crazy good sex, according to Connie, leaving Lacey to suffer every time.

The first movement brought on a crush of pain and memories of what happened. It was difficult to get herself out of bed, but she managed. This would get annoying, and fast. Being sick or injured was something she had neither the time nor the patience for. She walked gingerly into the bathroom to check the mirror.

A light rapping came at the bedroom door.

"Come in." The bruises painted unfamiliar colors over parts of Lacey's face.

Connie entered the bathroom to stand beside her friend. The top of Connie's reached a couple of inches above Lacey's shoulder. "You look like you've been in a boxing ring with a guy. A guy who's a lot bigger and stronger than you."

"I feel like it, too."

"I know the shoulder hurts, but how about your head? That big bruise must've come when you slipped out of that hole in the wall, huh? Looks like it's got a knot under it. And a little strip of rugburn."

"Yeah, I know. It only hurts when I touch it, so I'm going to try not to. Everything hurts."

"You're in good shape; just not for the acrobatics you put your body through last night. Come on out to the living room; breakfast is almost ready. Jonathan is cooking his famous bacon and eggs. I've already fixed your tea. And I've set out your next dose of pills for the pain."

"Okay. I should change first."

"Don't forget, you shouldn't try to shower today. I can help you wash up before we go to the police station. Getting dressed can wait until later. I'll help you get into your robe now instead. Come on out, while everything's hot. I even made toast, with grape jelly."

"You and Jonathan are great, even if he does like the temperature way too cold for my tastes. It's like the Arctic in here."

"I've already taken care of it, don't worry. I opened the windows to let the warm air in. I'll wrap a blanket around you when you sit down at the table."

"Speaking of worry...what did Reid say when he called last night? Or was it this morning?"

Connie cast her eyes to her feet, letting loose a big sigh. She shook her head, her lips set in tight lines.
"He didn't call."

The news came as a shock. "Didn't call? I wonder why not?"

"Well, I can give you three guesses, but the first two don't count," Connie said.

"Kate." Lacey's jaw clenching. That also brought pain, but it couldn't be helped.

"Exactly. I'd not only bet everything I own on it; I'd bet everything I'll ever own on it. Now, you come on with me and have some breakfast. After we've eaten our fill, we'll try calling up the ranch and see where it gets us."

***

As the three of them watched a movie, Connie sat beside Lacey on the couch, continually pressing the redial button on her cellphone. For a solid hour. She almost hung up on the woman who finally answered as her finger dropped to end what had always been a busy signal so that she could hit redial.

"Collier Ranch, this is Becky speaking. How can I help you?"

Connie's eyes met Lacey's, surprise in both. Jonathan grabbed the remote to mute the movie. Connie huddled against Lacey with the phone resting on her palm.

"Becky!" Lacey answered over Connie's speakerphone. "Becky, this is Lacey Freemont. Do you remember me? I'm Russell's mother."

"Yes ma'am, I remember you. I just finished putting the phone back in order. Someone had it disconnected. It was unplugged and from the angle, I didn't notice it."

Connie's brow furrowed at the information, her eyes meeting Lacey's with an unspoken accusation. Entirely too coincidental.

"We missed seeing you here for Mother's Day weekend. Russell was upset. How're you doing?"

"Oh, I'm going to be okay. Thanks for asking."

"Is something wrong? Are you sick?" Becky asked.

"No. I got hurt yesterday. Didn't Reid or Russell tell you?"

"No ma'am. All I know is, I was told by Kate last night that the room Mr. Collier reserved for you was to be made available to the very next caller."

"Evil piece of..."

"Connie, please," Lacey pled. "Becky, where's Reid? I need to speak to him. Or Russell."

"Well, if you'll hold on, I'll see if I can find one of them for you. Oh, I see Kate in the dining area. Let me go get her. She probably knows where Reid is."

"No!" Lacey's knee-jerk reaction at top volume made Jonathan jump. She lowered her voice. "No, please don't. I don't want her to know I'm on the phone. Please, Becky; you know how she is. Only Reid or Russell. Or Robert."

"Okay. I understand, believe me. Oh! You're in luck. Reid's right here; he just walked through the front door. Hold on."

Lacey waited, holding her breath, praying Kate wouldn't grab the phone instead. Then someone picked it up, with a shrill voice audible in the distance.

"Hang on a second, Kate. Whatever you want, it can't be that big of an emergency. Becky said I have a phone call, so let me take care of this first. No, I can handle a phone call on my own. I don't need you to take it. No, no. Just wait there. Hello?" Reid sounded gruff.

"Reid. Thank God. It's Lacey."

His voice remained calm but had a hard edge to it. "Lacey. What do you want? I'm kind of busy right now."

He had her at a loss. She never expected this kind of reaction, her face resembling that of a swatted puppy. No words came to mind.

"Hey now!" Connie inserted herself, swinging her arm, and thus the phone, away from Lacey.

"You just take it easy there, big boy. Lacey could've been killed last night, and you're so busy you can't give the mother of your son five minutes of your precious time? Where's Russell? At least we know *he* cares about Lacey and whether she lives or dies. Why don't you make yourself useful for something besides a hat rack and go find him for us?"

"Who is this? What're you talking about? Lacey, are you still there?"

"This happens to be Connie, Lacey's roommate, the person who's been taking care of her since I picked her up at the hospital last night. She can't take care of herself, thanks to the man who nearly killed her."

Lacey had been tugging on Connie's arm the entire time, to little avail. "Connie, stop. Let me have it, please."

"What're you talking about? What man? What happened to her? Lacey? Lacey, are you still there?" His words came in a sudden rush of clear panic.

"I'm here, Reid."

Jonathan turned to his girlfriend. "Come on; let's go for a walk around the complex. We should give them some privacy." He removed the phone from Connie's grasp and placed it in the palm of Lacey's right hand.

Connie stood, stiff and reluctant, keeping her voice elevated. "We'll be back in a few minutes. Don't let yourself get upset by Reid or try to move around and hurt yourself more. The least you could've done was call us back, Reid! Someone who cared about Lacey would've called." Connie yelled the words as Jonathan finally plucked her up and carried her away, his arms wrapped around her waist.

"Lacey, what's going on there?" The fear in his voice couldn't be missed. "What happened? Who tried to hurt you?"

As the apartment door closed, Lacey took a deep breath. "Reid, I'm sorry about last night, about not being able to come out for Mother's Day. My cousin Jonathan and a police officer spoke with Kate and made sure she had all the information. Kate was supposed to call you. Did she catch you before you got to the airport?"

"Sort of. It doesn't matter right now; all that matters is you. Are you all right? I mean, you're not, but what's going on there?"

"I'll be okay; it's just going to take some time." She related the ordeal, answering a few questions of his that popped up along the way. "The police are investigating. They saw the guy and chased him, but he got away."

"I'm grateful you're safe now. I wish I'd known."

"Didn't Kate give you the message about all this?"

"She said there was a bad connection. She told me you had your boyfriend Johnnie call and say you'd decided not to come this weekend after all and that I was not to call you. When it looked like you'd decided not to come it broke Russell's heart."

"That's not the message she was given; not even close. The police officer who placed the call told her I'd been in an accident and was in the hospital. He also gave her Connie's name and cellphone number. He read it twice, so she'd be sure to have it right, because I wanted, needed, to hear your voice. And to talk to Russell. The officer even made her read the phone number back to him because Jonathan insisted. He told me that."

"Damn it. You needed me and I wasn't there for you. Kate gave me a number to call. Because I thought you had a boyfriend and had stood up Russell and me to spend the weekend with him instead, I was upset. So, I didn't try calling until early this morning. I woke up some guy named Kevin, who wasn't amused. It was a wrong number. Then, I called your cell and there was nothing.

"I'm sorry. I'm sorry you were injured and I'm sorry I thought you were capable of hurting us like that. I shouldn't have. I should've given you more credit and tried harder to reach you."

"I'd never drop a commitment to you and Russell, not for any man. And there isn't a man in my life, anyway. Kate's Johnnie is my cousin, Jonathan, by the way. He's also my roommate's boyfriend. I think I mentioned him before." The medication was slurring her words, fogging her memory.

"I think you did. It's a surprise to me you aren't seeing someone. I'll admit to it being a pleasant surprise." His voice softened, deepened. "How do you feel?"

"Lousy. But the worst of it is not being able to spend Mother's Day with you and Russell. My first Mother's Day. The doctor won't let me fly."

Reid sighed. "If there was a way to do it, I'd grab Russell and get on a plane for Charlotte. But he's got school Monday, with a couple of important tests coming up. And we have a lot of guests here. We had more bookings than usual for Mother's Day, a lot more. Several members of my staff were given the weekend off to be with their mothers or their wives and children. Kate mismanaged the leave approvals this time around, but I didn't want to destroy my employees' plans at the last minute."

"It'll be okay." There was no hiding her disappointment.

"We'll have to make up for it the next time we see you. I should tell you we left early for the airport yesterday to pick up your Mother's Day present on the way to get you."

"You bought me a present?" Her spirits lifted.

The smile on his face came through the phone. "Yes, we did. I let Russell pick this one himself. You're going to love it, I promise. We'll hold it for your next trip out here."

"That might be the Fourth. I've got recovery and rehab. Starts Monday."

"Waiting will be hard on Russell and me. I need to see you for myself. I want to make sure you're okay." He sighed. "When you come back, I intend to make a concerted effort to get you to move to Texas as soon as possible.

"That way I'll be able to keep an eye on you and keep you safe. It's the only way Russell and I will be comfortable after everything that's happened. He's going to be worried when I tell him what happened to you. And speaking of safe, you said your cousin is your roommate's boyfriend. Does he live with you and Connie?"

"No. Sometimes Connie stays at Jonathan's place or vice versa. I'm not worried. We've got locks on the door and friends around the apartment complex." She moved her legs to the couch and tucked in the blanket as best she could, pinning the phone between her right cheek and shoulder.

"That's good, but not too long ago someone slashed your tires in the parking lot, which still bothers me. Did you ever find out if anyone else's tires were slashed besides yours and Connie's?"

"No." Inhale, exhale; and then respond. "It was only us."

"So now, especially after what happened to you last night, I'm thinking someone's targeting you and Connie. Or just you."

Verbalized by someone else, it sent a shudder through her. "Honestly, Reid, I don't know. I didn't connect the two events. There's no reason for someone to come after either of us."

"A grudge. A jealous ex-boyfriend comes readily to mind as a strong possibility. If he found out about Russell and me, it might've set him off. It sounds like he's trying to prevent you from coming to visit us.

"I don't like this, Lacey; not one bit of it. This person is unstable. I want you here with us as soon as possible. Now more than ever." Reid wished he were on his cellphone. That would allow him to pace. He needed to move around. What he needed was to see Lacey again, as soon as possible.

"I seriously doubt what happened is the result of a jealous ex-boyfriend, Reid. I haven't dated anyone in a long time. It's been somewhere around eight months, I think." The last guy freaked her out with his choices in music and clothes. And long fingernails. Connie had zero skills as a matchmaker.

"Well, you be sure and tell Connie I'm grateful for what she did for you, even though she seems justifiably angry with me."

"I'll explain it to her. I'm going to need to keep the rest of this call short even though I want to talk to Russell. It was a long night and I have to go make an official statement at the police station. I just hope they don't take more pictures." She tried to stifle a yawn.

"Do you mean for evidence?" Reid asked.

"Yes. They took some last night, but I've got a big knot on my forehead that popped up overnight. It's from where I hit the wall and serves as a great compliment to the ugly bruise."

"Good God. Lacey, I feel horrible about what's happened. Do you need me to fly out there and be with you? My dad can probably handle things here for a few days, at least after Monday. Even if it didn't make you feel better, I'd feel better. Or I could bring you back here with me. You can rest and be spoiled rotten at the same time."

"Thank you, but no. I'll be okay. I'm under orders not to fly, remember?" The order might be rescinded by then. But she didn't want to be anywhere near Kate, which wouldn't be restful at all. She'd prefer taking her chances in Charlotte, even with the unknown. After her shoulder recovered, it'd be an entirely different story.

"All right, but I want you to think about it and give me a call anytime, day or night. It doesn't matter. I'll have my phone with me constantly, no matter what I'm doing. I'd move any mountain to get to you, even in the middle of the night. Just say the word."

"I appreciate it, but I'm okay and I'll be sleeping a lot." It sure sounded like he cared. A lot. "Connie's taking the first half of the week off from work to stay with me. And Jonathan got his hours changed for the coming week to spend the nights with us. Security is taken care of; he's a big guy, kind of like you, just leaner. Jonathan would never let anyone hurt me. We're fine here."

Reid released a loud sigh. The woman he was undoubtedly falling for had been in terrible danger. Most likely still was. And she was in no condition to defend herself. "I understand what you're saying, but I don't like this, having you so far away from us when you need our help. I'd rather have you near me for protection."

"I've got help here. Everything will be fine. Could you get Russell for me, please? I'm getting tired." Reid's reasoning seemed to be escalating toward her being in mortal danger, which wasn't at all the case. But that might be why Jonathan and Connie were taking time off to keep an eye on her. They might be thinking the same thing as Reid, just not verbalizing to avoid planting additional fear.

"I'm going to go find Russ and we'll call this number back. It's showing up on the phone display at the registration desk. I'll use my cellphone to get it down now, so I'll have the number in mine and when I call back Connie will have mine in hers."

"Okay. That sounds like a good idea. I'll be waiting for you. I need to hear Russell's voice. He was all I could think about last night."

"Listen. Russell came up with an idea a while back. Not being as technologically inclined as he is, I'll leave the details to him. He said we could video chat instead of just talking on the phone. I think that'll help all of us get through the times when we aren't together. What do you think about that?"

"It sounds good to me. I'd like to wait on that until maybe Friday evening. The swelling and bruises should've gone away some by then. I don't want Russell to see me the way I look right now. In the interim, we can just do phone calls." She tried to stifle it, but the yawn that followed was loud.

"Hang in there. I'll be back with you in a few minutes. And Lacey, I can't tell you how glad I am you're going to be okay. I don't know how I'm going to manage the wait until you're back with us here at the ranch. Even Russell's video chat idea won't be good enough for me."

***

"Done with your shower yet?" Connie called from the doorway to Lacey's room.

"Yes, I'm drying off. Not easy with one hand," came the response. Monday mornings weren't Lacey's favorite. Especially not this one.

Everything was more difficult and physical therapy would be painful. "I don't suppose you're willing to help me get dressed, are you? Physical therapy is in a couple of hours. Otherwise, I won't even have time for breakfast. Starved by my best friend."

"Whine, whine, whine." Connie giggled as she entered the bathroom to her roommate's glare. "Just kidding. You're so serious. Here, let me have that." She snatched Lacey's underpants.

After helping dress her friend, she combed through the hair that was a soppy, tangled mess. Grabbing a hand towel, she squeezed the hair to soak up more water without putting tangles back in it. "That's better. I'm going to blow it dry partway."

"I'd rather let it air dry. I'm hungry."

"You'll be okay. It's only a few minutes. I insist." Connie grabbed a brush and the hairdryer, switching it on quickly to avoid hearing Lacey's protest. Three minutes later, it was over. "There. See? That didn't take long. Just enough so it won't be dripping on your plate. And I'm sorry, but I have to leave you on your own today. They need me at work."

The realization took a few seconds. "Wait. You're leaving me alone? To drive?"

Connie nodded, grinning.

"You're kidding me? On my first day going out of the apartment with one arm you're making me drive? You were supposed to stay with me all day. Is Jonathan coming instead?" It didn't take much effort to conjure up a vision of serious discomfort from simple navigation maneuvers behind the wheel. At least on the first day or two, until she got the hang of it. What a nightmare.

"Come on out with me. I found somebody to take care of breakfast and get you to PT." Connie walked into the living area, rounding the corner for the kitchen.

Lacey followed, frowning. That Connie would leave her alone all of a sudden made no sense. Until she saw Reid, a dishtowel over one shoulder, smiling. Her eyes widened as her jaw slackened. "Reid? Oh my God. What're you doing here?"

He tossed the towel on the counter and strode over, carefully wrapping his arms around Lacey. "I had to come," he whispered, his voice husky and deep, his cheek nuzzling against hers. "Had to." He took a step back, looking her over.

His jaw twitched several times in succession, his eyes narrowing. "All I want is one shot at the man who did this to you. Just one. It's all I'll need."

Her arm was in a sling, her face a variety of purples, with a few yellows around the edges, and her lips were swollen, with stitches. It was the first time in his life he had genuinely wanted to kill a man with his bare hands. Jail time would be worth it.

Lacey raised a hand to cover her mouth when Reid stared at it. "I didn't want you to see me like this."

"Don't worry about that. You're beautiful no matter what. I can't believe what that monster did to you. How much pain are you in?"

"Not as much as when it happened. I can't believe you came." Her right hand moved from covering her mouth to caress his cheek.

Reid turned his head and kissed her palm. Even if she weren't Russell's mother, he would have these same feelings for her, the same ideas in his head about a life with her. Karen had chosen Lacey to be Russell's mother. Surely, she would have approved of Lacey being his wife, especially after he'd spent so many years alone.

"Okay. Well, then. Since I'm clearly not needed here and you're in good hands, I'll go to work now. Jonathan's bringing Mexican for dinner. I'll text him that you're here, Reid, to be sure he gets extra food."

"Sounds good, thanks," Reid said, glancing briefly at Connie.

"Thanks, Connie. See you when you get home," Lacey said, returning her attention to Reid.

As the door closed, Reid took Lacey's hand and led her slowly to the table, in full view of the kitchen. "You sit right here and relax. I'm making pancakes and bacon. Got a whole pack and there's just the two of us. I hope your appetite is good." He scooted in the chair for her.

"It is. I'm starving. I can eat my half of the bacon, no problem." Reid turned with one eyebrow raised. "Half? I was figuring on a third." He patted his stomach.

"Nope. Half. My body's trying to recover from trauma. That takes lots and lots of bacon. It smells delicious, by the way." She took a deep sniff.

He leaned down to apply a butterfly kiss to her forehead. "You can have as much as you want." He returned to the kitchen to tend to the food.

"So, you're driving me to physical therapy, I assume? I was afraid I'd have to drive myself this first time."

"I'm here to take care of you for the next three days and nights. That includes driving you wherever you want. Your limo awaits us in the parking lot."

"Limo? My car gets me where I need to go, but I wouldn't call it a limo." She giggled. This was wonderful, having him here. A dream come true. If only she weren't injured. Or at least if her face weren't so messed up.

"We're not taking your car. You're going in style and comfort. I rented an SUV. Cadillac." He grinned her way.

"Wow. That'll be cool. I've never been in one of those before." Not only did she have companionship, but she had utter confidence in her safety with Reid around.

Relaxation and healing would come easier now. An added benefit would be spending time together, just the two of them. If she could stay awake for it.

The smile she sent him warmed his heart. The thought of finding the man responsible and planting his fist squarely in that man's face drove him. Eventually, the private investigator Reid had hired would locate the guy. Then, Reid would have his revenge. The police could have what was left. It'd be convenient if all that happened before he had to return to Texas.

Independence Day

ELEVEN

Jayden picked Lacey up at the airport, along with several guests. So many in fact, that he drove a large van that seated fifteen people. He informed her both Russell and Reid were busy, as the ranch was filled beyond capacity with visitors for the next several days, and some folks were going to be around into the next week. They were on overload, struggling to handle everything.

It sounded as though it might be difficult to spend any real quality time with Reid, which was unfortunate. But perhaps she could spend extra time with Russell. Since this was the Independence Day holiday, it added a freebie day to her time off, giving her nine days in full or in part to spend in Texas. Anticipation had her antsy.

Jayden occupied most of the drive with relating historical facts about San Antonio to the new arrivals, bringing it to life. She'd been too nervous on the first trip to appreciate Jayden's colorful anecdotes and masterful storytelling. Jayden also told the tourists how much fun he had at Fiesta, winning a trophy for his dancing.

He glanced at Lacey in the rearview mirror then, grinning, and she responded with a wink. It had been an entertaining and impressive performance. As they neared the ranch, Jayden switched to an overview of the area and what could be expected on their visit.

They made good time. Once there, it was a wildly different scene from her first trip to the ranch. Guests swarmed everywhere, practicing on the firing ranges, heading out on afternoon trail rides, going for hikes, bike rides, or a swim in the massive in-ground pool. The ranch was enormous, but the sheer number of guests made it seem small and crowded. Definitely crowded.

Jayden helped with luggage as the guests admired the scope of the building, the fireplace, the beams, everything, just as on Lacey's first trip. Like a normal guest, she checked in at the front desk while Jayden continued unloading luggage. After receiving her room key, Lacey hurried up the stairs.

After making quick work of putting away her clothes and toiletries, Lacey passed Jayden on her way back down the staircase. He toted luggage. "Do you need any help, Jayden?"

"No ma'am. Thanks for offering, though. I hope you find your family quick enough for your liking. Russell might be out in the barn. There's no telling where Reid is. Until all these guests started arriving, he was counting down the days on his calendar, waiting for you to get here."

"Oh, yeah? Thanks for telling me. I'll see you later!" She tore down the staircase.

"No problem, Lacey!" he called out to her back.

The barn was quiet, devoid of humans. It was the only place she'd seen so far without throngs of humanity. Behind the barn she found Russell.

He was busy preparing the wash area for the arrival of horses, setting out buckets filled with bathing supplies. Not far away, a ranch hand tossed her long, blonde ponytail over her back while squatting to point out a hole in the ground near some brush, explaining to her group of twenty tourists about how rabbits burrow. Her voice carried well.

"Russell," Lacey called.

He spun on a dime. "Mom!" He dropped a loaded bucket that tipped and spilled its contents. He bounded over to hug her, lifting her off her feet.

"Whoa, take it easy now!" Lacey laughed as he returned her feet to the ground.

"Sorry, Mom. I didn't hurt your shoulder, did I? Is it sore from the trip?"

"No, honey. It's fine now. My physical therapy is done and I'm as good as new. Better, even. My upper body strength is probably twice what it was before. That's an exaggeration. But not by too much."

"Good, I'm glad. Dad couldn't stop talking about going out to Charlotte to take care of you. He said you two got to talk a lot."

"We did. I didn't like getting hurt, but your dad did a great job taking care of me. I've never been pampered like that before. He cooked for me, and we watched movies. When I wasn't sleeping, that is. I slept a lot. Your dad made sure of that."

"He told me he was glad he went because you were stubborn and wouldn't admit to it if you needed help. And he wanted to be there to protect you."

"He called me stubborn?" Her brow furrowed. Stubborn. Not that it wasn't true; she just didn't think he'd figure it out as fast as he had.

"Yeah. He was worried."

"I'll bet you were, too, weren't you? I'm sorry about scaring you."

"I was scared, but not like dad. The night we got the call from Aunt Kate while we were at the airport, he was mad. I've never seen him mad like that before, not even close.

"All he did was ask me if I knew you had a boyfriend and I said no. He didn't say another word, just drove us home. I heard him pacing around his room most of the night or watching his TV with the volume cranked up."

"He did?" Lacey walked with Russell to the bucket and supplies to help pick up what had been spilled.

"He likes you, Mom. He likes you a lot. After he talked to you on the phone the next morning, he came running to find me. He told me what happened to you. He felt bad about how he'd acted the night before, even though you didn't know about it. I was scared until I talked to you. Talking to you didn't make dad feel better, though.

Russell began spacing out the buckets to allow everyone to spread out. "He didn't like that the guy who hurt you wasn't in jail. He talked about doing all kinds of things, like hiring a private investigator to find whoever it was and teach the guy a lesson himself."

"He told me about that idea. He actually did it, but the firm he hired is still looking. I need to tell him to call them off. He doesn't need to be wasting money like that. My friends are watching out for me now. Real close, too. For a few weeks, I couldn't even go to the bathroom at work by myself."

"Dad's favorite idea was going to your apartment to conduct a friendly kidnapping, as he called it. He was going to bring you back here to live with us to keep you safe. Then he wouldn't have to keep worrying about you all the time. I figured he'd bring you back here with him when he went to Charlotte." Russell returned to the barn for additional supplies and Lacey followed to help.

"He asked me to come, but my roommate and my cousin had everything under control. Plus, I had my physical therapy and I started work that Friday because I did so well with the therapy. Your dad helped me with all that, too." Reid cared, but the friendly kidnapping thing sounded permanent. She wasn't sure she liked that part of it but knew what the intent behind it was.

Russell ran a hand through his unkempt hair. "It was his idea to call you every morning and evening before he went to see you and after he got back. Aunt Kate tried to talk him out of the trip.

"She said it'd make you mad because you'd think he was being presumptuous, pushy, and another "p" word, I think. She said women like you are independent and would get offended, and he should leave you alone or he'd drive you away from us. Is what she said true, Mom?"

"No, honey; none of it. I did tell your dad not to come, but I was happy to see him. We had a great time. He did a wonderful job taking care of me and keeping me company, even though I slept through a lot of it. Probably wasn't much fun for him." Lacey grabbed two buckets of supplies. Russell managed four.

"So, Aunt Kate was wrong about you?" Russell was confused. How could his aunt be wrong? Most of the male ranch hands said women were all alike. He knew that had to be a grownup thing to say, just from his own experience around the girls at school.

"Yes, she was. Next time she gives you an opinion about the kind of person I am, just tell her thanks and walk away. Then, you can go tell your dad what I said today."

"Okay, Mom, I will. I missed you. Did you have a good trip out?" They placed their buckets on the ground, then went for the hoses to add soap to the array of buckets and fill them with water.

"Yes, I did. But I'd rather talk about you. And while you're talking, we'll both keep working. That way you'll get finished sooner and maybe we could go for a walk or something after dinner."

"That'd be great. I've been busy today. We've got more guests than usual for the Fourth of July weekend, a whole lot more. It might be the fireworks show our neighbors are shooting off this year. They've hired some company to do it up big, they said. They're just as packed with people as we are."

"We'll be able to see them from the front yard, just not hear as much of the boom sounds. Some of our guests are planning to take a bunch of folding chairs out by the road to sit and watch from a closer spot. It'll be crowded." Russell shook his head at the craziness.

"Speaking of which, Russell, this place is big but there aren't enough rooms for all the people I've seen. Where are they all sleeping?"

"Some are staying in the cabins we have around the lake; those are all full. The ranch hands who live out there year-round are all cramming into one big cabin to make more room for the guests. We've got a couple of groups who are due in here later tomorrow. They're heading out on camping trips because they want to rough it for a couple of days. Dad brought in extra workers for that."

"Speaking of your dad, where is he? I haven't seen him yet. I only got here about twenty minutes ago, though." Lacey glanced at her watch.

"He might be leading one of the trail rides out to the overlook or a couple of other places. I'm not sure if he took any of them out or if some of the other guys did it. They'll be back in time for a late dinner."

"Okay then. I'll just have to wait. When I first got here, I didn't know if I'd be able to find you in the crush of people. I kind of figured I'd have to wait on you to get back from whatever chores you were doing. I thought I'd have to occupy myself with Spark for a while or help out in the kitchen. Speaking of Spark, where is he?"

Russell shifted his feet and looked out to the pasture. "Hey, guess what we're having for dinner?"

He didn't wait for her to try to guess. "A big cookout! We've got enough extra guests that Grandpa had to buy some extra grills. He'll be standing out there for hours since there're so many people to feed. Everybody in the kitchen is doing overtime, too. Grandpa's grilling steaks with baked potatoes and all the fixings. He makes the best steaks in the whole world."

"That sounds nice. I'm not a big meat eater, but I can go for a juicy steak occasionally."

Russell headed for the barn. "You'll love my grandpa's; he's legendary. I've got to check the grills and bring out the charcoal. You can go ahead with your idea to help in the kitchen. We're having grilled corn on the cob, too. I know you said you love corn on the cob."

"Yes, I do." She followed close on his heels. "You didn't answer my question from before."

"I didn't? Sorry, Mom, there're just too many chores to do."

"Obviously." She grabbed his arm, stopping him. "Where's my horse? If he's in one of the farther pastures, it's no big deal. I can wait to ride until tomorrow; it's late anyway and there's lots of work to be done. If Spark is close, I'd like to at least give him a carrot. Do I need to clean his gear or anything?"

"No ma'am." He studied his feet. "He's out."

"Out. Where? He's a horse; he's supposed to be out. Thus, I'm assuming you mean something else."

"He's out on a trail ride." His mother would be upset. He bit his lower lip.

"Oh. Someone else is riding him?"

"Yes. I'm sorry, Mom. There was a lady who was nervous about horses, but her family wanted her to go on the trail ride after lunch. Aunt Kate told her all about Spark and made him sound so good the lady said she'd think about it. Aunt Kate even took the lady out to meet Spark. She's never done that before.

"I told them Spark belonged to you and you were coming in today, but Spark was acting sweet around the lady, and he made her laugh. Aunt Kate kept saying you wouldn't mind, because..." He stopped, looking more uncomfortable than before.

"Because why, honey?"

"She said you wouldn't mind because you always like to say how you're family, whether you are or not."

Before responding, Lacey took a deep breath, exhaling in slow motion. "It's okay. I'm sure Spark will be fine. You didn't want to tell me someone else was riding him?"

"I was worried you'd be upset, or your feelings would be hurt on account of my dad giving him to you. And I didn't like how my aunt talked about you. You *are* family."

"Oh honey, that's sweet of you. But I don't want you to worry about anything your Aunt Kate says about me. I'm a big girl; I can take it.

"And as for Spark, your dad was just being nice to me. I don't believe Spark is mine, not really. Your ranch is here to make money, not to have a good horse grazing in the pasture for weeks or months on end waiting for me to come back here for a few days to ride him. It isn't fair to your dad and grandpa, or Spark."

"But he belongs to you." His eyebrows were raised, his lips pouty.

"As long as I can ride him while I'm here, or even just spend time grooming him, I'll be fine. He's not my horse. I enjoy thinking he is, though. I blew up that photograph of Spark you texted me and framed it. It's sitting on my desk at work, beside the photo of you and your dad."

"Okay. I'll be sure and tell dad. He was worried. He didn't find out about all this until Spark was already gone."

"Your dad is sweet, like you." She rubbed a hand over his shoulder.

"He wants you to have a good time while you're here. He thinks that'll make you come back more than you've been doing. He said it's been too long between visits, and we need to see you here on the ranch a lot more often than how it's working out."

Her eyebrows rose at the information.

"We were disappointed we only got to talk to you on Mother's Day instead of seeing you. Dad said it wasn't right and he was going to do something about it, but he said the timing had to be perfect. He wouldn't tell me what that meant."

Interesting. She'd like to know what Reid had meant herself. "Well, let's not worry about that right now. We'd better get going. Those chores aren't going to take care of themselves."

***

It was late in the afternoon when they finished. Robert manned the grills with a few of the ranch's cooks. Extra picnic tables had been set out, mostly beneath massive live oaks scattered around the guesthouse.

Bottles of condiments and baskets containing a variety of bread slices helped secure the tablecloths in the warm, gentle breeze. Several guests were already seated, waiting for their steaks, listening to music strummed by Jayden on his guitar as he wandered from table to table. A few people danced.

Inside the guesthouse, several families milled around with their luggage. Lacey attempted to visualize the size of the ranch and its habitable buildings in her head versus the number of people she'd seen wandering around. Where in the world would everyone sleep?

Before she spotted him among the throngs, Reid surprised her by striding over and enveloping her in his muscular embrace, holding her so tight she could scarcely draw a breath. It was a wonderful feeling.

"Lacey. I'm glad you're here. I've been worried and I missed you. How's your shoulder holding up?"

Before she could formulate a response, Reid eased back just enough to take in her eyes. Then, without any indication, he took her face in his hands and leaned forward until his lips met hers. They were soft, pressing against hers, electrifying her body. It was brief, but a very public display.

He had kissed her on the cheek or forehead every night in her apartment after tucking her into bed. He hadn't wanted to cause pain to her wounded lip. She still remembered how loved each of those kisses had made her feel.

"Reid. It's..." Lacey wasn't sure about her capacity to complete a sentence after his kiss. Breathe. "I'm fine now. I've missed you, too. More than I'd realized." Her hands rested on his chest, her heart beginning the familiar pounding Reid Collier brought on.

Russell stood a couple of feet away with a huge grin on his face. Reid shouldn't have kissed her where their son could witness it and get ideas in his head. Then again, ideas were running through her head with reckless abandon.

"Good. I'm glad to hear it. How was the ride?" Reid took a step back, dropping his arms to his sides. He'd overreacted, lost control. Russell had seen them kiss. How would he explain it to him? Besides, the news he had to break might change Lacey's mind about that kiss. And him.

"We didn't ride, Dad. We set up the stalls with fresh bedding and gave the horses their dinner. Most of them needed baths and grooming after the trail ride, so we helped some of the guys take care of it for the guests who didn't seem capable of handling it."

"Or for those who showed no interest," Lacey offered, wondering if Reid stepped back because he regretted the kiss. "Like the woman who rode Spark and tried to put him in his stall while he was sweaty from the ride, *and* with his saddle and bridle still on."

Lacey wanted to add a request to forbid the woman from ever going near her horse again, but this wasn't the time. And she didn't possess the standing for such a demand. She still might ask later.

"Sounds good." Reid's eyes shifted to Lacey's, his hand rubbing the back of his neck. "Lacey. I need to talk to you."

"Sure." She noted that Reid seemed flustered, but his reluctance no longer seemed to have anything to do with the kiss.

"I'm sure you've noticed all the people behind me." He tilted his head toward the busy dining area. Several guests had chosen to eat inside.

"It'd be hard to miss them. I didn't realize you could accommodate this many people." She glanced to the masses, then to Reid.

"We can't. There seems to have been some sort of a mix-up, a glitch, I guess you'd say. A massive one."

"What kind of glitch?" Lacey asked.

"The computer seriously overbooked us for the next few days."

"How'd that happen, Dad?" Russell's eyes were wide.

"I don't know, son. Kate's tried to straighten it out, but these folks got themselves a bargain here."

"What do you mean?" Russell asked.

"They've gotten our bed and breakfast for a few nights at half price, first night free. They said our website was running a tenth-anniversary special. There was also a special for weeklong guests."

Russell gaped in astonishment. "It's the ninth anniversary of the bed and breakfast part of the ranch, not the tenth."

"A computer can't do something like that; not on its own, it can't. It would have to be a programming error." She attempted to imply the problem would be Kate and manufactured on purpose. Lacey wasn't sure why Kate would've done that, though. It didn't make sense.

"Kate can't figure out what's happened. None of us can understand it, but it'll have to wait. We certainly don't want to turn these folks away. Some of them have driven hours to get here. Lots of families came from out of state, and many of those are loyal, repeat visitors."

"Where are we going to put all of them?" Russell asked.

"We're packing them in wherever they'll fit. Most of them are understanding about it and a few are doubling up with friends or family who also came. Some are going into our family wing, son." Reid cast his eyes to Lacey. "Kate's been juggling people, switching them around to avoid having any of our guests put out too much. She's done the best she could. Lacey, I'm sorry, but I'm going to need to ask you to move into another spot."

"Oh. That's okay, I don't mind. I'm happy to do whatever I can to help." Switching to a different room wouldn't be a problem. It certainly wasn't anything to make Reid this uncomfortable. Could there be something else?

"She can stay in my room, Dad. I'll sleep in your room tonight." Russell put a hand on his father's arm as he spoke.

"No, son. With all these people here to take care of, Kate volunteered to surrender her room to a group of guests. She insisted. She's rearranged where all the ranch's family members and staff will sleep for the next several nights.

"Your room will house Kate, Becky, and all of the female kitchen staff, including Mrs. Gordon. They'll be packed in, but it'll work. They're going to be on-call in a rotation, watching over the kitchen and the guests tonight in case there're any special needs. It's a certainty there will be with this many people. Plus, the breakfast shift will start early.

"Kate and Mrs. Gordon get your bed, while the other ladies will use sleeping bags and blankets on the floor. They're wall to wall in there, like a can of sardines. Sounds uncomfortable to me.

"We've got waiters sleeping on the kitchen floor. Your grandpa's room has been rented out, so he'll be sharing my bed with me, and you'll have to use your sleeping bag on the floor in my room, along with Gil and a few other guys." He took a breath, noting the change in Lacey's expression. Wary.

"The couches out here near the fireplace are being occupied by some of the more accommodating male guests. Some of our male staff will sleep in recliners or the last of our sleeping bags to help handle issues that crop up overnight. We don't have enough tents or sleeping bags for everyone. We won't be able to walk around anywhere tonight without the risk of stepping on someone. We'll have to be careful."

Lacey's brow furrowed as she crossed her arms. Something else was definitely on the horizon for her. Another bomb was about to drop.

"I even called our neighbors across the street. With their fireworks display, they're completely out of space, like we are, but they managed to cram in nineteen of our guests."

"Then, which room is Mom taking?"

Reid's gaze shifted to Lacey again. "Kate said she would've tried to catch you before your flight left Charlotte, but by the time she realized the magnitude of what we were up against, your plane was already in the air. She said you should come regardless because of what happened to you back in Charlotte. Said you deserved this vacation more than anyone she knows."

"So, where am I sleeping?" She reworded Russell's unanswered question, ignoring Kate's sudden interest in her wellbeing.

"Well. Kate came up with a last-minute idea and we can't think of an alternative. We were thinking you could stay in the barn. She wanted me to be sure to tell you what a huge help it would be. She's taken special soaps, shampoos, a guest robe, and towels out there for you to use. And a vase of fresh flowers as a thank you. We can't ask any of the guests to stay out there, since it'll only hold one person. And you're our only single."

Her eyebrows rose as her eyes widened. "The barn? Are you serious?"

"It's not what you think, not a stall or anything. Jayden lives there. We've got a nice studio apartment attached to the office. It's peaceful and quiet, nicely furnished, and sealed against drafts and insects. The place used to be part of the office, but we renovated it last year and turned it into Jayden's quarters when I promoted him to barn manager.

"The floors came out great and the kitchenette has black granite with white cabinetry, a small fridge, and a microwave. The bathroom was also renovated. The place is clean as a whistle. The apartment is tiny but it's comfortable. I wouldn't consider it for you if it weren't.

"There's another room above the studio with a daybed that Jayden's already moved his belongings to. His place is nicer, so he wanted you to have it."

"Why does my mom have to stay in the barn? That isn't fair." Russell's complexion showed hints of red.

"She's the most likely person to do it," Reid said.

"Why? Is it because she's my mom? Or because she tried hard to keep in touch with me in the beginning, just like she promised, and nobody can understand what happened there, either? It's just like with this computer problem." Russell's voice rose with increasing outrage. He'd grasped the situation perfectly in Lacey's estimation. But she couldn't let it escalate.

"Russell, no. Don't think like that." She didn't want him to start anything, even though she wasn't thrilled about the situation. "It's okay; I'll do it. There isn't much of a choice if I want to stay at the ranch and see you. I'd go through anything to spend time with you."

"Thank you, Lacey. Kate and I appreciate this. She's already taken the liberty of packing your things. They're over there by the side door. She said she knew you'd be willing to help us out of a jam since you're family."

Slumped against the doorframe, her belongings were old and not worth much, but they were hers. Now, suddenly, Kate referred to her as family. "She did, did she? Cold and efficient at the same time. I appreciate how you and Kate know me so well. Not to mention how the two of you came to this conclusion and knew I'd be willing to cooperate. What a great team you and Kate make." She shot Reid a glare.

"Lacey. That's not what's going on here." Reid's brow furrowed.

"It's clear to me this situation had some serious forethought to it. My arrival, coupled with a sudden, inexplicable computer glitch, and all these guests arriving the very same day. It's an interesting turn of events." Lacey's hands jabbed onto her hips. Her fury had reached the boiling point. Reid Collier could keep his kisses from now on.

His furrows grew deeper. "What do you mean?"

"I'm not blind, Reid, or stupid." Lacey shook her head, deciding it more prudent to back off, rather than instigating in front of Russell. Although she wasn't the one who started it. Neither was Reid, most likely. At least, she hoped not. All this made her wonder, though, how he really felt about her. Probably nothing like what she'd imagined.

"Lacey, I can promise you, if there was some other way..."

"Oh, there're other ways. I can think of a few on my own easily enough. I'm sure you could figure out something if you bothered to put your mind to it, instead of taking Kate's word. Or if you were willing to listen to my suggestions. But since you didn't even bother asking, there's no point. It won't change anything. Not for me, it won't."

She looked to her son. "Goodnight, Russell. I guess I'll see you in the morning. Since there're so many guests, I'll help you with those extra chores I imagine you'll have for the next several days."

"Lacey, I don't expect you to do any work around here because of what's happened. You're sacrificing enough as it is to move into the barn and be farther from Russell. It's supposed to be your vacation. And even though you're feeling better, I'd prefer to see you taking it easy on your shoulder." She misunderstood everything about the situation.

Her expression spoke of anger and betrayal. He didn't want to lose her over something so minor as a bed. Had Kate been trying to help or harm with the idea she'd insisted on? There hadn't been time to consider.

Reid extended a hand toward Lacey, and she sidestepped out of his reach, repeating the glare, making sure it lasted longer this time to be sure he couldn't miss it. Innocent or not, Reid had just shown her where she ranked, and it was nowhere near where she'd imagined, especially after his kiss.

"What about dinner, Mom? Maybe you and I could get our steaks first. You were telling me how hungry you were while we were working."

At the bottom of her priority list was returning to the house or its vicinity anytime soon once she went through that side door like she didn't even matter. "I've lost my appetite, honey. You go ahead without me."

"You've had a busy day Lacey and I know they didn't serve a meal on your plane. You have to be starving. Just because you're bunking out in the barn, it hardly means you're not welcome in the house for dinner." Reid spoke with a firm tone, hoping it would make a difference.

He didn't know her at all, as he was about to find out. "It looks to me as though you have more mouths to feed than you have room for at the table. If I do decide to get anything, I'll eat it elsewhere. The mother of your son seems to be the last person you need to concern yourself with, considering all the complete strangers here who need your attention, Mr. Collier. Now, if you'll excuse me." Lacey stormed off and didn't look back when he called her name. It was a weak effort on his part anyway.

She scooped up her duffel bag and satchel, scarcely stopping as she strode past where they sat, exiting through the side entrance. On her way out, Lacey made sure to give the screen door an enthusiastic shove, causing it to slap shut behind her with a sharp, resounding crack loud enough to be heard over all the voices, both inside and out.

TWELVE

"Mom?" A knock came on the apartment door.

The tentative call of her son awakened Lacey. She was worn out and went to sleep early to ignore her growling stomach. Pride wasn't worth starving over, but the choice had been made. Reid wouldn't even notice. Or care.

Even though she hated to admit it, the apartment was a wonderful space, homey and well-constructed. Not much sound transmittal, but the horses were tired. She'd hear them at dawn when they stirred, to snort and whinny for breakfast. Couldn't find a better alarm clock than that.

"Hang on a second, Russell. I'm coming," she mumbled.

The lamp on the bedside table had her shielding her eyes as it pierced the darkness, illuminating the vase of white peace lilies Kate brought. Lacey had seen enough of them at her parents' funerals that she didn't care for them anymore. Beside the vase sat a dish filled with a variety of high-quality candies, chocolates, and mints, untouched. Possibly poisoned, Lacey thought as she donned the guest robe. Two strides across the Saltillo tiles had her at the door.

Russell stood in the office, bearing a wooden tray. It held two bottles of water, two small salads, and two narrow slices of pecan pie, topped with a scoop of melting vanilla ice cream and a heaping mound of whipped topping. "You didn't come back to the house for dinner."

"Oh, Russell! I love whipped cream and pecan pie with vanilla ice cream. You're such a sweet boy."

His face turned pink under the olive. "Let's use the desk out here since the apartment is so small. Even if we put Jayden's Murphy bed up, there isn't much room."

"Good idea." She followed him.

"Hang on a second." Russell placed the tray on the desk before moving to the other side to pull out a chair for her.

"Aren't you a gentleman?" It made her proud.

"My dad taught me. He said you should always be respectful to women and take good care of them because they're precious."

And yet, Reid stuck her out in the barn. Russell didn't notice the inconsistency. "We are?" It would appear there were exceptions to Reid's rules. Maybe she was his sole exception.

"Yes ma'am." He sat to dole out the food. After he'd said the blessing, they ate. Sometimes she neglected to say the blessing. Her ways needed to change to be a good example for her son; it'd be good for her, too.

"You guys serve excellent salads here." It was one of the tastiest she remembered having. Then again, she was very hungry.

"My dad grows it out behind the house."

"Oh yes. I remember you telling me about it when we were together in Charlotte. Russell, I'm glad you found me."

He gave her a huge grin as he swallowed. "Me too. And I'm glad you came to visit me again. We'd be able to see each other every day if you moved out here." He scowled at the ceiling. "What's that noise?"

"Jayden." She stuffed in a forkful of salad.

"Jayden? He sure is being loud."

"He promised he'd stop by eleven. He told me he likes to unwind before bed by dancing."

"He does?"

"He's practicing for next year's Fiesta." A grape tomato burst with tremendous flavor between her teeth.

"Already? I guess he wants to win again."

"I suppose he does. He got some ideas from watching his competition this year. Jayden's a nice guy; I don't mind if he makes noise up there for a while longer. I slept right through it already anyway. Now, why don't we talk about something different, like the plan for tomorrow's chores? You're why I came. And I'm family too, right?"

"You are, but you shouldn't work too hard. Dad said."

"I don't care what your dad said. He doesn't know me or what I'm capable of. And he has no say in what I can and can't do. We'll work hard and have fun while we're at it."

***

As they left the barn behind, the sun was rising, brightening the sky. It should be a clear, beautiful day, just the way Jayden said it'd been the past couple of weeks. Lacey had worked hard at physical therapy and in the gym, harder than before her shoulder was injured. She was up for a physical test. But not this.

"Do you mean to tell me your father allows you to drive this truck?" Her hands were planted on her hips, and she wore a skeptical expression. The words and voice were her mother's. Becoming a mother must have brought it out in her.

"Since I was ten. I'm a good driver. I'll show you."

"Ten, huh? Seems young, but I suppose the world is different on a ranch. Well then, what am I supposed to do since you'll be driving?"

"You get to throw the hay out."

"Throw the hay out?" Good thing she'd been conditioning herself.

"I'll drive around the pasture while you toss out flakes of hay. Just spread it around so the horses don't bunch up too much. Sometimes, they bite or kick each other over it. The ones in the big pastures don't need hay with all the grass. This hay is for the ones in a couple of smaller pastures and the paddocks. We've got them up close for all the trail rides coming. There's less grass in the places we're stopping at. The weather's been kind of dry."

The pickup's bed was packed tight with bales of hay. "I'm going to be sitting up on top of all that? I trust you'll be driving extra slow, right?"

"Always. Come on. You can ride inside with me until we get into the pasture. And you can eat the breakfast burrito grandpa made you. He also fixed you a thermos of sweet tea." Russell walked to the passenger side to open the door for her.

"Your grandpa is such a sweetie. You must get it from him." No mention was made of Reid, and Russell didn't seem to notice. They drove off along a well-worn dirt road. "You sure are doing a good job."

"Thanks, Mom." He glanced at her, quickly resetting his eyes on the path before him.

"What'll we be doing after this?" Lacey took a big bite of the burrito's deliciousness.

"Oh, there's lots to do. We need to saddle the horses some of the guys moved into the barn last night to get them ready for moving cattle."

"Even Spark?"

"No. I don't think dad listened to us last night, he seemed distracted and upset after you left the house. He kept me up with his groaning and snoring. Anyway, I told grandpa what happened, and he put his foot down. He said Spark was off limits to everyone except you whenever you're here or on your way here. He made sure all the workers knew and he talked with Aunt Kate. She didn't look happy."

The corners of Lacey's mouth rose. "I love your grandpa." She continued munching her breakfast.

"I think it's mutual. Anyway, after the horses leave, there're the stalls to muck out and water troughs to fill. And we have to bring in more wood for the firepits for tonight. We've got to be sure to watch out for snakes while we move the wood, though. I'll show you how to do it, don't worry.

"Oh, and then we'll need to find and trim up enough sticks for the guests to use for roasting hot dogs and marshmallows for dinner; most everyone's signed up for it. The rest are having barbeque chicken. After we finish, we can break for lunch, unless something else comes up. It happens sometimes."

"All that before lunch?"

"It's not too bad. If we finish early, we can start on the afternoon chores and maybe get done in time for a break before dinner."

"Great." Exhaustion crept in before the day even got started.

"You don't have to do any of it if you don't want to, Mom. Or you can help with some parts and skip the rest."

"I know. I'm sorry, Russell. I didn't sleep well last night." She licked her fingers before wiping them with the napkin.

"Did Jayden make too much noise?"

"No. He'd stopped by the time you left, right after we finished our last game of checkers. I don't know what it was. I thought I heard someone in the barn, maybe out in the office, and it spooked me even though I knew Jayden was right upstairs. I maneuvered the heavy dresser over to block the door, but I still had trouble sleeping." Lacey opened the thermos and took a long drink, glad the dirt road was relatively smooth.

"You should've just called me. I would've come with my sleeping bag and slept on the floor."

"You're the best kid. I didn't think about calling you. But there's not enough room in there for you to spread out. I'm sure it'll be better tonight. Jayden promised to check all around the barn before he goes upstairs."

"Just let me know if you change your mind. I could squeeze in between Jayden's bed and the counter on the kitchen floor." He eased the truck to a halt. "I'll need you to open the gate and then close it behind the truck."

"Okay." After handling the gate, it was time to climb on top of the bales. She balanced on the edge of the truck's side and hoisted herself up by pulling on the twine holding the bales together.

The first two horses were visible, cresting the nearby hill at a fast walk that turned into a competitive trot. "They must've heard us coming," Lacey called.

"They always do. Hold on back there."

"Go ahead." Her fingers grasped the rough twine as her lower back braced against the back of the pickup's cab. Russell drove with the utmost care, but it was still a bumpy ride. They stopped halfway up the slope.

"You can cut them open now and throw some out," Russell called.

"Okay." Lacey clambered across the bales to those at the far end and used Russell's pocketknife to slice open the first bale. One of the horses leaned in to grab a bite from an unopened bale beneath Lacey's foot. "Hey, back off now," she admonished, tossing the first flake of hay.

It didn't go far. The second horse began to munch on what had been thrown as the first tried for another stolen mouthful, her ears pinned back against her head. Lacey tossed another flake, this time more like a Frisbee. It landed with a thud, attracting the attention of the first horse.

Lobbing a couple more before they drove off, Lacey slung hay as they went, as additional horses ambled or trotted over the crest of the hill. Twice she nearly toppled from the pickup, too exuberant with her tosses. The first time, Russell was afraid she'd gotten hurt in her struggle to remain on the hay bales, what with the high pitched squeal. The second time, he laughed at her. So did she.

***

After a long morning, a lunch break had never been more appealing. Lacey sat at a picnic table in the backyard with her head resting on her arms while Russell got their food. She'd fallen asleep by the time he returned.

"Mom? Here's your lunch." He slid a plate in front of her as she roused.

"Thanks, Russell. This looks good."

"It's just a peanut butter and jelly sandwich with pretzel sticks, Mom. You must be tired."

"I am, but I'll be okay. I needed food and a chance to sit down and not do anything. I'll be fine after we eat."

"If you change your mind, you can always catch a nap or rest in the rocking chairs on the front porch or by the fireplace inside. There's no fire in it, on account of it being hot outside. The ceiling fans and air conditioning in there will cool you off."

"I promise I'm fine, but thank you anyway, honey. I'm just not used to this much physical labor." She took a big bite of the sandwich. Simple, but good under the circumstances. Russell had two on his plate.

"Just don't overdo it. Dad's worried you might."

"Sometimes worrying's good for a person." Reid needed to think about how he'd treated her and how he was allowing Kate to manipulate him.

Russell swallowed the last bite of his first sandwich and washed it down with water. "If you'd like tea instead of water, I can go get you some, Mom. They've got plenty in the kitchen for whoever wants it."

"No, water is best for us while we're working hard in the heat. Wouldn't your dad agree?"

"Yes. Aside from his morning coffee, water is all he drinks. He's got me to where I don't like sodas much anymore."

"Good. I agree with your father there." Resentment rose in her at the thought of Reid. It couldn't be helped.

"Hey, you're halfway done already. Good job."

"So are you, and you've got twice as much food as I do. You're a growing boy for sure." Lacey took another big bite.

Sitting still for a while was great, but the sooner they got back to work, the sooner the chores would be done. Skipping dinner seemed like a good option. Being away from Reid and Kate would provide a bonus. She'd been doing her best to avoid thinking of them all morning, which meant they were in her head constantly.

The kitchen door opened, and Reid emerged, a big smile on his face as he strode their way with three bottles of water. The smile Lacey had worn vanished at his approach.

"Oh, no." She hadn't meant to say it out loud. Forced chatting could delay her sleep plans by as much as a half hour. Plus, there was the fact that she didn't want to speak to Reid, or even see him. Maybe ever.

"Are you still mad at my dad?"

"Sorry, honey. I shouldn't have said it. I'm just tired, that's all." And the unspoken answer was a resounding yes.

"Hey, you two. How are the chores coming?" He sat across from Russell, his eyes taking in both of them, hoping some of Lacey's anger had faded. He placed the bottles of water on the table. "I didn't realize you already had water. Take the extras with you for this afternoon."

"The chores are mostly done. Mom's a big help."

"She is?" Knowing her, she'd pushed herself too hard already. That shoulder could give out on her. If that happened, he'd find a way to convince her to rehabilitate on the ranch this time. But the appealing idea of having her with him wasn't worth seeing her in pain. She needed to relax for a while.

Lacey attempted to conceal her exhaustion, holding her head high.

"I can believe it," Reid said. "But you look worn out to me, Lacey. Why don't you take the afternoon off and rest your shoulder? I'm worried about you. Jayden told me you didn't sleep well last night."

"I'm fine. I came here to visit my son. He's got a way of making even mundane tasks entertaining." She took a long drink of water to avoid talking, turning away to look back toward the barn as she nibbled on a few pretzel sticks. She'd rather be shoveling manure than sitting here with Reid, although the two tasks had similarities, come to think of it. The thought had her smirking.

Reid turned to Russell. "You're keeping a close eye on your mom for me, right?"

"Reid!" Their attention was drawn to the kitchen door, where

Kate waved frantically. "I'm bringing your lunch! I'll be right there!"

Now they'd have to stick around until Reid finished eating to avoid being rude. She'd sure like to be rude. That went double when Kate came over, carrying a bottle of water and two plates heaping with food to the picnic table. Rude behavior might have its place after all. Lacey wanted to test it out and see.

Kate put the plates on the table, positioning herself close to Reid.

Lacey was angry with him, almost beyond words, but the ugly head of jealousy arose in her. Snapping out of it would be more productive. If he wanted Kate, he could have her.

"Oh, my goodness. I'm exhausted from all the extra work I've been doing thanks to the computer mix-up," Kate said. "The alarm clock woke me out of a sound sleep at six this morning to give me time to get ready for my day. I haven't even had any time to investigate what went wrong."

So fake. Lacey couldn't believe Reid and Russell were incapable of seeing it for themselves. She sent Kate a blank stare while they ate.

"We're tired too, Aunt Kate. Mom and I have been outside since before sunrise, way before your alarm clock went off. She's been working as hard as me out there. I'm proud of her."

Reid nodded. "So am I; and grateful to you, Lacey. Don't worry about the mix-up, Kate. Whatever went wrong, we'll handle it. I'm sure it won't happen again."

"You never know about these things. Sometimes, they're what you call cyclical, which means it could happen every couple of months or so. You just never know." She stared pointedly at Lacey.

Like coinciding with her trips out here? Lacey would love to say it out loud. Instead, she selected a different tactic, one Kate wouldn't be able to combat. "Kate, are you a computer programmer or something?"

"Me? No, no. I took a computer class at the community college years ago and my professor said I had a gift." She beamed at Reid.

He didn't notice, lost in thought. There had to be a way to get through to Lacey. The anger still bubbled in her, just under the surface. If it festered, he could lose her. That couldn't be allowed to happen.

"Interesting. Hey, I was thinking maybe I could look at your computer to see if I can figure out what happened. You know, seeing as how you're so busy and all."

"You?" She laughed. "You'd have to know that computer like I do to get anywhere with it, no offense."

"None taken, Kate. Say, did Russell ever tell you what I do for a living back in Charlotte?"

"No, it never came up. I'm too busy around here for a lot of small talk about matters not important to the running of this ranch and my family."

Come into my parlor, said the spider to the fly. This was going to be good. Lacey's smile spread.

"Aunt Kate, what Mom does for a living is important to me."

"Of course it is, dear." She verbally patted Russell's head.

Condescending jerk. Lacey's smile vanished with her opponent's veiled strike. "Well, since you didn't ask, I'll tell you. I work with computers, all day, every day. I manage complex software systems and troubleshoot computers and other equipment when needed. I've had extensive training and experience in computer programming.

"When I was in college, I even learned how to take them apart and put them back together again and how to build new ones from spare parts. I think I could handle a simple system like the one you've got here."

The color drained from Kate's face and her lips parted but no sound came out.

The information surprised Reid. "We'd appreciate it, Lacey. I know you work with computers, but I had no idea you were so talented." If she moved onto the ranch permanently, he knew of a job she'd be great at. Since she was so determined to have one.

"It's not talent. It's education and experience. If there's time, I'll check into it once the guests have thinned out a bit. It should be easy enough for me to find out what happened and when."

"You can do that, Mom?" Russell asked enthusiastically. "Can I watch?"

"Yes, and yes. I can show you the insides of a computer. If it's as old as I imagine it is, I can bring back some new parts with me on my next trip and increase its speed and efficiency for you, Reid. I'm sure you're way overdue for a software upgrade, too."

"That would be wonderful, wouldn't it, Kate?" Reid asked.

"Wonderful." Kate's eyes were cold.

***

Lunch had gained Lacey valuable knowledge and it shook up Kate to boot. Lacey made her excuses so she and Russell could get back to the chores early. Unmentioned was the desire to get away from Reid and Kate. Reid had risen from the table as they were leaving, off to handle more chores himself. Kate remained, stewing and angry, leaving her food untouched.

The afternoon was long. They plowed through until Lacey could scarcely move. All she wanted was to collapse on her bed in the barn and sleep until the alarm clock made what would no doubt be a valiant, though unsuccessful, attempt to awaken her at dawn.

"Okay, we're done for the day," Russell pronounced.

"You just made me so happy, honey." Lacey was ready to cry for the sheer joy of being able to stop and rest. Beads of sweat rolled down her face and neck, carving unwelcome channels through the dust and dirt. A moistened handkerchief offered modest relief when she wiped it over her face and neck, smearing the dirt.

"You're tired, aren't you?" Russell asked.

"I've never been more exhausted. I admire people like you and your dad, who do this kind of work every day. Me? I'm a wimp compared to you guys. There's no way I could do this on a full-time basis."

"You just need to get used to the routine. Your muscles are already strong enough. Or you could work inside the house."

"No. Thanks anyway." The glares Kate shot whenever Lacey had seen her since lunch sent chills along her spine. No doubt she felt threatened by what might be revealed in an exploration of the computer. "I don't care much for housework. If I can't be on a computer, I'd rather be outside."

"Dinner is served! Come on, you've earned it. Take a load off!" Robert called from the kitchen door, waving them inside.

The aromatic scent of barbeque chicken hung heavy in the air, bringing a loud growl from Lacey's stomach. Reid could be in there. And Kate would be prowling.

"Come on, Mom." Russell took her by the hand and gave a gentle tug, but she refused to budge. "What's wrong?"

"I'm sorry, Russell. I don't want to go in there."

"But you have to eat."

"We ate dinner together last night and you brought me breakfast this morning. Those meals were better than being inside your house with all those people. Even though I live in a big city, I'm not a fan of crowds. Not like that. Besides, I'm worn out enough to skip dinner. Just tell your grandpa I said thanks but no thanks. I'm going to shower and get straight to bed."

It was all in avoidance of mentioning she didn't want to be near Kate. Or Reid. They had turned out to be a surprise. Lacey was well on the way to convincing herself she didn't care about Reid or who he spent his time with. She'd been a fool to have allowed herself to believe a romance might be kindling with Reid.

***

Hot water pounded, soothing aching back muscles after harder physical labor than she'd ever performed in her life. Russell was worth it. Lacey could take partial credit for his existence, but not his personality. His other parents got the credit there, especially Reid.

The big showerhead was set for a thumping massage. The body wash Kate had furnished carried the distinct aroma of lavender, making for a relaxing shower and adding to her sleepiness. She still didn't care for being dumped out in the barn, even though it was a nice space.

Considering how well built the apartment was, it surprised her to feel a sudden draft, accompanied by the sound of a thump. She paused with her hair sudsy. There were no additional noises, just the one. It sounded as though a door on this level had been opened and closed. Nearby. She remembered locking the apartment door. It must've been the office door.

"Hello? Is someone out there? Hello? Russell? Jayden? Gil?" Gil and Jayden had been preparing the firing ranges when Lacey nearly crawled into the barn. The two men were going to teach guests how to safely use firearms. They were both so nice. Neither of them would have come in here, especially unannounced.

No one would've used the hidden key to enter the apartment and then not responded to her call. It must've been someone in the office for a minute and then gone. There was nothing to worry about.

After a quick rinse, Lacey turned off the water to conserve resources with extra guests in residence. She reached through the shower curtain for the towel and poked her head out. Nothing was out of place. The bathroom door remained closed, providing a wave of relief.

The towel was thick and soft and smelled of lavender. It was one of the ones from the guesthouse. Lacey was determined to move back into the house before her vacation ended, possibly through a bold move that involved asking Reid for a favor. If it worked, it would leave her spending only two nights in the barn.

She intended to convince Reid that her barn stay should be taken over by Kate. How fitting that would be. After all, Kate was family, too. Right? Lacey snickered at the idea, at seeing the expression on Kate's face. Talk about priceless.

Sunset would come in an hour, which meant activity at the firing ranges would wrap up soon. After things quieted down, sleep would come with ease. She was famished but more worn out than hungry.

So far, this trip was proving good for weight loss. Not that she needed much of that.

Lacey pushed aside the shower curtain and stepped onto the plush mat. That was when she realized she wasn't alone in the apartment after all.

THIRTEEN

It lasted for less than a couple of heartbeats, but she still heard it, clear as day. There was no mistaking the sound, even though she'd never heard it in real life before. Instinct brought her to a dead stop, thanks to an unmistakable jolt of primal fear. Movement in the small space would prove deadly. Was it even safe enough to breathe?

Fright left her paralyzed. She didn't know what to do in such a perilous situation. Since she couldn't see her would-be attacker and had no means of escape, there was nothing to do except wait until she was missed.

But that might not come until the next morning. She wouldn't be able to tolerate the waiting or the standing. If someone came to the office, they'd be able to hear a scream and hopefully come to the rescue. She prayed for someone, anyone, to come before the killer decided to draw closer and eliminate her from the world.

Her absence didn't go unnoticed for long. Someone knocked at the apartment door. Lacey found herself wishing she hadn't locked it after all.

"If it was Russell, rather than a guest out exploring, he'd know about the hidden key and use it. Jayden was a possibility, coming for something of his he'd forgotten. He'd be armed. Please be Jayden. Please.

"Mom? Mom, are you finished with your shower yet? I know you said you weren't going to eat, but Grandpa's made dinner for us anyway. He told me to come and get you. I'm not supposed to take no for an answer. He said if you don't want to come inside, you and I can eat at one of the picnic tables.

"And if you still don't want to come, he's going to bring your dinner himself and you two will have a conversation. About Dad, I think." Russell yelled to be heard through the outer door and the bathroom door in case she was in there. Or asleep.

"If we eat fast enough, I can get you in on the firing range lessons before sunset. There're some guests at both sites now. I was thinking you might want to learn how to shoot." Why wasn't she answering?

Right about now Lacey sure wished she had a gun in her hand, even with no idea of how to use one. Why did she ever come out here where the wilderness areas of the ranch were so near the homes? She didn't belong here. What she should've done was refuse to stay in the barn, but it was too late now.

Russell knocked again, louder this time, before trying the doorknob. The silence following his knock stabbed at her heart. What if he assumed she'd gone, and he didn't come back for a while? Wouldn't it start slithering around? Slithering. What a bloodcurdling word.

The clicking sound of the apartment's door being unlocked was followed by footsteps, then a tentative tap on the bathroom door. She was afraid to speak. Snakes couldn't hear, could they? The doorknob turned, followed by the door opening a crack. Her heart hammered.

"Mom? Mom, are you in there? Are you okay?"

She had to take a chance. She couldn't allow him to come any closer for fear he could be bitten. "No, Russell! Don't come in here!"

"I'm sorry, Mom. I thought you'd be finished with your shower by now." His words came in a rush of embarrassment. "I was knocking on the door and talking to you. Didn't you hear me?"

"Russell, stop talking and listen to me. There's a rattlesnake in here."

"A rattlesnake? Are you sure?"

"Positive. Get Gil or Jayden or somebody with a gun and hurry!"

"I will. Don't move! I'll be right back Mom!"

Gunfire echoed beyond as guests practiced on the dual firing ranges. Gil and Jayden were out there, providing instruction. They weren't far.

The sound of more footsteps, arriving far faster than hoped for, signaled the help she needed. One of the guys must be coming for the snake. Salvation was just outside the bathroom door. The deep voice called out from the other side.

"Lacey, it's Reid. I'm coming in now; only me. I don't want you to make a move unless I say. Do you understand?" The knob turned and the bathroom door swung slowly aside.

"Yes," her voice quavered, even though a wave of relief swept over her. Reid had come to her rescue. He wouldn't leave her here or let her be hurt.

The slight creaking of the door was sure to rile the snake, wasn't it? Or the movement? Reid had a gun in his hand. His eyes met Lacey's and sent her a reassuring nod.

Fleetingly, she wondered how much of her body was covered by the big towel. Probably not as much as she preferred, not that her state of undress mattered under the circumstances. Reid's eyes skimmed down her body and back to her face in a flash. She detected the subtle twitch in his jaw, the slight narrowing of his eyes.

So beautiful, so sensual. But so frightened, her eyes wide, hands trembling. It churned his stomach, making him angry to see her like this. Like she probably was when that man chased her through the place where she worked in North Carolina.

Keeping her safe and happy had been his objective since her first visit to the ranch. It couldn't be a rattlesnake. There was no way for any snake to get in here.

Indeed, no rattlers had been discovered anywhere near the developed areas of the ranch in years. They were diligent. Had to be, for the sake of the tourists.

He glanced to the toilet and saw just how wrong he'd been. His eyes widened as he gave a hard swallow. The rattling resumed in earnest.

"He's a big one Lacey, but you're going to be fine. I'm not going to let anything happen to you. I've got his full attention on me. I want you to turn your head, nice and slow. Face away from him. Stare at the mirror for me and then close your eyes in case any porcelain goes flying from the shots. Don't open your eyes or move until I say."

Lacey rotated her head, doing as he asked, reluctant to utter a sound. They glanced at one another in the mirror. Her body shook like a leaf, visible in the reflection.

"Good girl. Now, when I shoot, it's going to be loud in here. All I'm asking you to do is hold your ground."

Still afraid to acknowledge him with words, Lacey shut her eyes tight. He had an unobstructed view of her in the full-length mirror and she was half-naked. No, from the glimpse in the mirror, it was more than half. Two items to be concerned with, one a lot more important than the other.

Reid gave her a countdown. "Get yourself ready now Lacey... three, two, one!"

Then came the ear-splitting sound of gunfire, so close and loud Lacey would've sworn she was the actual target. It had her flinching badly with each discharge of the gun. She wished she could cover her ears against the sharp, booming sounds, even if it meant dropping the towel. Survival over modesty.

But Reid told her not to move and she wouldn't. She trusted him. He was her salvation.

Before she was aware of his proximity, Reid wrapped her up in his arms, his hands on her bare back, holding on tight as he whispered in her ear. "It's okay now, Lacey. You're okay. I've got you. It's all finished now. He's dead."

She turned her face to nuzzle into him and the comfort of his presence, her shaking coming under control, replaced by tears. One of his hands shifted between them, readjusting her towel to better cover her body. His fingers brushed one of her breasts as he worked.

He applied a long, tender kiss to her cheek. Then he lifted her into his arms, carrying her out to the bed, where he sat with her across his lap. Her hands had such a firm grip on his bicep he'd be left bruised. He didn't seem to mind.

"Get it out of there for me," Reid instructed someone.

"Don't worry; I've got what I need to do the job, son," Robert said.

"Be careful; don't let it get you," Reid said.

"I'm the one who taught you about dead snakes biting when you were two years old, remember? You just take care of her; she's the priority. I've got this."

"Dad, can I come in now?" He wanted so badly to check on his mother. He'd heard her choke back a sob.

"No, Russ. Not yet. Keep back until your grandpa goes by with the snake in the bucket and the apartment's been thoroughly searched."

"Gil, I want you and Jayden to get in here and check the rest of the room, every inch of it. Even the dresser drawers. And watch yourselves."

"Yes sir, we're on it," Gil assured him, taking charge of the search.

Lacey didn't want to watch; all that mattered was the comforting strength and safety of Reid's embrace. Her heart still pounded with a frenzy. Reid rubbed her arm with one hand, the other around her waist. He periodically kissed the top of her head and whispered reassurances to her.

"I'm not going to let anything happen to you. You're safe with me. It's okay. It's all okay now," Reid said.

After a few minutes of hectic commotion, the verdict came from Gil. "It's all clear, Mr. Collier. We even checked the shoes and inside Lacey's luggage."

"Thanks, guys. You can go now, but I want everything in this barn searched, every nook and cranny, top to bottom; all of it. I want the horses out of here and into the pasture. Get every spare ranch hand in on this. The guests won't think anything of it. They probably just thought the shots in here were from one of the firing ranges."

"Yes sir," Gil said before dashing for the stalls to start evacuating the horses.

"How a snake managed to get past everyone's notice today, including the dogs, beats me. And I thought your apartment was sealed better than this, Jayden. We'll have to get to work on it later this week as a high priority. Until then, you'll sleep in the house, somewhere. Maybe you can put throw pillows on the floor. I won't have you living out here until we're sure it's safe."

"Yes sir. I appreciate that," Jayden replied. A poisonous snake. They needed to check beyond the barn. Everywhere around the house, the sheds, the pool. Guest safety was paramount. But he'd start those procedures on his own and tell Reid about it later. Reid had personal issues to handle now.

"It's okay now, Russell. You can come in." Reid stroked Lacey's hair a couple of times, kissing her temple. "You might want to make sure the towel stays up, sweetheart," he whispered in her ear.

Those words helped snap her out of it. She opened her eyes, placing a hand where Reid tugged the towel over to give her enough to grab. She noted the moist area on Reid's shirt caused by her wet hair and wiped her eyes.

Russell's face creased with worry as he sat on the bed. "Are you okay, Mom?"

She wanted to grab him for a big hug. He almost lost a second mother today. He must be so frightened. "Yes, Russell. I'm okay."

"Russ, why don't you go to the closet and pull out the guest robe for me? I know Kate brought one over here for her."

"Yes sir." He returned in a flash with the robe.

"Lay it here on the bed and stand outside the door to make sure no one comes in. And while you're there I want you to face away. Don't turn around and don't look back here."

"Okay, Dad. I won't, I promise." After giving his mother a quick kiss on the cheek, he rushed through the door, leaving it slightly ajar. He stood outside it to perform guard duty, back straight and arms folded over his chest.

"Lacey, we're getting up now, but I'm not letting go of you until

I'm sure you can stand on your own, okay?"

Thank God for Reid. Lacey wasn't sure her feet could hold her yet. She nodded.

Reid stood and lowered her feet to the floor. Momentary panic hit her, and she took a firm hold on the front of his shirt, her wide eyes searching his.

The response was a reassuring smile. "It's okay. The apartment's clean; there's nothing to be afraid of. I'm right here and I'm not going anywhere. Hang on a second." He reached for the robe, then moved behind her, holding the garment up to her back. "Drop your towel. I'll close my eyes if you want me to."

"No, you don't need to." She did as he instructed, allowing the towel to pool at her feet. It meant he had a full view of everything back there, but he'd already seen plenty in the mirror.

She pushed one arm at a time into the sleeves and he slid the robe onto her shoulders. He removed her wet hair from inside the material with a gentle touch. As Lacey wrapped the robe around herself, Reid slid his arms beneath hers with the sash in his grasp. He tied it from where he stood behind her then applied several long kisses to the side of her neck.

"Everything's going to be okay now, Lacey; I promise." His lips brushed her ear as he spoke, kissing her cheek before stepping back. "It's all right now, Russ; you can come in. She's decent."

On impulse, Lacey spun and threw her arms around Reid's waist, pulling herself close against him. He hugged her, rubbing his hands along her back, and making shushing noises. She felt more comfortable this way and didn't want to let go.

"Would you like to sleep with me tonight, sweetheart?" he asked with a soothing tone.

Her eyes widened and she pushed back to see his face.

The reaction made him realize what he'd said. "Oh. I'm sorry, Lacey. I didn't mean it like... not that I wouldn't want to..." He glanced at Russell and licked his tongue over his lips.

"I wanted to say I'm not letting you stay in here and there's no

room anywhere else, which means you'll need to be in bed with me."
He closed his eyes and sighed. "I'm still not saying it right. What I
meant was..."

"It's okay, I know what you meant. I'll take you up on it." Her
hands rested comfortably on his chest, his hands on her hips.

"Good, I'm glad it's settled. Otherwise, I'd have to insist."

"I don't want to be in this room anymore. And I don't want to
sleep by myself, either. Not tonight. Sleep would never come."

His hands moved to her shoulders and squeezed them, as he
rested his forehead against Lacey's and released a long sigh and a lot
of built-up tension. "Okay. First things first. Let's get some clothes
for you to change into and pack up your things. Then Russell and I
will escort you to the guesthouse for dinner. I'll have to find
someplace to put Jayden, my father, and the other guys. Russell can
stay on the floor where he was.

"Once you've seen the sunset, we can go to bed whenever you
decide you're ready. We can stay up late to watch a movie on the big
television or turn in early. It's all up to you tonight; you're in
charge."

"Do you want me to pick out something for you to wear, Mom?"
Russell asked, eager to help with something.

His mother smiled. "Sure. Thank you, honey."

Russell set to work rummaging around in the closet.

Reid whispered in her ear. "You'd better grab your underwear for
yourself. He's only fifteen, after all."

FOURTEEN

The meal of barbeque chicken, a side of salad, and yeast rolls was perfect, washed down with fresh homemade lemonade. After dinner, Russell and Lacey rocked in the porch chairs for a few minutes, passing the time enjoying one another's company and sharing in small talk.

Russell held her hand as they stood in front of the house, watching the sunset. Reid was on her other side, his arm in a secure grip around her waist. Guests remarked about the beauty in the sky. The deep blue was streaked with bright oranges and pinks from a scattering of high-level clouds.

"What do you think, Mom? This is better than last night's, isn't it? Did you even get to see the one last night?" Russell asked.

"I got a glimpse of it through the apartment window and you're right, it is better. It could just be because I have a heightened appreciation for sunsets right about now, along with everything else in life." She squeezed her son's hand.

Reid removed his hand from her waist, freeing himself to interlace his fingers with Lacey's. She met his gaze, and he placed a tender kiss on her temple. He nodded to Robert, who stood nearby.

"All right, folks. You can hang here and watch the stars come out, rock on the porch for a while, or head on inside to catch the movie on the big screen. We're making a fresh batch of popcorn and the cookies are due to come out of the oven any minute now. We have an outstanding selection of beverages to choose from, both kid and adult varieties." Robert began herding the group toward the house. "There's also marshmallow roasting going on at the big firepit. We have plenty if you want to join in."

Reid and Russell moved Lacey toward the house, keeping her between them. The guests with the youngest children gathered around the firepit.

"Do you want to watch the movie for a while Mom, or do you want to go to bed?" Russell asked as they took the stairs and crossed the porch.

"Definitely bed. I'm worn out."

"It's okay, I understand. I figured you would be. I'll get my sleeping bag. Grandpa's going to use it to sleep on the kitchen floor tonight."

Lacey hugged him. "You saved my life today, you know; just like your dad did. If you hadn't come along when you did..."

Russell smiled. "You're the only mom I've got. And I like having you around."

"All right, Russ. Go get the sleeping bag out of my room and then get yourself ready for sleep. We've all had a busy day. I'll fix up something for you to sleep on."

"Okay, Dad. I promised I'd help Grandpa and Aunt Kate with the refreshments since Gil is helping with the guests by the firepit. Then I'll be right in. I volunteered to help with breakfast, too. We're making something special in honor of you, Mom. Grandpa and I arranged it with the kitchen staff. You'll love it."

"You're thoughtful. You don't need to go to any extra trouble on my account. The regular menu will be fine."

"But I want to. And we've already made plans. I'll see you soon." He sent her a grin before dashing into the house and tearing down the breezeway at top speed.

Reid led Lacey in Russell's wake at a leisurely pace. It had been constructed like a conservatory, composed of a multitude of screened, tinted glass panels, trimmed in white. At the moment, they were closed against the heat of the day.

White wooden benches in a modernist style sat along the edges, amid beautiful flowering plants cascading from baskets or spilling from long, narrow planters painted white. The flowers were bright yellows and purples, lending cheer to passersby. The ceiling was light blue, like the sky, set with a few large skylights.

"This is an impressive spot. I've never seen anything quite like it."

"I enjoy it myself. It's exceptionally nice when storms roll through. It's like you're out in the middle of the elements without getting wet or risking a lightning strike."

At the end of the breezeway, they entered a rambling, single-story structure with soaring ceilings. The walls were painted a warm terra cotta. Large, colorful photos of wildflowers, many of them bluebonnets, adorned the expanses between doors and along hallways.

"This is as good as the breezeway. It's homey, and I love the colors and photographs."

"Thanks. This is the original homestead."

Russell ran from a room at the hallway's end, a sleeping bag under his arm, grinning as he passed them.

"Not much point in telling him to slow down now. He's a little amped up after everything that's happened." Reid laughed.

"Anyway, I didn't hire anyone for this. I redecorated everything myself a couple of years after my wife died. Good therapy for me. She had all the walls a stark white with prints of teddy bears and girls concealed behind giant bonnets. They kind of freaked me out, to tell you the truth. She was an intelligent woman with questionable decorating taste. I never told her that, though."

Lacey laughed. "I think it would've freaked me out, too. This is kind of artsy." He looked dubious. "I mean that in a good way. Like an art gallery."

"If you say so. Well, here we are." He opened the door to the room

Russell had exited.

The interior was spacious, with a window seat covered in turquoise pillows at one end, framing a soothing view of the far pasture, and shaded by a large live oak. A branch larger in diameter than Lacey's waist reached out invitingly past the window. The tree showed tremendous age by its girth and spread, its branches sturdy enough for an adult or two to sit on side-by-side.

The bedroom walls were a warm, soothing blue, reminiscent of a hazy summer sky. The floorboards were wide planks of hand-scraped dark walnut. Reid's bed was the room's centerpiece.

It had a presence all its own, also composed of dark walnut, etched with grooves and curves and a few flings of copper inlay. The bedcoverings and the window curtains were layers of white, coupled with an intense, vibrant turquoise. The large master bathroom was masculine, a combination of coppers, chocolates, and blacks, with terra cotta walls that leaned toward orange. Vibrant Mexican sinks were set in the dark granite countertop with veins of copper slashing through it.

"This place is beautiful, Reid. Did you do this, too?"

"I did. I guess you can tell my favorite colors are turquoise and copper."

"Yes. It all works together. It's soothing and vibrant at the same time. The bed looks comfortable."

"It is. You go ahead and change into your pajamas." He handed them to her. "Russell laid them out, so they'd be ready for you. He put your clothes in my closet and one of the dresser drawers. If you want, I'd be happy to double-check the bathroom before you go in there."

"No. If you're close by, I'll be all right. I feel safe with you around."

"I'm glad to hear it. I'll be right here when you come out. I'll get the covers turned down for us and you can climb right into bed. We should be ready by the time Russell gets here. I think all three of us can use a good night's sleep. I'll use the comforter from our bed for

Russ to sleep on."

"Okay." Lacey flipped on the bathroom light switches, bathing the room in a warm glow, and closed the door. She admired the room while brushing her teeth. Then she changed into her pajamas, simple short shorts, and a pastel pink top.

The potential difficulty of sleeping with her son's attractive father hadn't been a consideration on this trip. Not really. Fantasies didn't count. It was weird to think of being nervous about sleeping beside her son's father. Normally, that's the way their son would've come into being, by Reid sleeping with her. Totally different kinds of sleeping, though.

There weren't any sounds emanating from the bedroom. Reid might've gotten pulled away by a guest in need of help. Probably a safe enough time to get into bed.

When she opened the door, her breath caught in her throat. Russell hadn't arrived yet, but the comforter had been folded several times and spread on the floor for a bed, along with a pillow. Reid was changing, dressed only in boxers, pulling up his pajama bottoms. The resulting three-quarter view gave an immediate jolt to her heart rate. A sculptor would have difficulty carving those muscles. Lacey swallowed and cleared her throat.

Reid straightened, pulling up his pajama pants. "Lacey. You're fast. I didn't expect you out here this soon. I'm sorry."

She raised one eyebrow, meeting his gaze. "You don't have anything to apologize for. I should've checked first. You've got amazing muscle tone. I hope you don't mind that I noticed."

Reid grinned, his cheeks showing a touch of red beneath the tan, his eyes remaining steady on her. "Thanks, Lacey."

He scanned her body at his leisure as he moved. "I like what you're wearing. It shows off your sexy curves. I hope you don't mind I noticed, either." His voice lowered, boosting the room's heat.

"No, not a bit." Nerves were liable to cause a fall if she tried to move. Had she started something? Part of her wanted to. Calming down would help. There was no way to mute the attraction toward

Reid, though. It had grown too strong.

He walked to the bed, lifting the covers. "Climb in, sweetheart."

A careful placement of one foot in front of the other got her there without a stumble. The mattress was firm, the padding plush. When her head settled into the pillow, Reid pulled up the sheet to her ribcage and leaned over her.

One of his hands rested on the bed beside each of her shoulders, leaving her happily pinned in, unable to move away from him if she wanted to. He kissed her forehead. "I want you to get a good night's sleep."

"I'll try." He had no idea how nervous he made her, or how difficult sleep might be in coming.

"I can't begin to figure out a way to tell you how glad I am you're safe. Not to mention how happy I am you're in our lives. When we first met in Charlotte, this speech I had rehearsed went out of my head. My heart was pounding too loud for me to think at the sight of such a beautiful woman. I didn't know where any future with you in our lives might go.

"But Russell has a mother again. I've never seen him like this. He's more excited about the future than ever. He wants to share everything with you." He hesitated. "He's hoping to see you regularly. I guess I should say daily. You should also know I agree with him."

"I live too far away to see him every day unless we keep using the computer to video chat. It's better than a phone call. Even if I were to get a job in San Antonio, I'd still be far away. Relatively speaking."

Reid grinned as though at a private joke. There must be something she wasn't getting because what she'd just said wasn't funny. Was it?

"Unless I miss my guess at all the hints he's been dropping, I believe he's hoping you'll move in here permanently."

"Oh." Lacey smiled. "Well, that's sweet. I'd like to be able to live in the same house with him and see him all the time, but I'm not much of a ranch hand, I'm afraid. And I didn't struggle to put myself through college to go back into the service industry."

Reid chuckled. "The idea of you choosing between cowgirl and waitress wasn't in his head. The hope is for you to take up permanent residence in this room. With me."

It took a couple of seconds for her brain to catch up. The resulting flash of heat brought a blush.

"Just thought you might like to have a heads up, in case Russ starts talking to you about it."

Okay, no big deal. She'd taken it the wrong way. This was all about Russell, not Reid. She wished she hadn't overreacted, drawing attention to how she might be feeling about all this, about him. "Oh. I understand. I'm glad you told me."

"I decided to take advantage of it as a teaching opportunity with him. It was about how a man should take his time with the woman that he thinks might be the one he wants to spend the rest of his life with. It's a major decision for both of them.

"But I also pointed out how you and I have seen or spoken to each other every day for over four months since the day you came here to see Russell, and that we've grown closer during that time. I told him relationships shouldn't be rushed, although sometimes you know right off if a person is going to be the one."

What did he just say? "Right." She tried to swallow the uncertainty. "I'm sure he understands. He's old enough."

"He is. I also let him know I'm crazy about you, but I pointed out we're not quite ready for a big step like marriage. I told him we're going to be working on it, but your relationship with him will never suffer because of it."

Had she forgotten to breathe? She must have. This was heading in that direction after all. He was talking about marriage. The butterflies took off, pounding in her stomach. Butterflies with wings of steel.

"I didn't say the waiting would be easy for me, though. Sometimes, all the restraint just goes right out the window when I look at you." Reid gazed into her eyes, taking in her lips. Part of him wanted to propose, right here and now. He knew without a doubt she was the one. The only concern was that she might not be ready yet. Hearing her say no would bruise his heart. It wouldn't stop him, though.

A flood of electrified nerves coursed through her body. He had kissed her before. Always exciting, always leaving her wanting more. But this felt different. Lacey pulled her arms free of the sheet and lifted them, rubbing her hands along Reid's back. Those dark eyes of his held her future.

Reid leaned down to press parted lips to Lacey's. Her lips were soft, warm, and tender. Welcoming. The taste of her, the warmth, excited him.

He wanted to take her now, to find Russell fast and tell him to find someplace else to sleep. He had the woman of his dreams in his bed, kissing him back as he pressed his body to hers. One of his hands shifted to support his weight, while the other tugged the sheet out of the way.

A rush of warmth surged into Lacey's belly, spreading everywhere as the stubble on his face brushed across her face. Her fingers caressed his bare back, then dug in, encouraging him as he lowered to her, his upper body covering hers. A cascade of trembles followed his fingers as they maneuvered beneath the small of her back, applying gentle pressure to lift her body into an arch against him as he deepened the kiss. He had her on the verge of losing control already.

"Goodnight!" That came from Russell, in the hallway.

They broke from the rising intensity of the intimate moment just in time. The bedroom door opened, and Russell entered. He grinned as Reid straightened to face him, tossing the sheet over for Lacey to catch it and return the cover to its previous position.

"Is everything all set for the special breakfast tomorrow, son?" Reid interlaced the fingers of his hands in front of his groin to conceal the hardness, trying to make the move a casual one, natural. Kissing Lacey, especially with such intensity and with her lying under him in his bed, hadn't been the wisest idea. He should have been able to exhibit some control over himself, but it had fallen away.

"Yes sir. I'm going to brush my teeth and change now. I'll be right back." He rummaged through a drawer and grabbed pajamas before dashing into the bathroom.

"Don't brush your teeth too fast, Russ. Do a good job," Reid called as he pulled a shirt from the same drawer Russell used. Once he'd covered that tempting torso, which was an awful shame from Lacey's perspective, Reid climbed into the far side of the bed to pull up the covers on that side. "We'll pick up where we left off soon, okay?"

"Okay. I won't let you forget."

He smiled, tracing the outline of her lips with his finger. Where was that control he had under normal circumstances? Her mouth was perfectly shaped. So kissable. "I'd never forget that. I could develop the world's worst-ever case of amnesia and not forget that kiss, or how you taste..." He blew out a long breath and laid back on the pillow, thinking as he stared at her, as they stared at each other.

When Russell emerged a couple of minutes later, he came over. "Goodnight Mom and Dad."

"Goodnight Russ," they chimed.

Lacey extended her arms to him as he moved in for a hug. "I love you, honey."

"I love you too, Mom."

She rubbed a hand through his hair. "You need to go to sleep now. Tomorrow will be another busy day. We've got work to do."

"I don't want to," he protested, straightening. "Dad, can't I hang out with Mom tomorrow? Please?"

"Russ." Reid tried to conceal a grin.

"You can't," Lacey interrupted, sitting up and glancing at Reid. "I'm sorry, Reid. Russell, your duties here are important; just like with your education. You can't ever let any of your work at the ranch or your education slide. Not for any reason. I remember how proud my parents were, seeing me graduate from college. I made it before they passed away."

"I'm sorry, Mom." He sat on the bed and put a hand on Lacey's.

"Thanks, honey. My father was eighty-nine when I graduated, and my mother was seventy. They met late in life and had me even later. The point is, don't ever gamble with your future or shirk your obligations to your dad and grandpa, not even for me. I'll help you with your chores tomorrow and we can hang out."

"You won't be too tired? Dad said you should rest tomorrow."

"That's because your dad is looking out for me. I'm tougher than everybody thinks I am. I can survive anything for you."

"Okay. I'll take good care of her for you, Dad."

Reid chuckled. "I'm going to rely on you, son."

"Go to sleep now, honey. I'll turn out the light as soon as you're settled," Lacey said.

Russell sank onto the pile of bedding without another word, and she extinguished the light. When she laid back, Reid placed a hand on her shoulder in the darkness, his mouth by her ear.

"You did a decent job with the lecture in case you were wondering. Not bad for a new mother." He touched his lips to her cheek before lying down and rolling over to face the far wall.

***

Lying beside Reid gave her a pleasure and comfort far surpassing Lacey's imagination. His steady breathing reassured her of his presence and her safety with him around. It took time, but eventually, she drifted off.

Later, she realized Reid had awakened, because a tickling sensation came to her heel, then her ankle. He was touching her with his toe. It had to be his big toe, strong and a bit leathery because big, tough, outdoorsy men like him didn't get pedicures and soak to soften their skin. But Russell was in the room. Risky. Yet, Lacey had no intention of registering an objection.

When he began using the toes of both feet, confusion set in.

Something wasn't right. The realization of the true source impacted her chest, squeezing so tight it robbed her of breaths.

There were snakes in the bed, all varieties and sizes, dozens upon dozens of them. They were everywhere beneath the sheet that was tangled around her body, inhibiting escape. They slithered over each other and her legs, positioning themselves to bite. Lacey thrashed and kicked at the imprisoning covers, trying desperately to cry out for help, yet unable to do so. She whimpered with fear instead.

"Lacey. Lacey. You're having a nightmare; wake up. It's okay."

Reid's voice did little to soothe or calm. The snakes were real, not some nightmare. Flipping over, she slid on her back toward the headboard, frantic to escape, finding her voice as the venomous shapes writhed in the darkness. "No, no, no!"

"Lacey!" Reid took hold of her, trying to stop her movements as her hands pressed against his chest in an effort to push free.

"There're snakes in the bed! Oh, God! Help me, Reid! They're everywhere!"

"No, honey, no. There're no snakes in here. There's just you and me, okay? There's nothing else, I promise. Russell, turn on the light."

"Let me go. I have to get away! They're going to kill me." They tightened around her legs, their tongues tickling at her skin.

Light bathed the room. Reid had a firm hold on her, his body wrapping around Lacey's, attempting to control her. It must be what wearing a straitjacket was like, and she wanted to be free.

The snakes were climbing, ready to strike. Didn't Reid understand? They were down there, writhing and tangling, the scales rubbing across her skin. There must be hundreds of them.

"Pull back the covers, all the way. Throw them back onto the floor and let her see. That's good, son. Now, I want you to look down there, Lacey. Go ahead, it'll be okay; I'm right here."

Glistening beads of sweat had broken out across her trembling body, chest heaving, hands shifted to grip Reid's arm like a vise, just as in the apartment earlier. She did as he instructed, risking a quick, reluctant glance to the foot of the bed, finding it devoid of snakes.

Safe. Where had they gone? Seeing with her own eyes brought de-escalation, belief in Reid's reassurance.

"You see? Nothing there. Everything's okay. Take a deep breath now and hold it for a couple of seconds. Good girl. Now, let it out, nice and slow. Good. Now, do it for me one more time." Reid rubbed her back, one hand on her cheek, his forehead resting against hers.

Russell climbed onto the bed. He put his arms around his mother's waist from behind and laid his head on her back. "I'm sorry, Mom. It's okay. I love you. Dad and I will keep all the snakes away."

"I'm sorry. I didn't mean to freak out. It was so real. They were everywhere. I was terrified. I had to get away." Even though she knew it was a dream, part of her mind still held doubts.

"I know, I know, sweetheart. It's okay." Reid brushed his cheek against Lacey's as he continued holding her. His breath blew at her hair, warming her ear. If only he hadn't put her in Jayden's apartment. She was terrified. There had to be a way to counteract the fear.

"Mom, you're safe with dad and me, remember? We saved you today. We'll always save you; I promise."

"Me, too," Reid offered with a long, soft kiss to her forehead. "Always."

Lacey took another deep breath and released it, then leaned into Reid as he applied another kiss, this one to the side of her head.

"Come on now. I want you to lie back down and get some sleep. Russell, move up here onto the bed. You lie on the other side of her. Maybe with both of us in here, she'll be able to sleep soundly."

"Is there enough room?" Russell asked.

"It's a California king-sized bed and your mom is small enough for all three of us to fit, no problem. If it feels too tight we'll all just sleep on our sides."

Once they were in position and covered, Russell extinguished the light. The glow from a crescent moon cast a faint, bluish light into the room through the gauzy curtains. She smiled as Reid snuggled up close against her, slipping an arm over her waist. After a few minutes, she drifted off into contented sleep.

***

Awareness of morning came as her hair was stroked, the hand slow and gentle. Tingling came to her scalp, spreading via nerve endings. Her eyelids fluttered open. Reid gazed into her eyes, his lips holding a sweet smile.

"Good morning," he said in a low whisper, his hand shifting from her hair to caress her cheek.

Her stomach fluttered at his touch. "Good morning," she whispered a reply. Russell stirred once behind her. "What time is it?"

"Almost time for the alarm clock to go off. How'd you sleep?"

"Much better. Thanks for helping me through my nightmare. I'm sorry about my reaction, about losing control."

"You don't need to be sorry. It was bound to happen after what you went through in Jayden's apartment. I'm glad I was here for you. It would've been terrible if you'd been alone when it happened." His hand stopped moving to rest on her cheek, his fingers extending into her hair.

The gesture relayed a sensation of desire and belonging. "I'm glad you were with me, too." She removed a hand from beneath the sheet and placed it over his.

He took her fingers in his grasp and lifted them to his lips, applying a kiss to the back of her hand. Now her stomach leaped into somersault mode. She wasn't sure what to do or how to react.

"Mom?" The mumble came out scarcely audible.

Lacey shifted to lie on her back. "Good morning, honey."

"Good morning, Mom." He wore a grin despite bleary eyes and applied a gentle hug. "Did you sleep better?"

"I did. I had a wonderful man on either side of me. How could I have been afraid of anything?"

"You'd better go ahead and get yourself ready, Russ. You wanted to wake up early since you and your grandpa are making a special breakfast for your mom," Reid said.

"Oh yeah! Thanks, Dad." He hopped from the bed, wide awake with remembrance. "I'll see you downstairs later, Mom! And sorry, Dad; I forgot to say good morning to you."

"It's okay son," he grinned. "You go ahead and change your clothes in the bathroom and then go downstairs so Lacey can get ready."

"I'll be out in a minute, Mom." He kissed her cheek before rushing to the dresser to pull out clothes. Then he tore off into the bathroom.

"You've raised the sweetest, best son. Not that I'm prejudiced in his favor or anything."

"Thanks, Lacey. I'm prejudiced myself. He makes it easy; he's a great kid. I couldn't ask for better because they just don't make 'em like him."

Reid propped up on one arm, tracing a forefinger across Lacey's bare shoulder in tiny circles, sending chills through her every pore.

FIFTEEN

"Okay, Mom. You sit right here. Dad, you sit beside mom."

She sat in the chair her son pulled out and let him scoot her in. "Thank you, Russell." Lacey sent him a smile.

"Yes ma'am." Then he whispered in his father's ear before rushing off to the kitchen.

"So, you're supposed to keep me distracted, huh?" She locked her gaze on Reid's.

"You heard that?"

"I have good hearing." She smiled.

"I'll have to be sure to keep that in mind." He tucked her hair behind an ear. Emotions shifted into a higher gear when he rested his arm on the back of her chair and began absent-mindedly running his fingers along the back of her neck, sliding them down her shoulder.

The twinge of her skin under his fingers gave him a thrill. The physical contact must be exciting her as much as it did him. The softening of her face and the narrowing of her eyes provided that clue. "What other special abilities do you have that I should be aware of, for future reference?"

It was difficult to keep her focus on Russell alone when his father looked at her the way he so often did. She hoped it wasn't simply her overactive imagination. "Well, there's nothing much else I can think of." Especially with him touching her and leaning in the way he was doing. Was he going to kiss her here, in front of everyone?

He kept coming until their noses touched. Lacey closed her eyes as his lips applied another of those feathery kisses, the barest of contact. So extraordinarily tempting. He did it again, this time parting his lips and holding the kiss a heartbeat longer.

"Close your eyes, Mom!" She turned from Reid and caught a glimpse of Russell's back in the swinging doors of the kitchen, checking to make sure the coast was clear.

She did as he asked and waited, missing the warmth of Reid's lips on hers already.

"Sit straight back in your chair and keep your hands in your lap," Reid advised.

Hushed whispers and footsteps gave away Russell's presence. The thump of items being placed on the table was followed by enticing aromas.

"Okay, you can open your eyes now!" Russell announced.

A large, lime green ceramic plate rested in front, filled with steaming hot food. On it sat a small, terracotta-colored bowl of grits with melting butter that had been capped with brown sugar in a tiny mound on top. Along with a thick slice of French toast sliced on the diagonal and adorned with pads of butter, sprinkled with cinnamon, confectioners' sugar, and topped with fresh fruit. Beside that sat a single baked egg, held in place by a long strip of bacon-wrapped snugly around it.

Robert held a huge mug of English breakfast tea and a vase of summer flowers in deep yellow and white. He and Russell grinned from ear to ear.

"This is wonderful! Thank you all so much!" Lacey's hands clasped at her chest, surprised at how much trouble they'd gone to for her.

"You're welcome, Mom."

"Come here!" Lacey extended her arms to hug her son and gave his cheek a quick kiss. "You're sweet. You too, Robert."

Robert placed her tea and the flowers on the table by her plate, then put a hand on her shoulder and kissed her cheek. "Happy to do it, dear. And even happier you're still with us. I hope you always will be."

"That goes double for me," Reid said, kissing her other cheek.

"This is so special," she said.

"Like you, Lacey," Reid said. He had a look in his eyes that she hoped was indicative of extra meaning behind the words.

A waitress brought plates of food for Reid and Russell. "I'll be right back with your drinks," she said.

"You enjoy it, Lacey; I've got to get back to my cooking, so nothing burns. Guests are coming down," Robert noted, a bright red dishtowel draped across his shoulder. He rushed back to the kitchen.

"My father loves what he does. This whole bed and breakfast idea brought him right out of his crusty shell," Reid said. "You and your grandpa did an excellent job on breakfast, Russ."

"Thanks, Dad."

"You sure did." Lacey savored a bite of the egg and bacon combo.

"These bacon egg muffins are great, aren't they, Mom?"

"Yes, they are. Do you serve these a lot?"

"This is the first time. I searched online for special breakfast items and found these. Grandpa said he knew we could make them easy enough. And I remembered you telling me how much you loved good French toast. My grandpa makes the best."

Reid smiled and nodded to two guests taking seats across from them. "Good morning."

"You three sure do make a lovely family," the older woman noted.

Reid glanced at Lacey and smiled before focusing on his guests. "Thank you, ma'am; I think so, too. How're you folks enjoying your stay?"

Leaving Reid to his duties, Lacey turned to Russell. "So, what'll we be doing today? I think I should forewarn you... I'm not going to be able to work as hard as I did yesterday. My muscles are already fighting me in my efforts to lift this fork to my mouth."

Russell laughed. "The usual. We'll take it easy today, though."

That laugh warmed her heart. Any amount of time spent in Texas on vacations wouldn't be near enough. Lacey needed to hear more of that laugh and Russell needed her. Then there was Reid. A sigh louder than she'd intended came out.

"You'll be grown up and off to college before I know it. Then I won't have much of a chance to get to know you. When you're finished with college, you'll get a job and meet a nice girl who won't be anywhere near good enough for you by a long shot and you'll get married. I'll see even less of you then.

Another sigh escaped her efforts at suppression. "This isn't right. You're my son. We just found each other, and we've already lost fifteen years. There's no way to make up for so much time, but I'm going to do my best. I want to spend every moment I can with you, Russell." Lacey's lower lip quivered by this point, tears spilling from her eyes.

He slid his chair back and then Lacey's, to allow them to stand and embrace. "It's okay, Mom. It'll all be okay, I promise."

Lacey pushed back from him, with a rash decision that'd lurked in the back of her mind since her arrival. "Russell, I can't keep flying out here to visit you like this."

"You can't?" His voice came out small, thinking the worst. The snake had scared her off.

"No." Her fingers combed through his hair. "It's not enough. I'm quitting my job in Charlotte as soon as I can. I'm going to find a job and an apartment in San Antonio. Charlotte's too far away. I need to be able to see you more than this. I love you so much!"

"Mom!" He hugged her harder than ever, temporarily robbed of speech.

Those at the table near them burst into a round of applause. Reid, clapping loudest of all, paused to wrap his arms around them.

"Go ahead, son. This seems like the right time to me," Reid said.

"It isn't wrapped yet."

"She won't mind. Give it to her." Reid's arm rested snug around Lacey's waist.

"Okay." Russell fished around in one of the deep pockets of his khaki shorts and withdrew a sealed plastic bag. "Here you go, Mom; it's your Mother's Day present, the one we couldn't give you because you got hurt trying to get out here to spend the weekend with us."

"What's this? Oh, it's a pretty silver necklace. Thank you, honey." Upon opening the bag and upending it, the sparkling twirled rope chain pooled into her palm, an embossed silver disk attached.

"Open it, Mom!" Russell jittered in place.

"Open it? What do you mean?"

"Here, let me show you." He took it and flipped his thumbnail at the edge. The disk popped apart into two halves.

"It's a locket; a beautiful locket." Emotion had the words sticking in her throat.

Russell handed it back to her. "Look at the pictures."

Renewed tears came into her eyes and a lump found a home in her throat. One photo held Russell's face, the other Reid's. She swallowed at the lump but found it impossible to come up with words. Russell put his arms around her, and she rested her forehead against his shoulder, so glad to be with these people. Her family.

***

She'd just sat down on a bale of hay for a break, leaning back against the wall, eyes closed. Russell had gone to the public restroom beside the barn's office after Lacey cleared it. She'd never have allowed her son to go in without it being checked for snake intrusions first.

She exhibited great caution, even peering into the toilet before sitting, just in case. Wouldn't want to get herself bitten back there. Besides, the ranch was far from medical care, and anti-venom treatment.

"Lacey, why are you in the barn?" Reid asked.

Her eyes popped open. "What're you doing here, Reid? We've got the barn covered. The last job for the day is carrying these two bales out for the horses in the nearest paddocks. I'm just taking a rest break while I wait for Russell. He's in the bathroom. I checked it first, don't worry."

"You shouldn't be in there or even out here until we figure out for sure how the snake got inside the apartment. Next time come up to the house for the bathroom. I'm concerned being in here might give you more nightmares tonight."

"Russell didn't want me coming into the barn either, but I told him I felt like I had to. It was important for me to be able to come back in here and do chores or just walk around. I can't let fear rule my life."

A frustrated sigh escaped Reid's lips.

"Reid, I can't go around being afraid all the time. I even..." Would he approve? He should. "I even took a few self-defense lessons in Charlotte. Did pretty well, too. It makes me feel more confident in my ability to protect myself in case I ever need to."

He sighed again. "Let's talk about a different solution to the problem, shall we? You've occupied my thoughts since this morning when you said you wanted to move to San Antonio. I'm glad to hear it. You'll be safe here with us."

The rattlesnake came instantly to mind, but Lacey refrained from verbalizing.

"I've been working on coming up with a solution to our problem. Kate's had the room across the hall from me since Karen got sick all those years ago. Now she only uses it when she works late because we're slammed, or on rare occasions when the weather is bad enough to make driving back to her house hazardous. It's a spacious room with a good view of the pasture where the horses congregate under the trees.

"Since you're in our lives now, I'm converting it into your room. The first thing we'll do is redecorate. You'll be able to choose the colors you want, and I'll have everything taken care of by the time you move in. What will you need to do, give the city two weeks' notice?"

Her head swam. He must mean for the room to be for occasional use like Kate did. But he used the word move. "Yes. But I've got to find a job before I move out here. And jobs for the skills I have don't just grow on trees. It may take a few months to a year before something comes open. The thought of a delay that long depresses me." Her voice trailed off.

"That's going to take too long for all of us. We'll figure out something. Russell shouldn't have to be away from the mother he's been missing most of his life. We're a family and we should be together. When you get back to Charlotte, I want you to go ahead and resign. Two weeks later, the moving van will show up at your apartment. I'll make the arrangements the day you leave here to go back to Charlotte."

He paused, thinking. "I don't want you driving out here alone. I'll make sure the moving company I hire can also tow your car. You'll fly here. Russ and I will pick you up at the airport."

"You've thought of everything, haven't you?" The words came with a reluctance she doubted he picked up on, considering his enthusiasm.

"To be honest, I haven't been able to think of anything else since breakfast. You said you wanted to move out here and I started working through the plans in my head. I'm looking forward to it as much as Russell is. Maybe more." He grinned.

She didn't relish the idea of ruining his mood. "It sounds great, Reid. But the reality is that I need a full-time job first. And it's easier to get a job when you've already got one. I won't turn in my resignation until I have a new job. I have to be able to provide for myself."

"Lacey." He shook his head as his hands moved to his hips.

"I mean it, Reid. I'm not going to live in Texas without a job. And I won't accept financial handouts from you, either. It's not how I was raised. I just can't do it."

Russell emerged to join them.

One of Reid's eyebrows was raised, but it was clear he didn't want to discuss any of it in front of Russell. "This conversation isn't over. I'll stick around and help you two with the hay. Then it's inside for dinner and bed."

Labor Day

SIXTEEN

Lacey shouldered her satchel and extended the handle of her new suitcase, giving Connie a wink.

"That sure is a nice piece of luggage Reid bought you. He's going to marry you. If I were you, I'd be hinting around that I was ready."

Lacey's free hand went straight to her hip in a fist. "Not yet. I don't want to push it with him. I don't know how he feels. I mean, I do, but marriage..."

"Reid likes you a lot. It's implied through the gift you've got a hand on right now; not to mention those kisses you told me about."

"A piece of luggage implies a level of closeness between a man and a woman?" Lacey shook her head. "Gee, and to think of all the years I've wasted my time waiting for flowers or jewelry when what I should've been looking for was a nice, sturdy suitcase."

"Silly. It's not the bag, or how much it cost. Which, by the way, was a lot. That's top of the line, right there. Anyway, as I said, it's not the quality or expensive label on it. It's what the purpose is. You're moving in."

"That's what you think?"

"It is. You should think the same thing. You're taking some of your most precious knick-knacks along with some clothes. All of it will be left behind in your new room. Then there's that. He's given you a room. And not just any room, the one directly across from his. And he had you decorate it the way you want, so you'll feel comfortable and at home. Next thing you know, he'll be paying you a late-night visit."

The image painted by those words sent a wash of warm pleasure over Lacey, sending the corners of her mouth upward. "I sure do hope so."

"Then you'll be moving to San Antonio permanently. And you'll have a fancy diamond ring on your finger to match those pretty earrings he already bought you. If you've forgotten, just reach a finger up and touch an earlobe."

Despite Connie's silliness, it had Lacey thinking. "You don't believe that, do you? Could he mean all that by giving me this piece of luggage?"

"Wow, somebody's over-analyzing the situation." Connie straightened, folding her arms over her chest.

"But you said..."

"*This* is the time you decide to start listening to me? Good grief, Lacey. I was teasing. There might be some truth to it, but time will tell. If I were you, I'd be making it come true. He's a real doll-baby, with sex appeal going to waste out on that ranch." She made a purring sound.

"How am I supposed to make it come true?"

"You're a woman." Connie slapped her palm on the countertop.

"So? What's that supposed to mean?"

"Give him some hints, for starters. Let him know how you feel about him. Most of the time, guys don't have a clue about reading women, about what we want. We think they're born with a radar system to detect how a woman is feeling or what she's thinking, but they're confused, just like us."

"And? How do I feel about him?" This should prove interesting. Lacey twirled her hair up and clipped it in place on top of her head.

"You've got to be kidding me. The guy is ruggedly good-looking and saved your life. He's got a heart-stopper of a smile and he put you in his bed."

"Because there was no other place to put me. Russell was in there, too." Lacey smirked.

"Yeah. A bit of a mood-killer, no doubt."

"There was no mood to kill. I was terrified. I nearly died, Connie. Romance wasn't involved." Not the complete truth, but she didn't want to share every detail of a kindling romance just yet. Not kindling; more like... smoldering. "Russell's first mother died, and I almost made it two in a row for him."

"Okay, okay. Suit yourself. One of these days, I'll be listening to you tell me how right I was all along. Connie the matchmaker."

Lacey's brow furrowed. "I'd never call you that."

"You will." She grinned.

"Won't." Lacey shook her head. "First, you didn't set me up with Reid, so you can't take any credit there."

"Can so. You used my phone to call the ranch and my name for check-in." She grinned.

"Okay, maybe that. But you did introduce me to two or three different guys, and none of them worked out at all. We didn't even remotely connect."

Connie held up a hand, all five fingers extended, shaking her head. "It was five guys. Your memory's not good sometimes."

"I must've blocked one or two of them out. I wish I could do the same with all of them." Lacey closed her eyes, regretting the conversation had ever taken this turn down a bad memory lane.

"You're such a kidder! Come on, Jonathan should be pulling up out front any second now."

"Jonathan, the wonderful guy *I* introduced *you* to. Remember? Are you coming with us?" Lacey rolled her pre-engagement suitcase past her roommate.

"Yes ma'am. Jonathan and I are heading out on a romantic weekend getaway as soon as we slow down just enough for you to tuck and roll at the airport."

"Nice. With a friend like you, who needs a Kate in their life?"

"Ha, ha. Very funny." Connie grabbed her luggage and followed Lacey out.

***

Lacey arranged photos of her parents and a few of Jonathan with Connie. She carried around an old stuffed palomino pony with long legs, its mane and tail missing some hair where she'd brushed too much as a kid. The perfect spot for it was found on a plush gray chair by a low shelving unit filled with books by her favorite childhood authors: Sam Savitt, Marguerite Henry, and Walter Farley. Then she put away her clothes in her new dresser, in her new room.

All she'd done was give Reid an idea of colors for the room. He'd handled everything else. The formerly deep pink walls were now a soft sage, mimicking the silvery color carried by some of the native vegetation Lacey found appealingly different from Charlotte.

The furnishings were white, with a worn, distressed look to them, gray showing through from underneath. The outside had been brought in. It couldn't be more perfect.

There was also a large photograph of Reid, Russell, and her, all of them on horseback, cattle roaming through scattered trees in the background. It hung over the king-sized bed, with its coverings of bold turquoise and white, a match for those on Reid's bed, a welcoming reminder of the man who did this for her.

The room was wonderful. Lacey couldn't wait to tell him how much she liked it, demonstrating with a hug. Or maybe a quick kiss on the lips; or a long one, depending on who was or wasn't around at the time. The tingles rising in her belly signified the need to find him. To ensure Reid's attention, she'd changed into a tank top and cut-off jean shorts.

Rushing from the breezeway into the check-in area of the lobby, she came face-to-face with Kate. Smoke practically rose from the woman's ears. She wore her typical tight clothes, a red silk blouse with a plunging neckline, black fishnet stockings, a black leather miniskirt, and long, black boots laced all the way up from her toes to above her knees.

The sight of her had Lacey thinking yet again how she disliked having her son exposed to the woman. And thinking it was time to finally say something about it. She took a deep breath.

Studying her attire, Lacey selected an opener. "So. How long does it take you to lace up those boots?"

The scowl chilled, as intended. The contempt and jealousy had been supplanted by pure hatred. "You're stealing everything from me; my room, my Reid, and possibly even my job."

"Your job? I don't want your job. I don't even live here, Kate. And I didn't steal your room; Reid gave it to me. It's his room and his idea. As for Reid himself, he was never yours in the first place. He's not mine, either. His life is his own to make. You've never understood that."

"Reid and this ranch belong to me, like my sister before me. I was right here when she died. My only sibling. I've worked longer and harder for it than she ever did. But she gets all the credit and I get none, the way my whole life has gone. Never good enough to compare.

"I've been here to watch this place grow from a bunch of stinky, muddy cows to a major tourist attraction, way bigger in size and scope than how it started. I helped make it happen. I deserve this ranch and the money from it more than anyone else does. Certainly, more than you do."

"More than anyone else? More than Reid?" Lacey had felt a twinge of sympathy when Kate spoke of her sister's death. Then it all changed. The true Kate emerged.

"We've had people making reservations just to spend time watching those buffaloes. I told Reid to start a zoo out there. Because of my suggestion, he bought those weird-looking buffaloes. My contribution toward growing the wealth of this ranch. I guess Reid didn't mention that. Probably forgot my input, like usual."

"Mom, where's Dad?" Russell, baseball bag on his shoulder, charged around the corner, nearly barreling into Kate. She quickly retreated a few steps. "Oh, sorry Aunt Kate; I don't want to be late for the game."

"I haven't seen him. Have you, Kate?" The entitlement of Kate's words had rattled Lacey. Caution around the woman would be required. And Reid needed to be warned.

Kate blatantly glared. "No." She whirled on her high-heeled boots, strutted into her office, and slammed the door.

"Is she mad?" Russell asked.

"I think she's busy. You look great in your uniform."

"It'd be better with Astros colors."

"Gold and white look good together. Should we check around back for your dad?"

"There he is. He's just pulled up to the porch in a Jeep. Come on." His free hand latched onto one of Lacey's and they dashed for the front door.

***

"Thanks for letting me drive the Jeep, Reid. I love it. It's so much fun."

"It suits you. A pretty woman in a tank top and shades, hair swirling in the breeze. Not to mention your smile. It creates the perfect picture. You're what's been missing in our family," Reid said.

"I think my other mom would've liked you a lot. You two would've been friends. I don't think she'd mind you being my mom now." Russell said from the backseat.

"I love you, honey."

Reid smiled, nodding in approval.

"There it is, Mom." Russell pointed to a wide turnoff. In the distance were several parking lots. There were also multiple fields, with kids in brightly colored uniforms playing games or warming up.

"This is exciting. I love baseball."

"You're not just saying it because, well, for some other reason, are you?" Russell asked.

"No," she reassured him. "I played softball when I was in middle school, high school, and college. Why would you ask me that?"

"Well, I think Aunt Kate only came to that one game of mine to impress Dad."

"Maybe she did, but I imagine she was proud of you anyway," Lacey offered. "And I'll bet she surprised herself by having fun." She tried to sound upbeat.

Russell opened the car door for his mother after they parked. "She never came to another game, even when I asked her to. I'm glad you're here."

"Thanks, honey. And I plan to attend as many of your games as I can. I loved playing when I was younger. Connie always said I didn't need a gun, that a bat would be plenty deadly in my hands. She used to pitch to me in college for practice until I hit a ball close enough that it had her refusing to go near a diamond again. The grassy kind, I mean. That was only if I was playing."

Lacey handed the keys to Reid, who was still laughing. "Was that close hit on purpose or an accident?"

"I was fairly good. So, it was on purpose, totally controlled," she paused. "Okay, mostly controlled. We'd just argued."

"Remind me never to argue with you. After I show you the bleachers, I'm going to get our snacks from the concession stand," Reid said. "Do you want anything in particular, or do you want me to surprise you?"

"I'm assuming baseball food is universal. That means you can surprise me with one of those giant soft pretzels and cheese dip if they have them. If not, you can surprise me with whatever you like."

Reid chuckled, pointing to the bleachers. "Sit anywhere. There's already a line at the concession stand, which means I'll be a while."

"Oh, Reid. I almost forgot. I wanted to thank you for my room. It's perfect." She threw her arms around his neck and kissed his cheek, something more appropriate with Russell and other kids around. Otherwise, it would've been on the lips.

Reid returned her kiss, his hands low on her hips, adding several squeezes. "Russ, you'd better get a move on."

"Okay, Dad. Come on, Mom. What position did you play?"

"Left field in middle school. They shifted me to third base in high school. I was decent at it. We never won a championship while I was there, but we came close one year. My parents loved coming to my games and cheering me on."

"That's all cool, Mom. You're cool."

"Thanks, Russell." Her son thought she was cool, an unexpected ego boost. He walked beside her, not abandoning her to charge ahead and join his friends. He even took her to the dugout first to introduce her to his coaches and teammates.

As the teams warmed up, Lacey found a seat as instructed and spread out to enjoy the warm sunshine, leaning back to prop her elbows on the bleacher seat behind her, her feet on the one ahead. She'd love to take more photos than the couple she'd snuck when the team had started warmups and drills, but she didn't want to embarrass Russell too much.

The view had become blocked by parents gathering around the dugout. Lacey responded by closing her eyes, enjoying the heat sprinkling her face, the result of dappled shade beneath a massive live oak. Vibrations came through the warm metal bleachers, but she assumed the person would sit somewhere else. Or ask her to move. There were plenty of places to sit.

"Hi, there."

Lacey glanced up into the face of a man whose dirty uniform indicated he'd just gotten off work. The pocket of his emerald polo shirt bore the name of a landscaping company. Cool blue eyes were warmed by his smile.

"Sorry, I'm taking up an excessive amount of real estate," she said.

"No problem. There won't be a crush for seats until the game starts. I've been on my feet all day and I'm ready for a break. Do you mind if I join you?"

He might've been intending to sit where she was leaning. Lots of people preferred to occupy the same seat game after game. "Help yourself. I'm saving one spot here for someone else." That was added in case the guy had any amorous ideas.

"Thanks." He settled in and extended his hand. "I'm David. My son is on the home team. I don't believe I've seen you around before."

Her lips spread wide. "My son is on the team, too. My name's Lacey."

"Lacey. Pretty name, like its owner. Which boy is yours?"

"Russell Collier, number three."

"I know Russell and his father. I didn't know Reid remarried. He sure did keep it quiet." He glanced down at her left hand with a frown.

"We're not married. Our story is complicated."

"Well, whatever it is, I'll be sure to congratulate Reid. I don't suppose you have a sister out there somewhere, do you?"

A giggle popped from her mouth. "No, I was an only child."

"That's a shame."

Over by the concession stand, Reid looked their way. It encouraged Lacey to sit up, abandoning the lounging. She didn't want to give Reid the impression she was flirting with David. He wasn't the man she was interested in at all.

***

"Are you cold, Mom?"

"A little chilly is all. I should've worn my jacket. These clothes are good for an afternoon baseball game, but not so useful after dark."

"Let's go sit by the fire. That'll warm you up. We can have s'mores with the guests."

"Sounds like a good idea." Her hands dug for deeper cover in the pockets of her shorts as they strolled, but it failed to prevent her teeth from chattering. "I should've gone to the house for my jeans."

The dry Texas air often had a chill at night. The current temperature was 71 but dropping with the lack of sunshine. And there was a breeze out of the west-northwest. She was sensitive to the cold, which meant anything below 75. And her clothing was skimpy.

"I'll go in and get your jacket in a minute, Mom."

"That'd be great." Then again, if she had the opportunity to cuddle up against Reid, it would make the chicken skin worthwhile. If he was able to spend time with her. The guests would need tending to. "I haven't had an authentic s'more in my whole life. Not like this, melted by a real fire outdoors and all."

"Hey, Dad! Guess what?" Russell hollered.

Reid was on his way to the fire. "Hey, there you two are. Have you recovered from the excitement of the baseball game, Lacey?"

Her face glowed at the mention of the game. "Yes. I'm surprised at how tired I am. It's almost like I was out there playing myself."

"I noticed you took photographs. I'd like to see what you've got sometime before you leave us. Unless we can manage to talk you into staying permanently this time."

"You can't. Not yet anyway."

"You know I intend to try my best." They stood gazing into each other's eyes, the tension building until it crackled, sizzling in the air.

"Dad."

"What is it, Russ?" Reid's eyes remained on Lacey's.

"Mom said she's never had a real s'more over a campfire before. This is going to be her first time."

"Well then, you're in for a treat. Come on, I'll get you a nice spot by the fire before it gets too crowded. I think about half the guests are still on their way back from the sunset trail ride. It'll give us plenty of time to make sure you're stuffed and happy." He placed a hand on her lower back, guiding her path to a location of his choosing.

Reid maintained close contact as he helped her select a sturdy roasting stick. He held it steady while she skewered a gigantic, plump marshmallow with it. He tested her nerves by standing behind her, his arms wrapping around to guide her in the toasting.

His cheek pressed to Lacey's as he nuzzled and whispered instructions. The proximity warmed, adding to that provided by the fire pit.

"You're doing a great job. There, that's good for you, a nice golden brown," Reid whispered in her ear, then nibbled at her lobe, sending her heart into a furious pounding. "You belong here with us, you know."

"I know. I'll get here one of these days." Her voice came out in a low hum.

Russell and Robert stood nearby. They smiled as they nudged each other, whispering.

"Russ, bring me a chunk of chocolate and a couple of graham crackers for your mom," Reid called, releasing her after applying a soft kiss to her cheek.

As soon as Russell arrived with the needed ingredients, he handed them to his father and moved off to pass out supplies among the guests approaching from the house.

Reid helped Lacey assemble her s'more. "There now, press it together. You'll need to let it cool for a minute; just keep holding it and don't let the hot marshmallow ooze over the edge and burn your fingers. I'll get mine toasted while you're waiting." He jabbed his marshmallow into the hungrier of the flames, catching it on fire before withdrawing it.

He chuckled at the mild alarm on her face. "It's okay, this is how I like mine. Watch." He blew on it until the flame died, then held it close for her to examine.

"The outside's burned. Won't it taste bad?" she asked.

"No, not at all. My dad taught me to do them this way when I was a kid, younger than Russell. I guess I got used to it. And it's more fun." He slid the marshmallow off, capturing it between the graham crackers and a slab of chocolate.

"Can I take a bite of mine now?"

"Yes. I just didn't want to risk you burning your lips or tongue on the marshmallow. I want to protect those luscious lips of yours for other things. The tongue, too." Reid watched with interest as Lacey took a bite. He leaned in to apply a slow-motion kiss to her lips and in the process licked his tongue over the corner of her mouth, where a little marshmallow remained. "What do you think?"

Using one hand to block his view of her mouth, she chewed a couple of times before answering, but a response wasn't easy. "The kiss was amazing, and the s'more is delicious. Probably crammed full of calories, isn't it?"

"Glad you liked them both. Don't worry about the calories." His eyes took their time sliding over her body, not missing a single detail. "You don't have anything to be concerned about in that regard. Your body is completely perfect. Another few pounds wouldn't hurt anything. It's fine to indulge yourself now and then. You're on vacation, after all." He stuffed in a mouthful.

"Reid, can I see you for a minute?" Gil called from the other side of the firepit.

Reid waved and nodded in response, his tongue stuffing the bite to one side of his mouth. "I'll be back honey. Why don't you have a seat on the knee wall? Save room for me." He kissed her cheek before turning away, immediately turning back. He stepped closer to lean in and press his lips to Lacey's, long and slow. The kiss was marshmallow and chocolate, mixed with raw heat. "We can pick up where we just left off when I get back." He strode off, still holding his s'more as he made his way around the guests.

"Can I sit here, Mom?"

Russ's arrival snapped her back to reality, away from daydreams of kissing Reid. "What? Oh. Sure, honey. I see you like your marshmallows just the way your dad likes his."

"And grandpa." He shifted his head to indicate Robert, in the midst of flaming his dessert and assisting a jovial cluster of guests who wanted theirs the same way. They were all laughing and having a wonderful time. "Here's your jacket, by the way; I didn't forget. How do you like your first real s'more?"

"Oh, it's great. Even better than I thought it would be. This was a good idea. And thanks for bringing me my jacket." Russell helped her slip into it, enabling her to keep hold of the remains of her s'more.

"You're welcome. We have s'mores at least once or twice a week when we have guests; sometimes more often. They love it."

"I'm sure they do. I liked the way your dad helped me make mine."

"Yeah. Grandpa and I noticed." He chuckled, attempting to stifle it.

Her head swiveled in his direction with one eyebrow raised. "And just what's that supposed to mean, young man?"

He knew her well enough to recognize surprise, not anger. He grinned. "I told you dad likes you."

"Do you think so?" On the other side, Reid talked with guests as Lacey's head filled with ideas, none of them PG rated.

SEVENTEEN

"Okay, time to go," Reid announced as he strode through the front door and onto the porch. "We're going for a drive. And it's a surprise, so don't even ask." He extended a hand.

Lacey had been sitting in a rocking chair on the front porch, waiting as instructed by Russell. He said a surprise was coming, that she had to be patient. Questions concerning the surprise went unanswered.

Gil pulled up in a battered olive Hummer with oversized tires and no doors. They hopped in the back. This vehicle was used in the backcountry, as affirmed by the sign on the back reading Collier Ranch Tours. There were loads of things to see and do here. She'd barely scratched the surface.

She recognized some areas, including a few trails. And the yearling calves she'd helped Reid and Russell round up when the animals had broken through a fence. They'd found the bovines wandering amongst a grove of trees.

Rounding them up had been fun and was something she looked forward to doing again sometime soon. But even then she'd been distracted, wondering if she needed a bulletproof vest at the ranch. Kate was out for blood.

They drove northwest along a dirt road, passing endless pastures with grazing cattle or horses, and a distant one with the recently acquired bison. They seemed to be adjusting well to the new digs.

The vehicle moved deeper into hillier terrain where vegetation became sparse, and fences fell away. Reid pointed out interesting landmarks or told her stories of events from his youth. Turning off the road, they followed a well-worn trail of tire tracks.

"There's a river not far from here," Reid said. "We've got less than ten miles of it on our land. I'd like to get more one of these days. We could add in some river tours, maybe get a boat. We'll be stopping short of it but within eyesight. I'll take you on a walk to get you a view."

"I'd like to see it up close someday." Since a San Antonio move was in the future, there'd be plenty of opportunities. Here and there, Mesquite gained footholds on outcroppings, between boulders, or wherever else the wind had blown their beanlike seeds. Texas sage and other hardy plants did likewise. "Are there fish?"

"Yes. Russell and I will have to take you fishing. There's a good fishing hole near where we'll be. A large stream feeds into the river from underground near that spot. I've protected the land around it, which gave the vegetation time to regrow. With the water shaded and now clean as a whistle, the native fish and wildlife are thriving.

"Cattle used to roam freely out there. They trampled everything, muddying the water, using it as their toilet if the mood struck them. Can't blame them since they didn't know any better.

"With the river and the area around it restored, we take guests out for fishing trips. Clean and cook up the catch on the spot, camping under the stars. It's a great experience. The guests gain a heightened appreciation for taking care of the environment. I like to think so, anyway."

"You're a good steward of the land, Reid. You should be proud of what you've done."

"I appreciate it, Lacey. I am proud of it. This was a long project. It took years and a lot of dedication and demanding work, not to mention convincing my dad of the rationale behind it. Eventually, I'll show you everything we've got to offer here." He placed a hand on Lacey's.

"That gives me something else to look forward to. Texas and this ranch are incredible. I've never been out West before I met Russell. I have to say I'm in love."

Reid raised an eyebrow as he studied her face. "I like hearing you say those words."

He raised her hand to his lips for a kiss. "The land around here has a way of getting to people. I'm glad you like being here. This evening, you and I need to have a serious conversation about your impending move to San Antonio. After we eat, we'll take a walk to watch the sunset and have that conversation.

"I can understand wanting to stay in Charlotte until you find something in your field. But the holiday season is rolling back around, which means before you know it, the anniversary of Russ flying to Charlotte on a trip that changed all our lives for the better will be here. I want you to know I'm determined to have you living here with us permanently by Thanksgiving." His jaw was set in stone, matching the breathtaking terrain around them. There were columns of rock, cliffs, and steep drop-offs.

"Sorry to interrupt folks, but we're here." Gil slowed the Hummer as they crested a hill. A Jeep was parked nearby. They rolled to a halt and Gil climbed out to offer his hand to Lacey as she slid from the seat.

"Thank you, Gil," she said with a smile.

"Yes ma'am." He gestured toward the backside of the gentle slope. "That's where we're headed. The path is safe enough, but if you even think you see or hear a snake, you just let me know."

Eyes following where Gil pointed, the surprise became evident. Halfway down on a level spot, three people were gathered on a red and white plaid cloth under a small cluster of trees with silvery leaves. In the center of the cloth sat a picnic basket and a spread of colorful plates and food. "Thanks, Gil. I appreciate that."

"Gil," Reid called in a low voice as Lacey moved ahead. "What is Kate doing here?"

"You said this was for the family and she told me that included her. Especially since you were generous enough to include me as a member. She asked me directly where you'd be eating. I didn't know there'd be a problem with telling her."

Lacey wasn't going to let Kate ruin this outing with her family. Her smile widened as Russell charged up the hill. "This was a pleasant surprise, Reid. Thank you," Lacey said as Reid came alongside them.

"It's nothing fancy, but it's good. It's Mrs. Gordon's fried chicken and buttermilk biscuits." His face was set in a scowl.

"She could work in a high-class restaurant. You're lucky to have her," Lacey noted as Russell joined them.

"She and my grandpa are kind of sweet on each other," Russell whispered, casting a glance toward his grandfather.

"Is that a secret?" Lacey asked.

"No," Russell said. "Everybody knows it."

"Except Mrs. Gordon and my dad," Reid chuckled.

"What're the guests doing for dinner, with your dad out here instead of at the grill?"

"I've brought in a few extra hands for this, and all the guests are having the same meal. The picnic baskets and blankets have been distributed at various locations, wherever there's a pretty spot with shade. Those on staff who are musically inclined roam around from one group to another, singing or playing an instrument. It's always been a popular event. Our older guests are eating in the dining room, then taking in a movie on the big screen. It's all covered. We're good for a few hours yet."

"Come on, Mom. It should be a pretty sunset tonight with the river and all the cool rock formations out here," Russell said, leading the way down to the spread.

***

They ate until they were stuffed. Russell left to pick wildflowers as a surprise, according to Kate, who'd sent him off on the mission.

236

Knowing his mom's favorite color, Kate had told him where he could find some little ones in deep pink. That all raised Lacey's suspicion.

Unfazed, Kate turned her back to Lacey and made herself the center of attention. Wearing a revealing red dress with a flared skirt, Kate kicked off her shoes and began performing the sexiest dance Lacey had ever witnessed. Robert strummed his guitar in accompaniment.

Gil's attentiveness was rooted in Kate, his face brightening by several orders of magnitude whenever she faced his way. Lacey had the feeling Kate didn't see the big picture. Instead, she was fixated on Reid to the exclusion of any other man. Maybe someone needed to point out Gil's interest. That someone shouldn't be Lacey Freemont.

The dance ended with rousing applause and whistles of appreciation. Then a second one began. Kate held the full interest of the men.

Reid had said he wanted to go for a walk to see the river, just the two of them. From where she stood with her hands fisted on her hips and her jaw clenched, it seemed that wasn't going to happen. Men. Reid could go for a walk by himself for all she cared now.

There was no solid reason for the mounting jealousy, except feeling ignored and inadequate. Outclassed in the realm of sexy dancing, for sure. And men seemed enamored with sexy dancing. If Reid wanted a woman who could dance, he didn't need to look at Lacey. Kate might come out on top after all.

Unable to stomach the display any longer, Lacey decided to find Russell instead, storming off in the direction Kate had said he'd taken. Picking wildflowers with her son would give her something else to think about. And Russell certainly didn't need to witness those dances.

A final glance over her shoulder before leaving the group's line of sight revealed a changed scene. Robert had ceased playing, looking her way. Reid waved her back. Kate tried giving Reid a spectacular view as she leaned down, reaching for his hand.

Lacey blew him off with an angry swipe of the air. If not for Robert being there, she would've thrown him the finger instead. Still might.

As soon as she was far enough away, she began calling for Russell. No response came, leaving her to wander a bit, cupping her hands around her mouth. Pausing to listen, her sense of trepidation crept in. He'd only been gone ten minutes at the most.

While stopped, she surveyed the area. It was quiet, making it easy to hear Reid calling, getting closer. She was in no mood to acknowledge him and had no interest in his presence, aside from gaining his assistance in locating their son.

That's when the faint call registered, crying out for help. With Russell's next call, Lacey's ears pinpointed the origin. Instinct told her to fly. She sprinted for the slope ahead, that instinct guiding her on a route preferred by a crow in flight.

The slope wasn't especially steep but taking that crow route had her going straight up, which was slow. Everywhere there was loose material underfoot, like walking on marbles, plenty ending up inside her shoes. Near the top, she scrambled on all fours for better traction. At the peak, she paused to catch her breath, her eyes scanning the terrain.

Almost as far as the eye could see there were boulders, rocky outcroppings with sheer cliffs. They came with meager scatterings of brush and scraggly, low growing trees. Not far away flowed the river Reid had spoken of, winding along until concealed by steep hills.

Deep shadows sliced the landscape with the lowering sun. The sunlight glared off slabs of rock. Here and there where soil sat in depressions among or within the rocks, tufts of stubborn wildflowers in brilliant yellow or white had taken root.

Along the edge of one of the outcroppings, Lacey spotted a pair of hands, fingers attempting the impossible, to dig into bare rock. A collection of carefully plucked wildflowers blew away on the breeze, one by one. Her heart surged into her throat.

"Russell!" Screaming his name, she dashed forward and leaped into the air over a sizeable gap to land hard and square on an outcropping below, the one her son clung to. Even as she shoved herself up and bolted forward at her best speed, Russell's hands slipped away. He was disappearing into unknown danger. And he had to be afraid.

There was no other thought besides saving her son. Close enough to taste it, she threw herself toward him in a slide reminiscent of those in her softball games. The surface was unforgiving to her ribcage compared to the red clay surface back home, which was hard enough.

This was so much worse. So was the damage. The chance had to be taken, the stakes incalculably higher on that boulder.

Lacey emitted a loud yell of pain as the impetus propelled her forward and fire shot through her chest. The momentum of her body was enough for her to clamp her hands over her son's like talons before he slipped completely out of reach. "Gotcha!"

The sense of triumph was short-lived, as the realization hit. The inexorable creep over the arch of rock hadn't stopped, just slowed. There was no way to prevent him from going over.

Gravity had him and she didn't possess the strength to fight it, especially considering the rib damage from the impact. She could release him and perhaps save herself from the dark void glimpsed well beyond his feet. But a life without him was unthinkable.

"Mom! Pull me up," he cried.

"I've got you. I've got you, baby."

The hope in his face flickered and died as the loss of hope in hers registered. "We're slipping!" The panic rose in his voice.

"It's okay, honey. We'll fall together and see where we end up." She fought to remain calm for his sake.

"Let go, Mom. You've gotta let me go."

"Never as long as I live." Pain seared with each breath.

The rock was a relatively smooth downward curve. It had little on the surface to afford Russell a grip. Nothing aside from the occasional effort by a ragged sapling tree, a shrub, or a scruffy clump of green sporting deep pink flowers to establish a feeble foothold.

A ledge caught her attention, perhaps twenty feet below her head. That meant, with a frantic calculation run in a split-second of terror, it was less than twelve feet under Russell's toes. He had a chance, a decent one. Perhaps the only one.

"Lacey! Hold on, I'm coming!" Reid yelled, choking on fright. He'd witnessed Lacey's impact, heard her cry out. As he ran, he realized his son must be over the side and Lacey was trying to save him.

The pair continued slipping toward a rendezvous with fate, and Reid wasn't there to help. It was all up to Lacey. "Russell, I'm letting go. Break up your slide with one of the plants growing between the rocks. Grab them, then catch the ledge under you." Her voice steadied for him. Steadied with the only hope she saw.

Russell glanced down as Lacey forced herself to release the grip. It came with the right hand first, serving to angle him to her left as he dangled above the precipice. It got him nearer the center mass of the ledge.

He was too heavy to hold any longer. She had to let him go. His fingers were already nearly out of hers, gravity too much to fight.

Russell slid more than dropped. On the way down, his hands grasped a young Mesquite, yelling when a thorn skewered the base of his thumb. He released it on reflex and dropped the rest of the way, ending up on his side on the ledge. Uninjured, except for the stab of the little tree that helped ease his fall. Could his mother do the same? The thorny plant had been sufficient to slow his descent.

A headfirst slide gave Lacey a glimpse of Russell's slow-motion fall, landing on the ledge in a heap. Frantic, she pressed her hands against the outcrop, but the slope was too steep and her position too unstable. Too late to stop.

Just as gravity took her, Reid's fingers brushed her ankle in vain, pulling off a shoe as she went over. In frustration, he yelled for his family. He could only watch as the woman he loved dropped away from him and the rescue he should've been able to provide. The scream she issued ripped his heart to shreds.

The Mesquite waited. Despite the risk of thorns, there was no choice. Lacey grabbed for it. And missed.

But just below and to the side of it grew a scruffy clump of Texas sage, sporting a few purple flowers. Lacey's fingers plunged into the little clump of stems and closed tightly on three small branches, capturing them in a fist.

The hearty shrub halted her forward progress for only a moment before the inexorable pull from below overcame. No way was she releasing those branches, wispy though they were. Lacey had a fleeting vision of her body flipping over from a combination of gravity and not letting go of the plant, resulting in a collision that would punch her back against the rock wall. Surely a fall would follow.

The sage might not be capable of supporting the maneuver she rapidly conjured up, but no alternative sprang to mind. She wriggled her feet, one in a sock, the other in a shoe, against the rock, her hips lending assistance. Like a sideways-moving inchworm, she maneuvered to one side, managing a couple of feet before gravity performed a rapid reversal of her orientation.

This was a fall rather than a slide. Lacey prayed in that heartbeat for the scrappy shrub to hold through the weight and the pendulum that her body became. She swung left, then right, and back to the left. Using her free hand to alternately push and pull her body on the cliff face, her movement stopped.

Bits of dirt, leaves and small blossoms trickled down into her hair. Lacey knew what was happening, how little time she had. She allowed herself a single whimper.

"Mom! Drop and I'll catch you!"

A glance below showed her son, closer to the side of the ledge than his mother would prefer, arms stretching upward.

The decision to let go came simultaneously with the surrender of the shrub, eliciting another scream. Arms tightened around her as Russell grunted. Both of them went down, Russell absorbing most of the blow. On her side, Lacey looked down past the perimeter of the ledge and pushed back in fright, getting herself to safer territory as Russell scrambled up to assist.

In moments, she sat breathing heavily, her back against the rock wall. This wasn't solid ground, but it was close enough. Her ribs were broken or badly bruised, considering the pain in breathing. She lifted her left hand and conjured up a weak smile for Russell. The shrub was still clutched, dropping bits of soil from its roots.

"Lacey! Good God. Are you all right down there?" Reid called. Russell was moving around. Lacey wasn't. Not as far as he could tell, not after that frantic push away from the edge.

"My ribs." She braced them with pressure from one hand. "Tell him I'm hurt."

"Dad, she's hurt. Pretty bad, I think. She slammed into the rock up there hard when she tried to save me."

"We'll get her to a hospital. Hang on, you two. I'll be right back," Reid called.

Lacey closed her eyes to focus on shallow breaths that generated less pain. Russell sat quietly, worrying.

Less than ten minutes later, Reid called down. "We're getting both of you out at the same time. Russell. Here comes the rope. Wait for it."

The rope dropped inches from Russell's left shoulder, a few feet of it pooling onto the flat shelf of rock near the edge, a knot at its end. Russell grabbed it and looked at his mother. "Do you want me to help you stand?"

"No, Russell. Climb. You get out first. Then it'll be my turn." She looked up into his eyes.

"Russell, you keep that grip tight once you get on the rope. Lacey, get on. The winch is plenty strong enough to pull both of you up together. I'm not leaving you down there. I'll climb down to get you if you can't make it your own."

"Tell him no. I can do it." She didn't want to risk having Reid climb down.

Russell relayed the message before helping his mother stand.

Lacey grasped the shrub in each hand and pulled in opposite directions. One diminutive branch tore loose from the rest, sporting a hunk of roots. The resulting pain made her wish she'd asked Russell to do it for her. She passed the thin branch to Russell. "Put this in a pocket and get it to the top for me. I'm planting it outside the window of my room at the ranch."

He smiled and nodded as he accepted the responsibility, tucking the piece into what he hoped was a safe spot.

They each established a grip on the rope, Russell instructing his mother on how to hold securely. He climbed up the rope several feet to be above his mother and give her room. Russell called for the pull to begin. Reid passed the word to Robert, who cupped his hands and bellowed across the distance for Gil to start the winch.

A strong tug came through the rope, followed by a slow, steady pull toward the top and salvation, lifting them inch by precious inch. In a minute or two, they'd be safe.

"You okay?" Russell asked.

"Just focus on your hold, honey. Don't worry about me. I'll make it." Her legs and feet were clenched together, holding tight.

A chilling sound echoed as a sickening jolt tore through the rope. Lacey's hands lost a few precious inches, the rope slipping through her fingers before regaining hold.

"Hang on you two. Lacey, you all right down there?" Reid called.

Russell relayed the message of her security, wondering what might have gone wrong. Their upward movement had stopped. They hung waiting, mostly in silence. And worry. Russell hoped his mother could maintain her hold.

A moment later came Reid's call. "Russell, climb up to me. Then we'll pull Lacey up together. The winch is malfunctioning, and Gil can't get it moving again. Grandpa is holding me so I won't slip."

"Go, Russell," Lacey insisted. Reid's body spread over the curve of the rock. Russell had less than three feet to go.

Russell nodded, then made his way up, hand-over-hand with

relative ease. The rope jiggled in Lacey's hands as he went. She'd been less concerned about her safety when trapped in the bathroom with the rattlesnake.

Then the tremor in the rope repeated, multiple times in succession. This was something different, not caused by Russell's movements. Lacey's grip was firmer this time, the jolts not as substantial as the initial one, but still unnerving. A loud pop reverberated, followed by a lull, lengthy enough for several causes of trouble to blaze through her mind.

"Russ, climb faster! Get up here. Now!" Reid ordered, his voice deep, his words rushed.

Russell worked his way up to cover the remaining distance. Lacey wondered if she should be doing the same. Fearing it would be more difficult for Russell, she waited for instructions. A sense of self-preservation fought her mother's instinct tooth and nail.

"Keep a good hold on my legs, Dad," Reid called. "Okay, Russ. Reach up to me and I'll take your hand."

Reid lay prone, reaching toward Russell. The consequences should Robert's hold on Reid falter might prove fatal.

"That's it, son. Come on, just a little more," Reid encouraged. "Lacey, we'll get you next. Grab my hand, Russell! There!"

The proclamation filled Lacey's heart with relief. She glanced up to see both of Russell's hands grasping one of Reid's. Reid braced himself and Russell on the sloping edge with his free hand.

That's when everything changed. Another loud pop, like a small explosion, accompanied a distant scream. The detonation came with a horrifying sensation. There was no longer any security in the rope Lacey clutched. It had gone limp in her fingers, like in an old-time kids' cartoon.

As her impending demise registered and the sensation of falling hit, the rope firmed with a massive yank. The sudden change in tension dislodged her. She slipped a foot before reestablishing her grip, the rope strands burning through the uppermost layer of skin on her hands.

A whipping noise from above warned of the rope, freed and slithering through the air, arching toward her. The analogy of the rattlesnake came into her mind for a fleeting instant. The other end of the rope passed her by, then dangled alongside.

A glance down at the two ends of rope had her mystified. She looked up to see what had happened, how the laws of physics had been overcome, how it was that she was still here. Instead of dead at the bottom of the precipice.

The scene amazed her. She was alive thanks to her guardian angel, Reid Collier. He held Russell's dangling body with one hand, Lacey clinging to the rope in his other. The strain on Reid's body became readily apparent.

"Mom!" Russell glanced down; wide-eyed.

"Russell," Reid called through gritted teeth. "I can't pull you and your mom up at the same time. You've got to find a way to climb over me. Dad, can you pull me back?"

"I'll try, but I'm afraid I'll lose all three of you!"

"Call for help then. Yell for Gil or Kate."

Robert called, thundering the command at the top of his lungs, his voice echoing. No response came. "Something must've happened up there. No one's coming. Let me try pulling again, but I can't risk losing my grip on you, son!"

Seconds ticked by with no change, and still no help from anyone else. Reid's arms shuddered, his face reddening, eyes closed tight. Russell's attempt to climb his father's arm wasn't working. The sleeve of Reid's shirt gave an audible ripping sound at the shoulder. Russell stopped.

Not just stopped. Russell had begun to slip from Reid's hand, loosened by sweat and strain. They were at an impasse that couldn't hold. Robert couldn't let go of Reid, nor could he pull everyone up in their human chain by himself. Reid couldn't continue to support both Russell and Lacey.

The rope slipped, just a fraction. Then another, and another. Even as Reid's fingers dug in. He refused to give up, to acknowledge the pull of fate. He couldn't lose either of them. But the battle was being lost on both sides.

There were only seconds remaining before Russell slid from Reid's hand. Not enough time for Lacey to climb to the end of the rope and let go, to drop a few feet. The angle didn't look any better than on her first trip over, either. Possibly another jump for the ledge would work a second time around. There might be a chance.

Regardless, the decision had to be made, and fast. It was simply what must be done, the only way she could fathom to save her son. Reid could never choose for himself. It would be too much to ask, something he might never fully recover from, mentally or emotionally.

This was a worthy sacrifice, not suicide. She'd do anything for this boy who'd been in her life and heart less than a year. He was more important to her than her own life. He was her life. She'd never risk his.

"I love you, Russell!"

They stared down at her.

"Reid." Her voice wobbled as she tried to keep it steady, tears choking her. "You save him. Remember Russell, if this doesn't work out, I'll always be with you."

The realization hit Reid hard. "Lacey, no! Don't!"

As her gaze met Russell's, Lacey did the hardest thing she'd ever done, fighting every instinct in her.

She released the rope.

EIGHTEEN

"Mom!" The long, bloodcurdling scream bounced off the rocky walls.

Lacey scarcely heard anything above her own cry, the blurred faces above her of little consequence as she fell to her death.

The impact of her feet on the ledge she'd just gotten off of was unanticipated, more than she'd hoped for. But it jarred her from soles to skull, as her back and head followed. The distance hadn't been nearly as far as it was for Russell when she'd dropped him minutes before, but he'd landed much better.

Lacey lay on the ledge, unmoving and dazed, watching as thousands of tiny, brilliant white stars swarmed in to saturate the black void filling her vision. They moved when she tried staring at them, like they were alive, swimming in darkness. How odd. What could they be?

A trickle of warm, thick liquid with a metallic taste made its way between her lips by the right corner. It tickled her face as it followed gravity. Blood. Trickling along her cheek.

Whether it was from a bitten tongue or cheek, it was the least of her problems. Vague recollections of the past minutes seeped into the flow of imaginings, pushing at the stars. Trying to gain attention and figure this out before it was too late.

"Hurry!" Reid's frantic voice echoed. There was a pause, then he spoke again. "Find a place to tie off the other end of this or else just wrap it around you and hold it, you and Russell.

"Lacey, can you hear me? I'm coming down there to get you. Just hang on," Reid said.

"Mom, can you hear us?"

Russell. That was Russell. It wouldn't be wise to move; not yet. There might be some broken bones, like maybe the skull. Most likely a concussion. Her second. The first one came from a girl on the Little League team who hit her in the head with a bat over a boy Lacey never even noticed.

The spinning in her head eased, the stars clearing, as when a new day dawned. Her eyes opened a crack to see an overall feeble illumination. She groaned through the pain of moving a leg, just a bit. It didn't feel broken, but the subtle movement sent a cascade of pain through her body. The hope was that being able to move her leg also meant her back wasn't injured. The pain brought a flood of dizziness.

"She moved, Dad! I saw her move. I saw her."

"Are you sure? I don't see her moving. Lacey honey, can you hear me? Whatever you do, don't move. Stay still."

Reid didn't realize how much his voice echoed down here. He must be cupping his hands around his mouth to make it project better. It reverberated inside her skull. She wished he'd stop.

"Dad, hurry. She's going to fall. You've gotta save her."

"Lacey, I'm coming for you. Don't move." Reid's voice was steady and confident.

Clearing darkness in her head revealed rock and shadow. Shouldn't there be sky from overhead? It took a minute for the facts to register. The view came from her skewed orientation.

Most of her body rested on the ledge, but not all. Her head hung past it, along with her shoulder and an arm, stretching out into the air, over the chasm. One leg laid securely atop the ledge, the other along the very edge of the rock. If she tipped to the side, the fulcrum would be gone. Essentially half on, half off. Situations didn't come much more precarious than this one.

Wisps of hair laid across her sweaty, dirt-streaked face, some stuck to her skin, the ends of them waving in the breeze of her breaths. Her eyes closed, surrendering to the pain and swirls in her vision that came when she tried to move.

In her dream state, Reid rappelled down to rescue her. She'd be taken home and get to see Russell again. She wouldn't die on a slab of rock, all alone.

Reid moved her body fully onto the ledge and pressed at the side of her neck, searching for a pulse. His head lay against her chest.

"You're breathing. Thank you, God. Thank you so much. Lacey?" His voice quivered, unsteady. "Sweetheart, please...wake up for me. Can you hear me? Lacey?"

It wasn't a dream. He was here. She opened her eyes, blinking, her voice a whisper. "Reid?"

"I've got to get you to the top, and then we'll drive you to the hospital. Just hang on. I'll be as gentle with you as I can." He lifted her up and over his shoulder. "Stay still now. I'll have you out of here before you know it."

***

"So, what happened?" Lacey asked. She'd been alert for some time. She couldn't stop the memory replaying in a loop through her pain-filled head, of Russell crying over her on the way to the Jeep, hysterically asking Reid if his mother was dead.

After the men changed a flat tire, apparently punctured by a chunk of metal from the winch, Robert drove them to the hospital. Lacey sat in the back seat, wedged between Reid and Russell, her head on Reid's shoulder. Each of them held one of her hands. And talked the whole way there, making sure she responded and stayed awake. Whenever her words slurred, they made her wake up. Russell's pleas kept her fighting.

Sleep was still desirable, but less so now, despite the pain medication. Too much had been going on. Now, they waited for the doctor to return from examining the x-rays.

Reid refused to leave the room even when Lacey's anger flared, and she told him to go. He informed the nurse they'd have to call security to make him leave, and they'd better have more than one guy to handle it. That threat had caused Lacey to rethink and relent.

There was a temporary truce. Reid assisted with removing her clothes and getting her into the hospital gown, then into a wheelchair to be taken for x-rays, and back to the room, under the covers. Moving around, however insignificant the effort, resulted in searing pain almost everywhere. She needed Reid's help and wasn't happy about it.

He sighed, sitting on the edge of the bed, first rubbing her shoulder, then smoothing her hair. He couldn't seem to stop touching her, somewhere, anywhere, simply to maintain the physical contact. A part of her was glad for that. She wanted the reassurance of being here, alive and loved.

"The winch must've malfunctioned, blown itself apart. There were a few pieces strewn around on the ground, one embedded in a tire. We had to change it before we could get you to the hospital. There was no cell signal, no way to call for help.

"Kate and Gil were long gone in the Hummer by the time we got you to the top of the hill. I found them here at the hospital a while ago. Gil was having a CAT scan on his head. Kate drove him here. Gil was trying to get the winch working again when it snapped loose. Some of it hit Gil in the head, knocking him out. The rope tore free and went flying over the cliff."

"And you grabbed the rope to save me."

"Yes." He reached out and took her bandaged hand, squeezing it just enough for her to feel it. He'd been holding her hand a lot. So close to death. His son and his future wife. He'd nearly lost everything today, the day he'd planned on proposing to Lacey.

"I still can't believe you were able to do what you did. I'd probably be dead if not for you."

"And Russell would be dead if not for you." He kissed her

forehead. He'd been kissing her a lot, too.

"Kate said she was reacting on instinct. She dragged Gil into the Hummer and drove off to get him to the hospital. She wasn't thinking straight after seeing all the blood from the gash on Gil's head. Those two have developed a friendship over the past few years."

"How nice for them."

"Lacey, I know we came close to losing you today. I know how terrified I was, how helpless I felt. Russell lost it. And I left him there with my dad and didn't give it a second thought.

"All I could think of was getting down to you on that ledge before you tipped over it. Anyway, the point is that I don't want you to take anything out on Kate. She was trying to save Gil's life. I know how she felt."

"Do you believe what you just said? You can't see past the past, Reid. Russell almost died out there. I almost died. Kate knew the situation she was leaving us in. She left us. She left us to die; Russell and me."

"Lacey, you've got to try to see this from my perspective." He rested a hand on her shoulder.

"Why? You don't care to attempt to see it from mine. I know what's going on. From an outsider's view, from a target's view, I see it." Escalating volume brought pain to her head.

"A target? Lacey, you can't think that. They were simple coincidences, nothing but." Kate couldn't have been responsible for what happened today. Impossible. And she isn't evil. Couldn't be. She was Karen's sister. Family.

"Not simple. Two of them almost cost me my life; or did you forget about that part of it? Why do I need to keep risking myself? She might succeed next time."

"There's no proof Kate was involved in any of this." Rational thinking was required here, but Lacey couldn't see that yet. Everything else was just a coincidence. Right?

"I have proof of some of it, strong suspicion for the rest. You just don't want to listen. It's what lets me know where I stand with you, Reid." Lacey wriggled aside until she dislodged his hand from her shoulder.

"Sweetheart..."

"Don't you call me that. I'm not your sweetheart and I never will be. The only name you'll ever use with me is Lacey."

"Sweetheart," he emphasized the word as he took one of her hands between both of his and held on tight. "Kate may be jealous of you, but it's nothing more. You can't blame her. She's spent the last ten years of her life taking care of Russell and me. And the ranch. She feels redundant."

"You're wrong. I *can* blame her," Lacey snarled. She's the one who sent Russell to pick wildflowers. Told him to look at the boulders and crevices in between, especially near the edges. Ask him.

"I should've told you this before, but one time I was successful at getting through on the ranch phone, right before Christmas. Kate threatened me, warned me to stay away, especially from you. I'll bet she never told you about that, did she?"

It was high time to unload. If he still didn't believe her after this, they'd be finished. He was either too nice or oblivious. Whichever it was, it had contributed to the near deaths of her and Russell. A man with a heart of gold wasn't worth dying over. It would crush her to leave him, but she'd do it. There was a backup plan she'd use if necessary.

"No. She never said anything about it. You got through? And she never told us." Reid's eyes grew wide as he stood. This couldn't be.

"When Connie finally reached the ranch to tell you what happened on Mother's Day weekend, Becky said the phone at the registration desk had been unplugged and arranged to where it wouldn't be noticeable. Just like the phone at my workplace, the room I was trapped in. I'm not saying Charlotte was her. I'm saying she hired someone."

"Russell said you leave your phone with her during the day to keep an eye out for messages because you're worried you might drop or damage the phone with the work you're doing. Perfect opportunity for her to delete voice messages and texts from me. She was hoping I'd give up and go away.

"Then she'd be there to comfort you, and to some extent Russell, over being rejected by me. The only other person who could have deleted those messages is you." Lacey paused, watching the puzzle pieces fall into place for him.

"I never saw any messages or phone calls from you Lacey. I would never have done that to you or Russell."

"Then think of the alternative. I have the proof I made them and proof they went through to the right number. You're not unintelligent, just naïve when it comes to Kate for some reason. And that's probably not all she did.

"Since no one uses Kate's computer except her, she would've been the one who altered the ranch's website to change the anniversary date. Or she paid someone else to do it. Something like that can't happen on its own. It's impossible."

Reid touched her arm. "Kate doesn't do any programming or changes. Not like that. She manages the contract with the company handling the website. They do what she tells them."

"Friends of mine in Charlotte can get evidence strong enough to stand up in a court of law through an examination of the hard drive. Kate, or someone she hired, purposefully stacked it so there'd be too many guests for the Fourth of July. She's the one who came up with the idea of me staying in the barn. That's what you said."

Reid's expression hardened. "Yes. She came to me with the idea. Made it sound appealing. You're implying she's responsible for the rattlesnake?"

"I'm not implying, I'm saying. The contractor you brought in to investigate said there was no way for a snake, especially one that size, to get inside on its own. To get inside the way it did, the contractor said the snake would've had to use a key."

"I can't imagine it. She couldn't handle a rattlesnake." He

hesitated as the wheels began turning, "She would've had to hire someone. But she's my sister-in-law."

"Your wife passed away a long time ago, yet you've kept Kate around all this time. You need to do some serious thinking about your life, Reid. Just go ahead and marry Kate if she's who you want, for God's sake. Do it and save my life again."

Reid frowned. "I don't have any feelings for Kate. I just can't see her carrying things this far, that's all. There's got to be something else here, something we're missing. What you've told me makes sense. It fits. She's interfered with my family, and I intend to get answers from her about it.

"But I can't imagine the rest of it. You can't blame her for your slashed tires, or the man who locked you in that room in Charlotte. She was at work, both times. Maybe it's someone from your past."

"How do you know it wasn't her? I never had trouble like that before I met you. They also got Connie's tires, not just mine, remember? They could've been trying to prevent me from making my flight.

"Maybe she hired someone for the things that happened in Charlotte. It would've been someone who wasn't smart enough to think I might resort to a taxi or hire a driver if it had come down to that. There're other ways to get to the airport.

"And she didn't think I'd made it to San Antonio, so she showed up to keep you company at Fiesta in my place. She was surprised to see me there. Remember?" Come on, Reid. See her for what she is. She's dangerous. Figure it out.

Reid rubbed at his chin, one hand on his hip as he stared at the wall. He did remember. It had been strange that she came, especially after explicitly being told not to.

"Never mind, Reid. Just forget it. At this point, I don't care what you think anymore. I'm tired of listening to you defend her. She could pull out a knife and stab me in the heart in front of you and I swear I'd die hearing you say she didn't do it." Nothing had gotten through to him. Or Kate was more important.

"Now you're being ridiculous."

"Am I? You can't see straight when it comes to her. Strange how everyone else can."

"What do you mean? Who do you mean by everyone?" He leaned on the bed's edge.

Lacey's temper rose. "Why don't you have the winch examined by a professional? See what really happened to it."

"Can't do it. Kate was in such a tizzy over Gil that she left the keys in the Hummer with the engine running. Someone stole it." He straightened.

"Wow. Convenient," Lacey said.

Reid's brow furrowed as his eyes narrowed. "What do you mean by that? She can't help how she feels."

"All this adds up to you caring so much for Kate that it overwhelms whatever good business sense you have. It's going to lead to ruin one day. You'll deserve it, but your father and Russell won't.

"She wants your ranch and says it belongs more to her than it did to her sister. She told me that herself. So, it's not just about wanting you. She thinks she deserves the ranch for all the time and work she's put in. If you continue to reject her advances, you'd better watch your back. I hope she's not in your will."

A knock came at the door.

"Come in," Lacey called, grateful for the presence of someone else in the room, an interruption in the pointless arguing that only made her breathe harder and her ribs hurt more. The doctor entered.

"Ms. Freemont, you'll be glad to know you have no major bone breaks. It shocks me, considering the nasty falls you endured. You've got a concussion and some bruising of the muscles over your ribs. Two of your ribs have suffered short hairline fractures. Healing will be long and painful, but it'll come. You won't need a cast, so we'll give you a brace to help."

"I'm relieved nothing's seriously broken, Tom. This could've been so much worse." Reid shook the doctor's hand. "Does this mean I can take her home now?"

"Sure. I understand the patient has already refused to stay overnight for observation." He faced Lacey.

"You're going to need time off from work to rest. Full recuperation in your case will be eight weeks, hopefully no more than that. The concussion you suffered will also take time to recover from. Knowing Reid as well as I do, I'll accept you being under his watchful eye instead of being in the hospital. If your tests hadn't come back as well as they did, I'd have you remain here until tomorrow," Tom said.

"Reid, I'd appreciate it if you'd leave now. I need to get dressed."

"You're not steady on your feet yet. I don't like the idea of leaving you alone. Besides, I helped undress you earlier, remember? Let me help you get everything back on."

"I don't need you." It hurt to be hard on the man who got her off that ledge. Not to mention saving Russell's life. His incomprehensible affinity for a spiteful woman kept putting Lacey, and now Russell, in danger.

Something had to change. The time had come to end the budding relationship with Reid. It would prolong her own life if nothing else. They'd need to work out a custody arrangement.

"I'll be outside the door if you change your mind," he said, casting his eyes to the floor. He left the room, dejected. He'd brought it all on himself, defending Kate the way he'd been doing for months now.

The doctor stepped out with him, the two men talking as Lacey changed into her clothes. The door was open enough to allow sounds in the hallway to pass through. Reid had left it ajar, most likely to listen for any call for help. Reid cared, but it wasn't enough anymore.

Tom was a loud talker. "Cute girl, but she needs rest worse than she thinks she does. Recovery will also be more painful than she likely believes. If she's staying with you, she'll have help. Does she belong to you?"

Lacey froze in the middle of buttoning her jeans. Belong? Never. Belonging would mean a different kind of connection, something deeper, truer. Belief would be part of that, and he didn't believe her.

"Yes, she does. At least, I'm hoping she does. If she doesn't, I'm going to do whatever it takes to make that happen."

"What about Kate? You two aren't together?"

"Why do people think the two of us are together? We never have been and never will be. I have no interest in her whatsoever. She works for me, that's all. And that'll be ending tomorrow. The cute girl in there? She's a computer whiz and everyone at the ranch loves her.

"I've had guests ask if she's my wife, or if she'll be staying on permanently. Those are the next items on my to-do list. I'm not letting her get away from me."

Lacey's stomach turned a somersault. Did she still care what Reid said? Emotions warred with logic. She sat to put on shoes before remembering one of them was somewhere back at the top of the precipice. A single shoe wasn't helpful. That meant wearing the ever-stylish hospital socks with the grips on them.

"Be sure to let me know when I can officially congratulate both of you. How does Russell feel about her? I mean, I know she just went over a cliff for him, but..."

"He loves her. She's his mom."

"I'm to hear they're close."

"No. It's a long story, but Lacey is Russell's biological mother."

"Now that's something you don't hear every day. She's his mother. It explains a lot, including the similarity in their appearances. And why she willingly fell into a canyon with him. You're going to have to give me a night at your B&B. It'll give me the chance to hear the story and give Kate a shoulder to cry on."

"Watch yourself. You're a grown man, which means what you do is your decision, but you remember how she was with Karen. They never got along and rarely saw each other. Kate took over Karen's job and only spent a few minutes a day with her sister. And then there was how little attention Kate paid to Russ when he needed it most; he was so young. She broke his heart into pieces and tossed them away. I can never forgive her for that."

"She was focused on you back then."

"Even while her sister was dying. It made me so uncomfortable I finally had to speak to her about it. I figured she'd given up by now because she backed off then, but I was wrong. I've got some serious thinking to do and blinders to remove where Kate's concerned."

Now Lacey didn't know what to think. He'd listened? Then why did he continue defending Kate?

"Tell you what, I'll swing by after work tonight. Spend the weekend, get me one of your dad's legendary steaks. Considering how much you say that young lady means to you, it'd be best if I were close by, just in case. I'll bring my doctor's bag and see if I can teach Russell how to use some of the instruments."

"You've got yourself a deal. Having you nearby will give me a higher comfort level taking Lacey out of here sooner than she probably should go. Plus, it'll earn you leftover fried chicken tonight."

"And a biscuit. Don't forget the biscuit. Count me in. I'll be about an hour behind you. Be sure to tell Robert to prepare for an extra steak for tomorrow."

"Count on it. I'll give you the room across the hall from mine. It'll put you closer. We just redecorated."

"Sounds good. I'll see you later then." Footsteps clipped down the shiny hallway beyond.

How dare he give away her room? Lacey stood to pull on her ripped, stained tank top but yelped when a fiery jolt of pain stabbed her. Her teeth gritted and her eyes closed tight against the tears as Reid rushed over.

"Hang on a second, Lacey. Let me help you." He assisted her the rest of the way, sucking in a sharp breath as Lacey grimaced. Reid lowered the tank top, tugging it down gently. "Do you want it tucked in?"

The pain hit hard enough to make her feel faint, so she leaned forward to rest her head and hands on his chest. "No," she whimpered.

"Do you need to sit down for a minute?"

"Yes. The chair, not the bed." He eased her into the chair she'd been sitting in.

"Do I need to get Tom back in here?" He crouched in front of her, his hands on her thighs and his eyebrows raised. She should remain in the hospital overnight. It was safer here, even with Tom coming to stay at the ranch.

"No. I'll be okay. I'd like some water, please." She stared at the floor. The desire to ask him to hold her rose strong, but she fought it down.

"All right hold on. I'll get it for you. The nurse brought you a cup." He retrieved it from the nearby counter. "It's got some special ice. I think she called it barrel ice, whatever that means. She said everybody loves it." He handed it to her and hovered as she lifted it to her lips.

"Thanks." She handed it back after a long drink.

"How's the ice?"

"Cold."

"Funny girl." He chuckled. And she did have a good sense of humor, even when feeling lousy. The urge to propose came over him strongly, but the timing was off. "When we get home, you're going straight to bed. You're spending the next couple of nights in my bed. I need to keep an eye on you."

"I could stay in my bed if you hadn't given it away to your doctor friend." Lacey stood, wobbling until Reid braced her. He continued to provide her with stability, no matter what happened.

"Your unsteadiness is confirmation. If it'll help, you can consider yourself kidnapped to my bed."

"Kidnapping's illegal."

"Do you think that makes any difference to me?"

She stared up into those brown eyes, filled with resolve, and rubbed her hands over his chest. "No."

He pressed his lips, warm and tender, against her own. A simple kiss, filled with meaning. "You sit back down and wait here while I find a wheelchair and then we'll go home."

***

Russell slept soundly in Reid's big bed next to his mother, despite the lights and television being on. She sat propped up with pillows, trying to focus on the local news; anything to distract her from thinking about what happened. The door swung open to admit Reid, carrying a tray with three large mugs of hot chocolate.

He closed the door, grinning at the steady rise and fall of Russell's chest. Placing the tray on the dresser, Reid extinguished the main light in the room and brought two mugs over with him. He sat beside her, handing over a drink.

"Would you like me to hold it for you?" he whispered.

"No thanks. I can do it." The mug wasn't easy to lift with all the tired, sore muscles involved. After blowing across the surface a few times, she took a small sip and ended up with mostly melted marshmallows, but it was tasty and added to the sense of being home.

"If it's too hot, I can set it on the nightstand for you."

"It's fine. While I appreciate the drink, I'm ready for sleep. You know you could've given the doctor a regular guestroom. You should be beside Russell."

"If he wakes up, he'll be worried about you and then he'll want to check on you. This will make it easier for all of us. Selfishly, I wouldn't be able to get any sleep unless I was with you both. And I'll be beside you to render aid during the night if you need help with the pain or have bad dreams.

"The unofficial family doctor has your room for the next couple of nights. That way, we'll all be more comfortable. Speaking of which, I'll help you lie back when you're ready."

"Reid, I'm sorry I was hard on you in the hospital."

"I had it coming. I haven't taken the time to put two and two together. I've been preoccupied wondering if you felt the same way about me that I did about you. I guess it means I was obsessed and thinking like a teenager when I should've been paying attention to what was going on around me."

"I suppose I can understand. It must be hard to believe someone you've known for years and trusted could turn out to be such an awful person." Lacey took a long drink before passing the hot chocolate to him.

He placed their mugs on coasters atop the nightstand, slid over to her, and put an arm around her shoulders. She settled into him and fell fast asleep.

***

Rolling over in bed wasn't supposed to hurt, but this time it did, everywhere.

Reid stroked her hair while making soft shushing sounds. "It's okay, baby." He kissed her forehead.

Bleary eyes opened to a smiling face. It was nice waking up next to Reid. That would be an easy thing to get used to.

"Good morning," he whispered. A faint, bluish light filtered around the edges of the curtains. "It's early yet. Why don't you try to get some more sleep? Russell's still out."

"Okay," she mumbled, snuggling up against his chest as he wrapped his arms around her, his chin on top of her head.

"God, I love you, Lacey," Reid said.

"I love you, too." Her whisper fought its way out against sleep.

He eased back from her. "What did you say?"

Still half asleep, Lacey repeated herself. "I said I love you." Then the significance of saying those words out loud, to Reid, came to her. Her eyes fluttered open. She shouldn't have taken more medicine earlier. "Reid."

"Nope. You said it. There's no way I'm letting you take it back, or blame it on the medication, even if it's true. You're stuck with me now."

He pressed his lips to Lacey's, light and soft. "You're my dream come true. I love you with everything in me. You're going to have to go ahead and quit your job now. I won't have you in Charlotte without me. You belong here with us. I suspect you already know that, though."

"I do." Despite the importance of the events unfolding, her eyes closed.

He smiled. "Since you're under the influence right now, I'll hold off on asking you the question associated with those two special words you just used. We'll get around to it later. For now, go back to sleep. I'll be right here when you wake up."

NINETEEN

Everything was stiff and sore. Showering presented a challenge, as did dressing. Reid had assisted her in getting into the bathroom and started the shower running before he left.

He informed her Tom had gotten in late, but the doctor would check in on her after breakfast. Then Reid left, saying he had something to handle, and he'd bring her breakfast in bed later. The shower made her feel worlds better.

But she didn't want to wait. The possibility of seeing Kate was unappealing, but she needed to move around. Plus, her stomach refused to stop growling.

Most of the guests were finished with breakfast and busy with preparations for a daylong cattle drive. That, combined with the wall clock reading well past eight, explained why no one was at the dining table.

"Lacey. I figured Reid would bring you breakfast in bed," Robert said as she shuffled into his open arms. "How're you feeling this morning?"

"Russell and I are alive. Doesn't leave much to complain about. Reid left while I was in the shower. He was planning on bringing breakfast later, but I wanted to come in here and get some normalcy back and move around some. Russell's coming in after his shower. Shouldn't be long."

Robert patted her shoulders. "My son couldn't have picked a

better woman to fall in love with."

Her eyebrows rose. "He told you about that?"

"He did. It's nothing I haven't been aware of since the first time you came for a visit."

"The first time?" Did he mean Reid had feelings for her even then?

"Yes." Robert chuckled. "My boy couldn't stop talking about you after you left us; made all kinds of plans. He's had it bad for you for a long time now. I haven't seen him like this since he met Karen all those years ago; maybe not even then. It's a good thing and about time."

The revelation brought a smile. "Where is he? He's not leading the cattle drive, is he?"

"No. He's staying home with you and Russell. I've got to get going because I'm taking his place out there. I love those things, even these short trips. We'll get you involved in the big one in the spring."

"Sounds good."

Robert walked away, then paused. "Reid was headed for the office last time I saw him. You might want to hang back, give Kate some room for the tantrum she's about to throw. I always knew she was up to no good.

But Reid's got himself a big, soft heart the way his mother did. Can't see the bad in anybody and can't stop giving those bad ones a second chance, and a third, and so on. I'd like to see Kate locked up. Still might come to that, with any luck. I've got my fingers crossed for the maximum sentence.

"You take a seat and I'll get your grits and a few prime slices of bacon I held onto for you. I'll be back in a few minutes. I'll grab your tea, too. Reid's made sure we have plenty on hand ever since you first came here, and he found out it was your favorite." He patted her shoulder again and returned to the kitchen.

Lacey scavenged a few leftover chunks of fruit from the buffet and took a seat. Jayden and Becky stood stiffly by the reception desk, glancing around, not speaking. In the blink of an eye, the office door flew open. Reid emerged with Kate close on his heels. There was no need to strain to hear the conversation.

"Wait, Reid. You asked me a question. I'm giving you my answer."

Question? What question did he ask her? Lacey listened carefully while keeping her eyes on the modest bowl, picking at the half dozen pieces of fruit. Even her growling stomach had quieted.

"You asked about my future and said I needed to make plans. For my future, I want what my sister had. She was happy, even as she was dying. I want a full-time life on the ranch. It belongs to me; it's my home. And you belong to me, Reid."

"What about Russell?" Reid growled.

"Oh. Him too, of course."

"You've never considered Russell at all, and it's your loss. You've never even tried to be a mother figure to him. I don't want you; never have, never will. Get out of my house and off my property. I don't ever want to see or hear from you again as long as I live.

"I know part of what you've done to Lacey, Russell, and me, by keeping us apart. You deleted messages from the computer, my cellphone, and the ranch phone. You should know I've spoken with the sheriff and I'm hiring a private detective later today.

Kate stood rigid, her eyes wide.

"Someone's tried to hurt Lacey, more than once. Both she and Russell nearly died yesterday, after *you* sent him to find wildflowers in that dangerous spot." He jabbed a finger in Kate's direction.

"No one can convince me you aren't the mastermind behind all the problems revolving around this family since Russell went to North Carolina to find Lacey."

"Reid, I couldn't help what happened at that cliff. It was an accident."

"The wheels were set in motion. I have suspicions; I plan on turning them into proof." He firmly planted his hands on his hips.

"You'd better set your affairs in order and pray you're arrested before I see you again. Jayden and Becky are going to watch you gather your personal effects from the office, and then they'll follow you to the front gate. You're a monster of your own making. I'm sorry I ever allowed you into this house the first time.

"The only good thing you ever did was buy that plane ticket for Russell and drive him to the airport so he could meet Lacey. It's the sole reason I'm not having a deputy escort you out instead. Now go!"

"Reid," she began a plea, extending her hands toward him. Tears, real or pulled out of thin air, ran down her cheeks.

"You heard me!" he bellowed. She took a step backward, dropping her hands to her sides. The tears ended as quickly as they'd begun, replaced by a cold glare. "You're making a mistake. It'll prove to be a big one. You'll regret this in the worst possible way."

Jayden and Becky, carrying moving boxes, followed Kate as she returned to the office in a fury.

Reid wandered over to stand by the registration desk, gazing around the massive room, remembering the hard work, the planning, the saving. Until his eyes fell upon Lacey. He visibly relaxed as the tension evaporated. He strode into the dining area.

Lacey stood and made her way around the long table to meet him. "Are you okay?"

Instead of responding, he wrapped his arms around her, burying his face in her damp hair. They stayed that way for a full minute before he began rubbing his hands along her back. "She almost took you away from me... and Russell. She could've succeeded. She almost did. It's nothing short of a miracle you're still alive. I'm sorry I didn't see it coming. I'm sorry it took me so long to believe you." His voice broke.

"Everything's okay now, Reid."

"I'll make sure of it." He straightened and wiped at his eyes.

"As soon as you feel up to it, I'm thinking two weeks from now at the earliest, we'll fly to Charlotte. I'll help you pack up your belongings and go with you to turn in your resignation. I'll be able to help you with gathering all your personal belongings at work. Once the movers collect everything, we'll come back home by plane."

After everything that happened, how could she say no? This was where she wanted to be, with Reid and Russell, wherever they were. Her home was with them. A job didn't matter. "Sounds good to me."

"And don't think you'll have it easy here, young lady. You'll be busy most days."

Part of her wanted to point out she'd been busy whenever she'd come, but Lacey kept her mouth shut and let him go.

"You're going to handle our website, payroll, and everything associated with the computer. I want you to explore ways to increase our efficiency with some serious upgrades, and I'm not just talking about the old machine sitting on the desk in there. I know we're way behind the times and we can do a lot more than the one computer.

"I'm thinking you can make maps for us, too. You know, for the guests to find their way around? And Russell told me about the ones you make at work for analysis. I've read about those being used to improve the management of farms and ranches to increase productivity. You can do that for our ranch and word will spread. You might have more mapping business than you can handle.

"But we'll also need you to help with the phones, the guests, and you'll be in charge of me." He smiled as he fished a gray velvet box from his pocket and went down on one knee.

Lacey's eyes widened as her mouth sagged open. After everything they'd been through yesterday, she didn't expect this. Not right now.

Reid opened the box to remove a ring, taking hold of her left hand. It was a beautiful, sparkling round diamond, with a smaller one to either side, set in a silver band.

"Lacey. I could never have dreamed up a more perfect woman, partner, and companion. You're beautiful, kind, smart, and everyone loves you. You've given me a child I love more than my own life and you were meant to be here with us. I love you with all my heart and I want to spend the rest of my life with you. Will you marry me?"

"Reid, I didn't expect this." Seeing his face begin to fall, she hurried. "I love you, too. You surprised me. Yes, I'll marry you."

The smile that followed lit the deepest recesses of his heart. He slipped the ring onto her finger, scooped up the box to shove it back into his pocket, and stood to kiss her.

It took a moment for her to realize they were surrounded by well-wishers, jubilant to have witnessed the joyous event. They clapped and patted them on the backs.

"Dad! Mom!"

They parted for Russell, as the small crowd around them had done. Russell hugged each of them, followed by Robert.

"I almost missed it, Dad. I was coming in for breakfast and you were on one knee in front of Mom."

"Same for me, Russ. I was in the kitchen when somebody pushed me out here, said I had to see what was going on. Otherwise, I would've missed out. I thought you were going to wait until tonight, by the fire outside." Robert slapped Reid on the shoulder and kissed Lacey on the cheek.

"I was, but this just felt like the right time." He stepped forward, placed his hands on either side of her face, and kissed her so long Lacey grew concerned about forgetting her name. It didn't matter. That was about to change anyway. Applause and whistles erupted.

A Thanksgiving Wedding

TWENTY

It was just the same at their wedding several weeks later, the clapping, whistling, and cheering. It was the day before Thanksgiving, the anniversary of the day Russell found Lacey. The day all their lives changed, for the better. Reid insisted on marrying her on that special day.

The ranch was adorned with balloons, ribbons, and flowers in turquoise, yellow, and white. Reid had an elegant white arbor constructed in the backyard for the occasion and the guests sat in rows of white folding chairs with colorful bows. Tables were set up near the house, decorated with sprays of flowers and white tablecloths. The weather cooperated, giving them a warm day without a single cloud to mar the depth of the turquoise sky.

They kept the ceremony brief, as once everything was finished, preparations for the big Thanksgiving meal the next day had to commence. After Russell and Robert congratulated them, Connie and Jonathan were next. They'd been with Lacey for a week, helping with last-minute preparations. Jonathan gave her away and Connie was her Maid of Honor.

The two of them were engaged. From Lacey's calculations, it happened about the time she hung from the cliff with Russell. Reid extended an invitation to host their wedding and honeymoon on the ranch in the spring, an offer gratefully accepted.

Lacey's ribs had healed well enough for a wedding, tossing flowers over her shoulder, and the heavy breathing about to follow as their short honeymoon began. Since the next day was Thanksgiving, Reid decided they would begin their honeymoon at the ranch. The unusual honeymoon would pick up a few days later with all three of them leaving on their first family vacation to Disney. That was already predicted to become another traditional vacation.

***

Reid carried Lacey through the breezeway and across the threshold of their room before placing her feet on the floor. He kissed her and closed the door as Lacey removed her veil. Large vases of fragrant flowers were staged around the room, the curtains were already drawn, the bedcovers turned back. Red rose petals had been scattered liberally across the bed and along a path over the floor leading from the door to the bed. Vanilla scented candles burned, their light setting a mood.

"Hang on; let me handle the dress. I've been fantasizing about this for a year now. I want to see how close to accurate I am," Reid whispered in her ear from behind.

The unzipping came slow, seductive. After sliding his fingertips up along her spine, they traced her shoulder blades to the straps of the dress. He slid it off her shoulders, one at a time, pausing to place several long kisses on each of them. Thus far, his fantasy was being decimated by the reality of physical contact and mounting heat.

Stepping out of the material, Lacey released her hair from its clip. After Reid hung up her dress he began shedding his tuxedo. Watching him remove the sexy suit, she kicked off her shoes, stripped away her underwear.

She was about to unfasten the lovely freshwater pearl necklace Reid had sent Russell to deliver to her that special morning. Reid came up and took her hands from the clasp, positioning them at her sides. Rising flames of desire followed his fingers as they skimmed up her arms and across her shoulders to the clasp.

After placing the necklace on the dresser, he returned to her. With each touch, caress, and kiss, the heat inside her grew until it became a roaring bonfire. He lifted her, Lacey's legs wrapping around him, her arms encircling his neck as he took her to the bed. He laid her back, and she rubbed her hands over his shoulders as he gazed into her eyes.

Reid lowered his head to Lacey's and pressed his lips to first one cheek, then the other. The kiss to her mouth lingered. His lips parted as they slid across hers lazily, slowly deepening the kiss. A subtle growl and the addition of his tongue made her insides quiver, aching for another. And it held the taste of punch and wedding cake.

"I love you, Lacey."

"I love you, too. Please kiss me like that again. Exactly like that one."

His eyes narrowed. "Okay, I can do that; as often as you'd like." He kissed her again and again.

The kisses grew in their level of heat, in the clarity of their desire, as he rubbed his body over hers. The heat of his skin caused her to tremble. She moaned as Reid's lips feathered their way along her neck while his fingers moved up her side, the hand sliding beneath her, pressing her against him.

As he kissed her, she took in his strong back with her hands, studying him through her sense of touch, noting the location of each muscle, taut and bulging with power. There was a long scar from years before when a horse threw him into a fence, a few bumps from moles. She wanted to know everything, how his skin felt against hers, the rhythm of his heartbeat under her hand, the way his eyes penetrated her soul as they made love.

Reid kissed, explored, caressed, and finally took her, making them one. The sensations mounted inside Lacey until a strong wave of pleasure washed over. She released a long, low rumbling in the back of her throat as Reid whispered her name, his body shuddering as he poured himself into her.

***

The dawning of Thanksgiving was just beginning to brighten the room when Lacey awakened. Reid's hand dangled from her hip and his deep, regular breaths moved his chest against her back. It gave her a feeling of contentment, unlike anything she'd ever experienced. There was so much love and happiness in this home.

It would be considerate to let Reid sleep. But she wasn't feeling considerate. Lots of work needed to be done before the big meal, leaving essentially no time for newlyweds to be newlyweds. Sleep could wait.

As she rolled over, Reid's eyelids fluttered. She rubbed her hands across his broad chest, relishing in the sensations brought on by those muscles.

"Umm, good morning, Mrs. Collier," he mumbled.

"Good morning, love of my life."

He gave a low hum as he stretched. "I like that."

"Good. You are without a doubt the most wonderful man on this earth. I'm very blessed to have you. And I love you more than any words could express. I can't believe we found each other. All three of us, I guess it would be. An instant, amazing family."

"Lacey." He applied several long, tender kisses before taking a lock of her hair between his fingers to rub it. "There's something I haven't told you. When I first saw you at the airport in Charlotte, something came over me. Part of it was a huge wave of primal lust, I'll admit.

"But your eyes tugged at my heart, even though I didn't have time for romance in my life, and that I feared risking my heart again by sharing it with another woman. It'd been a long time and I didn't know what to do with those feelings, or with the hope shining clear and bright in your eyes.

"I needed to get away from you, to think. That's why I hurried Russell out of there, without allowing you two to say a proper goodbye. I was afraid of losing my heart, but I already had. And then we didn't hear from you, so I tried to put those feelings aside and get you out of my mind. It was one of the hardest things I've had to do in my life.

"Then suddenly, there you stood in front of me, literally hat-in-hand. When I looked into your eyes again, instead of hope, I saw fear. Fear of me. You'd found a way to get here despite me, despite Kate, and you were afraid of me. You were afraid I'd keep Russell away from you after you'd made such a bold effort to reach him.

"And there was the worry over Russell's feelings, making sure you were serious about being there for him, but I decided I needed to trust you. Your eyes told me I could. And then you saddled Spark like a pro. That's when I knew you belonged here with us."

"I was trying to make a good impression. I wanted you to like me and let me stay. And come back." She traced a forefinger over his jawline.

"It worked. Even if you hadn't known how to do any of what you did, I was already impressed by your grit and determination in getting here the way you did. And your creativity. Connie." The corners of his mouth turned up as he ran his fingers over her body.

"You still remember my secret identity?"

"Yes. I remember everything about your visits here, every detail of every minute. I've played them over and over in my head during the times you weren't here, to keep me company."

Tears came to her eyes. "I should've come to live here so much sooner. I love you."

"I love you, too. You're everything I've ever dreamed of." He kissed her long and deep, one hand sliding to her back, pressing her close. His other hand reached down to touch. In an instant, the heat swamped, leaving her teetering. Reid pressed on, his mouth moving over her with enthusiasm while his fingers found the sweet spot and held her there until she was overcome.

Lacey's release came well-vocalized, muffled by her mouth as she pressed it against Reid's shoulder. He shifted her to lie on her back as her legs hooked over his hips.

Reid's sweet talk of falling in love, his slow, tender kisses, had lulled her into a romantic place, then the roaring fire returned. His head lowered to lie alongside hers, hot breaths blowing at her ear. She emboldened him by groaning and whispering his name, over and over.

Everything turned white-hot. There was nothing in the entirety of the world except the two of them. When Reid's rapid motions transitioned into deep spasms, he brought them to a joint release.

The fantasies and dreams had come true. He had the woman he loved in his arms. Nothing would ever tear them apart.

"How about a shower after we catch our breath?" she asked.

Reid raised his head from her shoulder, his breaths coming hard, preventing speech. Instead, he managed a knowing grin.

TWENTY-ONE

Lights beamed warmth from inside the house, while the grounds illuminated the deepening Thanksgiving Day twilight. The barn stood apart. There, only a pair of solar security lights shone, incapable of being snuffed out by a switch.

It had Lacey curious as to why the others weren't on, what with all the guests in residence. Reid liked to keep the area safe in case of wandering tourists until nine o'clock when most exterior lights were doused for stargazing beneath the clear, dark skies.

Someone must have extinguished the other lights. But the barn's front doors were closed. That was only supposed to happen during periods of snow. Her forehead wrinkled at the oddness of it all. She'd have to let Reid know when she returned from giving Spark his daily carrot a little early today in preparation for packing for the trip to Disney.

But the curiosity continued. Spark wasn't waiting at the pasture gate, nor was he anywhere in sight. A familiar squeal came from the barn. The horses were supposed to be out to pasture for the night. Jayden had gone to his mother's house for a late Thanksgiving dinner. No one should be in the barn. This called for an investigation.

One of the two rear doors was closed, the other open. Stepping inside revealed a smell that didn't belong. Gasoline. The hair on the back of Lacey's neck stood at full attention, requiring her to proceed with caution. The thought of moving into the wide center aisle gave her pause.

Instead, she decided on caution, crouching to the side of the first stall on her right, by the rear entry. Spark's stall. His hooves swished through the straw until he stood on the other side of the wall from her. Knowing she was there the animal emitted a soft, extended nicker.

The desire to respond tore at her heart. Horses tended to be uncomfortable when alone and confined. They needed the company of others. And they didn't like the odor of gasoline.

Tiptoeing, she moved to the stall's front corner. Spark moved with her. One more step and Lacey would be in the main aisle. Instinct screamed it would be a bad idea.

"Almost done in here," a man's voice said. He stood close, which had Lacey pressing herself against the side of the stall. "Don't worry, Spark. It won't be quick for you, but your owner's going to follow right on your heels. You'll see her on the other side. She won't make it to her precious Disney."

Heightened attention came with the threat as Lacey attempted to identify the familiarity, shuffling through memories of voices. A cellphone rang.

"I'm here." Then came a pause and footsteps, pacing down the aisle away from her. "Yeah, he's in his stall. From the way I've positioned everything, he'll have time to squeal for help before the smoke and flames get him, enough to make Lacey suffer when she hears it.

"When she comes running, I'll get her and make sure she joins him. If she doesn't come, I'll take care of her in the confusion that'll go along with the fire. I've only got about ten minutes before she comes looking for Spark to give him a carrot. Predictable idiot."

Her eyes widened. This man did indeed plan to kill her horse. Then her.

"It ticks me off that Jayden caught me. He was supposed to be at his mom's." The voice paused again. "I don't care. This is murder.

Lacey's one thing, but this is different. He's my friend. I should've taken out that useless city girl in Charlotte that night or slashed her throat instead of her tires the first trip out there."

Jayden was here. Was he still alive? And this man didn't care about killing him, or her? The rattlesnake was certain to be his handiwork. The voice came to her. Gil.

Monster and murderer. Kate and Gil. Lacey's fists clenched, trying to direct her fears toward anger, hoping to squelch her shaking. Her efforts weren't working well, but she had to overcome it. Her fingers flexed, the carrot dropping, forgotten. What could be used as a weapon? Gil had to be stopped.

"Just let me worry about that, Kate. You finish getting what you want from the wall safe and get out of there. I don't like you risking yourself for any amount of money, or the stupid diamond ring Robert wants to give old Mrs. Chicken and Biscuits for Christmas."

A large hand clamped over Lacey's mouth from behind as another wrapped around her waist. Her body stiffened, ready for a hopeless struggle against a much stronger, larger opponent. "Quiet. It's me, honey," came the whisper.

Reid released his grip, freeing her to turn. When she faced him, her eyebrows were elevated, her eyes wide. She was trembling.

The memory of seeing Lacey's expression standing in that bathroom when he'd pushed the door open to shoot the snake had struck his heart the same as this moment did. It had been emotionally painful to see the bruises and swelling when he visited her in Charlotte. The man who just admitted doing all that to her, terrifying and nearly killing her, his wife, was close. Talking to his co-conspirator. Kate.

He held a finger to his lips. "Get out. We need help. I have to stop him from killing Jayden."

"It's Gil," she whispered.

"I know. I recognized his voice. Get me that help. Find my dad and call 9-1-1. Hurry."

The phone conversation continued, with Gil unaware he had an audience. "This whole ranch should've been yours. Then Reid had to spoil everything by marrying Lacey instead of you. I was looking forward to killing him before your honeymoon started. No way was I gonna let him have you. Anyway, be careful and we'll meet at your house and go from there. I've got to finish up here. Okay."

Lacey wanted to stay, worried for his safety, but he was right. She nodded, sprinting for the house at her best speed once clear of the barn. As she flung herself into the kitchen, she plowed directly into Jonathan, sending his saucer of pie to the floor with a clatter.

"What'd you do that for?" he asked, miffed. Pie was his kryptonite. And that was the last piece of the best apple pie he'd ever tasted.

She grabbed fistfuls of his shirt. "Jonathan! You've got to get to the barn! Go around the back side of it. Reid's out there and he needs help."

"Reid?" Robert moved into view from behind the open refrigerator door. "What's going on?"

"It's Gil. He's the one who's been working with Kate, trying to get me. He's done something to Jayden and plans to kill him and burn down the barn. He'll kill Reid, too." Lacey turned back to Jonathan, her eyes pleading.

"Stay here." Jonathan pushed past her, shoving the screen door open, leaping the steps in one bound, barreling toward the barn, Robert not far behind.

"Mrs. Gordon, we need the Sheriff!" Lacey looked at her and saw the landline phone to her ear as she nodded. The kitchen staff was aghast, motionless with shock.

"Let me at that guy," Connie growled, trying to rush past Lacey.

"No. I need your help. Come on. We're going after Kate! She's here, too!" Lacey grabbed Connie's hand and yanked her friend around, then started running. They passed through the kitchen and across the dining area and registration, stopping near the office door. Lacey put a finger to her lips and whispered. "Stay right here. I'm going to the outside entrance. If she comes through this door, take her down."

"Don't worry. Go. I've got it."

Lacey bolted through the front door, down the steps, and around the house to the far corner. There, a brick patio with a low wall had been built for Kate, complete with outdoor furnishings and planters of lovely flowers, illuminated by solar lighting. This would be the last time Kate ever saw it.

A single light burned in the office and the French doors stood open. There was no reason for stealth. Lacey charged into the office at full speed and with a slight course correction, jumped onto a surprised Kate.

The momentum rolled them over the desk, sending a heavy, elegant lamp smashing to the floor, the air filling with floating papers. The cashbox tumbled away when Kate hit the floor, scattering thousands of dollars in Christmas bonus cash, the payroll, and a dark velvet ring box.

Delivering an elbow to Lacey's stomach in a frenzied attack, Kate yelled as she snatched hold of the broken lamp. She swung it as she rose to her knees, aiming for Lacey's head. Lacey threw up her hands to cover her face.

Connie burst through the interior door and body-slammed herself into Kate, sending them both into the front panel of the desk, the lamp sent flying. Kate shoved away from the diminutive opponent and decided that two against one meant it was better to leave empty-handed. She clambered for the exit.

No way that was happening. Lacey shoved to her feet, pursuing Kate through the glass doors. Kate's legs were longer, but Lacey was determined to stop the woman who'd jeopardized her son's life.

Throwing herself forward, she wrapped her arms around Kate's legs, tackling her to the bricks. Kate screamed, trying to right herself while putting a hand to her bloody nose.

There was no opportunity for recovery. Lacey scrambled op to plop herself down on the small of Kate's back. Kate thrashed from side to side, but Lacey grabbed one of Kate's arms, twisted it around to her back, and held tight as Kate screamed that she was being killed.

"I just might, so you'd better hold still. Connie, bring me the phone cord!" Lacey called, without turning an ounce of attention from Kate.

A few seconds later, Connie joined her. "Here, I've got it. Can I tie up her hands?"

"We're doing better than that. Wrap up her wrists, then I'll show you how we handle thieves here in Texas."

Connie bound Kate's hands behind her back with obvious glee, then handed over the other end of the cord.

"Hold her down while I do this."

"Happy to." Connie swapped places with Lacey, bouncing down onto Kate's back, resulting in another high-pitched scream. They now had an audience of amused onlookers and enthusiastic supporters.

Shifting to Kate's feet, Lacey bent them at the knee and looped the cord around them. Next, she lashed them to Kate's hands, good and tight. Then she jumped to her feet and lifted her hands clear. "Get up, Connie. She's not going anywhere. That's called hogtying. Jayden taught me!"

"Ha! I love it!" Connie said, meeting Lacey's palm for a slapping high five. "I'm still not leaving this spot. I don't trust her as far as a toddler could throw her. We'll wait for the cops to get here. They're going to haul your lousy keister to jail. You'll rot for a long time, Kate."

Momentary triumph shifted for Lacey to concern. "I need to go check on Reid and the others. But I can't risk her getting away. The bad guys always manage to slip away somehow."

"Don't worry. Sheriff's on his way. Miss High and Mighty isn't going anywhere," someone from behind said with glee.

Lacey turned to see Mrs. Gordon, wielding her favorite cast iron frying pan, with one of her assistants standing beside her, gripping a meat cleaver. "You run on , Lacey. We've got this useless mother trucker."

All eyes widened. Mrs. Gordon never used language like that.

"That's right. We'll watch her close, Mom. Go help Dad." Russell stood in the doorway.

"Russell, you be careful."

"I will. Nice hogtie, Mom."

"Thanks, honey." With a nod to Connie, Lacey ran through the guesthouse and out the backdoor, sprinting for the barn. The front doors had been opened and the lights were all on.

"Now that we've taken pictures of the scene for the sheriff, get the wheelbarrows and start scooping up all the contaminated soil. Spread out some straw and pile it over. We'll take care of proper disposition tomorrow," Reid instructed Jayden, Jonathan, and three other men, who nodded and set about their work.

"Jayden!" Lacey ran to him, bestowing a bear hug. "You're okay?"

"Yes, thanks to Reid. He beat the stuffing out of Gil. It was great!" He grinned.

She turned to Reid, who smiled and met her for an embrace. "I'm glad you're okay. I was worried."

"We're all fine. Gil's hogtied and gagged. Jayden did the tying. Taught Jonathan how to do it, for future reference. I'm thinking of offering your cousin a job, and he's thinking of taking it. Connie can help you with your work. Jonathan said she'd make a great waitress, though. If they accept, we'll let them build a place on the ranch, somewhere nearby. How does that strike you?"

The grin she wore was huge. "Wonderful! Connie just learned hogtying, too. From me. We've got Kate down on the patio by the office, ready for the Sheriff."

"That's my girl," Reid laughed.

"Connie, Russell, Mrs. Gordon, and a few dozen other people are watching her. I had to come to see if you needed help."

The laughter came again. "It's under control. My dad took Spark to the pasture after I fed him the carrot you dropped. Now my family's safe. Everything's going to be fine."

"We can live our lives without worrying anymore," Russell jogged up to them. "Two deputies' cars just pulled up. They're wrangling Kate into one of the cars. They added handcuffs to make sure she didn't go anywhere. More sirens are coming."

Reid released a sigh. "All these years, we had a couple of... rattlesnakes hiding in our midst. And now it's over." He kissed Lacey and welcomed Russell into the warmth of their family group hug.

THE END

If you'd like to follow the progress on upcoming novels, you can follow the author on Amazon: https://www.amazon.com/A-L-Nelson. Another option is to grab the free novella that is a prequel to Dangerous Offer when you sign up for the author's newsletter at: https://alnelsonauthor.com/newsletter.

Additional novels by the author are available on Amazon:

The Chaperone (part of the Superstorm series)
The Stranding
Winning Wonderland
Dangerous Offer

A note to the reader:

You have the power to increase the reach of my books, which means helping those charities I support. If you enjoyed this book, please recommend it to your friends and most importantly, consider leaving a review on Amazon. It is amazing the power those reviews carry for authors, and it only takes a couple of minutes of your time. All it takes is a sentence or for comment or leave some stars. It not only helps me, but increases the reach of the book, which earns more money for the charitable organizations supported. Thank you so much for purchasing this book and I hope it entertained you.

Sign up for her newsletter and stay up on all the latest book news, because there are plenty more novels to come. And follow her on:

Website: alnelsonauthor.com
Facebook at: ALNelsonAuthor
Instagram at: a.l.nelson
Twitter at: ALNelson13
BookBub: a-l-nelson
TikTok: alnelsonauthor

ABOUT THE AUTHOR

The author writes romantic suspense novels, where people unite to overcome seemingly impossible odds. Writing is her passion, recently discovered but now ingrained in her life. She lives with her husband, two children, and a dog afflicted with a joyous case of the zoomies in sunny Florida. When she isn't working at her fulltime job to pay the bills, she enjoys spending time with her family, swimming, and walks on the beach in search of shark teeth.

Most of the profits from her novels go to charity, with information about these on her website. So, buy a book to enjoy and help a good cause in the process.

Made in the USA
Coppell, TX
21 June 2024